Also by Robert Rosenberg
CRIMES OF THE CITY

SIMON & SCHUSTER

NEW YORK
LONDON
TORONTO
SYDNEY
TOKYO
SINGAPORE

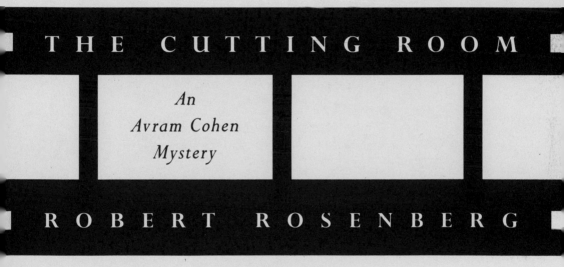

THE CUTTING ROOM

An
Avram Cohen
Mystery

ROBERT ROSENBERG

SIMON & SCHUSTER
SIMON & SCHUSTER BUILDING
ROCKEFELLER CENTER
1230 AVENUE OF THE AMERICAS
NEW YORK, NEW YORK 10020

DESIGNED BY SONGHEE KIM
MANUFACTURED IN THE UNITED STATES OF AMERICA

1   3   5   7   9   10   8   6   4   2

LIBRARY OF CONGRESS CATALOGING-IN-PUBLICATION DATA
ROSENBERG, ROBERT.
THE CUTTING ROOM : AN AVRAM COHEN MYSTERY / ROBERT ROSENBERG.
P.   CM.
I. TITLE.
PS3568.O7878C87   1993
813'.54—dc20   92-37187
CIP

ISBN: 0-671-74344-9

for Silvia, as always,

and for Amber, forever

DURING HIS LONG REIGN as the top detective in Jerusalem, Avram Cohen sometimes joked that he'd rather have been chief of investigations for King Solomon. But he lived the nightmare of the twentieth century and had been in the holy city from the birth of his country to the end of the millennium. He believed he had seen everything.

Tourists and true believers could drink up the rhetoric of the politicians and religious leaders, saying they saw God's golden sunlight reflected in Jerusalem's limestone ramparts. But Cohen had no illusions about what could be hidden behind those walls. As head of the Jerusalem District Criminal Investigations Department, he knew that there were crimes that could happen only in Jerusalem.

He had pursued corrupt holy men and politicians, terrorists of every religious faith or political inclination, and all kinds of extremists preying on everyone's fears of the future. He had chased on foot after suspects down the darkest alleyways of the Old City, raced against ticking bombs on crowded Ben Yehuda mall, and trapped the corrupt in the offices of the Knesset. He was never the highest-ranking policeman in Jerusalem. But after nearly a generation as chief of investigations, he was the most informed.

As the years passed, the risks grew greater. Loyalists feared for him, enemies waited in ambush. Caring more for the city than for himself was his mistake. It finally caught up with him in the bright, sweaty lights of the television cameras aimed at him and the politicians at the end of his last case. Suddenly he was off the force.

Never able to plan ahead further than the cases took him, he had not planned for his own future. Set adrift, he was purposeless. For the first time he could remember, since before he chose survival instead of surrender in Dachau concentration camp, he felt helpless.

More than anything else, that was the reason he was in the VIP lounge at Ben-Gurion Airport, nursing his second cognac while waiting for the boarding call for the flight halfway around the world to Los Angeles, trying to force himself to call Ahuva.

Their last conversation had been a disaster, and he knew he had only himself to blame. She was a magistrate known for strict judgments, especially when the victim's tale was told. Her fairness was as famous in Jerusalem as their affair was secret. She dealt in opinions, handing down thoughtful rulings that were garlands made of the soft grays hidden between black and white. He dealt in facts, hard and tough.

But in their haven at Cohen's apartment in the German Colony, over candlelit Friday-night dinners and afterward in bed, they shared the feelings that their vocations had deemed too dangerous to display on the job. For ten years, she was the pragmatically wise one, counseling caution and realism. Cohen, twenty years her senior, used their secret oasis as the one place where he could reveal his buried idealism, his belief in the Sisyphean purpose to which every devoted cop is loyal.

But once he was off the job, the sanctuary became a prison. Purposeless, he felt old. Alone, he spent his time looking back over incomplete cases, digging in the unwritten archives of his memories. He thought of convicts who might have been innocent, deaths that could have been avoided. He drew mental maps of intersecting choices, becoming lost in questions about himself he had never needed to ask before. Self-pity and impotence, bitterness and despair, crept into his life as quietly as Suspect, his cat. But unlike the old tom, these new visitors to his life disrupted all the routines he had so carefully nurtured. Especially his relationship with Ahuva.

It didn't help that her career was spiraling upward. Not that he would have denied her success. But when he heard the rumor about her name going onto the short list for the next year's nominees to the district bench, he was shocked to feel anger, instead of pride, rising instinctively inside him. He had clenched his hand tightly around the thick, cheap water glass of cognac that was his regular drink at Café Atara, until even the self-absorbed rumormonger noticed the tension and asked sympathetically about Cohen's health.

For nearly six months, Cohen had kept stoically silent while the café jackals snacked on what they thought they knew. He had refused to testify in the habitués' debates over whether he was a martyr or a scapegoat. But after hearing the rumor about Ahuva, he stopped going to the café, spreading his own rumor: Cohen was at work on a memoir and didn't want to be disturbed.

Though he did buy the pads and sharpen the pencils, the words had refused to come. The gossip about the nomination simmered in him like a potion. Instead of reporting it to Ahuva right away, he made up excuses for his silence. She was always strict about not lobbying for her own cause, so he decided that telling her would be a violation of that ethical self-discipline. It should be her proud privilege to offer him the news, he told himself. But he knew that it was his envy of her youth, with its hope for the future, that bothered him. And that only made him feel older.

For a few weeks, he tried hiding it from her. But it was a lost cause. Like any jail full of echoing self-recrimination, their haven had turned into hell. She wanted to talk about the future. All he wanted to think about was the past. Finally, in that last conversation, she raised the issue of a child. The doctors had told her it might be difficult for her, but still possible. In his painful paranoia, he saw it as a test of his commitment. He half-joked selfishly that he'd never live long enough to see the child become an adult. More seriously he claimed he wouldn't want her to be burdened by the lonely responsibility when he was gone. She called him selfish and stubborn and foolish. He didn't put up an argument.

Thus for the first time in ten years she finally turned the sanctuary into a courtroom, passing judgment on him with the angry disappointment of a former believer. "When you know what you want," she said, "let me know." It was a stiff sentence, but from Magistrate Judge Ahuva Meyerson he expected no less.

Suspect had jumped onto his lap, surprised by the midnight click of the door and complaining in a soft wail about the woman's angry departure. "Don't you know?" Cohen asked the cat. "She always warns the losers about what will happen the next time they show up in her courtroom."

Cohen scowled at a rustle of activity in the carpeted and tapestried lounge behind him. He looked up from the phone to the mirror behind the bottles. It was the American woman with the taut orange skin that bespoke expensive sun and surgery.

Earlier she had complained at even first-class passengers' having to abide by security regulations requiring their presence in the airport two hours before takeoff. He had not been impressed by her loud references to friendships with generals and prime ministers past and present. Her voice reminded Cohen of the Moroccan newspaper hawker on Ben Yehuda mall, sawing through the Friday-morning shopping crowd. But he had also noticed how she enjoyed the spectacle she made of herself, full of the self-confidence of a stage performer at work. The old Yemenite on Ben Yehuda was sarcastic about the headlines he mongered. She seemed to create scandals for her own pleasure, convinced she was entertaining her audience.

Now she was complaining about the price and strength of her vodka martini, calling for the manager as she strode to the bar. "Nun's piss," she called out in English, holding up the glass as if it were a laboratory specimen. "You think I don't know what a real one is supposed to taste like?" she groused, making sure he understood her meaning as she handed it over to the chagrined bartender.

Cohen checked his watch. Fifteen minutes to boarding. He eyed the phone beside his elbow on the oak bar. He still had time to call Ahuva. What could he say? That he knew he was missing his chance with her? He'd said it so many times in the past—to himself, to her. But saying it didn't make it any easier for him to go to her, to stay with her like a young man with no past to remember and only a future to anticipate. Disgusted with himself, he drained the cognac. As he put it down, his eye was caught in the mirror by the American woman. She was smiling at him while she lit a cigarette. Her gestures, betraying everything else about her, were tiny and ultrafeminine.

He reached for the phone, punching in Ahuva's home number. Three, four times he let it ring, until halfway through the fifth buzz he hung up. Realizing he was relieved, he signaled the bartender to fill his glass. But before the man could reach for the bottle on the shelf below the mirror, the American was sliding onto the tall stool beside Cohen. He looked her over from the corner of his eye. She was dressed for the West, from her rhinestone-studded jeans jacket to the silver-toed cowboy boots.

"Goldie, Goldie Stein," she announced. "I *definitely* don't recommend the martinis," and she winked at him in the mirror, making him turn to face her.

In the dim light of the lounge, he had guessed her to be Ahuva's age. Now, up close, he adjusted his guess drastically upward, realizing that her tight-fitting costume was advertising either a health club or a surgeon, but not authentic youth. Her eyes revealed her age as they worked to conceal her feelings. He had seen their almond shape turn quickly to narrow suspicion when the waitress presented the bill for her drink. Now they were squinting at him with a politician's effort to remember his face for the future.

But her fragrance surprised him. Again he thought of Ahuva, trying to remember if he had ever asked her for the name of the perfume. He winced with shame, and his eyes flickered to the phone. Nine at night on a Saturday. She was practically religious about the nine o'clock television news. He wondered where she was.

"Good thinking," Goldie said, eyeing the bottle of Martell as the bartender poured Cohen a drink. "You can't fuck up straight liquor, I always say. Let *me* have one of those too," she ordered the barman.

Cohen snarled a short, silent smile and then drained half the miserly measure the bartender had poured into the short water glass Cohen had requested for his drink.

"But put mine in a *real* cognac glass," she called, shaking her head at Cohen's tumbler before smiling at him again. "So, as I was saying, I'm Goldie." Disappointment fluttered across her face when he didn't respond to the name. "Goldie Stein? The tinseltown tattletale?" she added in a lilting tone and with a self-deprecatory grin that both asked him again if he had heard of her and questioned her own statement.

"Cohen, Avram Cohen," he said quietly, glancing at her sidewise and then looking back at his drink, wishing she'd go away.

"And you are a . . . ?" she asked. When he didn't fill in the blank, she tried a different tack. "I'm in the media. Newspapers, TV," she boasted casually.

He raised his eyes from the polished brass liquid to the mirror. Now doubly distrustful of her prying, he believed that silence would finally drive her away.

"It's a living," she defended herself, reading his mind. "But I'm *good* at it," she said proudly, "and *that's* what counts. Right?" She peered at him in the mirror, waiting for his response.

Her manner of emphasizing words reminded him of an informer who worked for him once. The memory of the *shtinker* increased his resistance to her.

But she wasn't deterred by his silence. "Your turn," she said.

He raised an eyebrow at her in the mirror.

"You're dressed too casually for a businessman," she guessed, "and God knows you're not one of those *lousy* politicians." Discreetly she leveled one of her long red fingernails, to point across the almost empty lounge. The back of her hand was tanned dark, but the skin was like a soft flimsy leather, grained and loose, aged and angrily spotted liverish.

Cohen, of course, recognized the politician, and it was easy to pick out the businessman, with his open briefcase. A pair of honeymooners nuzzled on a corner sofa. The ground attendants were gossiping by the door to the tarmac. He wondered why Goldie wasn't bothering the national-team basketball player drinking alone in the corner.

"Come on, you don't have to play hard-to-get with me. We're *both* too old for that." She leaned closer with her mocking smile. He raked his fingers self-consciously through an unruly lock of hair that had flopped over his forehead; it was more white than black, with almost no gray. Her mouth pursed, as her expression changed to expectation.

But instead of answering, he looked away. Six months ago, he thought, he would have sent her packing with a snarl. But six months ago he wouldn't have been sitting in the airport, waiting for a flight halfway around the world.

"You look like you're sitting in jail instead of waiting for a first-class flight," she said, her bracelets jangling on the counter. "What's with the *attitude?*" Her elbow shoved the phone slightly. He pulled back, as if by touching it she had touched him. "You do have thoughtful eyes," she finally said, not noticing his flinch. "A scientist maybe?" She glanced at the book on the bar in front of him. "Moshe Dayan? Jeez. Light reading or what?"

"A biography," Cohen said, hating himself for falling into the trap.

"Touchdown!" she exclaimed sarcastically. "I was beginning to think you really are an asshole." She took a sip of her drink, picked up the book, and, opening it in the middle, frowned sadly. "I should have paid more attention in Hebrew school," she said, as much to herself as to him, and then with a surprising seriousness she asked, "Is it any good?"

"I'll decide when I finish," he said softly.

"I *knew* him," she bragged.

He remained stone-faced, uninterested in her insinuation.

"I guess you don't jump to conclusions, do you?" she asked. When he said nothing, she made a decision. "A professor of history," she said, "that's what you are."

Cohen's abrupt laugh surprised him as much as it did her. He realized he was uncomfortable with the momentary pleasure he took from what he regarded as flattery.

"So?" she asked.

"It doesn't matter," he said. He sipped his drink to douse the bitter truth, and became aware that she was the first genuine stranger he had spoken with in more than a month.

"Tough guy, eh? I'm going to give it only *one* more guess," Goldie said. "And then the gloves come off," she threatened with a laugh. She studied his eyes again, and he stared back, daring her to try. A smile grew on her face. He thought she was going to lose.

"A cop." She suddenly grinned with realization. "You're a cop."

He unwillingly lost his poker face, causing her to laugh again.

"A cop!" She chortled. "Boy, I got to admit that's a surprise. *Never* would have expected a cop."

Cohen reached for his green packet of Noblesse cigarettes on the bar beside his book, wondering what gave it away. Before he could get a cigarette out of the packet, she was holding up a gold lighter. He sucked deeply at the flame and then turned away to exhale the gray smoke. A cough followed. She waited for him to catch his breath. At least she didn't tell him the cigarettes were bad for him, he thought, as she plunged on. "I sure could have used you," she said. "You see, my camera was stolen."

Her tale began with a dinner with some movie star she said she was interviewing at a restaurant in the heart of intifada country. For a moment he wondered what fool had recommended it for an evening dinner party, no matter how celebrated the diners. But then, watching her through the mirror behind the bar, he realized she could probably hold her own against both the masked Arab teenagers of East Jerusalem and the crack Border Police troops on patrol against them.

He paid less attention to her words than to her face and its changing expressions. Her eyebrows rose and fell with each emphasis, her pink-lipsticked mouth wrapped the words like packages for delivery, and, occasionally, the bridge of her nose wrinkled, revealing tiny pale scar lines that even the most expensive surgeons could not hide. He thought of Ahuva's pale skin and its even paler lines of age, and how she had kept her shape but her skin had turned softer over the years. His eyes flickered to the phone.

"Well, for the insurance, I needed a police report. I got to tell you, that police station," Goldie gasped. "Talk about central casting. They had everything except goats."

Her mention of the Russian Compound pushed open the door to Cohen's memory of his office on the second floor of the ivy-covered building. He thought of the magic of the dawn light pouring in through the tall, narrow window directly behind the desk that had served him for more than a decade. He settled into the memories the way he used to settle into the old chair behind the desk, closing his ears to her voice the way he used to close the door to the echoing stone floors and arched ceiling of the corridor outside his office. Half a year had passed since he last sat behind that closed door listening intently to a much different tale of madness.

"The craziness of it all," Goldie shrieked, bursting into his thoughts. "I don't need that kind of *meshugas*," she said. "They sent me round and round. The last thing I needed last week was more drama. For godsake, I had Jenny Garson, *exclusive,* for a week," she summed up, demonstratively admiring her fingernails.

But while he recognized the gesture, he had no idea who Jenny Garson was, and he certainly didn't care. Out of the corner of his eye he saw the ground attendant pushing at the door to the tarmac and one of the stewardesses picking up a hand microphone from behind the attendant's desk. In one swift movement, Cohen leaned over, reaching for his canvas bag on the floor. Standing straight, he swept the book into the satchel, his only luggage for the trip.

"Hey, what did I say?" Goldie complained. "I didn't mean to rag you," she said, in a tone that implied that she was the one who had been insulted. "Besides, you still haven't told me how a cop can afford first-class tickets to L.A."

But Cohen already had the canvas bag zipped up and over his shoulder. He made a small gesture with his free hand, pointing a finger upward as if referring to a higher presence. Goldie frowned with incomprehension. The loudspeaker chimed its bell, and the stewardess's accented English came on, informing passengers that boarding for the Tel Aviv to Montreal to Los Angeles flight had begun. "It's time to go," Cohen said simply, shooting Goldie a short, humorless grin before turning to the open door to the tarmac.

Two men move swiftly through a dark house. They wear black masks and signal silently with pointing guns. Slowly they edge around the curve of a flight of stairs, steeling themselves for their burst through the open doorway at the top, where a couple makes love. The woman is riding the man. Her back twists. The gunmen enter. The man springs as the first bullet rips her off him. The second strikes his forehead.

Cohen cringed in his seat. He hated violence as entertainment. When the woman's blood-soaked hand started crawling across the screen to the fallen telephone on the carpet in the bullet-riddled bedroom, Cohen yanked off the earphones. Dropping them on the empty seat beside him, he scowled at the suddenly silent movie. In real life, he thought, blood spills black, not red.

He slouched uncomfortably for what seemed the hundredth time, finding a spot from which to peer through the half-open plastic curtain over the window to an unmade bed of clouds. The sun was somewhere ahead of the plane. He stared into the bright center of the purpling sky ahead, trying to imagine how Der Bruder would look fifty kilos lighter than he had been only four years before, when they last met.

Maximilian Broder, the man Cohen called "the brother," was born to make movies. His father had worked with Fritz Lang, and his mother had danced for Ziegfeld. Unlike those bigger names, Broder's parents—like Cohen's—didn't get out of Germany in time. Cohen's friendship with Max Broder had nothing to do with show business.

It was the three days on the run together, years together in Dachau, and, finally, one more year as *nokmim,* avengers hunting down Nazis in the ashes of Germany, that Broder and Cohen shared. It had been forty years since Cohen quit Europe and the assassination team in favor of the Jewish war of independence in Palestine, wanting to realize a future instead of chase after the past.

Half a decade passed before they met again, as accidentally as the first time, when both were youngsters trying to make it across the Swiss border.

An American film crew was doing a movie about the war of independence. Cohen was a young patrolman in the Jerusalem police, on crowd-control duty while the Hollywood people shut down a neighborhood for three days of shooting. The American movie star, playing an Israeli war hero, gave the crowd their thrill and some autographs. But Cohen stared only at the tall, heavy man who was sweating profusely as he relayed the director's commands to the local extras.

Memories stung Cohen's face like the *sharav* dust in the air. Der Bruder had made it to America. But at that tearful reunion in divided Jerusalem, on the street corner half a block from the Jordanian border, neither Cohen nor Broder mentioned the last time they had been together, when Cohen finally disobeyed Der Bruder, choosing life over death.

The Jerusalem reunion ended with promises to stay in touch. Broder wrote three letters. Cohen responded with two postcards, at first telling himself that he let his last answer lapse because he was busy.

But the truth ran deeper. More than anything else, he had wanted to forget. He had already decided he could never speak German again, and using the same willpower Der Bruder had helped him learn, he sealed his past away, determined to forget. For a while, he even took to wearing his shirt sleeves rolled up only one fold above the wrist, to hide the number tattooed on his forearm. He reinvented himself, becoming an Israeli without a past and with only a future to create. He worked on his accent, replacing the clipped tones of German with the slurred melodies of spoken Hebrew. Indeed, he was always secretly pleased when a new acquaintance, accidentally spotting the number, would be unable to hide surprise that Cohen was not a *sabra,* native-born to the land.

But Broder wouldn't let him forget. It took four years, but Broder made it back to Israel; by then he was a director of his own movies. He, too, had remade himself into someone else: an American, a rising star in Hollywood, wealthy enough to be courted by the new Jewish state, seeking donations. "Come back with me," Broder had said, visiting Cohen's spare one-room flat in the German Colony apartment. "You'll live a lot better than this," he said scornfully. "We'll make our movie. Our story," he added, in the familiar conspiratorial whisper. But Cohen said no; he was enrolled in a police investigators' course, hopeful about a future of his own. He was done with his past.

Since then, Broder had come to Israel after every war, each time making sure to spend at least an hour with Cohen. Broder would do most of the talking, but Cohen had no interest in Hollywood, and the past was a subject he never discussed. Not even with Der Bruder. So the visits would descend into strange silences between Max's speeches, in which the offer to join him in Hollywood was never specifically repeated but always remained hanging, like all the other unresolved dilemmas between them.

Cohen fidgeted in the airplane seat, remembering. On Broder's last visit to Israel, four years before, the director had proudly announced that he was finally going to make the movie about their years together. It was during a season that Cohen, by then chief of investigations for the Jerusalem police, remembered as the first long hot summer of intifada, and Cohen had little time to spare his old friend.

"I'm calling it *The Survivor's Secrets,*" Broder had said. They were standing in the lane outside Cohen's apartment house on a late Friday afternoon. Starlings out of Africa were heading north for the summer in Europe, flocking in the branches of the aged cypress that shaded the taxi waiting for Broder. "You'll come. All you have to do is be there. Tell me who to trust and who to believe." The starlings were louder than the cars on Emek Refaim, rushing home for Shabbat. Broder had to raise his voice to add, "And who to question closely."

Cohen had looked up to the treetop. In the fast-growing darkness, it took a moment to spot the birds amid the dark leaves of the tall broad tree. He knew that a sudden noise could break the singing, and the thick leaves would shake as the flock leapt as one into the sky. But they'd only fly once around the tree and then roost again until it was truly time to leave Jerusalem. "The movies are your business," Cohen said simply, "not mine." There was no way a movie could claim priority over the flesh and blood of Jerusalem. "I'm not interested," he said softly, pulling open the back door to the taxi. Broder frowned, shrugged, and sighed, getting in. Cohen closed it on him with a strong slap that seemed to make the flock take a deep breath before leaping into the air as the taxi turned right on Emek Refaim and headed back to the King David Hotel. Cohen had stayed in the lane, watching the birds sweep upward into a helix that finally collapsed in a great swoop back into the treetop.

But still Broder wouldn't let go. He made phone calls to report the process. Not many, and they came sporadically, but over the years Cohen heard that Epica Studios had signed on. Casting had begun. Shooting was scheduled. Each time, Broder would hint, but never say outright, that Cohen was wanted. He always had a question that he wanted to ask. "Just one thing," he'd say, "a small detail" he needed to remember. Was the bullet in Bernard Levine's left leg or right? The shade of blue of Manheim's eyes. The kapo they called "the Beast"? What was his real name?

Cohen had always said he couldn't remember; Broder would laughingly call him a terrible liar.

But when the phone call came a few days after Ahuva walked out, Broder's first call since Cohen's departure from the force, it was a much weaker Avram Cohen who answered. A *Los Angeles Times* report had mentioned Cohen's case in a story about political interference in Jerusalem police investigations.

Cohen had been less shocked by the pre-dawn phone call than he had been by the letter from manpower division asking to which bank account he wanted his pension payments deposited automatically.

"You're out of excuses, my brother," Max had shouted down the line at three in the morning. "It's time for you to come," he ordered. "I finished the movie. I'm at the final cut." His throaty rumble had been made hoarser by the slight echo of the long-distance line. "But you don't even have to see it if you don't want to," he said, surprising the Jerusalemite. "Just come. We'll have fun. In twenty years you haven't taken a vacation. It's time for you to get some enjoyment out of life. Come on. Get your *tuchus* over here."

For the first time in years, Cohen couldn't answer truthfully, "I am enjoying my life." And Broder knew it.

Cohen gripped the phone tightly, listening to his breathing. If he went, he thought, he wouldn't have to commit himself to anything, feel guilty about his pain, or be reminded of his uselessness. As if all the years had never passed, Der Bruder once again was offering Cohen an escape.

Broder had said the same thing Ahuva had accused him of only a few days before. "You're out of excuses, Avram," she had said. But unlike Ahuva, Der Bruder won.

Cohen's stomach was rumbling. He clenched the fleshy fold over his belly as if trying to draw the fat over the muscle to cover the hunger. Like all survivors of starvation, Cohen could be compulsive about food. For most, it was a matter of stockpiling, always making sure there was more than sufficient supply. Two or three refrigerators full were not uncommon in survivors' households.

For Cohen, it was the quality of food that mattered. He could cope more easily with hunger than with unidentifiable food. The camp had taught him hatred for the inedible. Years of bachelorhood had refined the compulsion into a passion for fine cooking. So he had turned down the stewardess's offers of the airplane's microwaved dinner, thinking of Broder's promises about the best restaurants in Los Angeles. Cohen had protested he couldn't afford such luxuries. It's all-expenses-paid, Broder had insisted. But Cohen thought about the letter from personnel and the pension payment to his bank, one more bit of evidence of his age. Old men, he thought bitterly, always had to worry about their money. Then he laughed cynically to himself, thinking of Der Bruder, who had weighed barely thirty kilos on the day the Americans arrived at the camp, ballooning to more than a hundred and fifty during the years in Hollywood. But soon after Broder began work on *The Survivor's Secrets,* he reported in one of his calls to Cohen that he was planning to lose fifty kilos from his huge frame.

Cohen shifted uncomfortably again in the seat. He hated flying. He wished the engines behind and below him could lull him into a dreamless sleep instead of nag him into searching the even tone for a hint that something was wrong and the plane was about to fall from the sky. It badgered him like the question of whether he should be grateful to Der Bruder for giving him the opportunity to flee Jerusalem, or curse his old friend's penetration of his defenses. A braver man would have said yes to Ahuva, he thought. A stronger man would have said no to Broder. He remembered when he had been that strong, and wondered if he would ever be brave again. He was weighing the predicament when he sensed someone taking the empty seat beside him. He opened his eyes. It was Goldie. He had avoided her in Montreal, ignoring her smiles and winks across the waiting room of the terminal, hoping his rudeness would keep her away the rest of the trip. But she was incorrigible.

"There's a really good scene coming up," she said eagerly, picking up the earphones Cohen had dropped and making herself comfortable in the aisle seat. "Here," she ordered, holding out the earphones for him.

"Doesn't matter," she said when he only shook his head. "I know the words." Indeed, with the gossip columnist beside him Cohen didn't need the earphones, or have to read the lips of the actors. Goldie recited by heart as the figures moved on the screen. " 'Ralston, you bastard,' " Goldie hissed while a brunette in spike heels glared at a sharklike businessman behind a desk. " 'You think getting rid of me is gonna get me off your back? Well, you're wrong. I know who you really are. And I'm gonna expose you. D'you know why?' " The leering man on the screen leaned back in his chair, oozing crass sexual innuendo. " 'No, why?' " Goldie whispered in a guttural basso as the Ralston character spoke. There was a pause, and then she turned on the steam for the brunette's next line. " 'Because you're slime, Ralston. Slime.' "

Cohen couldn't prevent a short laugh at the columnist's enthusiasm, and she took it like bait, chortling, "I love it. 'Slime!' " she howled. "God, I love the movies. I mean, I know it's crap." She lowered her tone in mock apology. "But don't you love it?

Make the PI a dame. Great concept. They took in more than thirteen million the first weekend it opened." She leaned toward Cohen and, changing her tone completely, whispered in a seductive rasp, "So?"

"So what?" he asked.

"So are you going to *tell* me?"

"Tell you what?"

"How does an Israeli cop have enough money to pay for a first-class ticket to L.A.?"

"I was invited by an old friend. For a vacation."

"Really? Who's the Daddy Greenbucks?"

"Pardon me?" he said, not knowing the expression.

"Whoever it is must be rich," she said. "*And* value your company," she hinted with even more curiosity.

He shrugged slightly.

"Let me guess," she offered. She tapped one of her fingernails on her pouting lips, and before Cohen could protest, her eyes widened with excitement. "I've got it. Many years ago you fell in love with a suspect in a big heist, a beautiful woman, and you're on your way to see her because she was so beautiful and smart. She wasn't some over-the-hill bitch like me. Am I right?" She leaned closer to him, using her half-open blouse the way an interrogator offers a suspect a cigarette.

It was true that Der Bruder had seduced him. And saved him. Maybe they had even loved each other, he thought. But brothers sometimes fight too. He winced slightly.

Anticipating whatever answer he could make, she leered suggestively and said, "Or *maybe* your friend is an old customer. Israeli mafia," she whispered, either ignoring or not noticing his recoil. "You *were* on the take, and *now* you're on the *run*."

Six months earlier, he would have exploded. Exhausted from the sleepless flight, drained by weeks of self-pity, he could only scowl at her and look back to the movie screen, shaking his head with dismay.

"Kidding, I'm only kidding," she protested. "Come on," she pleaded. "What's the big secret? Remember what I said? We're both too old to play hard-to-get."

Cohen sighed. From the moment she had identified herself as a Hollywood gossip columnist, he knew she would recognize Max Broder's name. The last thing he wanted was her kibitzing about Der Bruder. But she had given him no choice.

"Max Broder," he finally confessed, feeling foolish for all his delaying tactics. From the start, he thought, he should have followed his own advice to every suspect he ever had questioned. Tell the truth.

"Max Broder? The director?" she asked. "*The* Max Broder?" she demanded excitedly when his silence confirmed her question. "He's friends with a cop?"

"A retired cop," Cohen protested. He pronounced the word like the Yiddish word for head, *kop,* as he deliberately turned away from her excitement.

A car chase had begun on the movie screen. Cohen opened the biography on his lap, hoping it would make her go away. But though she remained silent at his side, out of the corner of his eye he could see her right hand clicking two long red fingernails nervously against each other. The hum and rumble of the jet engines camouflaged the sound, but their insistent rhythm soon had him imagining the beat of her annoying tic. He looked up when he realized he was concentrating more on her thumb and forefinger than on Dayan's archaeology. But before he could ask her to stop, she finished her private deliberations.

"All right, what's Max Broder doing with a *retired* cop for a friend?" she demanded suspiciously, grabbing hold of his left forearm to get his attention.

He turned slowly to look at her hand on his arm. Her eyes fell in embarrassment to her fingernails on his thick wrist. They were like drops of blood alongside the sans-serif digits of the purple number tattooed on his broad left forearm, halfway between his elbow and his hand.

"Oh, God, I'm so sorry," she gushed, staring at his arm. "I didn't know. I mean, I knew that *he* was . . . I mean, everyone knows *he* was a . . . I'm sorry. I didn't realize . . ."

"It's all right," Cohen said in a comforting, almost paternal tone. Her stare made him self-conscious, and again he brushed a stray lock from his forehead, wondering if he had deliberately waited for her to notice the camp identification number. "There's no need to apologize," he said, and added in an almost officious tone, "I am on a long-overdue vacation. He has been inviting me for many years, but I never went. Now I am retired. So I am going." It spilled out of him like groceries from a torn bag, surprising him.

"Just in time, if you ask me," Goldie said eagerly. "What with all the *trouble* he's been having."

"Trouble?"

"You know, the studio pulling out of the project," she said.

"We never discuss his business," Cohen said bluntly.

"Right. Gimme a break. What do you talk about? The Lakers? Don't give me that bullshit," she complained.

His eyes fell reflexively to his forearm for a second and he looked back up at her.

"All right, sorry. I guess you do have other things to discuss. But still, you must know what's been going on with him. With the movie, I mean," she insisted.

He shook his head.

She studied his face. "This your first trip to Hollywood?"

He nodded.

"You don't know anything about it?" she asked.

"I don't go to the movies very often," he said. "And I don't believe everything I read in the newspapers," he added.

"Good thinking." She surprised him with her sincerity.

They both fell into silence. She tapped at her cheek with a finger, her eyes on the screen but her mind elsewhere. He waited patiently. She had much more to tell him, and he already knew he could count on her to show off what she knew, or thought she knew.

"God knows *somebody's* got to tell him there are limits," she finally said, as if to herself. Then she turned angrily on Cohen, stabbing at his broad chest with a long red fingernail. "I'll tell you something. I haven't reported half the things I've heard about him lately. You know why?"

Cohen listened to her with all the skepticism he knew how to muster. Gossips sold rumors, the cheapest bargains in the bazaar. Anyone could invent one, if only it was told with enough conviction.

"Because I *understand,*" she said in a stage whisper, nodding with conviction. "He couldn't help being obsessed with this flick. His masterpiece, they say. But I know it goes even deeper than that. Back to . . . to . . ." She tried to finish the sentence, but instead glanced again at the tattoo.

"His past," Cohen filled in for her.

"Exactly," she said, relieved. "But now that he's supposedly *finished* it, it's like he's doing everything to keep it from coming out. Not that I can blame the studio for canning it. Who cares about the Shoah nowadays?" she asked rhetorically, using the Hebrew word for Holocaust. "I mean, *except* us Jews?"

From the start, when Broder announced that the film was going to be made, Cohen had made clear his lack of interest in it. Now this woman's talk was making him feel guilty about his deliberate refusal to discuss the movie. The guilt primed, he defended Broder. "He won't do anything to jeopardize the movie," he said.

"Yeah?" she said doubtfully. "What about last week? He tried to kill Andy. And don't give me that look; there were witnesses."

His impulse to laugh drained away. She was serious.

"Andy?" he asked.

"Andy Blakely. He's studio chief at Epica."

"This Blakely—he is dead?" he asked.

"Of course not," she said, astounded by the question.

"So," Cohen said without trying to hide a patronizing smile, "Max has been arrested for attempted murder."

"Don't be silly," she blurted.

"You see?" he said sternly.

"Listen to me," she said, sitting upright, trying to be even more serious than he. "Your friend Max Broder made quite a scene. At Ma Maison, no less, which quite frankly is *not* the place to attack a studio chief. He tried to kill Andy with a *steak knife*. That's right," she said to his disbelieving eyes. "He was out of control. From what I hear, it was eleven points on the Richter scale of breakdowns." Satisfied with her testimony, she adjusted herself comfortably in her seat and smiled triumphantly at Cohen.

He didn't even blink. "When?" he asked.

"Tuesday night."

Broder had called Cohen in Jerusalem the following night, wanting to know which Hollywood actress Cohen wanted to meet. Cohen had demurred, but Broder insisted until finally Cohen threw out a name. Broder chortled, telling Cohen he was completely out of date. The actress had been dead for a decade. If anything, Cohen remembered, Broder sounded euphoric, describing his plans to have dinner at the best restaurants in the city and to arrange at least one good party. No parties, Cohen had protested, but Broder insisted. "What's the good of coming to Hollywood if I can't throw you a party?"

Cohen clenched at this memory as if it were a lone fingerprint on a murder weapon, and he reprimanded Goldie. "You don't know what really happened. You weren't there."

But the authority in his tone confounded her. "Of course not. I was too young."

"No," he corrected her. "I mean, you were in Jerusalem last week. You don't know what really happened."

"Listen, buster," she charged, "I'm paid a lot of money to know exactly what happens at Ma Maison *every* night of the week."

"Hearsay," Cohen scoffed.

"I don't usually do this," she shot back. "But in this case, and *only* because of the circumstances"—her eyes flickered to his arm again— "and you being Max's old friend and all, I'll tell you who told me." She pursed her lips as if priming the muscles for the effort to give away her source's name. "Leo Hirsh," she finally said, as if it were a trump card in a game.

"Who?" Cohen asked.

She rolled her eyes at his ignorance. "Leo Hirsh. Epica board member *and* Max's executive producer on this project. Hell, Leo goes back to *Two to Tango* with Max. That's almost thirty years. In fact, until I met you, I thought Leo was Max's oldest friend."

"Was Hirsh at the restaurant?" Cohen asked.

"He was at the table!" she exclaimed.

"And he called you in Jerusalem to tell you about this?"

"That's right," she said proudly.

On the movie screen, the woman detective was sitting behind a newspaper, waiting for someone in a hotel lobby. Cohen covered his eyes with the palm of his meaty hand, cursing silently. He had known he wouldn't like Broder's friends. "Children play a game called broken telephone," he finally said. "They sit in a circle. The first one whispers to the second one. The second one to the third. The message becomes distorted." He paused before adding, "Among children it is harmless."

"Listen," she hissed. "Don't be such an asshole. I'm *trying* to tell you something. It's *suicide* for Max to attack Andy Blakely like that."

"Why?" Cohen asked.

"Because," she began, sighing with exasperation at his ignorance of what should have been obvious. "Andy's job is to get Epica out of the red, and there's no way any Holocaust flick is going to be a summer hit or take Christmas by storm. So Andy pulled Epica out of the distribution deal. The last thing he needs now is a flop. The stock market would kill him."

"So?"

She shook her head at his incomprehension. "Epica owns the movie. If they don't show it, *nobody* will see it."

He snorted. Broder would have had at least two fallback positions for every possible obstacle on the way to his goal. Der Bruder had made an art out of contingency plans. Cohen could already hear Broder's braying laugh when Cohen would tell him what the columnist reported. "Ridiculous," he muttered, shifting away from her in his seat, as he thought of all the ways Der Bruder knew how to kill. None of them included a steak knife across a table in a crowded restaurant. "Ridiculous," he repeated, punching at the hard, uncomfortable pillow propped between his seat and the window.

Goldie looked at him for a long moment and then tenderly touched his arm. He opened his eyes. "It really happened," she said. He couldn't help but notice the pity in her voice and for a moment wondered if it was for him, for Broder, or for herself.

He shook his head. "I doubt it."

"You're the one who says you haven't seen him in a long time.

Maybe he's changed." She paused. "Hollywood does that. Changes people. *You* don't know Hollywood. But *I* do." It sounded as if she was trying to break the news gently.

"And you don't know Max Broder," Cohen muttered back, not knowing whom he was defending, his old friend or himself. He huffily wrapped his arms around his chest, turning away from her.

"I'm sorry I'm the one to break the news," she said, patting his arm sympathetically. "I was only trying to help."

He refused to acknowledge her attempt at tenderness.

"Maybe *that's* why he invited you," she said, suddenly thoughtful.

But he only hunkered deeper in the seat, refusing to participate any longer in her gossip.

"Whatever," she surrendered, getting up from the seat. "If you're staying with him," she added from the aisle, "I'm sure we'll run into each other again. He gets around to *all* the right places."

He waited until her perfume faded before he opened his eyes to the dark night sky beyond the oval window. She had made him miss the sunset. He slapped off the reading lamp, readjusted the pillow, and pulled at the too-small blanket that had slumped behind him in the seat, drawing it over his shoulders against the cabin's chill.

He was suddenly aware that he had clutched Jerusalem around him like a *tallit*. Each knot on the fringed prayer shawl represented one of the Bible's commandments. But for Cohen the linen had frayed over the years, the knots of belief had come loose in one terrible blow.

He dozed fitfully for the rest of the flight, waking finally to the shifting tones of the jet engines in descent. For a second he didn't know where he was. The fright passed, and he made his decision. He'd stay a few days. Maybe even see Der Bruder's damn movie. But then he'd go home.

The engines screamed. As his stomach muscles tightened under the seat belt with the rumble of the wheels touching down, he wondered if Goldie was right and Hollywood had changed Max Broder in ways Cohen could never have imagined. But with the relief he felt when the plane's rush down the runway turned into a slow, smooth taxi to the terminal came the realization that at least he knew Der Bruder.

T W O

THE PILOT THANKED the tail winds for getting them to L.A. on time and thanked the passengers for trusting him with their lives. "It's ninety-eight point six out there. Body temperature," he quipped over the loudspeaker as the plane nudged into its slot at the terminal.

Cohen was the first passenger out of his seat, the first out of the plane. The customs officer raised an eyebrow at the long-distance first-class traveler with only a single bag of clothes. But the officer asked only a perfunctory "Business or pleasure?" as he noticed Cohen's profession on the brand-new blue Israeli passport with its single visa imprinted at the U.S. consulate in Jerusalem.

"Personal," Cohen said, adding, "I'm retired," in an almost apologetic tone, immediately embarrassed by what felt to him like a confession.

"Lucky you," the gray-haired official said, smiling broadly as he handed back the passport. Cohen didn't return the smile. He followed signs to the main exit. Through glass doors at the end of a long corridor, he could see the expectant faces of people waiting for arriving travelers, and as he pushed through the doors, he was already scanning for Der Bruder's face. Planning ahead was one of Der Bruder's keener qualities, a compulsiveness that tried to cover every detail. Only those who plan can improvise, Der Bruder taught.

The plane was on time. Broder would have been five minutes early. So it took only a few minutes for Cohen to realize that his

friend was not at the airport. He carefully checked the black-
boards and placards held up by a row of chauffeurs waiting for
arriving travelers. Even Broder could have had a last-minute ob-
ligation, might have sent a driver instead of personally picking up
Cohen as he had promised. But no sign advertised Avram Cohen's
name.

He used his free hand to reach for his flask and achieve the
sweet burn of cognac on his tongue. Shaking Goldie Stein's tales
out of his ears, he headed for a bank of pay phones across the
wide corridor. After a moment's fumble for the proper coin, he
punched in the number. A gruff, impatient "Yeah?" answered. It
wasn't Der Bruder's voice.

Cohen identified himself and asked for Max Broder.

"Avram Cohen, you said?" asked the man.

"Yes."

"Hold on."

Cohen's hearing was dulled, his ears were still ringing from the
pressurized cabin. But he was aware of voices in the background.
"You're the friend from Israel?" the man said. "The cop?"

"Is Max there?" Cohen demanded impatiently.

"I asked you a question," the man insisted.

"Yes, yes," Cohen said impatiently. "From Jerusalem, yes."

"I'm afraid there's some bad news," said the stranger.

Cohen gripped the receiver tightly. "Yes?"

"Your friend's dead," he said. "He hanged himself." A half beat
later, the man added, "I'm sorry."

The air conditioning in the terminal was powerful, but sweat
gathered quickly in the hollow of Cohen's palm clutching the
receiver. "Pardon?" he asked, hopeful that he had misunderstood.
He shifted the receiver to the other ear. "Again, please?" he asked.

"He hanged himself," the man repeated. "I'm sorry."

Cohen slumped slightly, grasping the phone booth's soundproof divider with one hand. "That's impossible," he said reflexively.

"It happened," said the stranger at the end of the line.

"Who are you?" Cohen asked in a shocked whisper.

"Madden. Detective Sergeant Mike Madden. Beverly Hills Police."

"I'm on my way." Cohen hung up without waiting for a response from the American policeman. He grabbed his bag from the floor and strode blindly away from the phones.

His mind was reeling, and he careered with it, walking twice as fast as everyone around him, dodging the pedestrian traffic like a racer moving through the pack. All the claustrophobia he had felt in the plane exploded into a need to get out of the terminal building. Grief propelled him forward blindly. Der Bruder. Dead. Suicide. It was so illogical, so preposterous—so impossible—that he suddenly froze in place, paralyzed by the contradictions.

Someone bumped into him from behind. Cohen spun, ready to strike. "Hey, man, I'm sorry, it's cool," the young man said, holding up a guitar case to protect himself and backing away from the fury on Cohen's face. He gave Cohen a strange look and then, mumbling about crazies on the Coast, passed the bewildered Jerusalemite, leaving a wide berth.

Deadlocked at an intersection of four brightly lit hallways and a confusion of signs pointing to terminals and avenues, exits and parking lots, Cohen stared into his own darkness. The airport bustle was dull and inarticulate around him. Faces passed, voices spoke. But he heard nothing and saw nothing.

He had the return ticket to Israel. Get out of here. Leave, he thought. Go home. He looked up at the signs, but all he saw were blurred letters and stubby arrows. His mouth was as dry as Jerusalem in September. He realized that he was shaking and a cold sweat was pouring from his forehead. His heart was beating erratically. He felt dizzy and tried to control the panic, looking around for somewhere to sit down. Plastic chairs lined the nearby wall. He forced himself to move first one foot and then the other. It was only a few steps. His knees gave way, and he fell into the seat. A memory of young Max Broder, whispering harshly at him, came into his mind. "You want to kill yourself?" Broder had whispered sarcastically. "I'll tell you how."

The dizziness was making him nauseous. Max Broder's face was suddenly replaced by the face of another young man: Ori, the doctor who had treated him less than a year ago for the knife wounds in his belly. Seeing Cohen's intake of cigarettes, he had run some tests. The doctor's voice echoed in Cohen's mind: "You're trying to kill yourself." Cohen convinced Ori not to pass on the results to the police medical board. Not that it had mattered. A month later, the prime minister himself made the decision that Cohen's career was over.

"Sir, sir?" A woman's voice was in his ear. "Are you all right?"

His eyes fluttered open, and he had to concentrate to focus. She was wearing an airline cap on top of her coiled blond hair. Behind severe glasses, she had worried eyes.

He blinked. There was a sour taste in his mouth, and though the dizziness was gone, he felt light-headed. He realized he had slumped over the armrest of the chair, into the next seat. He started to sit up, and she helped him, putting an arm under his to lift him upright. Pain, augmented by self-pity, crossed his face.

"Let me get you a doctor," the flight attendant said.

"No doctor," he answered hoarsely. "I'm fine."

"You fainted," she said. "That man over there saw it." She pointed toward a platinum-haired man standing beside a phone booth across the corridor. He was wearing a black sports jacket, a white, tieless shirt, and black trousers. If not for his uncovered head, he might have been one of the ultra-Orthodox of Jerusalem.

"I'm all right," Cohen insisted. His throat felt raw, as if he had just been shouting. He cleared it, and repeated the assertion in a stronger voice, fighting the impulse to shout her away.

"Can I get you anything? Water? Anything?"

"It's happened before to me," he lied. "I didn't eat very much on the airplane," he added. That was the truth.

"Yeah, I know what you mean," she whispered conspiratorially. "I can't eat it myself. Maybe you need something fresh and healthy," she suggested.

He rubbed a hand over his clammy forehead. "A washroom?" he asked, and she pointed across the wide corridor. "Thank you," he said. He took a breath and stood up, surprised at the wooziness.

She rose with him. "You sure you're all right?" she asked earnestly, touching his elbow for support.

The light-headed feeling passed. "Yes. I'm fine. Really. Thank you."

She picked up his bag. "There's an airport doctor," she offered again.

"No doctor," he snapped back, grabbing his bag. Her expression made him apologize. "I'm sorry. I'm just tired. That's all." He began a retreat. "Tired. Thank you. Thank you," he repeated, and then turned to concentrate on the door to the lavatory across the corridor.

He stood in front of the corridor at the first sink in a long row, and he stared at his gaunt face. The bags beneath his eyes were deep and dark. He ran cold water and cupped his hands under the stream, then rubbed the chilly water into his face, as if he could wash away the age and the pain that gnarled his face like an old olive tree. It wasn't enough. He plugged the sink with a paper towel and filled it with water. He dunked his head, once, twice, three times, each douse driving away another layer of the fog that had gathered thickly in his mind. Finally, he pulled a towel from his bag to wipe his face dry, and looked into the mirror again.

But instead of his own face, he saw Max Broder's. It was long and narrow, with deep-set haunted eyes that, even when Max grinned, were wry and full of secrets. Cohen gripped the porcelain sink for support, closing his own eyes tightly. In that darkness he saw worse than Broder's grinning face.

He saw the hanging victims. Cohen had seen too many of those. And so had Broder, he knew.

He blinked in the fluorescent light until all he saw was his own familiar gaze, the permanent imprint of weariness in his eyes. Der Bruder a suicide. Impossible, he thought. But there was only one way to verify the truth. He picked up his bag and headed out of the lavatory to look for a taxi.

Just outside the men's room door, in the wide corridor of the airport, he saw the concerned citizen who had pointed him out to the stewardess. Cohen smiled weakly, nodding silent thanks. But the man didn't seem to notice, disappearing past a line of departing travelers.

The cabbie studied a book of maps as thick as Jerusalem's phone directory before announcing that it would cost seventy dollars for the hour's ride to the Beverly Hills address. Maybe it was the look in Cohen's eye, or maybe it was a slow night, but the driver didn't put up an argument when Cohen pulled open the back door, saying, "Fifty dollars and no talking."

The seat was lumpy, and the air conditioning made him rifle through the canvas bag for his windbreaker. They rode north on a wide highway thick with cars. He leaned against the windowpane, the glassy chill a memory of the cold sweat that had accompanied his faint inside the airport.

He no longer felt the nausea. But his mind continued to whirl crazily. The car transported him like a lifeless bundle, and that, like the hunger in his belly, reminded him of another time, long before, when he had been certain he was riding to his death. But Broder had been at his side then. Calm and calculating, he was by then already Der Bruder to Cohen. Barely moving his lips, Cohen cursed softly. First at himself, for making the trip. Then at Der Bruder.

The scenery beyond the speeding car window was a blur of headlights and shopping malls, neon signs and skyscrapers, all as anonymous and meaningless to him as the stars. There was a salty taste on his lips. He thought about how far he had traveled, halfway around the world to the edge of this continent, aware that just to the west, where the earthbound stars of the city came to an abrupt halt, was the ocean. He told himself that the salty taste was either the ocean's breath or his own sweat, and concentrated on the instinct that had told him to order the policeman on the phone to wait.

For years he had been telling junior officers the exact same thing. He searched deeply within for feelings that had been dormant for six months. Disbelief merged with instincts embedded during years of investigation. He would see for himself. It's all he could do. He owed it to Der Bruder. At least, he decided, he would stay for the funeral. And go to the ocean. That was something he wanted to see.

He closed his eyes and attempted to force his mind to sink into darkness, below the surface turbulence. On the way down into the depths, he realized he was trying to think about anything except Broder. But just before touching the black bottom of sleep, he understood that he was trying to think about anything except himself.

It seemed only a moment later when a sharp turn knocked his

cheek painfully against the windowpane, waking him from a familiar nightmare that always ended just before Cohen thought he
had finally understood its meaning.

They were off the highway. He checked his watch. If the driver
had told the truth, the journey was finally coming to an end. He
was surprised to learn that Beverly Hills actually did have hills.
He had thought that everything in Hollywood was make-believe.
Maybe the policeman on the phone was make-believe. Maybe the
suicide was make-believe.

The car sped onto a ridgeline road that gave him a sudden view
of the city below. Streets and commercial strips, skyscrapers and
vast plains of roads and highways, pulsated with lights and color.
He fought the passivity that had overtaken him months before.
He had prepared himself for the rendezvous with Der Bruder but
not for the city itself. Just before the taxi entered a short patch
of thick fog, he looked down on the lights and wondered where
exactly Hollywood was, remembering Goldie's condescension.
"You don't know Hollywood," she had said, as if it were a state
of mind for which no road map could be drawn. And when he
answered, "You don't know Max Broder," he had meant she didn't
know Der Bruder.

The car came out of a dip, and he grabbed at the handgrip over
the door when the taxi turned sharply into a left-hand turn. The
headlights lit up thousands of tiny white objects on the black road
ahead. Straining to look out the rear window, Cohen realized that
they were broken blossoms from a stretch of oleander bushes lining
the road. The petals flurried in the wake of the car, and for the
first time, as he turned back in his seat, Cohen started paying
attention to Broder's neighborhood. They passed wrought-iron
gates and long circular driveways leading up to white haciendas,
gray mansions, and strange architectural experiments, all illumi-

nated by lights set into landscaped gardens. Each estate was walled, with shrubbery or stone, wooden fencing or stucco walls topped with broken glass.

He was thinking of the hidden courtyards of Jerusalem, when the taxi driver spoke for the first time since Cohen had settled into the back seat. "You with the cops?" he asked, startling Cohen as they pulled into a circular driveway fronting a gray-stone building that was more castle than house, with a tower at each end and a turret-topped portal at the entrance.

A patrol car and four expensive sedans were parked around the circle. The taxi drove slowly past the cars. Cohen recognized none of the makes, except a Mercedes like the one driven by a politician Cohen had always suspected but not quite caught. He scowled as the cab halted in front of the broad wooden door. On the patio, three steps above the gravel driveway, a short, square-jawed policewoman stood at attention in front of the arched doorway. She uncrossed her arms and propped her fists on her hips. "Weird," the driver mumbled.

Cohen sighed as he pulled a fifty-dollar bill from his wallet and handed it to the driver. He yanked at the canvas bag and opened the door.

"You have business here?" the policewoman drawled gruffly before Cohen was out of the car.

"Avram Cohen. For Madden," he said.

The policewoman hefted the heavy holster on her hip. "Wait here," she ordered, then opened the door to the house, disappearing inside.

Cohen stepped away from the taxi, and the driver immediately revved the engine. The yellow cab spat gravel as it fishtailed around the circular driveway. The red brake lights flickered once at the end of the drive, and then the car was gone. Cohen turned back to the house. Broder had been proud of it, bringing pictures to show Cohen in Jerusalem in the summer of 1967, the year after he bought it.

A large man was watching from the doorway, a silhouette in the bright lights that spilled from the portal. The policewoman was back in her sentinel's position on the porch.

Cohen sighed. He felt bedraggled. He needed food, a shower, a bed. He needed Der Bruder to explain where he was. He needed his life back. He nodded to the tall man.

"I'm Madden," the man said, backing up in the doorway as a gesture of invitation. Cohen hefted his bag, smiled weakly at the policewoman, and then crossed the threshold and limply accepted the American detective's handshake.

They were in a foyer lit by a huge chandelier. The bright light emphasized Madden's square-jawed face and reflected off the balding scalp beneath his graying red hair. His clothes hung on him as limply as his thinning hair. He had worn them past the point where they could pretend to trim a paunch or emphasize height. His shoes were a brushed leather that didn't need polishing, with rubber soles as silent as Cohen's sneakers on the quarry-tile floors.

"I've been waiting for you," Madden said, closing the door to the policewoman outside. They were alone in the silent air-conditioned chill. The polished tiles reflected the hundred lights of the chandelier hanging overhead. Directly in front of Cohen was a wide staircase, leading to a second-story landing. To his left was a wide entrance to a baronial living room. A vaulted ceiling exposed beams like an angry dog's bared teeth. To his right was a dining room, dominated by a long, burnished table with high-backed chairs for twenty guests.

"Again, sorry about your friend," Madden said behind him. "I hear you knew him a long time," he added sympathetically.

Cohen was looking at a tapestry hanging on the far wall of the dining room. Broder had bought it in the Old City *shuk* two weeks after the Six Day War, on the same trip during which he had told Cohen about the house. The tapestry was more than four hundred years old and showed St. George slaying a dragon to free the maiden on the rock of Jaffa port. It had been a quarter century since such discoveries could be made in the open market of Jerusalem, Cohen thought, sighing. "Yes, a very long time," he said softly, his voice hoarse. He coughed once deeply, feeling an ache in his ribs.

"If you could speak up, please," Madden said behind him.

"Since the war," Cohen said, more loudly. He was hearing his own words as if they were coming from outside his body. He realized his ears were still clogged from the pressurized cabin. He swallowed hard, trying to clear them. He glanced at Madden. The American was at least ten years his junior, he decided. A sergeant, he remembered. So he added a clarification. "The Second World War."

"Yeah, they told me." There was admiration in Madden's voice. "And the last time you saw him?" he asked, pulling a pen and pad out of his inside jacket pocket. He opened the pad, his pen poised.

"Four years ago," Cohen said. The American was a head taller than he was. In the bright light of the chandelier, Cohen could see the broken red capillaries on Madden's bulbous nose. "In Jerusalem," Cohen explained. "But I spoke with him several times in the last few days," he said, looking back at the tapestry. Grief filled his chest as he counted each call in his mind. "Six times," he said, speaking to St. George.

Behind him he heard Madden's book slap shut and then the sharp hiss of a match being lit. He turned just as Madden tilted his head back to blow a thick cloud of blue cigar smoke up toward the chandelier.

Cohen shivered, even though he was still wearing the jacket from the taxi ride. In the few moments he had waited outside in the heat, he had started sweating. Now he was feeling cold again. His body was as confused as his mind. He pulled his silver flask from his pocket and took a long sip. Madden smirked. Cohen looked down at the flask in his hand and then held it out, offering Madden a swig.

Madden deliberated silently for a second, looking from Cohen's eyes to the gleaming flask. "Fuck it," he said, reaching out. He sniffed once at the small opening, then smiled at Cohen before pouring a short stream of the cognac into his open mouth. He smacked his lips, then scowled at the taste as he handed it back to Cohen.

"I want to see the body," Cohen said.

"Shit," muttered the American. But before he could add anything, a shrill shout came from the dining room.

"Commander Cohen!" the man's high-pitched voice squawked loudly.

"Fuck," Madden snarled under his breath, but Cohen wasn't sure if it was because of the voice or the mention of his rank.

Cohen turned to identify the voice. Under different circumstances, he might have laughed at the metallic Lycra track suit that only emphasized the tiny man's roly-poly shape. The track suit would have been more appropriate on an Olympic competitor thirty years younger than the short man with barrel thighs, balloon belly, and weak chest. His tiny round spectacles reminded Cohen of the posters of rock-and-roll musicians on the walls of the record stores he frequented in Jerusalem. The man stepped delicately past Madden as if the detective were something more than furniture but less than a person. Madden looked down with his own distaste, exhaling a tiny stream of smoke at the little man's back, and with a haughty smile dared Cohen to protest.

"Leo, Leo Hirsh," the little man announced from a few steps away, holding out his arms as if to embrace the Jerusalemite like a long-lost brother. Cohen didn't reciprocate the gesture. But the producer wasn't deterred. He grabbed Cohen's hand and pumped as he spoke. "We had no idea you were coming. None at all," he said, rising on the balls of his feet in order to look straight into Cohen's eyes. "If Max had only told me, I would have had a limo waiting for you. What am I saying? 'If Max had only told me,'" Hirsh suddenly bawled, dropping back to his normal height. He reached into his pants pocket and pulled out a crumpled tissue. He blew his nose loudly and took a deep breath. He was about to continue, when he turned on Madden. "Do you have to smoke?" he snapped.

But the American detective was studying something beyond the narrow window beside the front door. From where Cohen was standing he could see only the rear end of a red convertible pulling up in front of the house. As Hirsh joined Madden at the window, Cohen noticed that the producer wore his hair in a small gray ponytail that only accentuated the absurd fight against age. Cohen unconsciously raked a hand through his own hair, guessing that he and Hirsh were close to the same age.

"Shit," Madden hissed.

"Oh, God, how'd she find out?" Hirsh cried. "Whatever you do, don't let her in," he said, backpedaling toward the dining room. "At least not until I get Vicki out the back door. Vicki will kill me if she finds her here," he said, talking as much to himself as to the others, "and *she'll* kill me if she finds out Vicki was here and I didn't tell her." He turned and bobbed through the banquet hall to the rear of the house, as Madden opened the front door. Cohen stepped into place beside him.

"Don't tell me," Goldie Stein called out cheerfully to Cohen, her high heels crunching on the gravel as she walked around the car. She had changed into a pink jumpsuit, unzipped to create a dark backdrop for a rope of gold hanging knotted around her neck, its casual noose dipping into her deep cleavage. "You got a police escort from the airport. So?" she asked, approaching them. "Where's Max? How'd the *reunion* go?" she added. "I decided it was too good an item to miss, so I——"

The policewoman stepped into Goldie's advance as the columnist reached the front step. "I'm sorry, ma'am, you'll have to stop right there."

"Don't be absurd," Goldie said disdainfully, and tried to move up one more step. The policewoman held up her hands to stop her. "Avram, will you tell this *person* that I can come in," Goldie ordered over the policewoman's head. But before either he or Madden could say anything, Goldie's expression changed to relief, and she was looking past the two men to someone approaching from behind them.

"Phyllis," she called out, relief in her voice. "Thank God, at least there's *someone* here who'll tell me what's going on."

Cohen turned. Like Leo Hirsh, the woman was dressed in the costume of a professional athlete. But while the producer's tight track suit emphasized the grotesque shape of his body, hers smoothed out all the curves into a too-sleek physique of flat plains instead of curves. Diets and exercise controlled her body. She was almost as tall as Madden, with the slightly hunched shoulders of a woman who had been ashamed of her size as a young girl. Her hair was drawn tightly back into a bun, tightening the skin of her face, which was pockmarked but tanned as leathery as Goldie's. She was way past thirty, Cohen thought, wondering how close she was to fifty.

Looking as if she'd be far more comfortable in a suit, she offered a professional handshake to Cohen, ignoring the columnist.

"Commander," she said, presenting a large hand. "I'm Phyllis Fine. Max's lawyer." Cohen took the chilly handshake automatically, noticing that unlike Hirsh, she had no redness in her eyes.

"I'm so sorry," she gasped. "We had no idea you were coming, and to arrive to something like this . . ." She let a sigh finish the sentence.

"Phyl-lis!" Goldie whined from the driveway.

"I'm sorry. Goldie, this is Commander Cohen. He's——"

"I know who he is, goddammit. I spent eighteen hours on a frigging plane with him. What I want to know is what's going on here?"

The lawyer didn't break the news softly. "Max is dead," she said simply. Cohen noticed that the lawyer cocked her head immediately after she said it, as if studying Goldie's reaction.

"Yeah, sure. Who did it?" Goldie joked, disbelieving. "Andy Blakely? Gimme a break. What's really going on?" She took a step forward. "Max!?" she called out into the vast house. "Max, are you there? It's Goldie!" Half an echo came back. She looked at Fine, Cohen, and Madden, confused.

"He's gone," Fine said solemnly. "They took him away an hour ago."

Cohen glared at Madden, but the American was watching Goldie. She gulped, and her hand went to her throat. Her eyes scanned them all, stopping at Cohen. It was as if she needed his confirmation before she could believe it. She touched her breastbone contritely, the question in her eye. Cohen nodded gravely, noticing Madden and Fine exchanging their own glances. Madden finally raised an eyebrow, handing over the responsibility to Fine.

"It was suicide," Fine said softly.

Goldie's eyes darted between Fine and Cohen, finally settling again on Cohen for confirmation. But he remained stone-faced, only nodding slightly. "I guess he got his cop too late," she said. Suddenly her expression changed to worry. "Sophie?" she asked anxiously. "What about Sophie?"

The name startled Cohen. He hadn't thought about Sophie Levine since Broder had told him that Bernard Levine's daughter was finally safe. He felt as if he was being ambushed by ghosts. He tried to remember when Der Bruder had said that he had finally avenged Bernard's death, taking in the girl. Two years ago? Three? He wondered if, like his body, his mind was beginning to fail him. But noticing the slight sneer that crossed Fine's face at Goldie's mention of Sophie Levine, he forced himself to stay attentive.

"She found the body," Hirsh piped behind Cohen, startling them all. The producer was slightly breathless. "Hello, Goldie," he added.

"That poor girl. Twice an orphan," Goldie lamented, adding with resolve, "I've *got* to see her."

Hirsh frowned at the idea. "Not now, Goldie. Please," he said. "The coroner gave her a sedative. And there are still a hundred calls to make. To let people know." Goldie started to interrupt, but Hirsh guessed what she was going to say. "I phoned your hotel in Jerusalem. I didn't know you were back," he tried.

"Bullshit," Goldie snapped.

"But he hasn't told Chucky yet," Fine offered.

"That's right." Hirsh nodded enthusiastically. "So you still have it ahead of him. It's your story right now."

"Thank *God* for small favors," Goldie said cynically.

"Come on," Hirsh said, stepping onto the porch, past Cohen, Madden, and Fine. Taking Goldie's arm, he started to lead her away from the policewoman back toward her car. "I'll tell you what Andy said."

"As if *I* couldn't tell *you*," Goldie said contemptuously, halting in her tracks. " 'It's a terrible tragedy' "—she dropped her voice into the same kind of labored basso she had used to imitate the leering businessman in the movie on the airplane—" 'a loss for the studio and the entire industry.' Shit, Leo," she suddenly added in her own reedy voice, "I wouldn't be surprised if the son of a bitch said that he had no idea Max Broder was so . . . so 'troubled.' That's right—that's what the fucker would say. Troubled, my ass," she said with contempt. "Come on, Leo, tell me something I don't know," she demanded. "Tell me about the movie. Max is dead. The secrets can come out now. Start with something simple. Like the title. Or the story line. I know it's about the Holocaust. But give me something more. Why'd he make everybody sign those secrecy clauses in their contracts? And why didn't he let me on the set?"

"You weren't the only one," Hirsh protested. "He didn't let Chucky, either. You know that. It wasn't personal. It was policy."

Cohen shivered, but it wasn't his body that was troubled. Some of Max Broder's secrets were his too.

"Leo, why don't you tell her what Laszlo Katz had to say," Fine suggested.

"*Now* you're talking," Goldie said, smiling coolly at Fine. "What did his majesty have to say?"

Hirsh was about to begin, when Cohen spoke up, surprising them all. He knew the name. "Why does it matter what Laszlo Katz said?" he rumbled.

"Laszlo owns Epica," Hirsh said, turning back to the Jerusalemite. "Well, he's the chairman of Oceanic, and Oceanic owns Epica. He's always been interested in the movie. In fact, Max wanted to show it at the benefit. For HEI," Hirsh explained. Cohen thought he had said *chai,* the Hebrew word for "life." "You know," the producer said to Cohen's questioning eyes. "The Holocaust Education Institute? It's this coming weekend, Saturday night, at Katz's house. Max wanted you," Hirsh added, with a solemn gulp at the mention of Broder's name, "as one of the guests of honor."

Again Cohen cursed Der Bruder, and then himself for the folly of believing Broder's promises. Katz's name was on marble and brass plaques all over Israel. Some were in hospitals, others in universities. But it was Holocaust studies and memorials that most profited from Katz's philanthropy. A full-fledged Shoah Business, Cohen thought bitterly. At Laszlo Katz's house, no less. Broder never mentioned it. Cohen hated such events, and Broder knew it. Cohen wondered if he would have won the fight with Der Bruder over attending, and realized he was feeling queasy, thinking about what other ambushes Der Bruder had planned. The possibility that the suicide itself was one of Broder's surprises tried to pry at Cohen's mind. But he clamped down hard on its icy grasp, and it melted away.

"Max had this idea that Katz might overrule Blakely," Hirsh was saying. "I tried to explain it to him. But he wouldn't listen. Blakely made a decision when he canned it. That's all. Business. Laszlo had to stick by his man."

" 'Laszlo,' " Goldie scoffed. "You make him sound like he's a regular *pal* of yours. I'll bet he didn't even talk to you. I'll bet," she added, pleased with herself, "you got it from one of his *secretaries.*"

"That's not true!" Hirsh protested. "I spoke directly with him," he said proudly.

"So? What are you waiting for?" Goldie exclaimed. "What did he say?" She grabbed Hirsh's arm and pulled him away. Cohen heard a slight sigh of relief from Fine before she stepped off the porch to join Hirsh and the columnist. Politics, he thought, disgusted. He touched Madden's arm, a signal to step back into the house for their own conversation.

"They were trying to con Vicki Strong into going to the funeral," Madden said softly as they entered the house. "She lives next door and came over when the first siren pulled up. And everybody knows Vicki hates Goldie."

Even Cohen had heard of Vicki Strong. But he shoved her aside, rumbling, "He knew I was coming. Maybe they didn't. But *he* did. He sent me the tickets. It doesn't make any sense that he would do this on the day I was coming."

Madden lit his cigar again, considering Cohen's statement. "Tell you the truth," Madden said, exhaling a cloud of smoke. "You showing up gave them more of a jolt than him taking the big jump." He took another puff, eyeing Cohen over the burning end, silently asking why Broder didn't tell anyone in Hollywood in advance about Cohen's trip.

Cohen had been asking himself the same question, from the moment he met Leo Hirsh. He ran through the possibilities in his mind. Whom did Der Bruder want to surprise? And what was the surprise?

But Madden had already made up his mind. "Fuck, a guy jumps, who knows why he does what he does?"

Cohen sighed to himself. "Please," he said, "I must sit down." He went to the banquet table, ran his hand over the luxuriously polished wood, wondering if it was mahogany. As he pulled out one of the tall-backed chairs, he saw at the end of the room a pair of swinging doors that he decided went into a kitchen. But his hunger had to wait.

"From what they say," Madden said behind him, "it sounds like your friend was in deep shit. They worked with him daily. If you want to call what they do work." There was resentment in his voice. "You saw him . . . when was it?"

"Four years ago," Cohen admitted.

"And talked with him a couple of times on the phone," Madden said knowingly. "You got to admit, they knew him better."

"Six times," Cohen said softly, to himself more than Madden.

"What's that?"

"A note? A letter?" Cohen said, louder.

"Nope," Madden said. "Sorry."

Cohen sensed that the American's sympathy was turning impatient, and something in his tone augmented Cohen's suspicion. "You searched?" he asked, studying the detective's ruddy face.

The question startled Madden. "I looked around," he said defensively.

"You looked around," Cohen repeated slowly. Any of his former subordinates would have recognized the reprimand.

Madden did too. "They said you were some kind of Dick Tracy back in Israel," the American snapped. "Well, this isn't Israel. Fuck, up here," he said, looking around at the stately room, "I sometimes wonder if we're even in America. But those people out there say the guy killed himself, and I can't find any reason to argue with them."

Cohen tried to interrupt, but Madden cut him off. "This is Hollywood, man," the policeman continued. "People do funny things here. Like punching their own tickets because of a movie. The guy's masterpiece went down the tubes." He used the term as if he didn't understand artists but knew what they could do if their work was ruined.

"That's what Leo Hirsh says. And I'll tell you straight, I read the trades—got to, if I want to keep score in this town. So I know who Leo Hirsh is, *and* Phyllis Fine. But you?" he added, as if he had stumbled onto the conclusion. "You? I don't know you.

Or why you're here." He was trying to use the accusation as a lever.

But Cohen paid it no mind. He was struggling with the memories. Der Bruder had saved him from death many times. And once he had rescued Cohen from suicide. Cohen shook his head no, exasperating Madden.

"All right," the man blustered. "Here's something for you to chew on." He yanked his notebook out of his inside pocket. "Barbara something," he mumbled to himself. "Yeah, Darnaby. Barbara Darnaby. Ever hear of her?"

Cohen bowed over the table, resting his forehead in the palm of his hand. He, too, was frustrated. "Sergeant, until today I had never heard of Goldie Stein, Leo Hirsh, or Phyllis Fine. Vicki Strong I heard of." He sighed deeply.

"An English broad," Madden said, looking up from his notebook. "Worked for Broder as an assistant producer. That's the official version. But unofficially? It was probably something more than just work. That's what I heard between the lines when the lady lawyer was showing off. And last week the broad rolled him over. For Blakely, no less. According to Fine, when Darnaby showed up with Blakely at some business luncheon they were having, Broder went over the deep end. Completely. Old guy, young dame. I've seen it a million times. Speaking of which, there's the German broad. Sophie Levine. Now, there's a chick who could make a guy blow his brains out."

Cohen peered through his fingers at Madden's leer. He felt a momentary hatred for the American. But he couldn't complain about Madden. It was just one more day on the job for the man. Thirty years of sunburns instead of tans were creased across Madden's brow. Cohen wondered how much longer it would be before it was Madden's turn to retire.

Not long, Cohen decided, sitting up straight. He had searched

within himself for strength. For now it was enough that he wanted
to prove Madden wrong. He would be the first to admit that he
didn't know, or want to know, anything about Hollywood, and
that he certainly knew nothing about Max Broder's life there. He
summoned the only piece of evidence he so far had, and looked
up crookedly at Madden.

The sergeant was standing at the end of the table, admiring his
reflection in the sheen of the waxed surface.

"He couldn't commit suicide," Cohen said softly, his silver-gray
eyes grabbing Madden's. "Not over a movie"—he held up his
thumb—"and not over a woman." He extended a forefinger. He
implied that he could have ticked off a dozen other reasons for
suicide that might be considered normal in Beverly Hills but that
would have had no effect on Max Broder. "He did not survive
Dachau concentration camp in order to commit suicide," Cohen
grumbled, trying to control his temper as he explained what was
to him the obvious.

"I don't know about that," Madden admitted dubiously. "But
I do know about this place," he added with more conviction. "You
know how many suicides we get in this town? We get 'em with
ropes, dope, guns, razors; we get 'em with cars. And you know
what? Nowadays we get 'em with sex. Fuck, suicide's a way of life
around here. You just don't hear about it, that's all. You know
why?" He leaned forward, almost conspiratorially, and answered
his own question when Cohen remained silent. "Money. Suicide's
a fucking embarrassment for the assholes left behind. You saw
them," Madden said bitterly, jerking his head toward the outdoors,
where Goldie was still huddled with Hirsh and Fine. "They know
they can't cover this one up, so they're at work on Vicki Strong,
and God knows what else, trying to figure out how to make a
new deal out of the situation. Jesus," he groaned, "I don't know

why I have to tell you all this. They're *your* people. You ought to know better than me what I'm talking about."

Cohen's eyes narrowed as he grasped the implication. But before he could say anything, the other man went on. "Don't get me wrong," Madden said. "I got nothing against you. Hell, I wish America stood up for itself the way you people do. Shit, we're both cops. Right? So, if you don't mind a word of advice, I think maybe you're letting your emotions fuck up your judgment. Because I'm telling you, it's a straightforward suicide we got here. Nothing more, nothing less."

His speech over, Madden relit his cigar and, not seeing an ashtray, dropped the burnt match into his jacket pocket. He spat a piece of tobacco off the tip of his tongue. A blue cloud of smoke hovered between them. "Now, you still want to see where she found him?" he asked.

Goldie had said Cohen didn't know anything about Hollywood, and now Madden was telling him the same thing. Their condescension was infuriating. But Cohen knew they were right. He didn't know Hollywood. The proportions were different here, Cohen thought, recalling the endless sprawl of the city he had seen from the taxi. Jerusalem could fit into that basin, and there would still be room for the rest of Israel. But the truths always remained the same. Madden was right about one other thing, he knew. A policeman should not be emotionally involved in an investigation. Yet it was his very involvement that gave him certainty. For the first time in six months, he felt a familiar stirring deep inside. He looked up. Beyond Madden, in the driveway outside the dining room window, he could see Phyllis Fine and Goldie leaning against the car, Hirsh bobbing and feinting in front of them, feeding Goldie's hunger. The lawyer was looking over the columnist's shoulder as Goldie wrote in a pink notebook.

"Show me," Cohen said quietly, pushing himself away from the table.

"That way to the bedrooms," Madden said, pointing to the right when they reached the top of the wide stairs. But he headed in the opposite direction. "The Levine girl says she saw him when she went out on Friday night, and when she came back this morning, she thought he was sleeping," Madden explained.

"He was alone all weekend?" Cohen asked, following Madden's broad back.

The policeman was leading Cohen down a corridor that had a slight curve, so that it seemed strangely endless. "According to Fine, the housekeeper's mother died two weeks ago. Broder gave her air tickets home for the funeral." He reached the last door in the corridor.

"The Levine girl started looking for him at lunchtime. And she finally found him in here," he said, opening the door to a huge room.

The wraparound windows told Cohen that he was in one of the house's two towers. Track lighting set into free-floating wooden beams was aimed at floor-to-ceiling bookshelves, which held books and awards, photographs and folders. Across the room, between two of the library-type bookcases, he could see French doors that opened to a small porch facing south. He scanned the room further. A huge wooden desk, facing a large Degas oil—two ballerinas— hanging above a fireplace, dominated the room. A computer sat on a trolley beside it.

Cohen's eyes fell to a tiny tarnished Statue of Liberty perched on the computer monitor. Der Bruder had always loved America, Cohen thought, finally jerking his eyes away from the statuette to look around the room for signs of the hanging.

"It was in here," Madden said, striding past the desk to one of the tall bookcases. It was turned oddly askew to the wall, revealing a dark entrance.

"It was some kind of secret passage in the old days, I guess," Madden said, pushing slightly at the bookcase, which swung open smoothly. "He turned it into his cutting room."

The sergeant stood aside, indicating that Cohen could enter. Cohen started past the desk, which was piled with pads of paper and books, publicity stills, and blue-covered folders bound with brass clips. One folder sat apart from the rest. It was black, with gold lettering. He leaned over the desk. By habit he was careful not to touch anything. *The Survivor's Secrets,* the gold lettering said. The word *Treatment* appeared in smaller type below.

"I thought you wanted to see this," Madden growled.

Cohen looked up, to where Madden stood at the yawning entrance to the narrow room revealed by the displaced book-case.

Just past the entrance was a cumbersome-looking machine with a dark screen, rollers, buttons, and levers. He looked back at Madden. "It's called a Steenbeck," Madden said, like a tour guide. "It cuts film."

Cohen scowled, knowing he'd never be able to figure out how to work the machine without help. There were very few mechanical devices Cohen could manage proficiently. Most were in the kitchen. But he realized that the very idea that he would be interested in making the machine work meant that he was getting on track, back to work. He couldn't deny the momentary feeling of pleasure at the thought.

He looked away from the machine, down the long, narrow room. Hundreds of strips of film hung from clips attached to wires stretching just above his eye level from one end of the room to the other. Some were barely a few frames long. Others reached almost to the floor.

At first he was reminded of a slaughterhouse, of carcasses hanging in a row. There was even the chill of an air conditioner. But then he had another memory, which leapt vengefully at him from one of the murkiest corners of his mind. Bodies in the dark.

He shook the memory away and reached gingerly for one of the ribbons of film. Touching it made all the other pieces on the same wire quiver and rustle, as if the celluloid had come to life. Twitching bodies in the dark. He shivered, uncertain whether it was the memory, the air conditioning, or a fever that shook him as he held up the piece of film to the bright light pouring through the entrance to the cutting room.

All he could see was the endless repetition of a solitary tree in the snow. There was something oddly familiar about the scene, and he strained his eyes, trying to recognize the place. In the background he could see the distant spires and rooftops of a Middle European town.

"It's further down," Madden said, his hand blocking the light as he pointed down the corridor. Cohen let the film strip drop back into place. The quivering ribbons accompanied him as he went deeper into the darkness, reaching a black muslin curtain that stretched across the wall at the end of the room. He pulled at the thick cloth, and the outdoor lighting in the garden splayed across his face through the glass. He was surprised it wasn't dusty, then realized the film required as dustless a room as possible. He leaned close enough to look out and down, into the driveway.

The patrol car was gone. Goldie still stood outside her car. But instead of Hirsh and Fine, a raven-haired young woman in a pale-blue dress was standing in front of the columnist, whose hands suddenly reached for the young woman's face, pulling it forward. Goldie pressed her lips against the other woman's mouth. But it did nothing to change the young woman's posture, which remained almost military in its indifference to Goldie's squirm of passion.

"To your left," Madden called from behind him, surprising Cohen into dropping the curtain back into place and pushing through the Oriental curtain of film strips.

He entered a small alcove, almost a cell, with tall, narrow walls. Just beside the top step of a five-runged wooden ladder propped closed against the wall was a small piece of the same dark material that covered the window at the end of the corridor two steps away. He brushed the cloth aside, squinting in the sudden light that poured from a small portal, almost a peephole. He leaned closer to peer into the large room that was visible below. Its baronial furnishings of heavy dark wood and sets of tapestry-upholstered sofas and chairs matched the dining room's decor. It was like a legendary nobleman's hall, he thought, and for a moment, one of Grimms' fairy tales, remembered from his childhood, came into his mind. Madden coughed apologetically behind him, and Cohen brushed away the memory like a cobweb, dropped the cloth back into place, and turned to face the man. They were belly-to-belly, almost touching.

But Madden was looking upward to the high ceiling. Cohen followed his gaze. A white rope, cut just below the knot, was tied to a beam about three meters above the floor.

"What the fuck," Madden sighed, looking back at Cohen. "A guy punches his own ticket, he's already fucked up," he said, as if apologizing for Broder's choice of the tiny alcove as the venue for the suicide.

Cohen's heartbeat was a speeding metronome. He attempted to restrain its furious pace. There had been no sign of any forensic work. Either the Los Angeles police were extraordinarily neat or Madden had not done his job. He kept looking upward, aware of the American, a head taller, looking down at him.

"Where is the body now?" Cohen growled, trying to control his temper.

"Morgue," Madden said matter-of-factly. "It's the law. For suicides."

"At least that," Cohen mumbled under his breath.

"What did you say?"

Cohen only shook his head.

"He knew how to tie one, that's for sure," Madden said. "I got it down in my car, if you want to see." Something taunting in Madden's tone made Cohen finally move his gaze from the cut rope to the policeman.

"Yes," Cohen said, knowing all too well where Broder had learned the knack of a hangman's knot. He wondered if Madden's gibe was a test. If it was, he had only one answer. "I *must* see it," he added, to make sure Madden understood, and then looked around the room, settling on the ladder leaning against the wall.

"We found it like this," Madden said, reaching past Cohen for the ladder, to demonstrate.

"Stop!" Cohen commanded.

Madden froze in midmotion, then straightened up and looked down at Cohen. In the small room, Cohen could smell his own cognac on Madden's breath. "I've got the noose downstairs," Madden told him again. "Hirsh and the lady lawyer say he always kept one on his desk. Loved tying and untying it."

"You did nothing," Cohen stated, not wanting to hear what Madden was telling him. "No search. No taking of evidence. Nothing."

"There was nothing to do," Madden grunted.

Cohen took a deep breath, but he couldn't hide his anger the way Broder's house hid the cutting room. "You didn't even try, did you?" he grilled bitterly. "You got the call, those people down there told you it was suicide, and you accepted it without question." He compressed his rage to fit the tiny alcove, and it came out a barked whisper.

"Hey, fuck you, all right? Madden shot back. "Who the fuck you think you are? What the fuck do you know about it? You're a fucking tourist here. That's all. A tourist, get it?" He jammed past Cohen, slapping his way through the ribbons of film strips. A length of film fell from the wire, while its siblings cackled at Madden's march down the cutting-room corridor.

Cohen forced himself to hold back. He wished for something that could explain it all, make it all simple and clear and enable him to leave right now, go back to Jerusalem, back to what he did know. He knew all too well what it was like to work in a city where politics could pervert police procedure. He had fought it, but at least in Jerusalem he knew the rules and players, and had allies as well as enemies.

He suddenly realized that he had not been so lonely since the night he met Broder, another Jewish youth with a plan to reach the Swiss border. Cohen's family's summer home was in Bavaria, and he had followed his mother's instructions, taking the train to Munich and then hiking and hitchhiking to the place on the lake where Cohen had vacationed every summer of his twelve years. But the Nazis had expropriated the house. Cohen had been two days in the mountains alone, hungry and tired and ever more doubtful that he would reach the border, when Broder stepped out of the woods and said, "You're trying to get over there?" pointing southwest toward Switzerland. "You have a compass. I have food," Broder had said. "We'll share."

Cohen's chest rose with a painful sigh, and then he bent down for the fallen piece of film before leaving the cell where Broder's body had hung.

But in the semidarkness of the alcove, he couldn't make out

the picture repeated over and over in the meter-long ribbon of film. Frustrated, he tugged at the curtain over the window. Goldie's car was pulling out. The young woman was running gracefully across the oval lawn in the center of the driveway, until she disappeared from Cohen's view.

He was about to step away from the window when Madden appeared below, Hirsh and Fine at his side. Madden was gesticulating angrily as he spoke to them, Hirsh was shaking his head in obvious dismay. Cohen watched as the policeman marched to his car trunk, jabbed a key into its lock, and momentarily was hidden by the open lid. When he reappeared, he was holding a transparent plastic bag.

The repulsion on Fine's face was obvious as she stared at the bag when Madden stormed past her, disappearing from Cohen's view. Thinking he would soon be hearing the American policeman's return to the cutting room, he continued watching Hirsh and Fine. Her back was to Cohen, but he could see she was wagging a finger in Hirsh's face. Suddenly Hirsh said something, and she turned. Madden reappeared, without the plastic bag. Fine turned on him, but Madden snarled something at the lawyer, going past her to the unmarked police car.

Cohen's mouth twitched in a slight smile. Through the glass window, he could hear the slam of Madden's car door and the revving of the engine. A moment later, Madden's brake lights flickered at the end of the driveway, before disappearing into the night. Hirsh and Fine exchanged a few more words and then drove out of the driveway in convoy. Fine owned the Mercedes, he noticed. But he could only guess at the make of Hirsh's car—an Italian-made sedan?

He waited until the last of the brake lights disappeared into the darkness at the end of the driveway before he walked slowly out of the cutting room, his fingers absentmindedly grazing the film strips. His mind was reeling.

But he knew enough to stop at Broder's desk, to get the treatment of *The Survivor's Secrets*. Clutching it to his chest thoughtfully, like a religious man who knows the prayers by heart but keeps the book close to his heart, he made his way down the hallway.

There were three objects on the dining room table: Goldie's card, a handwritten note from Hirsh, saying he'd be in touch about the funeral preparations, and the plastic bag that Madden had left behind.

St. George looked down on him with pity as Cohen stared at the noose. Like an albino snake coiled with deadly poise, the white rope inside the plastic dared Cohen to test its bite. Cohen's hand shook slightly as he reached for it. But he didn't need to open the clean bag to see what he was looking for: the last twist of rope, where the spiral coil was closed by a practiced hand. The fray-preventing tape at the end of the rope was peeking out of the gap between the sixth and seventh wraps of the rope, woven between the second and fourth. It was as recognizable to Cohen as Broder's signature. Broder had learned to tie the knot while he worked in the camp carpentry shop. There were hangings almost daily. The gallows had to be well maintained. Broder learned his job well.

But that wasn't why Cohen's hand trembled. He suddenly remembered the familiar solitary tree in the film frame in the cutting room. He had first seen it in a cow pasture, on the outskirts of a village south of Munich. Levine had noticed the tree in the meadow. After all, Bernard had pointed out, the butcher had always shown great interest in the effects of hanging. Both Cohen and Broder had laughed at that. But it had been Broder's idea that they take the Nazi's boy as well.

Cohen dropped the plastic package as if the snake had suddenly come to life. The Nazi had not believed the Jews would have the courage to kill the child. By the time the boy's legs stopped kicking, the tyrant had given them the information they had come for, and Cohen had made his decision. He was done with the *nokmim,* the Nazi-hunters.

He looked up from the noose, at the maiden on the rock in the tapestry. His head ached, his stomach roiled with hunger. He had prepared himself to open the sealed room of his memories with Der Bruder and finally put them to rest. But now he was alone. Like a sleepwalker, he made his way to the swinging doors at the end of the dining room, concentrating on his hunger lest his mind sweep him into the darkness he feared.

Moonlight glinted off the stainless-steel refrigerator door and sparkled across polished copper-bottomed pots hanging from a circular rack above a butcher-block table in the center of the darkened room. He dropped the treatment on the table and had started toward the stainless-steel refrigerator, when he heard water splashing from beyond the open sliding glass door to the rear of the house.

The simmering night enveloped him as he stepped through the doorway. He lit a cigarette and then started along a flagstone path that led down a sloping hill, around a terraced wall, and into a large patio surrounding a rectangular pool lit by underwater lamps.

She was swimming with the sharp, graceful strokes of an athlete trained for the sport and with the angry urgency of someone trying to beat a personal best. He stood at the end of the long pool, waiting for her to reach him. As she approached, he realized she was naked. The water was so clear and her method so smoothly repetitive, he could see the muscles rippling on her back. She took the last few meters in one long submerged stroke. Her arms pressed against her torso, like the long black hair streaming down her back, emphasized her long, trim body.

She came up and grabbed the edge of the pool with both hands, smiling at him as if he were her coach and she was expecting praise. She had Bernard's face, so Slavic it was almost Asian. She had inherited the high, wide cheekbones and the raven-black hair and the pale-blue eyes, which glittered like the pool's surface in the night lights. "You are Avram," she said, and licked away water from her upper lip. "I'm Sophie. Bernard's daughter," she added.

She was the only other flesh-and-blood survivor of the *nokmim*. But she was grinning lasciviously at him as she pulled back from the edge of the pool, not letting go of the edge. Instead of hiding the view of her body, she only revealed more, swaying slightly back and forth in the water. He looked away, embarrassed. Hirsh had mentioned a sedative. For the sake of Bernard's memory, he decided to blame her shamelessness on the drug and looked around for something with which to cover her.

The blue dress was crumpled in a soft pile beside the pool at the other end. He started for it, and strangely, a memory of something Bernard Levine had once said about Max Broder came into his mind. "Even when Broder saves your life, it's for Broder." He wondered why he remembered it now, as he picked up the dress, wondering, too, how much she knew.

She was too young to have ever known her father, a party official arrested by his own people in East German intelligence after the Soviet invasion of Czechoslovakia. Broder had come to Israel when he heard the news, trying to convince the Mossad to rescue Levine. But the Israelis weren't interested in helping an East German apparatchik who had never stuck out his neck for them, especially not a Jew who survived the camps in order to choose anti-Zionist communism as his cause.

So Broder asked Cohen to help resurrect the *nokmim,* devising a plan to kidnap an East German cultural affairs minister, due in Cannes for the film festival, and hold him hostage in exchange for Levine's release. Cohen spent three long nights and days of argument, talking Broder out of the plan. But Broder was a rich man, with the innocence of the rich who believe money can solve everything. He left Jerusalem, promising he'd spend whatever it took to buy Levine's freedom.

He never had the chance. A month later, word came over the Berlin Wall that Levine was dead. Broder made some efforts to get the widow and baby from the East Germans. But with Bernard Levine dead, Broder's enthusiasm flagged. The widow died a year later, leaving Sophie, the orphan. And by then all Broder's enthusiasm was gone.

Cohen had heard nothing more about Bernard Levine until Broder reported that Sophie Levine had shown up. When was it? Cohen tried to remember. Two years ago? Three? There had been a flurry of calls from Broder, but at the time there were more important things for Cohen to think about. Vigilantes had been at work taking their revenge on Arabs, and the politicians were interfering with investigations. Cohen had little patience then for Broder's self-congratulatory tale about his generosity to Bernard Levine's daughter.

The dress was light and soft, an expensive material that she had dropped like a used towel on the patio's stone terrace. He held it out behind his back and signaled for her to take it. There was a splash as she heaved herself out of the pool and padded over to him, giggling softly. While she dressed behind him, he drank from his flask, his eyes roaming from the valley of lights beneath him to the clouded night above the city as he drew deeply of the burning liquid.

"What about me?" she asked. He turned. The dress hung wet and dark from her breasts. She was pointing to the flask. He held it out. She toasted him with a flourish before tilting back her head to let a trickle of the cognac spill into her mouth. A drop missed, and she sighed with pleasure as she licked it away from her upper lip. "You knew him well," she said, her speech slurred.

"Who?" he finally answered, deciding it had been a question. "Max? Or your father?" He held out his hand to take the flask.

Her crooked smile appeared slowly. "To the brothers," she said, toasting him again and taking another swig of the cognac. "I've seen the movie," she said, handing him the flask. "So very romantic."

"Romantic?" he asked, surprised.

"All right," she conceded. "Dramatic." Again the sarcasm was not hidden. "That was Max Broder's way, no?" she asked, but she wasn't looking for confirmation. She already knew what she believed. "Larger than life," she said, almost hatefully. "And my father. He was the secret one. Hard." Her eyes flashed, and Cohen thought he saw pride as well as pain. "So what about you? In the movie you are the innocent. An innocent hero." She grinned at him, either daring him to deny it or taunting him into admitting it.

He raised an eyebrow, thinking about himself. "No, I don't think so," he decided. It wasn't modesty. He knew the truth.

She frowned.

"None of us were heroes," Cohen said softly.

The answer pleased her, the smile raising the corner of her wide mouth. But then she turned suddenly caustic and fierce. "Tell me," she asked, "if you are so wise: Why did he do it?" A sob wrenched her body. Her shoulders shook. Sniffling, she stared at him, her eyes full of expectation that he would embrace her.

He clenched his hand tightly, trying to control his temper. Of all the people he had met, she was the last who should believe that Broder killed himself. A survivor's child should know better, he wanted to believe, hoping it was a realistic faith. He shook his head slowly, his pale-silver eyes boring into hers. "Do what?" he asked softly.

Her sobbing came to a stop as suddenly as it had begun. "Commit suicide, of course," she said, stating the obvious in a coolly surprised tone.

He shook his head.

"Of course he did," she insisted.

But his insistent, silent rejection of the assumption sent her backward one step. Her eyes filled with shock and sudden mistrust. Then her features softened, and her tone changed once again. "I understand," she said gently. "I also didn't want to believe it. Even when I saw it, I didn't want to believe it."

"No," Cohen said softly.

"What are you saying?" she whispered, alarmed.

"I want to know what happened," he said. "Not what people think happened."

"It was suicide," she insisted nervously. "Everyone says so."

He shook his head. He could see her thinking: a slight quivering of her right eyebrow, a tension in her lower lip. "You're just like him," she finally said, the bitterness unconcealed. Shaking her head with disappointment, she added, "You won't let it go." Her hair caught a silver streak of sudden moonlight. She waited for his response, an angry look in her eye.

"I was the youngest," he finally said. "Your father was the

oldest. Max in the middle. They saved me. Helped me stay alive. Taught me. I learned from them."

He paused, trying to decide what to say next. But she didn't give him the chance to continue.

"Well, now I'm the youngest," she spat back. "And I'm sick of people saving me. Teaching me. Because in the end it costs. I end up paying for it. I paid for my father. I paid for Der Bruder. I'm not going to pay for you!" Her chest heaved.

He could hear his own heart beating strongly, the adrenaline made of anger and pain, and of confusion about her meaning. But he also couldn't help wonder if her sudden shifts in emotion were not a result of any drug but calculated.

Perhaps she saw the hurt in his eyes, or maybe she realized she had gone too far, because suddenly the anger was gone, and instead of waiting for his answer, she changed her tone one last time, whispering, "Trust no one."

For a moment it could have been Bernard Levine himself warning Cohen about informers. "No one," she repeated, and then she spun away, running up the path back to the house, leaving him alone by the underlit pool, his hand stretched out too late to catch her, his voice calling out her name once into the empty night.

A MAN IS BRAIDING a rag into a rope. Beyond his determined face, we can see bodies hanging from barracks rafters. The man, gripping his ragged rope, climbs the bunks like a ladder to the sixth tier. Weeping, he clumsily ties the rope to the wooden beam. Around him there is crying and cursing. A searchlight beam scans the room quickly every few seconds, lighting up faces staring from the wooden bunks, stacked like shelves. At least a dozen bodies hang from the beams running the length of the narrow corridor in the wooden barracks. The face of the man who has decided to kill himself contorts for a moment, and then he jumps from the tier. The camera moves past the jerking body, halting in front of young Avram and Max on one of the shelf beds. Avram is tearing at a piece of cloth. "They want you to do that," Max says matter-of-factly. Young Avram stops tearing but does not look up. "It would be better to kill one of them," Max says. There's a slight smile at the corner of his mouth. Avram keeps his face averted. "It will be easy," Broder promises in a whisper. "You bite him." Avram looks up. "Right here," Max says, tapping at his own throat. "He'll die. You'll die." Avram's finger touches his own throat. "Of course, why kill one, if you can kill many?" says Max, already knowing he has won. "You want to know how?" Max asks. Avram nods slowly. "By surviving," Max answers. The searchlight beam lights up his lopsided smile.

Cohen woke with the awful feeling of not knowing where he was. Light was pouring over his face. He sat up abruptly. Broder's movie treatment slid off the bed to the floor, to lie beside the plastic bag with the rope inside. He looked down and shuddered.

It was exactly what he had feared. His dreams and nightmares had long ago taken over his memories. Broder's movie was opening the sealed boxes in the attic of Cohen's mind. The image of the hanging bodies on the very first page of the treatment was dragged out of the darkness to which Cohen had relegated it so many years before. At least Broder had not opened the movie with their capture, for which Cohen still blamed himself.

So he shook his head at the treatment and lay back in the bed, his hands clasped behind his head as he thought.

He went from Hirsh's absurd animation to Fine's icy handshake and Madden's doughy anger. Goldie's kiss. Sophie. He had followed her slowly and wearily along the path, stopping in the kitchen to make a sandwich and pick up the treatment, before heading up the stairs, following Madden's directions to the bedrooms.

He had guessed it was her room when he reached it, the first to the right in the strangely curving corridor. He had paused at the door, listening to the muffled patter of a radio disk jockey, thinking he should say something. But he had not known what to say. Not yet. So he had moved down the corridor, past closed doors that he decided could wait for investigation in the morning, and had reached the end of the corridor, where an open doorway filled with light waited for him.

Like the study at the opposite end of the house, the guest room was built into one of the towers. But unlike the study, where the walls were taken up with bookshelves, the guest-room walls had floor-to-ceiling windows to the world outside, and if there was a hidden alcove like the cutting room, Cohen couldn't find it. He did find a note, pinned to one of the pillows on the double bed.

"Sorry," it said, the single word signed with only an *S*. He had slipped it into the treatment like a page mark, and belching the aftertaste of sliced onion, lettuce, mustard, goose liver pâté, and a quaff of cognac, he had lain down to read the treatment. Exhaustion had swept over him. He didn't get past the first page before sleep rescued him from the memories, plunging him into familiar nightmares.

Cohen shivered in the air conditioning as he checked his watch. Eight hours was a very long stretch of sleep for him. He was usually too nervous for such an extended rest. Jet lag, he decided, trying not to think about his fainting episode in the airport. Pulling the sheet toga-like around him for warmth, he rolled off the bed. His joints ached from rheumatic stiffness. He softly spoke his name out loud, relieved to discover that the compression in his ears had cleared.

He went to one of the southern windows, struggled with a latch until he finally managed to throw open a leaded pane. It was hot outside. A light haze hovered above the city, curling into the expensive canyons below. The mansions seemed moored in the smog like great ships in fog. He could hear the hiss of a distant highway. A familiar sound startled him, and he looked up. A moment later, a helicopter swept past at eye level, a hundred meters away in the open sky, close enough to frighten a flock of birds out of a huge weeping willow at the far edge of the backyard lawn. The pool below was a slate-gray reflection of the hazy sky.

He sighed deeply. The morning cough rose from his lungs, and he went to the bathroom, commencing his routine of steaming water, a shave under the shower, and then a freezing blast to wipe away the morning aches. Dressed in his usual white cotton shirt and gray twill trousers, he started down the corridor, thinking about a cup of coffee. His sneakers padded softly on the tiles as he went past the closed doors, reaching Sophie's room. The radio still played softly. There would be time for his questions later, he thought. He'd let the drugs wear off.

The night before, he had noticed an espresso maker in the kitchen. He found coffee in the freezer and then went to the Italian machine, hoping he could figure it out without too much trouble. As he fumbled with it, he longed for a simple sweet Turkish coffee boiled in a *finjan*. It took him two tries before he managed to produce a cup of coffee. And when it finally emerged, the serving was tiny and the water lukewarm. Jerusalem was where he belonged, he thought. Not in a castle with a swimming pool and a futuristic espresso machine and no one he could trust.

Angrily, he slapped open cabinets until he found a jar of American instant coffee. He set a kettle of water to boil and, scowling, shoveled three tablespoonfuls of the brown crystals into a mug, stirred in some sugar and a teaspoonful of water. By the time the kettle boiled, the coffee in the mug was a thick dark sauce that foamed as he poured in the steaming water. He added milk, took a sip, then lit his first cigarette of the day before going back up the stairs to the study.

Standing in the doorway, he sipped at the coffee and puffed on the cigarette, considering where to begin. The open door to the cutting room was at the center of his quest, but he knew he wasn't ready to reenter that dark place. He would look for fingerprints on the ladder, but that would come later. The desk drew his attention first. Manuscripts and documents, newspaper and magazine clippings—everything seemed piled up neatly. The office implements were lined up like soldiers in a row: stapler, letter opener, pens and pencils, masking tape, a magnifying glass, paper clips. The computer terminal frightened him. He had missed learning how to use one for the police, and he completely mistrusted his ability to figure it out now. He had never even learned to use a typewriter more than one finger at a time, and even then, only when he was between secretaries.

He had always relied on assistants for such mechanical skills, and he missed an assistant now. Ordinarily, upon arriving at the scene of a crime, he would have been accompanied by a junior officer, who would take dictation as Cohen recited his impressions from a general survey of the room. Only then would he focus on details. But there was nobody at his side today, nobody to fill the notebooks with his impressions. And he felt rusty, as if his mind were rheumatically constrained. He looked around the room, alternating sips from the coffee and puffs on his cigarette as he thought.

Only when he finished the cigarette, dropping the smoking butt into the puddle of coffee at the bottom of the cup, did he ease himself into the room, starting with the periphery, intending to move gradually toward the cutting room. He began with the bookshelves to his right.

Rows of framed photographs lined the shelves in front of the books. Most showed Broder with movie stars, including a few whom even Cohen recognized. Many were beautiful women. Cohen quickly gave up trying to decipher the expressions of the women. Some seemed to be looking up at the huge director's long, sorrowful face with admiration. Others had affection in their eyes. They were all actresses, Cohen decided, so maybe they were all acting. But there was something consistent in their postures, in the way they held Broder's arm to their breasts or thrust their hips toward him. The big man in the pictures smiled down at them all with a proud expression, as if they were prizes he had won.

Slowly Cohen moved around the room, picking up each photograph and turning to hold it to the light. After a while, he reached for them automatically, taking the framed pictures down from the shelf, scanning the faces, and returning them, all in one motion. Max's lopsided grin leered back in all its familiar self-assurance. None of the pictures said anything about why he was dead.

He put a photo of Broder with Vicki Strong on the shelf and reached for the next picture. As he stared into it, his hand began to tremble and he instinctively stepped backward.

It had all been so confusing when the Americans arrived, especially since the first Americans to reach Dachau were a Nisei regiment of Japanese-Americans.

One of the soldiers had fallen to his knees, tears streaming from his eyes as he bowed over and over again to Cohen and Broder, starved and skeletal, half lying, half leaning, against the wall of the barracks. They were certain that they were dying. Finally, the Japanese soldier who spoke American English gently covered them with his blanket. Only with that gracious gesture did the realization that it was all over begin to penetrate their minds.

The next day Cohen and Broder had gone to the main gate. Cohen had hesitated just before the last barbed-wire barrier. Broder had pulled weakly at him and, draping a bony arm over Cohen's equally emaciated shoulder, dragged him forward. "Look," Broder had said. "The whole world is out there. We can go as far as we want now." All that Cohen had been able to see was the road cutting into the woods, and railroad tracks slicing the road in half. But it was a sunny spring day, and just as he raised his face to the warming sun, an American soldier had taken the picture.

Cohen didn't take his eyes off the photograph as he moved to one of two red leather chairs that faced the fireplace. He had no idea how Broder had got the picture. The soldier had walked up to them afterward, embarrassed, cap in hand. Remembering made Cohen feel dizzy. He leaned back in the chair, staring into the inner space of memories that went even further back than the camp.

For the first time in more than forty years, Cohen thought of the day he had come home from school and seen his parents climbing onto the truck, the soldiers laughing as his mother slipped, her dress tearing to reveal thick, pale thighs. He thought of his father raising his hand to protect her, a soldier swinging his rifle in a short punch that immediately drew blood from his father's face. He remembered hiding in the garden, watching all this until the soldiers were gone, and how he had waited until dusk to slip into the house through a basement window. For the first time in more than four decades, he thought about how, like an automaton, he had moved through the house, enacting all the motions his mother had drilled into him for just such an emergency. He found the clothes and knapsack she had prepared, just where she had shown him they would be hidden. And just as he had promised her so many times, he began following the instructions she and his father had rehearsed with him for months.

Then, for the last time, he walked through the house in which he had been raised. He was three weeks from his bar mitzvah. By the time he sneaked out into the night, wearing lederhosen, the knapsack over his shoulder, looking like any carefree Hitler Youth, his childhood was over.

Cohen had many scars. Some pained him when the weather changed, others hurt when he moved his body the wrong way. He could catalogue pain from a tour of the healed wounds on his body. There were the scars on his back from whippings in the camp, and scars from three bullet wounds, each from a different time in his life. The first, on his upper right biceps, was like a second inoculation mark; it was made by a German who tried to fight back when the nokmim came. The second was from a Jordanian soldier's rifle. It was a deep hole in his thigh, where a field medic dug out the bullet as Cohen lay in the Latrun valley during the fight to break the siege of Jerusalem. The third bullet wound was much more recent, a ten-year-old scar on his back, made by an underworld assassin who had failed. There were other scars as well, the most recent made by the broken stem of a wineglass, a crystal awl that a madman had plunged into Cohen's stomach when the Jerusalemite had moved in for the arrest.

But no salves or medicines, no Dead Sea minerals or homeopathic pills, could ease the twisted tissues of the inner scars made by the fatal compromises survival required. So he had sealed off those scars, each one a memory he could not bear to face.

Like all survivors, he had no explanation of why he had lived while others had died. Broder had always claimed it was because they had a purpose: survival and revenge. But everyone who lived through only one day of that place wanted revenge. Levine, ever the Communist, had always said it was because they shared whatever they had, but Cohen knew others who had shared what passed for food—the rotten potatoes, the slugs boiled in water as gray as the autumn sky over the camp. And those others had not survived. Cohen had looked into their eyes as they died and he had looked away while they were killed. As he wrestled with the guilt rising nauseously inside him, his beating heart created the image that gathered like storm clouds in his mind. He closed his eyes, remembering Max Broder.

He is looking out over a snow-covered meadow, looking out toward mountains. It's a familiar, comforting view, from his grandfather's summer house. But the house is empty, and the temperature is dropping inside the empty house. He is freezing, the blood thickening his body into painful slow-motion movements as he goes to the door. Max Broder is standing in the snow-filled meadow, halfway to the woods. He is wearing a soldier's overcoat from the First World War, his head and throat wrapped turbanlike with a long wool scarf. Avram steps outside. "Brother," Max calls out. Avram looks back at the house. Through the open door he sees strangers in his grandfather's house. He looks back at Broder. "It's not far," Max shouts. "We can make it." Avram reaches out to him. The snow falls faster and faster, and he tries futilely to capture snowflakes in his frozen hands.

A deep bass bell rang once, jolting him out of the dream. The picture fell from his hands. He checked his watch, realizing that, again, memory had turned to grogginess and then to dreaming. It was near nine in the morning. Almost an hour had passed. He heaved himself up from the chair and headed down the stairs, pausing at the landing just before Sophie's door, thinking the bell must have wakened her as well.

But the door was still closed, and the radio played on. It bothered him. At the bottom of the stairs he could see through the tall, narrow window at the side of the door; he could make out the vague outlines of two men. He scowled at his intuition that one of them was Leo Hirsh.

He decided Hirsh could wait, and knocked at Sophie's door. There was no answer. He called out her name, knocking louder the second time. The radio played on, but the closed door exuded silence. He opened it. The doors to a closet that stretched the length of one wall were open. Clothes were scattered every-where—across the floor, the bed, the chairs. His eyes leapt to the open door to a bathroom. "Sophie?" he called out.

But instead of her voice, the Oriental bell answered with a second chime. He strode quickly to the bathroom. It was empty. He turned to scan the room. A closed door faced her bed across the room. He went to it quickly, cursing under his breath as the downstairs bell rang again. He yanked open the door.

Broder's vast bedroom gaped back at him, the huge bed mocking him with its insinuation of the meaning of the connecting door between the two rooms.

Cohen wearily opened the door to Leo Hirsh, who was standing with a man who wore a dark hat above a neatly clipped beard streaked with a dramatic flair of white. "Avram!" Hirsh began, stepping into the house past Cohen. "I wanted you to meet Rabbi Gould. Joe," the producer added, "meet Avram Cohen."

The shock of white in the rabbi's beard was in stark contrast to the man's young skin and unlined eyes. He can't be more than thirty-five, Cohen thought, a young man. Rabbis were much older in Jerusalem. For a moment, an absurd thought crossed his mind: Perhaps the rabbi dyed the beard for dramatic effect.

"I'm so sorry about your friend . . . our friend," Gould said with professional solemnity, following Hirsh into the house and holding out a hand.

Cohen nodded, quickly dropping the rabbi's limp grasp.

"I thought it would be a good idea for all of us to get together, to discuss the ceremony," Hirsh said, his head bobbing as if he was keeping time with some rhythm he could hear in his mind.

"Ceremony?" Cohen said.

"The funeral," Gould said. "Max was a great friend of HEI, our institute," he said. "And Leo said that you, of all people, should be the one to say Kaddish."

Cohen's eyes moved from Gould to Hirsh. The producer smiled expectantly, awaiting praise.

Cohen shook his head slowly. "He wouldn't have wanted any prayers," he rumbled.

"What are you talking about, no prayers?" Hirsh protested.

"You want prayers," Cohen grumbled, "you say prayers."

"My God, it's the Kaddish we're talking about. Not a whole megillah," Hirsh charged.

"No," Cohen said.

"I can't believe this," Hirsh shrilled. "This is the man Max called his brother?" he demanded rhetorically. He stomped a few steps away from Cohen, his Italian loafers sounding an angry tap dance on the stone floor. His voice rose half an octave. "Listen, you," he accused Cohen. "Twenty-five years I've heard about you from Max Broder. Always telling me what a great guy you are." He started back across the foyer. "Straight. Honest. One of the last of the just. So," he said, suddenly changing pitch from accusation to supplication, "for him, I'm asking you. Say the Kaddish." He held out his hands in the gesture of a beggar displaying his poverty.

Cohen shook his head, frowning. "I can't do it."

"He was a Jew. Every Jew needs someone to say Kaddish when they die," Gould said softly.

"He was a Jew," Cohen agreed. "But he never relied on God. No prayers."

"What the fuck are you talking about?" Hirsh cried, his voice rising another half octave. "There's a funeral. The whole town is going to be there. The consul general is going to be there. For God's sake, I think I can get Vicki Strong to agree to go. What are you trying to do, embarrass us all?"

"Why should anyone care if I say it or not?" Cohen asked, honestly surprised.

"Because everyone in town knows who you are, that's why!" Hirsh was practically screaming.

Cohen snorted. "What are you talking about? Nobody knows who I am. Except you people, of course."

Hirsh looked at Gould, perplexed, gaping. Gould grasped the problem. "You didn't see the newspaper this morning?"

Cohen shook his head.

Disgusted, Hirsh shook his head. "I don't think you understand. As of this morning, you're a celebrity in this town. It'll only last a few days, of course. But at least through the funeral. Max's suicide is big news. And you're in the story, pal. The movie and the story. You don't believe me? I'll prove it to you. Joe, get the paper; I left it in my car. You mind?"

Obeying Hirsh's command without protest, Gould started to back out the open door.

"It doesn't matter to me," Cohen said. "You can say that I am a Cohen. I'm not even allowed in a cemetery."

Gould paused in the doorway.

"What the hell is he talking about?" Hirsh demanded.

Gould explained. "Cohens are the high priests. They can't be contaminated by the uncleanliness of the dead. That's the Orthodox way."

"You're not Orthodox," Hirsh protested to Gould. "I'm not Orthodox. Max wasn't Orthodox. And you"—the angry producer charged at Cohen—"you aren't even Reform. So don't give me that shit."

But Cohen was adamantly silent.

"I can't believe this. He doesn't want to say Kaddish," Hirsh moaned. "Joe, please. Talk to him. Show him the paper. Talk to him. I'm going to take a piss," he announced, and started along the corridor between the stairs and the living room. Halfway down, he yanked open a door. Just before he closed it behind him, he shouted, "Talk to him!"

Cohen pulled a cigarette out of his shirt pocket and, keeping his eyes on Gould, dared the rabbi to follow Hirsh's order. Gould stroked his beard, a small smile growing at the corner of his mouth. "You call yourself Avram," he finally said, "not Avraham."

Cohen sighed. He had been through this with other rabbis.

"Like the Patriarch," Gould said solemnly, "before God gave him his name."

Cohen nodded.

Gould cocked his head with curiosity. "Your parents gave you that name?" he asked.

Cohen shook his head slowly.

The rabbi nodded back. "Maybe you ought to see the newspaper, after all," he said.

Cohen shrugged, and puffed on his cigarette as Gould went out to the driveway, where Hirsh's luxury sedan baked in the heat. A moment later, Gould was back with the newspaper. Broder's suicide was a front-page news story, while the obituary filled half a page inside. Goldie's column started on page one. The article gushed about how making the movie had caused Broder to "relive his personal history" and how the "obsession with the historic tragedy turned into its own personal tragedy." She detailed Epica's decision to shelve the movie, and Cohen couldn't help but smile at the quote from Andrew Blakely, using the exact words she had cynically invented the night before. "Industry sources" quoted Laszlo Katz as being "heartbroken" by the news of Broder's suicide. The same sources noted that despite Katz's known interest in the Holocaust, his traditional hands-off management methods made unlikely any intervention by the Oceanic chairman in Blakely's decision about the movie.

By the time Cohen finished reading the first page, he had to sit down. He moved to the dining room and took the first chair before going on with the article, dimly aware of Hirsh's return and Gould's signal for the producer to remain silent while Cohen finished reading.

On the plane, Goldie had given Cohen the impression that she didn't even know the title of the movie. He remembered her saying that everyone attached to the project had taken a vow of secrecy. Now, with Broder's death, the truth was surfacing. *The Survivor's Secrets,* she reported, was not merely about the Holocaust. It was autobiographical, she said, citing her "exclusive interview" with "Jerusalem Police Commander Abraham Cohen, Max Broder's oldest, closest friend." Cohen scowled at Goldie's misunderstood spelling of his name. But much worse, as far as Cohen was concerned, was Goldie's description of him as "an ace detective, who flew in from Jerusalem to help Broder in his hour of need, arriving just hours too late." Predicting that the funeral would be "a standing-room-only affair," she ended her piece with questions: "What will Andy Blakely do with Max Broder's masterpiece? Release it? Or bury it with the Holocaust survivor? And will the ace detective from Jerusalem, himself a survivor and a major character depicted in the movie, accept suicide as the reason for Max Broder's tragic demise?"

Cohen lowered the paper, trying to control his anger, remembering Hirsh gleefully feeding Goldie morsels of gossip the night before. But it was Sophie's disappearance and the meaning of the connecting doorway between her room and Broder's that chiefly disturbed Cohen. The producer and the rabbi, impressed as they were by newspaper stories, could be concerned about public ceremonies. Cohen had other worries. There was so much to do. He still needed to return to the study, to the cutting room, and to the strange alcove where the body was found. He wanted to fingerprint the ladder. He would have to search Broder's bedroom and Sophie's. He also needed to speak to Phyllis Fine about the estate, but that was a particularly tricky matter. Madden, Hirsh, and Goldie were already suspicious of his arrival's coinciding with Broder's death. If he were to start asking about the inheritance, they might start believing their suspicions.

Fuming, Hirsh had departed with the rabbi, leaving Cohen in the doorway watching the metallic-blue car pull out of the circular driveway. "Politics," he muttered under his breath as the name Andy Blakely kept coming into his head. "Politics got you in the end too," he said aloud to the empty driveway.

As he looked around in the daylight, the extent of the neighborhood's wealth became startlingly apparent to him. Broder's house was indeed a castle, with its slate-tiled turrets at each end of the curving stone building.

He scowled at the wasteful luxury of it all, yet he remembered Broder's pride on his acquisition of the house. In Israel right after the Six Day War, Broder had told Cohen the story of the castle, the duplicate of a fairy-tale set originally made in wood and plaster for a movie. Broder's father had once worked with the original owner, a director who managed to get out of Germany just after Hitler's election. The director died penniless in the house after a botched Hollywood career.

"I've come full circle," Broder had said proudly. "So now you tell me: you in your little apartment in Jerusalem, or me in my castle in Hollywood—who is closer to heaven?"

The taunt echoed in Cohen's mind as he looked around at the estate, all too aware now that to him Max Broder's life was as foreign as all the wealth on display in the neighborhood.

A large, dark bird watched him from the castle's western tower as he started across the perfect circle of grass enclosed by the driveway. Through the flimsy shade of ficus and down the eucalyptus-lined driveway that ran straight ahead, he could see a wide cul-de-sac and a driveway entrance much like Broder's, lined by two rows of trees. He moved along the driveway, and the bird took flight, its shadow momentarily flashing across Cohen's path on the white gravel baking under the sun.

The sand-colored hacienda across the street had a strange roof, composed of two domes, three slopes of red tiles, and Moorish arches framing two rooftop terraces. Two red-and-white-striped umbrellas stood closed, stiff as needles, on one terrace, and the lush foliage of a roof garden sprouted from the arches on the other rooftop patio. A large rectangular parking lot, bounded by a low white stucco wall, turned the end of the sparkling black cinder driveway into a corral, with an opening twice the width of the wooden double doors that fronted the house. But there were no cars in the driveway, indeed no signs of life at all. He rang the bell, hearing it echo through the house. Silence. Maybe later, he thought, looking around.

Across the corral was a lush garden of trees and shrubbery, and beyond it the second story of what appeared to be an Italian villa. He walked through the garden. The house had a large terrace from which two flights of stairs curved down to converge at three wide steps. Two wedding-cake wings extended from behind and beside the veranda. He took the stairs to the right, going two at a time up the annoyingly shallow marble steps. Walking past a wrought-iron-and-marble table long enough to seat a dozen people, he crossed the patio to the glass doors of the house and, using his hand to shade the glare, peered inside. Sunlight glittered off the gold enamel of an elegantly curved chair directly in front of him.

He tapped sharply, four short raps on the glass. A young, sharp-nosed man was sitting at a dining table, which filled the center of the room. He was wearing a heavy cardigan sweater and a scarf and was polishing a silver bowl. Cohen tapped again. The man's head bobbed slightly, but it was to the rhythm of the music in the earphones of a Walkman he was wearing. Only when Cohen drum-rolled with his fingers on the window did the man look up, with a nervous, birdlike manner. Seeing Cohen, he put down the silver bowl as if it were delicate crystal, then pushed himself away from the table with the same kind of deliberate motion.

"You must be the air-conditioning man," the man trilled as he opened the door. "Quick, get inside before the cold runs out."

It was freezing in the room. "I can't remember such a heat wave," the man whined, quickly shutting the door behind him. "You really should have come in through the side," he added, turning to face him. "But I hope you can fix it. It's gone completely out of control. Hot, cold—really, it's impossible. And nowadays we really have to keep the house at the proper temperature." He smiled wanly at Cohen, who held up his hands in an attempt to halt the rush of words. But before he had a chance to explain, the servant stepped backward, suspicion in his voice. "Wait a minute. Where are your tools?" he suddenly asked, dubious.

Cohen offered his most guileless smile. Already he could feel the sweat drying too quickly on his brow. "I'm sorry; I'm not the air-conditioning man," he said, and shivered once in the cold room.

"Oh, my God," the servant moaned, backing up. "That fool at the gate. All that brawn and no brains," he said, brandishing the polishing rag as if ready, if necessary, to use the stained cloth as a weapon against Cohen, who was holding up his hands in a gesture of innocence.

"My name is Cohen," the Jerusalemite said. "I am—"

"I don't care if you're Moses himself," the man interrupted cattily. "You are not supposed to be here." He backed up even further, eyeing an ornate phone on a side table that Cohen could see in one of the mirrors in the room.

"I was a friend of Max Broder's," Cohen tried again softly.

The man halted. Melodramatic sorrow crossed his face. The hand holding the rag went to his mouth. "It's you!" he exclaimed. "You poor, poor man." He then sighed, shaking his head knowingly. "I knew Max. We all did. It's such a tragedy, such a terrible tragedy. And poor Vicki," he added, shaking his head with even more sorrow, and lowering his voice to a whisper.

"I was hoping I could speak with her about it," Cohen said. "I understand she was at the house last night and—" Cohen was about to continue, when a woman's voice interrupted him from behind.

"Thank you, Matthew," she said. "That will be all."

It was the same breathy rasp, made of whiskey, cigarettes, and a promise of sensuality, that the whole world had known for nearly forty years as Vicki Strong's. Like the hills of Beverly Hills, her bedroom whisper surprised Cohen by being real, not something made up for the movies. Even primed to meet her, he had to brace himself to turn.

She stood at the far end of the room, framed by the doorway and dressed in jeans and a white blouse, with a multicolored robe thrown over her shoulders like a cape. Clenching it closed with one hand at her throat, she was not so much looking at Cohen as inspecting him. He had confronted a prime minister, but face-to-face with Vicki Strong, even Cohen felt clumsy and awkward.

"Please, sit down," she said when the servant had gone. She pointed to a seat at the dining room table. "And please pardon the chill. I'm afraid that our temperature controls have gone somewhat awry." As she approached, there was no doubt in Cohen's mind that she was referring as much to her body as to the house. The body had been famous for its curves, with an improbable defiance of gravity. But that was all gone, shriveled and shrunken, and all that remained of the Vicki Strong whom Cohen remembered from the movies was her voice and her eyes. But if anything, he thought, aging had only remade the beauty into something more ethereal, haunted and deeper.

He could feel the words stumbling over his tongue as he started to speak. "Miss, uh, Strong," Cohen said, "my name is, uh, Avram Cohen. I am——"

She interrupted him with a mere nod, as she slid into a seat at the head of the table, putting a full glass of a coppery liquid in front of her.

Cohen was shocked. This close to her, he saw there was more than aging in the unexpected frailty of the woman. She had emanated sexual promise from movie screens for almost four decades, but there was disease at work in her now. He could see the ravages of illness in the gray pull of her skin. He had a vague memory of a newspaper story about her reclusion. The paper had attributed it to the inevitable defeat of youth by age and hinted about a nervous disorder that affected her mind.

"*Max's* friend," she said, as if they had already met and she was merely renewing the acquaintance.

"I'm sorry to bother you," he began, "but I would very much like to ask you some questions. You went to Max's house when the police came, and——"

"Max's *friend,*" she repeated, the emphasis changing. "I read about you today, commander," she said, making the rank sound as if it impressed her. "Matthew," she called, keeping her eyes on Cohen, and when the servant reappeared, "Please bring Commander Cohen something to drink. Under the circumstances, instead of something cold, something warm?" she asked the Jerusalemite. "Or perhaps," she suggested, "you think it's late enough in the day for something stronger?" She held up her glass. The sunlight through the liquor matched her hair precisely.

"Cognac, please," Cohen said to the servant, who batted his eyes once before starting out of the room.

"And Matthew," she said, before the servant was gone. "My pills. I'll take them now." She waited until the manservant swayed out before she continued. "The 'ace' Israeli detective," she said, quoting Goldie's column. "From Jerusalem. So how fares the holy city?" she asked. "I was there once." She shivered lightly under her robe. A tiny droplet of sweat on her forehead sparkled in the sunlight pouring through the broad windows into the house.

He remembered her three-day presence in the city, nearly twenty

years before. Henry Kissinger had been shuttling between Golda
Meir and King Hussein. His stay required complicated security
arrangements, made more so by Vicki Strong's insistence that she
wouldn't be evicted from the King David Hotel, no matter what
the U.S. Secret Service said. Cohen was operations chief for the
Jerusalem police at the time, low-ranking as far as the VIP bodyguards from both countries were concerned. But he was high-
ranking enough so that his walkie-talkie picked up their frequencies.
"The tailor"—Kissinger's code name on the trip—had decided
that the actress could remain in the hotel, and a private dinner
was planned, so neither the singer nor the tailor would be leaving
the hotel that night.

"Yes, I know," Cohen said.

That pleased her. "So?" she asked. "Is there going to be peace
out there?"

"Eventually," he said. He didn't add that he wasn't sure he'd
live that long.

"I like that," she answered, conferring a smile on him. "I should
have guessed you'd be different. After all, you're a friend of Max
Broder's. Or so Leo told me. And any friend of Max's . . ." She
sipped delicately from her glass. "You had some questions?" she
said, putting it down.

"Why did you go to the house last night?" Cohen asked.

There was something self-deprecatory about her smile, as if it
acknowledged some joke played on her. "It was the strangest
thing," she said. "I heard the sirens, and went to the window, and
saw they were at Max's. He was a friend of mine, you know. We
worked together. It was a long time ago." Her voice turned wistful.
"A long time ago," she repeated, looking reflectively into the
sunlight. "It was as if the sirens were calling me, as if Max himself
was calling me." Her voice faded, and she shook her head. "It was
the first time I was out of the house since the hospital," she

whispered, her eyes focusing somewhere far from the dining room. "For Max." She sighed heavily and took another sip of her drink, and then, staring into her glass, she shook her head at some memory before looking back at Cohen. He wondered if she was drunk.

"I understand you might be going to the funeral," Cohen said, trying to take control but already knowing that it was a lost cause.

"Yes," she said pensively. "I'm considering it. Leo is right. I owe Max." She took a deep breath, looked up at Cohen. "It seems I'm past the point of saying no to producers," she added with a sad grin. "I used to be famous for it. But enough of me. You said you needed some help." The sadness disappeared from her smile. "You even asked for a cognac when I offered you a drink. Policemen aren't supposed to do that. So I guess you are different."

He grinned at her, deciding that she had flattered him. "I wanted to know if you noticed anything the night before. Visitors to Max's house?" Cohen asked. But he already knew that she didn't have any answers for him.

She issued the familiar chimelike laugh, always so surprising a contrast to the husky bedroom rasp of her speaking voice. "We don't sit on the doorstep in this neighborhood," she said, "keeping track of the comings and goings. Do we, Matthew?" she asked, startling Cohen.

He turned to see the servant returning with a silver tray bearing a bottle of cognac, a pitcher of ice water, two glasses, and a half-dozen bottles of pills. He put down the bottle and a glass for Cohen, smiling unctuously at him as he laid the tray in front of the actress. "Of course not," the servant said, taking up a position a few steps behind his employer and batting his eyes once more at Cohen, who looked away quickly to the bottle of cognac.

The movie star was waiting for him. "Please," she said, "help yourself."

He poured a few drops into the glass and stopped. "You're

right," he said apologetically. "It was a foolish question." He pushed away from the table. "I should be going."

"We used to be much closer," she said suddenly in a soft voice. "Max and me, I mean. I've always cared deeply for men like him," she added. "Big men. Strong, creative, with authority. When he was directing me, it was . . . it was . . ." She searched for the word. "Yes, it was symbiosis."

One hand was at her throat, as if trying to hold back sobs. Her other hand was on the table beside Cohen's own. A large emerald ring glinted on a finger, matching her eyes. He looked up at her face. A teardrop of sweat carved a glistening path down her forehead. "Afterwards"—she sighed, looking at some inward secret only she could see in her glass—"afterwards he was done with me. One more man wanting to try me on. I fit for a while. But there's always someone else. Younger, usually. But I was also done with him." She smiled at Cohen. "Because he taught me something. He taught me that I could use men the way they use women in this place. It was something for which I was always grateful—until last year."

The smile on her painted lips was humorless, inviting Cohen to ask his question; the realization that she had AIDS whipped through his mind. It was a disease he had read about far more than he had encountered it in Jerusalem. His eyes flickered instinctively to the servant and then back to her. He hoped his embarrassment wasn't obvious. "If you aren't well," he suggested apologetically, "I really shouldn't be bothering you." He stood up.

But she ignored him, beginning to open the medicine bottles lined up in front of her. "I don't mind, if you don't," she said, suddenly decisive, indeed careful, but not telling him to sit down. "I should have taken these an hour ago. I really should catch up." One by one and two by two, she built up a pile of pills and tablets on the table beside her glass. "Not that it matters, of course," she said to herself as much as to him.

"Now, Vicki," Matthew interrupted. "You know that it's all a matter of attitude."

She rolled her eyes at the servant, smiled apologetically at Cohen. "He tries."

"I didn't know you were ill," Cohen confessed, unable to pull his eyes off her. "I had no idea. If I had known, I wouldn't have disturbed you."

She shook her head, discounting his protestations. "It was a secret. A whole year, I kept it a secret." She poured water from the pitcher into her glass, diluting the whiskey into a pale gold the color of the sunlight reflected off the polished wood surface. "But Leo was right," she said pensively. "He told me I couldn't keep it hidden any longer. This way," she explained, "I can make a statement. A public statement." She smiled wanly. "Leo says that in my own way, I'm as big as that basketball player. What's his name? The wizard?"

"Magic Johnson," he whispered.

"Right," she said. "That's what Leo said. And then he begged. Leo has a tendency to rave and rant or beg and plead," she added with a cocked grin. "But you're not interested in Leo. You want to know about Max."

"Did he have any enemies?" Cohen said softly.

She laughed, a brilliant, chilling chortle full of pain and anger as well as cynical amusement. "This is Hollywood, darling. *Everyone* has enemies," she exlaimed.

"Enough to kill?"

She looked down. His eyes couldn't help following hers to the brightly colored capsules and the pale tablets. There were at least a dozen. "The paper said you don't think it was suicide," she said wistfully.

He nodded.

"There are a lot of ways to kill someone in this town," she said slowly, her sly smile about to teach him an important lesson. "For example . . ." She nodded toward the pills. Before he could understand her meaning, she collected the pills into one hand, like chips from a gambling table, and with the other held up her glass for a toast.

He hesitated. She urged him on, raising her glass even higher.

"Come on, express yourself." It was a command. But just in case he still refused, she added, "For Max."

He lifted his glass. She tossed her head back, dumping the pills into her open mouth and draining them with her drink. He put down his glass slowly, waiting for the pained scowl to disappear from her ravaged face. He was finished with her, hearing within himself only his pity. He knew it was useless to continue seeking answers from her. "Thank you for your time," he said. "I'm sorry to have bothered you."

Disappointment fell across the star's face. "That's all?" she asked, bewildered by the abrupt end to the interview.

He nodded, and started to the door.

"Why?" she asked from her seat. "Why are you asking these questions?"

Cohen said nothing as he went to the door.

"Answer me," she insisted, summoning all the authority of her regal roles from the past.

Cohen turned to face her, repressing an urge to bow. "Because the police didn't," he said, closing the door on her belated laughter.

He could feel the hot tar sticking to the rubber of his sneaker soles as he crossed the sun-streaked plaza of the cul-de-sac. Heat waves distorted his vision. He felt miserable and lost. It was too hot. So hot he thought his head would explode.

At first he thought the car coming into the circle was a mirage. But it screeched to a halt beside him. The passenger door flung open. "Get the fuck in here!" Madden shouted.

Cohen's brief hesitation only made Madden angrier.

"Get the fuck in the car right now, you fucker. Now!"

Cohen obeyed, and Madden spun rubber the hundred meters to Broder's front door.

"You're fucking lucky!" Madden barked. His brow and nose were red with anger. "I told the local security company to let me know if anything happened in the neighborhood."

"What did I do?" Cohen asked.

"You don't walk the street in Beverly Hills. Ronnie Reagan lives up the street. You might wake him up."

"Do they shoot first and ask questions later?" Cohen snapped back. "Like in your American movies?"

Madden shook his head in disgusted frustration. "They would have handcuffed you and held you until a black-and-white showed up. Maybe, just maybe, they would have sprung you after a dozen hours of shuffling paper," he said, then added another "maybe" for spite.

"And maybe if you had done your job, I wouldn't have to be walking in the streets," Cohen shot back.

"Look," Madden said, exasperated. "I told you, if you have something you want to ask, you come to me. Don't bother people with questions they can't answer. Your man killed himself. Coroner's office called me. A broken neck. From hanging. You find the package I left for you? You said you wanted to see it."

"Yes," Cohen said softly.

"Well?"

"He made it," Cohen admitted.

"I'm glad we got that straight," Madden said, satisfied.

There was a short silence. Cohen broke it. "Who complained?" he asked.

"None of your goddamn fucking business," Madden wailed, angrier than ever. "Leave these people alone. You make trouble for them, it makes trouble for me. And I don't like trouble."

"I saw that from the start," Cohen said, getting out of the car. He leaned in through the open door. "Tell me something," he asked Madden. "When do you retire?"

The question disarmed the American detective. "None of your fucking business," he snarled.

"That explains a lot," Cohen said judiciously. He turned away from the car.

The American shouted one more time: "You just leave these people alone up here." Then Madden gunned the car engine, spinning the car wheels and shooting gravel. The passenger door slammed shut from the centrifugal force of the car's swerve out of the circular driveway. Cohen waited for the car to disappear, and then, ignoring Madden's orders, he marched across the street, already knowing which neighbor had complained.

Back in the empty corral of black gravel, sparkling in the sun, he held up his hands, as if offering a truce.

"I'm a friend of Max Broder's," he shouted. "From across the street." He pointed. "I don't mean to bother you. I only want to ask a couple of questions."

A full minute later, the door opened hesitantly. A prematurely gray woman peered out. She had haggard hollows in her ashen cheeks and questioned him with her eyes.

He took a step forward, and she started to close the door. "Wait," he called out. "Please."

The door remained ajar. But the woman's face had disappeared. He asked loudly if she saw or heard anything on Friday night or Saturday.

She was silent behind the partially open door. He repeated his question three times, varying it each time, taking a small step forward, lowering his voice slightly, so by the time he had questioned her the third time—including a third apology for disturbing her—he was on the steps, speaking in almost a whisper. He reached for the handle as he concluded, "Really, that's all I want," and pushed open the door.

She was standing a few paces away, staring at him. Her eyes were bloodshot. She reminded him of a Jerusalem junkie he knew, a doctor's wife whose Central European manners had disintegrated after her husband's death, when she no longer had anyone controlling her intake of morphine.

"Madam," he said, with all the courtesy he could muster, "my name is Avram Cohen. I am a friend of Max Broder. Perhaps you heard . . ."

Her stare turned into a sharp intake of breath, which Cohen understood to be a confirmation that she knew.

"I am trying to find out if on Friday night or Saturday morning you might perhaps have been awakened by an unusual noise or perhaps have seen visitors to his house. . . ."

She tilted her head back and forth, as if to let the idea roll from one side of her mind to the other as she peered at him.

"Madam, are you all right?" he asked, worried by her appearance and behavior. "Can I get you a doctor?"

Her laugh chilled Cohen as it burst from her. "I'm sorry," she finished, breaking into a cough. "Doctors. They're the last thing I need."

"Max Broder?" he asked again.

"He hanged himself," she told him, as if breaking the news. "I always said he was courageous. After all, he tried to hit on me while Charles was still here." There was more disrespect to herself than to Broder.

"Perhaps you saw something, Friday night? Saturday?" He tried again.

She nodded slowly. "There was a car," she said.

Cohen leaned forward, the better to hear.

"I was sitting upstairs on the terrace. From up there I have a view of the entire neighborhood. Your friend had the best view, of course. He invited us over once," she said wistfully, remembering better times. "Of course, he almost won an Oscar, so I suppose he deserved it. All I ever won was a palimony settlement." Cohen could hear the bitterness in every syllable.

"The car?" he pressed.

"I thought it was Charles. I'm always thinking that," she said mournfully. "But it wasn't, of course. It went into your friend's driveway."

"Who was in the car? Could you see?" Cohen pressed.

"No. I stopped paying attention when it wasn't Charles."

"What time was it?"

"After Letterman," she said.

"Pardon?"

"Letterman, Letterman," she said, annoyed by his ignorance. "The show? The TV show?"

"I'm sorry." He was apologetic. "I am a stranger to your country."

"About one. Maybe a little later," she explained.

He pressed again. "The car, what kind of car was it?"

She thought for a moment and then decided. "A limo. Dark."

"What makes you think so?" he asked patiently.

"Isn't that how everyone gets around nowadays?" she asked back, her gaze floating away from him, her voice trailing off. He was losing her, and he still had questions.

"Why didn't you tell the police?" Cohen demanded.

She stared at him. "It's hot," she said suddenly, gazing out at the neighborhood. The look in her eyes gradually hardened into a strange distant stare, going far beyond Cohen. "Very hot," she added, and surprised him by stepping forward.

Instinctively he backed away from her face, twisting in the pain of rejection, and her hand went to the door. "I think you'd better leave now," she said, in a soft, tense voice.

"Please, one more question," he tried. But by then he was facing the brass knurl of the knocker on the broad wooden door.

Wearily he crossed the sun-drenched space, the questions in his mind drumming their rhythm, his hidden grief straining to be let out. The distant barking of dogs sounded to him as though they were mocking his attempts to enter Broder's world.

Manheim's raving echoes over the stubble-sore shaven heads. His boots crunch rhythmically on the crushed gravel. The sun is an aching light behind the smoke. Manheim's voice is near now. The words are simple. "Dogs. Shit. Insects." But the hatred rages. Sometimes the screaming halts, and then it starts again, a whisper that grows into a howl. Sometimes a laugh precedes a screech. Two rows ahead, Manheim comes into view. He is small and slender. In one hand he has a pistol. The other holds an ivory-handled riding crop. A man in a white jacket is a pace behind the SS officer. Thick glass lenses, set into the doctor's elegant gold-and-silver frames, enlarge his eyes to the size of a madness that cannot be disguised. He peers closely, inspecting but never touching. He pauses, nods, and continues. He selects by shaking his head. Manheim watches closely with his icy blue eyes. From behind, it is impossible to recognize the chosen man. Everyone—except Manheim in the black uniform and the doctor in his white coat—is gray. Der Bruder's voice, so near it is distinct even as a murmur, identifies the doomed man first. "The anarchist," he whispers.

"Will he talk?" Cohen mumbles back.
"Would you?" Broder answers.

Panicked, Cohen woke in the silent house. The curtains over the open window were red from the sunset. He had come back to the house intending to search Sophie's and Broder's rooms and then continue in the study and cutting room. He had started with a shower to wash away the sour smell of sweat. He had picked up the treatment from the floor where he had left it in the morning, and naked, he had sat down on the bed, unable to dam his curiosity about what happened next in the movie. But again, jet lag and the memories had ambushed him, driving him into a long afternoon doze in which memory and dream melded with the story in Broder's treatment.

The jet lag made him think of Jerusalem, and of Ahuva, but that reminded him of another, more urgent call, to Goldie Stein. He searched in his trousers pocket for the pad where he had tucked her business card. An answering service operator promised that Miss Stein would hear that he had called. He decided on food before calling Ahuva. A few minutes later, he was dressed, making his way through the darkening house, searching for light switches on his way. He paused at Sophie's room. Nothing had changed in the chaos. He could see Broder's bedroom through the open door in her room.

Sighing, he headed down to the kitchen. Despite the espresso machine, he had fallen in love with the kitchen in the morning. The refrigerator was twice the size of his own, and well stocked. The kitchen utensils were easily located, in drawers logically placed between the stove and the sink. Above the butcher-block table, the pots and pans hung from hooks. A set of Finnish knives mounted in a wooden block were on the table. He tried making espresso again, learning from his mistakes in the morning and surprising himself with a successful double, which he sipped at while slicing up a tomato, an onion, and a cucumber, all diced tiny and thrown into a salad bowl. He added salt and pepper, a squirt of lemon juice, and a shot of olive oil. He had to experiment with the microwave oven on two frozen steaks before he managed to defrost one properly, and then, using a drop of olive oil on a frying pan, salt, pepper, a dab of mustard, and a splash of cognac, he cooked the meat. For a few minutes, preparing the food took his mind off everything that was irritating him.

But the blinking light of the answering machine at the desk in the corner drew his attention as he sat down at the table to eat.

The first message was from the Israeli consul general, whose secretary asked Cohen to call. The second came from Andrew Blakely's secretary, offering the studio's condolences and asking if there was anything Commander Cohen needed. Both left numbers, which he duly noted in his pad.

The Los Angeles reporter for *Hadashot,* a Tel Aviv daily, was next, asking for an interview; Cohen scowled at the machine. That short message was followed by a call from a man who identified himself as Chuck Grant, asking if Cohen would be interested in appearing on his show. Cohen snorted, thinking of Goldie. Hirsh was next, reporting that the funeral would be at ten the next morning at a cemetery called Sha'arei Eden, the Gates of Eden. Cohen wrote the name in Hebrew while Hirsh's voice on the machine said a limousine would pick up Cohen and Sophie at nine. "And there will be a *shiva* at my place afterwards," Hirsh said, ending his message with a plea: "And please, Avram, no scandals."

The tape clicked, and then there were the sounds of a carnival. Cohen clearly heard a calliope and, beyond it, music with a heavier, angrier beat. Drumming. It was so unexpected that for a moment he forgot it was issuing from an answering machine and called out to the still silent caller, "Hello?"

"Der Bruder said you would come," the machine answered, in a voice pitched higher than the sounds behind it. "I'm always at Santa Monica pier. I look forward to seeing you again." It was a man's voice, speaking a familiar German, and it seemed unused to talking to answering machines. The music continued in the background for another three measures, and then the machine clicked and beeped, coming to a sullen halt.

Cohen fumbled with the machine's buttons, trying to rewind the tape to listen to the last message. He played it back twice. But the identity of the speaker remained out of reach. For the first time, he realized he'd need a map of the city. He had counted on Broder as his guide. It had never occurred to him that he'd have to find his way around alone.

He sighed, wondering where to find Santa Monica pier, and then, finishing his steak, he thought about politics. He understood politics. That's why he needed Goldie. He washed the dishes, then he went to the phone, planning to call Ahuva. Reaching for it, he found himself answering its ring.

"Cohen," he said.

"Well, it's about *time* I heard from you," Goldie began, her voice sawing through the hum of a crowd in the background. A laugh far too brittle to be Goldie's came over the earpiece of the phone, and she reprimanded it with a curse.

"So? You find your murderer yet?" she asked, the sarcasm undisguised.

"I have not called it murder," Cohen grumbled softly.

"What's that?" she shouted. "Listen, you want to talk to me, you gotta speak up. It's really loud here."

He held the mouthpiece like a microphone, almost looking at it, imagining Goldie in front of him. "Goldie," he said loudly, "I need your help." He hoped it didn't sound like pleading.

There was a brief pause. He wondered if she had heard him, or worse, he suddenly feared she might have hung up. "Goldie?" he asked.

"You see, I told you you'd need my help. What made you change your mind?"

"How soon can you be here?" he asked, ignoring her question.

"Hey, what do you think I am? One of your cops?" she shot back. "I don't take *orders* from anyone. You got that?"

"I'm sorry," he offered, spotting the circus-mirror reflection of his grimace in the dark glass of the microwave's door. "Please?"

"That's better," she said. "All right. I'll be up there in an hour. Maybe less."

"Thank you," he said sincerely.

"And you'll tell me what changed your mind," she insisted.

He couldn't tell her outright that it was because hers were the only interests he so far understood in Los Angeles. Hers and Madden's. He did not know what a producer did, and could only suspect what lawyers might be up to in a city where people sold pictures of themselves. He didn't trust journalists, but he knew how to use them. So he attempted flattery. "The power of the press," he said, shaking his head as he hung up on her transparent laugh.

There was no answer at Ahuva's apartment. It was almost office hours in Jerusalem. He realized he was worried about her, before he remembered the reason why. A week before he left Jerusalem, she had remanded a rabbi to a week in jail. The wild-eyed rabbi claimed self-defense. An eleven-year-old Arab boy was in the hospital. It didn't help ease Cohen's mind that it was an election season and the rabbi's followers were vengeful. He didn't feel any better when there was no answer at her office. It was none of his business where she might be. But when he began to wonder if her disappearance was connected with him, he realized he was feeling the vanity of the paranoid. He'd call back later, he thought. Meanwhile he'd continue his search.

Sophie's chaotic room was compensated by Broder's compulsiveness. The suits were hung by color, from dark to light, across half a wall. Broder might have lost fifty kilos, Cohen thought, but his clothes were still large enough to use as a blanket. Shirts, too, were shelved rationally, stripes on one side, solids on the other. Cohen touched or brushed, felt or squeezed, each piece of clothing. He went through the shoes the same way, and finding nothing, he went to the bed.

The silvery-purple silk sheets mocked Cohen with their pricey sheen and hospital corners. He pulled at the sheets and then at the pillows, finally struggling with the huge mattress as if it were an unhappy drunk, until it was off its platform. But there, too, no secret place was found.

He looked around, determined, by now ready to be happy with a scrap of forgotten paper that would prove Broder might have missed a step instead of being a long stride ahead of the confused Cohen.

Black-and-white sketches of Degas ballerinas looked demurely away as Cohen took each of the three drawings off the wall. But the framed pictures concealed nothing.

He tried the floor, flagstone by flagstone, searching for a hidden safe. Broder had once told Cohen about it. "I'm rich now," Broder had said, "so I had a safe installed. Guess what I'm using as a combination?" But Cohen had been in no guessing mood that summer, his first as an investigator in Jerusalem, a month shy of being a father. Broder had been slighted by Cohen's impatience. "I thought you ought to know," he had said, pouting. "It's your number. Twenty-four eleven fifty-one. Who else in Los Angeles is going to know your number?" The sulk gave way to a laugh.

"Except me." A month later, Broder was back on the phone, with the news that Levine was dead. But by then, so were Cohen's young bride and unborn baby.

He was sitting on the bed, looking glumly at the tattooed number on his arm, when the chimes of the front doorbell startled him out of the memory. Careful to close both Broder's and Sophie's doors on his way, he went down the stairs.

"Where's Sophie?" Goldie asked, stalking past him into the foyer. "Her car's not here." She was dressed in a short, tight dress that seemed modeled on a tennis costume and revealed surprisingly muscular thighs and calves.

"I saw her last night," Cohen explained as he moved casually around her. "I haven't seen her since."

It took a heartbeat for the flicker of surprise to reach Goldie's face. Her lower lip folded into a frown, but then she brightened, as her eyes looked past him. "I haven't been *inside* this place in years," she said, negotiating her way into the huge living room.

It was organized into three separate seating arrangements, each furnished baronially. There was a fireplace large enough to cook a calf, and a stagelike second level at the far end. But instead of medieval tapestries, like the one of St. George in the dining room, the dark walls were decorated with more than a dozen life-sized paintings, the originals of advertising posters for Broder's movies.

"The *last* time I was here," Goldie said, "there was a bar up there." She was pointing toward the landing at the end of the vast room. "It's not there anymore," she added, disappointed.

"I'm sorry," Cohen said. "A drink?"

Goldie threw back a curl as she turned to him. "What's in that *darling* flask you carry?" she asked.

"Cognac," he said, watching her from the arched entrance to the room. "You were drinking vodka on the plane."

"You *remembered,*" she said, pleased.

"There's some in the freezer," he said.

"Perfect," she said, following him out of the living room.

They were in the kitchen, his back to her as he opened the freezer door, when she asked the question: "Have you seen his movie yet?" She couldn't see the grimace cross his face as he shook his head. "Shit," she muttered to herself. But she quickly recovered. "When you do, can I be there?"

"I'm not sure I'm going to see it."

"Bullshit," she declared confidently, and then looked, surprised, at the bottle he had handed her.

He crossed the room to the table, pulling the flask from his pocket as he sat down.

"*You'll* see it," she said. She went to the sink to get a glass for her drink.

He fiddled with the cap of his flask. "Perhaps," he said. "But you're the one who said that if Epica doesn't want to show it, nobody will see it."

She collapsed mockingly against the kitchen counter, moaning, "You're so literal." She batted her eyes at him vampishly, saw he wasn't amused, and stood straighter. "I'm sure Leo can arrange it for you." She took a sip of water. "And all *I'm* asking is that you let me see it with you." She smiled at him. "Now, that's not so much, is it?"

"Why?" he asked, suspicious.

"Why?!" she shrieked. "Because it's a great *story.* And so far, I've got it all to myself. Well, at least your part of the story. That bitch Chuck Grant, he'd love to get his hands on you. Wait a second—you aren't gay, are you?"

"Pardon?"

"Gay? You *know,* homosexual?"

He shook his head with a bemused smile. She studied him for

a moment, smiled back, and then asked. "You think he had any lemon in there?" She nodded at the refrigerator.

"I know there is," Cohen promised, pushing himself away from the table.

"That's all right. I can get it." She pulled open the refrigerator door. "You want my help?" she said, smiling before she disappeared behind the stainless steel. Only her tightly wrapped broad bottom showed as she bent to pick a lemon out of the fruit drawer. She waggled her rear once and then stood up, saying, "I want yours." Turning with a stripper's gesture, she used her hip to slap the refrigerator door closed, then sashayed confidently back to the butcher-block table.

"What do you want?" he asked her as she put down the lemon beside the bottle and the glass.

"I told you. The movie."

"Maybe," he said. He hated negotiating.

"You've got to do better than that," she said, "if you want *my* cooperation." She pulled a knife out of the block on the table and made him wince at her clumsy attempts to cut the lemon. Just as he was about to grab the knife away from her and do it himself, she succeeded. She grinned at him and dropped half of the lemon into her glass, then finally poured her drink.

"Tell me about Max and Sophie Levine," he suggested quietly.

She froze in midtoast, vodka in hand.

"Why didn't you tell me about them on the plane?" He studied the flask cap in his hand as he waited for her answer.

She tossed down her vodka, but still hadn't made up her mind. He was about to use his final card, when she decided. "I'm the *only* one who knows," she said. "I'm sure of it."

"It is my turn," Cohen said, "to say bullshit." He took a sip from his flask, watching her forehead furrow slightly as she thought.

"What about the movie?" she finally asked.

He shrugged.

She put down her vodka glass carefully and pushed herself away from the table. Her high heels crackled on the tile floor as she started out of the room.

"Maybe," he said. But she didn't stop her march toward the dining room. "If it can be arranged," he added.

That made her pause in midstride and turn to the kitchen counter, as if it had been her goal all along. She opened the tap and drank a glass of cold water before sashaying back to the table and pouring herself another full measure of vodka.

"The relationship?" Cohen asked.

"He used her," Goldie said. "When there was nobody else, he had her. He thought he owned her. She thought she owed him. You can't blame them both, I suppose. He *rescued* her from East Germany, didn't he? And brought her to this," she said, waving a hand at the kitchen, to summon up the luxury of the house.

"Do you know where she is now?"

Goldie looked at him defiantly, trying to protect Sophie. "She's *out* of here," the columnist said. "That's where she is."

"Where?" he demanded.

"What difference does it make?" Goldie mourned. "Max is gone. She's free now." Her voice was slightly slurred. He wondered how many drinks she had had before coming to the house on the hill. Still, he wanted to hit her when she added, "Or does she have to be grateful to *you* now?"

He concentrated on the cognac in the flask instead, letting its warmth sink into him. He wanted to go home. The burn in his throat and stomach receded. "Goldie. Please. I don't want to hurt her. She doesn't have to stay here. She's an adult. Get her on the phone."

Goldie shook her head slowly. "She knows a lot of people. Max really showed her off. Like a trophy, you know? He took her everywhere, for a while. She knows a lot of the kids."

"The police say she was out for the weekend," Cohen said. "From Friday night to Sunday morning." It was a question.

Goldie shrugged, looking suddenly older and forlorn, as if she had been left behind. "A party starts up in one place, goes on someplace else. She partied. But she didn't mean any harm."

"They said something about a nightclub."

"They say it was suicide," she shot back, like a wounded soldier with enough strength to fire a last round.

"Maybe," he said, thinking of the noose upstairs.

She eyed him thoughtfully. "There are a lot of clubs," she finally said.

He pulled the yellow notebook from his pocket and leafed through it until he found a blank page, before looking up at her, waiting.

But instead of a recital of the nightspots of Los Angeles, she reached across the table, taking his hand. "Avram," she said, "maybe Max *did* kill himself. You're a stranger in Hollywood. A stranger to him. I don't know what he was like back then. Maybe when we see the movie . . ." She smiled ingenuously, letting her voice trail off with the hint.

"Maybe." He left his hand in place to encourage her to go on.

"But I'll tell you one thing—Max turned mean in the past few years. He could be gentle and charming, and he was always a *helluva* ladies' man. But he turned mean."

But something she had said earlier had distracted Cohen. "Who exactly *has* seen the movie?" he asked.

"*I* don't know," she protested, surprised. "They didn't do *any* previews. No parties. No PR. Max had *extras* signing secrecy clauses, for crying out loud. And that was just up in Oregon. I hear that in Europe he *really* laid on the security."

"Who would know?" he asked.

"Leo. He'll know. Or Blakely. You know what? Ask Barbara Darnaby. She'd probably know best, that cheat, walking out on Max the way she did. You know, I can't believe Leo could be so stupid, not to tell me that it was when Barbara came into the restaurant that Max went crazy. But if there's anyone who can help you, it's her. She can probably tell you who saw it and when and which cut they saw. It's what she gets paid for doing, and she does it well. That's one thing you can say for Max, he sure could pick 'em."

F
O
U
R

ANOTHER ROLL CALL. In the snow. The soldiers wear overcoats. Prisoners clutch rags as blankets. The only sound is the crunch of the kapos' feet as they patrol the rows, the occasional thud of a club, or the equally dull sound of a body collapsing. It's a blizzard. Past the rows of gray prisoners, past the gray kapos with their clubs, and the gray guards, Manheim waits in his black car. The snow turns charcoal where the blue smoke of the exhaust pipe burns. The car faces the gallows. The snow has drifted into caps and epaulets on the shaven heads and gray shoulders of a dozen hanging bodies. "Look," Der Bruder whispers at Cohen's side. Young Avram's eyes flicker. A prisoner has broken ranks. He is walking away from the parade grounds. "I can't understand them," Der Bruder says. He could be a ventriloquist, the way he can speak without moving his lips. "Walking to death that way." He shakes his head slightly. The view is distorted, out of the corner of the eye. Murmuring begins. Only when the slave is halfway to the fence, and drops his blanket like a black teardrop in the snow, does the kapo notice. His head swivels back and forth between the prisoner and Manheim's car. The indecision is obvious in the kapo's bulging eyes. He could let someone else report the madness of the walking man, who is steadily approaching the fence. Heavy breathing becomes the blizzard's dampened whistle and turns into the shrieking of the train. All is white. There's a gunshot.

Cohen woke to the crash of a glass vase, knocked from the windowsill by a hot gusting wind that turned the curtains into flapping wings. He sat up straight. The sheets were soaked with his sweat. A red dawn was breaking in the east.

A bead of sweat slid down his naked side. He wiped it away and checked his watch. It was early evening in Jerusalem. He looked for the treatment. It was on the floor. He reached down to pick it up. Goldie's card fell out. He had watched and listened as she made phone calls, trying to locate Sophie. But every call turned up a dead end. In some, she asked if "Sophie" had appeared. In others, she called her "Max Broder's companion." But no one reported back that the missing woman had made an appearance. Eventually Cohen had sent Goldie home, and a few minutes later he took the treatment to bed.

He got up wearily, body aching in half a dozen places. After a shower, he sat down on the bed, by the phone. It was too early to call anyone in Los Angeles, he thought. But in Jerusalem, it was the end of the working day. He tried her office.

It was a new clerk who answered. He asked for the judge. When he was told she had already left for the day, he hung up without leaving his name. Then he tried her apartment. No answer. He slammed down the phone, angry first at her and then at himself.

He had two days' dirty laundry. He picked it up and started a search through the house for a laundry room. But passing Sophie's room, he dropped the small bundle of clothes on the floor and went in. He checked her closet, but he had no way of knowing what was missing. He went to her private bath. There was no toothbrush. He searched for papers. A passport. Something that would prove she had to return to the house. But it was all hopeless. The door to Broder's room taunted him.

Cursing, he strode to the phone at her bedside, reached into his pocket, and pulled out his yellow pad. Again he got Goldie's answering service, where he left a message for her to call him. Then he tried Leo Hirsh. The producer answered before the first ring finished.

"Listen," he started before Cohen could identify himself. "Dump all that GM shit and move it to—"

"Hirsh, this is Cohen."

"Oh," said Hirsh, "I thought you were my broker in New York. So you got my message? About the limo for the funeral."

"Yes."

"You won't make any more trouble," Hirsh begged. "It's bad enough, all that *na'arshkeiten* about the Kaddish."

Cohen interrupted. "Where is Sophie?" he demanded.

"What do you mean, where's Sophie?" Hirsh asked, surprised.

"I haven't seen her since the night I arrived."

"Well, *I* don't know where she is," Hirsh said emphatically. "She didn't leave a note? Call?"

"Nothing," said Cohen. "Do you know any of her friends? Acquaintances? Somewhere she might be staying?"

"That girl," Hirsh sighed, as if this was not the first time she had made trouble for him.

"Her friends?" Cohen prompted.

"Good question," Hirsh said. "Don't get me wrong—she was with Max whenever he needed her, running the house, taking care of the little things. But in the last few months she's been running with some wild kids. I warned Max, but he said she could take care of herself."

"Wild?" Cohen asked. "What do you mean, wild?"

"Well, they're not *my* friends," Hirsh said. "I stopped that kind of fucking around thirty years ago."

"You must know some names," Cohen urged.

"Kids. That's all. They go around in packs. I don't know which one she was into. But why don't you ask Goldie? She'll know."

Cohen made a short note in his book. Hirsh couldn't stand the vacuum of silence on the phone. "What? You're really worried about her?"

"Yes," Cohen said.

"Poor kid," Hirsh said, surprised. "Truth is, she really cared for Max. You know, she gave up everything for him. She could have had an acting career. With her looks? But she gave it all up for him."

"How did he find her?" Cohen asked.

"He didn't. She found him."

"Pardon?" Cohen said.

"You heard me. She found him. He was in Sweden for a film festival. They were showing *Cost of Survival*. It's become quite a little classic, you know. And she just approached him. She had a part in this East German flick, something about a swim team, I think Max said. She was one of the swimmers. Max was one of the judges. She came up to him, introduced herself. Lousy movie, Max said, but she had stood out. At first he thought the Commies were trying to bribe him with her. But then she said she was Bernard's daughter and—"

"You know about Bernard?" Cohen asked.

"Well, I *am* executive producer of the movie," Hirsh said, offended by the question. "Of course I know who Bernard was. Just like I know who you are. From the story. Didn't he tell you anything about it? I thought you two were as close as brothers."

"We were." Cohen sighed. "It was a long time ago."

"I know what *that's* like," Hirsh moaned. "I've got a brother back East, hasn't spoken to me in years. Says I've let all the money go to my head. I don't know, maybe he's right. But I sure was generous to his kids when they had their bar mitzvah. And I'm the one who paid for— Wait a second," he said. "That must be my broker on the other line. I'm putting you on hold. Don't hang up," he added, before Cohen had a chance to say anything.

He held the phone for a long minute, and then two. Halfway through the third minute, he was about to hang up, when Hirsh was back on the line. "D'ya mind if I get back to you later? The bulls are running and—"

"One last question," Cohen said. "Who *has* seen the movie? Goldie said there were no previews."

"Well, we don't have a final cut," Hirsh said, annoyed. "Do we?"

"He told me he wanted me with him for the final cut. Please," Cohen asked, "what is this final cut?"

"Just what it says. The final version of the film. After all the editing. I'd guess that in rough cut, about fifty of us saw it. Production people. Management."

"I am told that perhaps Miss Darnaby will know exactly who has seen it," Cohen prompted.

"Probably. What about you? I guess you and Max had plans to see it together? Now that he's gone . . . ?"

"Can you arrange it for me?" Cohen asked.

"Talk to Barbara," Hirsh said. "She'll set it up for you. Need her number?" he asked, then recited it quickly.

Cohen asked for it a second time, to make sure he had it right, and then Hirsh was gone and Cohen went back to work.

The projection booth in the screening room above the living room intimidated him. There were racks of film canisters and videocassettes and a shelf of electronic equipment, as well as a thirty-five-millimeter projector. For a moment he had the feeling Broder was looking over his shoulder, worrying whether he might break something. He moved gingerly into the neatly organized chamber.

On a small desk there was a printout of the movie library, with each film numbered. He ran his finger along the three shelves, comparing the list with the orderly archive. The only discrepancy he found was in the three cassettes of *The Godfather*. Part Three was shelved before Part Two. All of Broder's films were there, except *The Survivor's Secrets*.

The screening room itself consisted of two dozen comfortable armchairs and sofas arranged on a carpeted floor. The screen, tautly framed, was built into the far wall. He slumped into one of the armchairs. There was a telephone on the coffee table at his side, and he eyed it angrily, wondering if he was mad. "Don't be such an *a'kshen,* Cohen," he mumbled to himself. He suddenly had a memory of his mother's voice, as close as if she were standing beside him. He could almost hear her admiration of his willfulness, as well as the worry that it would get her only child in trouble. She, too, had called him stubborn, with love as well as exasperation. He shivered in the air conditioning in the windowless room, remembering Broder making the same warning, and Ahuva making the same accusation.

He heaved himself to his feet, and a few minutes later, he was nursing a cup of coffee in one hand, trying to decide where to start his search of the living room. The paintings caught his eye. They were mounted instead of hung. Their frames were all natural wood, lacquered dark. He studied one in particular. Vicki Strong's eyes were flashing green at Jeremy Steele. The ghost of another woman was behind Steele. Intuition told him to put down the coffee cup. He ran his hands along the sides of the frame, finding a fake knot in the wood.

He pressed but nothing happened, until he also turned the finger. There was a click. He pulled, and the frame swung open. He saw a numeric keypad. Cohen didn't even glance at his arm. The safe door opened.

There was a copy of Broder's will, along with three bound stacks of hundred-dollar bills—he counted one stack, reaching five thousand dollars, and assumed the other two had the same amount—as well as a thick brown envelope holding stock and bond certificates, and a velvet drawstring bag containing a fistful of unset diamonds.

The last thing he found was the gun. He broke it down, sighting along the barrel. Broder kept it clean. Cohen used his thumb to quickly dump the bullets from the magazine. The first one had just finished dancing as the last one fell with a push at the bottom from his thumb. He reloaded slowly, slipped the clip back into the handle, set it with a slap, and flipped the safety on. It was uncomfortable jammed into the back of his waistband. But it was familiar. He wondered if he'd get a chance to try it out before he might have to use it.

He picked up the will. Phyllis Fine was named as the attorney who prepared the short, straightforward document. It made grants to several educational institutions, but the bulk of the estate went to Sophie—"the closest person I've ever had to a child of my own." She also inherited the house. If she should have children, they would get, from the time of their birth, and in equal shares, half of the royalties from existing copyrights owned by Broder. The other half was to go to four film scholarship funds, two in America and two in Israel. If Sophie did not have children, the royalties went to the scholarships. But she still had her million dollars and the house.

But it was two codicils that stunned Cohen. He, not Fine, was named executor. He had had responsibility for an entire city, had sent many people into possible life-and-death situations. But except for that single year of marriage, he had never been responsible for another person's life. Broder was asking Cohen to be Sophie's father and the grandfather of her children. He wondered if she

knew the contents of the will, and then he read the final codicil.
If the first stunned him, now he was shocked. Sophie's inheritance
depended on Cohen's verifying that she indeed was the daughter
of Bernard Levine.

He reached for the phone on the coffee table. An answering
machine at Green, Feldstein and Fine asked him to leave a message.
He sighed, said he hoped to hear from Phyllis Fine at her earliest
convenience, and, without taking his hands off the phone, checked
his watch and tried another number.

"I'm sorry about interrupting you during the news," he said
softly when she answered with an annoyed hello after the third
ring.

"I've been reading about you," Ahuva said softly, with barely
a pause for the surprise at hearing his voice.

"What?" It was his turn to be surprised.

"*Hadashot* today says you're in Los Angeles because your friend
Max Broder committed suicide. "Is it true?"

"Not exactly," he said, grimacing as he realized he had forgotten
the reporter's call. "He died while I was on the plane."

"I'm sorry," she said.

"I tried calling you the last three days," he said.

"Javitz is in the country," she explained. "He gave some lectures.
We had dinner one night, and there was a reception last night in
Tel Aviv. So? Is it true? Max Broder committed suicide?"

"Is he still smoking those foul pipes?" Cohen asked, unable to
suppress the gust of jealousy, almost enjoying its energy.

"It's no worse than your Noblesse cigarettes," she taunted.

He could imagine her smile, and suddenly he wanted her as
much as he had desired her the first time he saw her stride onto
the bench in the magistrates court in the Russian Compound. It
had taken him a year to work up the courage to offer her dinner.

She broke the silence. "Did he commit suicide?" she asked again.

"I don't know," he said. "I'm trying to find out."

"That's a good start for you," she said uncynically.

"Yes," he said. "That's one of the reasons I wanted to call you."

"Why?"

"I'm sorry," he said. He had thought it would be more difficult. He could hear her breathing. "I apologize." It was becoming harder. "I was lost."

"And Max Broder found you?" she asked. There was no wry anger, but the question cut deep.

"He kept a lot of secrets from me," he said softly.

She eased his pain. "The Max Broder you described to me would never commit suicide," she said. "But of course, that was always hearsay," something that Cohen knew was never allowed in her courtroom. "I'm sorry. You told me you used to idolize him."

"That was a long time ago."

"But it must be painful."

"Yes."

They fell silent, listening to their breathing and the eerie clicks and echoes of a wavering international telephone line.

"The newspaper says he made that movie," she finally said. "The one you didn't want to see."

"Yes."

"Well, he finally got you to Los Angeles. Have you seen this movie yet?"

"Not yet," he admitted. "But I've been reading it."

"What?"

"The manuscript. They call it a treatment."

"I don't suppose you've looked to see how it ends?"

"No," he said, smiling at the joke between them. She always wanted to know the ending first.

"Well, I wouldn't worry," she said. "It's an American movie. It will probably have a happy ending."

The silence descended again, but it emphasized their loneliness, not the tension between them. Again, it was Ahuva who broke it. "It's difficult?" she asked.

"It's difficult," he admitted.

"Probably not helping your sleep much," she said. "Your dreams."

"He kept a lot of secrets," Cohen admitted.

"So you're working." She sighed. "When do you think you'll be done?"

"I don't know. There are things I have to do here. And I'm alone."

"You'll manage," she said confidently. "You've been alone before."

"Not for the last ten years," he said. It was the closest he had ever come to telling her he loved her.

He got out of the limousine, grimaced at the ponytailed driver's obsequious salute, and squinted into the morning sun, trying to remember where he had left his sunglasses.

To the east, the cemetery was a vast field of headstones and statuettes, granite plaques set into green grass, and occasional trees casting broad shade. It was all so bewildering to Cohen that even the driver noticed, pointing the Jerusalemite in the opposite direction, where the gathering mourners clustered and knotted to the west.

A dozen huge firs, their lower branches pruned to enable people to stand beneath higher, shading branches, lined a ridge at the top of a smoothly rising hill. He realized that the limousine Hirsh had sent was one of many, indeed too many to count. There were chauffeurs in uniforms and a relay race of charcoal-jacketed valets in gray shirts and black pants taking expensive cars that Cohen could not identify to a far corner of the field.

In Jerusalem, there were people who tear the clothes they were wearing at the moment they heard the tragic news, and kept wearing those signs of bereavement until the end of the seven days of *shiva.* Here, Cohen thought, already recognizing some of the famous faces, mourners dressed in their finest. Cohen was the only man without a tie, and he was wearing the windbreaker jacket only in order to hide the gun tucked into the back of his waistband. Even the greenskeepers, who watched from a small red tractor under the western shade of the last of the dozen trees on the ridge, were dressed more expensively than he.

He set forth on the flagstone path that crisscrossed the lawn up the hill.

Beyond the spreading lawns, he could see an expansive residential neighborhood to his east, the back of a shopping mall to his south, railroad lines just to the west, and a run-down commercial strip to the north. Far beyond that, a mountain range's tallest peak hovered in the haze. For the first time, he realized he was in a desert. Despite all the green, the wide-open space felt familiar. It had been a long time since rain fell in this place, he knew. The sprinklers might have worked all night, but under the morning sun, in the trapped heat of the city on the southern slope of a mountain, he could feel the thick grass underfoot crackle with dryness.

On all four sides of the grave were five rows of a dozen chairs each, already filling with people. A chair trolley, like an airport baggage cart, was on the ridge in the distance, bringing more chairs for the growing audience.

Cohen took up a position a few paces from the green, tarp-covered pile of dirt by the open grave. He was under one of the long sweeping branches of the fir trees lining the kilometer-long hilltop. A television news crew was climbing the hill. Parked on the grass by the start of the path was a van; a satellite dish stood on a tripod beside it. From the ridge he could see four policemen directing traffic on the main road outside the cemetery.

The mourners were dispersed over both sides of the ridge, on all sides of the grave, standing in clumps and knots, as if they were at a garden party. But instead of the clinking of glasses, rattling silver, and chatter, there was the murmur of whispering and sober conversation, and the distant sounds of the city carried on the light breeze from the east. He was aware of people around him, whispering behind his back, knowing who he was. Eyes flitted across his face, and heads turned with the news of his arrival.

He wished he had his sunglasses, and for a moment experienced a kind of stage fright, avoiding eye contact. He hated all ceremonies, but especially public attempts to understand dying, for he knew it happened alone, to even the most beloved person. He had refused to share his grief for more than forty years, and he certainly wasn't going to start now, with these strangers.

He swept his eyes over the crowd like a stroboscopic camera, collecting still images of faces and tiny dramas. There were certainly many variations on the mourning costume, he thought, watching a slightly tipsy couple in matching tuxedos enter a huddle of friends on the lawn. Not that he hadn't seen drunks at funerals. He was aware that while many of the people were pointing him out to one another, none had dared approach him. So he concentrated on patience and restrained his anger, realizing that among all the strangers there might be one, or even more, with a secret wrath of their own.

He saw people kissing into the air at each other and a vaguely familiar bearded face peering out of an emotional embrace and winking at a busty woman. A woman in more red than black seemed to have tracked his eyes, for at one point, there she was waiting for him, blowing a kiss over Broder's grave. But she wasn't Sophie, so he scanned on, deciding from what he already had been told about the Englishwoman Darnaby that she would be too polite to either wear a red dress to a funeral or blow a kiss over an open grave. There were dozens of elderly men, many leaning on walkers of various kinds. He watched a nurse accompanying one white-haired man who was pushed up the hill in a wheelchair but then got onto his feet and seemed quite spry as he moved through the crowd, the young woman in her tight-fitting white uniform at his side.

Cohen's own body felt off-key. Muscles were aching, and he was light-headed. He couldn't tell if he had been getting too much sleep or too little. The extravagance and pretense around him were making him feel sick. He wanted to go home. He looked away, to the north. For the first time, he saw the famous Hollywood sign on the hillside. It was far to the north, but legible.

He was smiling to himself, thinking maybe he'd send a postcard of the sign to his former assistant Nissim Levy, when he heard Goldie's voice. "Hel-lo?" she sang, but instead of melody, it came out as squawk. "Earth to Avram—come in, Avram," she tried again. His faint smile turned into a brief grimace as she forced his thoughts back to the funeral.

"Hello, Goldie," he said softly, barely moving his lips.

She leaned in at him, and then whispered in his ear as she offered him a kiss into the air beside his cheek: "Press on, darling, press on." Then she stepped back and ran an appraising eye over his clothes. He could not tell if her charcoal-gray mannish suit, with its large, almost black carnation, pinned above a glittering scarab climbing the linen lapel, was dignified or clownish.

She shook her head at his simple clothes and clucked, "Amateur night," before taking his arm to face the crowd.

"Have you seen Sophie?" he asked out of the side of his mouth.

"No," she said, imitating his surreptitious whisper. "But here comes Alvy Landy. This is gonna be a gas."

The approaching youngster wore a deliberately grim smile under an oddly bent nose, his teeth a sparkling white in a wry mouth set into a meager four-day beard. A strawberry-blond girl wearing a robe of subdued colors was half a step behind him.

"He's you," Goldie whispered into Cohen's ear, "in the movie," she explained, startling Cohen into a perplexed stare at the boy.

"I've been waiting to meet you for three years," Alvy Landy began solemnly, "but I never thought it would be without The Brother."

The boy's use of the secret name shocked Cohen. For the first time he realized that Broder's movie might include the story of the *nokmim*. He had always assumed it was the story of the camp that Broder would tell in the movie. Not the *nokmim*.

Goldie was right: he needed to see the movie. Cohen looked into Alvy Landy's eyes, wondering how much Broder had told. Goldie yanked on his arm and whispered into his ear, "He's waiting for you to say something."

"And I never expected to meet you. With or without him," Cohen said reflexively, taking Alvy's offered grasp.

"So you don't lack *all* the social graces," Goldie snapped snidely, though she was obviously impressed.

But Cohen paid her no attention, surprised at how the actor's handshake reminded him of Nissim Levy's sharp grasp of the hand. That reminded him of something Sophie had said about the movie and doubled the urgency of his need to find her. He scanned the crowd, ignoring Alvy's expectant face and Goldie's curiosity.

Sophie was behind the last row of chairs, in the midst of the crowd, wearing both sunglasses and a wide-brimmed black hat with a veil. At least he thought she might be Sophie, but then he lost sight of her for a second when she passed behind a movie star whom even Cohen knew was famous for doing his own stunts. Cohen watched the place where she would reappear. There were two other tall, elegant women, wearing oversized sunglasses and shiny black dresses that Cohen decided were probably designed for night, not mourning. His eyes moved quickly across the entire gathering, and he almost laughed out loud, for there were at least two dozen other such women, dressed in the same way.

"What's so funny?" Goldie asked at his side.

"Maybe he doesn't see the resemblance, Alvy," the girl at Alvy's side suggested. "Hi, I'm Pam," she said to Cohen, sticking out her hand. Cohen smiled at her, and he gave her hand one short, abrupt shake.

"Pam," Alvy moaned, making a sheepish expression of apology to Cohen. The girl shrugged slightly and fell contritely silent.

Cohen tilted his head, studying Alvy's face.

"It's obvious," Goldie said, disgusted with them all. "It's the eyes."

Alvy smiled. Like Cohen, he had silvery-gray eyes. But it was the boy's teeth Cohen noticed, thinking of his own fine teeth before Dachau. Cohen grinned once at the actor and then looked over his head, relying on his instincts and seeking out the first woman he had thought might be Sophie.

She was backing away from a barrel-chested man with a long braid running down his back.

Cohen yanked his arm out of Goldie's grasp, nodded curtly to Alvy Landy, and turned away just as a photographer took a picture of the actor with Cohen.

But he had gone barely two steps when Leo Hirsh latched onto him, Rabbi Gould in tow. Over Hirsh's head, Cohen could see across the lawn. The man with the braid was holding up his hands as if proving he had nothing to hide. But the woman—Cohen still wasn't sure it was Sophie—backed away, disappearing into the crowd where it melted over the ridge.

"So you've met your alter ego," Hirsh said, pulling Alvy with a paternal hand on the actor's shoulder, as he put a friendly one on Cohen's.

Cohen twitched, and Hirsh removed his hand. Alvy imitated Cohen's gesture.

Goldie smiled. "So, Leo, when do we get to see Alvy as Avram?"

"Goldie," Hirsh whined, "this is neither the time nor the place to be talking business. Don't you have any sense of propri-etry?"

"You mean propriety," she said condescendingly. "No, I must admit I probably don't. Avram would also like to know," she added, glancing at Cohen. "If I have any propriety, that is." She grinned.

Cohen barely heard. He was still scanning the crowd.

"He offered us the movie," Gould interjected, "for our benefit. He even met with Laszlo Katz about it. But I never got the cassette. You didn't happen to find it in his house?" the rabbi casually asked Cohen.

Before Cohen could answer, Hirsh broke in. "Joe, I told you. There is no cassette."

Gould shrugged. "All I know is what Max told me. He said he was going to have a cassette made for us to show at the benefit. If we wanted it. And we do." He looked at Cohen, expecting a response. Cohen's silence drew all five pairs of eyes to his face, waiting for his reaction. Goldie interrupted the silent search for a clue in his face. "He hasn't found any cassette," she announced. "For godsake, he knows less about the goddamned movie than any of us."

"Is that true?" Alvy asked.

Hirsh looked at Cohen hopefully, but the Jerusalemite couldn't tell whether it was because he wanted Cohen to have found the tape or not.

Cohen was still unsure of whom to trust. He looked around at them all and then asked, "Have any of you seen Sophie?"

"I saw her," Alvy said. "Over that way." He pointed away from where Cohen thought he had seen her, toward a knot in the crowd halfway to the next tree on the ridge. At least a dozen of the women in short black dresses, wide-brimmed hats, and large dark sunglasses were in view. Like spies in a bad movie, the young women in their stylish black at the funeral appeared obvious in their disguises. Cohen tried to remember something particular about Sophie. But all he had in his mind was her naked body in the water and her pale-blue eyes. Again, he thought he spotted her. But the woman turned, and she was a blond, with long hair spilling out from under her hat.

"Oh, my God!" Goldie exclaimed, grabbing Cohen's arm in excitement. She pointed toward a rustle of activity at the bottom of the hill, where limousines, sedans, and sports cars were still depositing mourners. "I can't believe it," she blurted. "I can't believe it!"

A tall, silver-haired man was helping Vicki Strong out of a limousine. Goldie turned to Hirsh. "Leo! How'd you do it? Getting Vicki to come out!"

"You can thank Avram here for that," Hirsh said, making Goldie raise an eyebrow. "She called me yesterday and said that after his visit, she decided to come, after all. What *did* you say to her?" Hirsh asked Cohen, who was looking at Goldie. She kept shifting her gaze between him and the rabbi and then down to the actress walking slowly up the hill, accompanied by a pack of reporters.

"Sorry," Goldie finally said apologetically, and she took off her high-heeled shoes and started running across the lawn, to meet Vicki Strong halfway up the hill.

Alvy Landy still wanted to be helpful. "I'm sure Sophie's here," he said to Cohen. "I can find her for you, if you want."

"If you would, please, yes," Cohen said gratefully.

Alvy grinned and backed out of the circle, going to a clump of people closer to the grave. Cohen watched the boy, his girlfriend in tow, approach a huge bearded man, who pointed down the ridge. The actor headed in that direction.

"There's the coffin," Hirsh announced, pointing to the flower-covered roof of the hearse. It seemed to float along the edge of the hill in the distance, as it approached from the direction opposite that which all the other cars had taken to the cemetery. "I have to make sure about the pallbearers," the producer announced. But before hustling away, he appealed to Gould. "Joe, keep the commander company for a few minutes before we get started."

"He wants me to make a last effort to get you to say Kaddish," said Gould after Hirsh was gone.

Cohen thought for a moment. "I haven't said Kaddish in almost forty-five years," he rumbled.

"Maybe it's time to say it again," Gould tried.

Cohen only stared back at the young rabbi, and then he turned away, still looking for Sophie.

Several faces spun, following his gaze. Others offered him sorrowful looks, trying to convey sympathy. A few he recognized from television shows, others made him think of the American tourists he knew from Jerusalem. Standing behind the last chairs on the western side of the hill, he saw Madden, towering over a pair of whispering women. The two detectives exchanged somber nods.

Then his eyes fell on Phyllis Fine. She was on the opposite side of the crowd, standing beside an empty chair at the end of the fourth row.

Gould was still at Cohen's side, waiting for an answer. "Don't worry about me," he reassured the rabbi. "Just living in the Land of Israel is enough to have won me a place in heaven." He was being as sarcastic as the rabbi had been saccharine. "Now, if you'll pardon me," and without waiting for the rabbi's response, Cohen started around the crowd, heading toward the lawyer, signaling Madden that he needed to speak with him, and still vigilant for Sophie.

Faces peered in at him, hands grasped his. Sympathy was offered with cloying familiarity. It was all polite but insistent, based on the assumption that he knew who they were—indeed, that they knew who he was. "My condolences." "He was such a wonderful man." "Such a tragedy." The phrases came at him out of scented smiles, from elderly men and blue-haired ladies, and from sexually ambiguous fawners and tight-lipped power brokers. Hirsh had kept his promise to gather together the Jewish and industry elite of the city for the funeral, and Cohen was a stranger in their midst, ignorant of their identities while they all believed they knew him well. It doubled his loneliness.

The *Hadashot* reporter and the Israeli consul general approached together. Cohen knew the diplomat was a political appointee, with better connections in the ruling party's central committee than he could ever hope to have in Los Angeles or the foreign ministry. He thanked them both for their condolences and reprimanded the reporter for getting the story wrong, then he moved on without further explanation.

"Commander," said Phyllis Fine, extending her hand. "Again, my condolences. Please let me introduce my partners, Lawrence Green and Jerome Feldstein." She turned to a pair of white-haired, leather-faced men. Both were a head shorter than she. They might have been twins.

"Larry," said one, offering his hand. "I'm sorry about your friend."

"Jerry," said the other. "Condolences."

Their grim expressions of concern were belied by body language that said he was Phyllis Fine's problem, not theirs. They didn't mind when Cohen indicated his need for a private conversation with Fine.

"I read his will," he began softly, taking her a few steps out of the crowd, down the ridge.

"Ahh," she said, "the codicils."

"If he didn't believe it was her," Cohen insisted, "why did he take her in?"

"*He* believed her," Fine said. "*I'm* the one who insisted on it. Well, not on you as the person to confirm her identity or even to put it in the will. That was his idea. But it was my idea that we have her checked out right after she came."

"Why?" he asked, confused.

"Precaution. Because my job is to protect him. I mean, *was* to protect him. And I thought he was putting an awful lot of trust in someone he barely knew—especially when it became obvious that she was doing more than running his household." She was unable to hide the undercurrent of distaste in her tone.

"Did you have her investigated?" he asked.

"Thoroughly," she said. "Sophie Levine is who she says she is."

"So why the codicils?" he demanded. "Why am I still in it that way?"

"That was his idea," she protested. "I thought he was kidding. But he had made up his mind, insisted on it."

"Why?" Cohen demanded.

"He said it would guarantee one thing that he wanted more than almost anything else."

"What?"

"It would force you to come to America. He said he didn't think he would ever get you here any other way."

Cohen's feelings were raw, his emotions clouding everything. But he willed himself to concentrate on the task instead of himself. "What about the conflict of interest?" he asked softly. "If I prove her to be an impostor, I get the inheritance. What's to prevent me from just saying it's not her?"

She shook her head with a wry smile and peered at him almost innocently. "Commander, you seem to have a much lower opinion of yourself than Max did."

"You told Madden that Max kept the rope on his desk."

"It started when he was on location. Like a nervous habit," the lawyer said. "Like worry beads."

Cohen rubbed at his brow, thinking as he looked around the crowd again, trying to hide his emotions from both of them. Instead of Sophie, he spotted Goldie, on the other side of the chairs. She was waving to him, while hinting with exaggerated nods that he should notice a man in her circle. The man bore a vague resemblance to George Bush, with the same sharp chin below a thin-lipped mouth, and a high forehead over an equally sharp nose, on which functional steel-rimmed eyeglasses were perched.

"That's Andy Blakely," Fine said, following Cohen's gaze.

Blakely was standing with Leo Hirsh, who was holding Vicki Strong's hands and beaming at her. A startling squeal of electronic feedback rent the air. Cohen could see Hirsh's face pale, and then the producer dropped the actress's hands and hustled toward Gould, who was struggling with the microphone. Hirsh called over a young man, he made some adjustments, and Gould tapped the microphone again.

"Ladies and gentlemen," the rabbi began, his sonorous bass rolling out over their heads. "Friends. If you will all take your seats, we can begin."

"Have you seen Sophie?" Cohen asked, as the lawyer started edging away.

"She didn't come with you?" Fine asked, surprised.

He shook his head. "I haven't seen her since the night I arrived."

"Well, she's here someplace. I saw her, I'm sure."

"Did you talk with her?"

"No," Fine admitted.

"Are you sure it was her?"

She eyed him suspiciously. "Of course. Listen, I'm going to my seat. Won't you sit down? Leo will be offended."

"I never sit at funerals."

She raised an eyebrow, before leaving him with a business card, which she slipped deftly into his hand. He ignored Hirsh, motioning that he take the empty seat in the front row. Exasperated by Cohen's refusal, the producer signaled to Landy and a second young man to join four older actors at the hearse.

They carried the coffin from the hearse, which had backed into place several yards from the open grave, and set it on a hydraulically controlled bier. Photographers closed in, snapping like desert whippets running after camels. Gould announced that the service would begin with a reading of the Twenty-third Psalm by Vicki Strong and Jeremy Steele. A slight muffled clapping began as the actors rose from their front-row seats and went to the microphone.

Cohen almost guffawed. Broder never called on any lord as his shepherd. Restraining himself, Cohen glared at the first person he saw applauding, while a few voices called for quiet. Cohen watched from the side, thinking about funerals in Jerusalem, where anguished mothers fell on open graves, and professional mourners recited psalms nonstop while the friends and family did the burying. He tried not to think about Broder, who had said that he would go to America, where people could afford to die in their beds. Except when they're murdered.

All the while, he kept up his visual browse through the crowd, looking for Sophie, wondering about the will and its meaning.

The actors finished their performance. Again there was a scattering of softly gloved applause, quickly hushed by the same shocked, muted whispers. Gould took the microphone, scanned the crowd, and stopped at Cohen, who shook his head slightly. The rabbi sighed and began the prayers.

Cohen wanted to drop his handful of dirt on the grave, and he wanted to find Sophie. Instead, Fine and Goldie both latched onto him as soon as Gould finished.

"Here comes Blakely," Fine whispered in his ear as the studio president approached in the midst of an entourage. Hirsh followed.

"That's Barbara with him," Goldie added.

Cohen's eyes went to a rosy-cheeked young woman at Blakely's side. She had honey-colored hair and a Roman profile to go with her dark eyes. A white lace blouse was visible under her navy-blue suit. She didn't need high heels to be almost as tall as Blakely, who was in a gray business suit and burgundy tie.

"Well, Andy," Goldie said as Blakely approached. "Fancy meeting you here."

Blakely ignored the columnist. "We are all terribly saddened by this tragedy," he said to Cohen in a raspy voice that eradicated all sympathy, turning the condolences into a transaction that cost nothing.

"Yes," Cohen said.

"You know, I feel like I know you so well," Blakely said. His smile displayed teeth as polished as his manicure. He gave Cohen a head-to-toe appraisal, and then explained, "From the movie."

"You always were so tactful, Andy," Goldie cynically chided the studio chief.

Blakely scowled but didn't take his eyes off Cohen.

"I hear that you don't want anyone to see it," Cohen said gruffly. All eyes turned on him, some in amazement, others with suspicion. He held his ground, staring at Blakely. Gradually the onlookers' eyes shifted to the studio president.

It took a moment for Blakely's smile to return.

"Avram," Blakely continued, "if I may call you Avram," he added, "perhaps we could have a private word." He held up an arm, as if to put it on Cohen's shoulder to lead him out of the circle. Cohen backed up. Blakely followed.

A dozen strides away, mourners were filing past the grave, burying Broder with flowers. In Jerusalem the body slides off the stretcher into the dusty arms of religious men standing deep in the hole they dug. Afterward everyone helps to bury the dead, even if it's only to add a single stone to the pile of dirt. Here, Cohen thought, nobody wants to get his hands dirty.

"I know you heard about that contretemps at Ma Maison last week," Blakely said softly but bluntly once they were out of ear-shot.

"Well?" Cohen asked.

"Max Broder was stronger than that. He knew it was a business decision. At least he should have known."

"You don't think he killed himself?" Cohen asked, surprised.

"I understood from the newspapers that there was no suicide note," Blakely said grimly.

"You shouldn't always believe the newspapers," said Cohen.

Blakely raised an eyebrow and then tried another tack. "You know, I've learned from the past months at Epica that it's sometimes very difficult for people like us to fathom the passions of an artist." His matter-of-fact tone patronized the dead director's eccentricities, but his attempt to claim something in common with Cohen was also offensive to the Jerusalemite. "Max Broder's funeral is not the first funeral of an artist whose death was a final message in the body of their work." He sounded as if he was quoting a press release.

Cohen remained silent.

"I don't know how much you know about our business," Blakely said tensely, trying yet a third approach. "I think you ought to know that it is just that. A business. Max knew that. There was never, ever, anything personal in any of this. Nothing at all. Not for me. And I'm sure not for Max."

"Why don't you want to distribute the movie?" Cohen asked.

"As I've explained many times, both on and off the record," Blakely said officiously, "Epica is in a struggle for its survival, and though we certainly can appreciate the importance of Max's project, our short-term goals simply do not include such a noncommercial venture as *Survivor's Secrets*."

"What about his promise to the Holocaust Institute?" Cohen asked. "Your boss," he added, choosing the word deliberately. "I understood he was expecting to see the movie there—"

"Mr. Katz asked me to pull Epica out of the red," Blakely interrupted haughtily. "I'v explained to him the financial reasons for my decision, and as in everything else since I took this position, he has given me his full backing. I must add that he's most upset by this whole matter. But he knows that my decision about the film was business. And final. Speaking of final," he added, "Max never even finished the final cut. Barbara?" he called out to his assistant, who quickly slid into place beside him. "What was it I said today?" he asked her. "About the real tragedy here?"

She nodded at Cohen. "The real tragedy here," she quoted, "is that the press interest in Max's death might enable us to distribute the movie anyway."

"In a much shorter cut than the one he wanted, of course," Blakely added. "Three hours was really a bit much."

"I don't care about final cuts," Cohen said. "I intend to see the movie. And I would also appreciate it if you, Miss Darnaby, could give some time to me—I want to hear about Max's activities in the last few months," Cohen said.

She turned to Blakely, who again looked Cohen over, this time making obvious his distaste for the Jerusalemite's entire manner. But Cohen held his ground, staring back at the studio president. Blakely nodded slightly, and Barbara opened a glittering small handbag, covered in shiny black scales. "My card," she said. "And of course I know how to reach you at Max's house."

"I'm free now," Cohen suggested.

"*She's* not," Blakely interrupted angrily, taking her arm. "We're already running behind schedule."

Cohen, too, felt his time running out. Many of the mourners had gone, and he had still not seen Sophie. He held up Darnaby's card in surrender. "I will make an appointment," he said, and walked away without saying goodbye.

He searched futilely in the lush grass for a rock or pebble to place on the grave. He finally dug a handful of dirt from the pile under the tarpaulin, and dropped it on the pile of flowers that had already overflowed the deep hole in the ground. Then he turned, looking for the girl again. He saw long black hair over the bare shoulders of a young woman in black making her way quickly down the path to the cars lined up at the bottom of the hill.

He recognized Sophie's athletic gait. Walking quickly, Cohen cut down the lawn past the headstones, almost running and nearly knocking over an elderly woman who suddenly appeared in his path from behind a large headstone.

But by the time he reached the road, he had lost her again.

Three limousines, a pair of Mercedeses, and a sports car drove by. He stood just out of the middle of the road, forcing the drivers to slow down so he could peer inside. Dark windows mocked him with a reflection of his wild-eyed expression. If Sophie was behind one of the smoked-glass windows, she didn't roll it down to show her face.

But a simple sedan did pull up beside him. It was Madden, who wound down the window as he paused next to Cohen. "Nice funeral," Madden began.

Cohen scowled at him and looked up, continuing his search for Sophie.

"I'm sorry about yesterday," Madden continued. "Shouting at you, I mean."

Cohen looked back at him slowly, as if both accepting the apology and giving Madden permission to continue.

"It's official. Jack Wilson's report says very clearly that your friend died of a broken neck and ensuing asphyxiation consistent with a hanging." He reached into his jacket's inside pocket and pulled out a few stapled pages. He handed the photocopied report to Cohen.

"There was a dark limousine in Broder's driveway on Friday night," Cohen said softly. "One of the neighbors saw it."

Madden nodded thoughtfully, as if pondering the information Cohen had just given him. "I see you've learned your way around," he finally said. "Tell me, do you know how to get to the airport?"

"I think I can find it," Cohen said, trying not to show too much eagerness.

"Good. Go there. Get on a plane and go home," Madden said roughly. "This isn't Jerusalem, and you're not a cop anymore. Go home," he commanded, and then gunned the engine.

His car swerved slightly to avoid hitting a limousine nosing its way toward Cohen. The Jerusalemite looked up one last time at

the grave on the ridge. The red tractor was pushing dirt into the
hole. He inspected the dwindling crowd. Funerals always ended
faster than they began, he thought. There was no sign of Sophie.
He had attended the ceremony. He guessed the *shiva* Hirsh had
planned would be worse.

The limousine that nearly collided with Madden was stopped
beside him. The ponytailed driver jumped out and started running
around it to open the rear door for Cohen. But Cohen opened
the door himself and instructed the driver to return him to Broder's
house on the hilltop via Santa Monica pier.

"That's a helluva long way around," the driver said, looking at
Cohen through the rearview mirror.

"Take your time," Cohen said, pulling open the door to the bar
facing the back seat and yanking out a bottle of cognac and a glass.
He leaned back into the comfort of the leather couch and looked
through the smoked windows as they drove slowly from the cemetery. Just as he was getting his last view of the grave site on the
top of the hill, he remembered what had struck him so clearly
while he stood alone on the hill: Der Bruder's legacy to him.
Cohen was the last of the *nokmim*. It was an inheritance he never
wanted.

There was no sign of Sophie at the house, but he remembered
a set of car keys in the kitchen and the rear end of a Jaguar sedan
parked in a three-car garage open to the driveway beside the
house.

It took him a minute to figure out the air conditioning, which
he turned off, preferring an open window. Then he opened the
glove compartment, looking for a road map. Instead of a map, he
found two thick spiral-bound books. He pulled out the top one
and flipped it open. Hundreds of street maps confounded him with

the enormity of the city. An index led him to a pair of pages in the second volume. He laid the open book down on the passenger seat and started his journey, hopeful that between the book and his own carefully paid attention to the limousine ride from the pier to the house, he would find his way.

Easing out of the gravel driveway, he tested the brakes with a couple of jerky stops before aiming the car down the short, steep hill. Oversteering the left-hand turn onto the three-lane road that rambled along the ridge, he jerked the wheel to the right and left, trying the suspension and the car's grip on the road. The Jaguar handled better than anything he had ever driven, including the cars used to train VIP bodyguards for the Mossad and the Shabak, the Israeli secret service. He had suffered through those courses twice over the last fifteen years. But as always, he had learned his lessons well.

Uncertain about his location when he reached the first intersection, he pulled onto the gravel embankment to check the map again. It took him a few tries to find the page he needed, and he traced lightly with his pencil until the road went into the next page's quadrant. He was turning his head to read a street name printed at an angle, when the entire car jerked forward and the pencil tore into the page.

"What the . . . ," he shouted, wrenching his head left and right. In the rearview mirror he saw the radiator grille and the lower half of the windshield of a cream-colored van pushing at the rear end of the Jaguar.

Through the open windows of his car he could hear shouting: "Kill Kikes Kill Kikes." It was raucous, drunken, and rhythmic. It took him a moment to decipher the screams, but the intentions were instantly recognizable.

Keeping his eyes on the mirrored reflection, he yanked the

automatic shift into drive and floored the gas pedal. He could hear the rear wheels machine-gunning the van with gravel, and the car swerved onto the asphalt, burning rubber.

Mulholland's curves and turns demanded concentration. He pushed the car as fast as it could go, speeding and drifting through curves, hoping that nothing was coming in the opposite direction. The squeals of rubber on asphalt accompanied the tilts of the car body as centrifugal forces hugged him close. But the Jaguar held true, and it was faster than the van, which faded into the distance and disappeared behind corners. Yet every time Cohen believed he had lost the van, it reappeared on the straightaways. He passed slower-moving cars, honking at them to get out of his way, wishing he had a siren. And still the van followed. He shifted uncomfortably, reaching behind him for the gun in his waistband.

He was almost certain he had lost the van, when ahead he saw a huge truck pulling slowly out of a left-hand turn, filling the road with its bulk. Whiffs of gray smoke belched from the exhaust pipe above the diesel engine, and Cohen applied pressure on the brakes. The truck moved slowly. He glanced in the rearview mirror. The van was approaching fast.

Cohen braked sharply. The truck was still easing through the turn, and the van was directly behind him.

In the mirror he could see three young men in the van's front seat. Their heads were shaven, a mockery of the shaven heads in the camps. Again they bumped his rear end, their shouting and chanting lost in the screeching of metal against metal. The driver of the van pumped the brakes, and its front end jabbed at the Jaguar's rear fender. He could vaguely see the driver's face, its open-mouthed screaming.

The truck finally pulled through the intersection, blasting its horn in amazement at the van's attack on the Jaguar. As soon as it had moved far enough to give Cohen room to pass it on the left, he jabbed the gas pedal. Just opposite the turn, he swung left, leaning into the curve, hoping the car would stick to the road and not slide into the steep ravine to his right. The tires tried to tear away from the tar, but the car held its ground.

He had no idea where he was and searched for the sun to get a bearing on his direction as the road dipped steeply into a canyon. For a short minute he was alone on the road, flying down the snaking pavement.

Aging olive trees with silver leaves and the low shrubbery of wild mustard and mint made him think of home. The ravine was a threatening presence on his right, and as he entered each curve he tried to estimate the apogee of the angle of his entry to keep the car off the slippery embankment.

But thinking about his position slowed him down. The van was behind him, the driver blaring his horn as he smacked the Jaguar's rear end. Cohen swerved, riding onto the gravel roadbed.

The guardrail scraped the passenger door, firing a stream of sparks at the vehicle behind him. He wrenched the wheel to pull back onto the road and sped ahead, trying to keep his eyes on both the road and the rearview mirror. He wanted them in front, not behind.

The road was too narrow for a sudden U-turn, and with each entry to a left-hand curve Cohen worried that he'd meet another car coming in the opposite direction.

"In pursuit—press; pursued—pull," he remembered the driving instructor saying. He held his hand on the horn, blocking out the screaming he could hear whenever the van behind him closed in, trying to warn any approaching cars. It could not go on like this. He made a decision.

He moved gradually into the center of the road, the van in his wake. The road widened as it dipped into a tight U-turn curve that swung upward, away from the ravine bottom another hundred meters below. Entering the curve, he was in the right-hand lane. But halfway through, he glanced once into the rearview mirror and swerved to his left, hitting the brakes once with both feet, letting the steering wheel slide through his fingers until a second brake slam spun the car one hundred eighty degrees. He had hoped the car was too heavy to flip. He was right. It skidded to a halt in the middle of the curve as the van flew past on the right.

For a flicker of a moment he saw identifying details of the van's passengers. An ear decorated with rings. A clenched fist and a wrist decorated with tattoos. A mustachioed face with an open-mouthed scream. "Fucking Jew!" Cohen heard before the expression of the driver changed from leer to panic, and they were past him, the burnt rubber of tires an acrid cloud in his eyes.

On the rear doors he saw a crude drawing of a clenched fist and the slogan ARYAN NATION spray-painted in black. The driver tried to skid to a halt, and at first the van's slide seemed controlled. But the van wasn't as heavy as the Jaguar. It began to seesaw sideways until it was out of control, tipped over onto its side, bounced and flipped, leaping over the guardrail and disappearing into the ravine.

Cohen flung open the door and ran the twenty-five meters to the guardrail. The van was still falling, crashing through the bushes. It came to a halt against the wide trunk of an ancient olive tree. He started down after it. About halfway down, he could smell the gasoline. He halted his sliding dash down the hill, grabbing hold of a tree branch to stop the fall. A half breath later, the van exploded, the shock wave a hot angry wind blasting into his face.

His hands were shaking. He pulled a damp cigarette from the crumpled pack in his sweaty shirt pocket and then reached into his pants pocket for the silver flask, realizing too late that he had not refilled it. He scowled and lit the cigarette, puffing from it deeply as he watched the black smoke of the burning van join the haze in the sky. Only when he finished the cigarette did he start the climb back up the hill. He could smell burning human flesh, another memory from the past. He was grateful he didn't hear screams.

Reaching the top, he got back into his car. The car phone was identical to the Motorola-made device he had wanted installed in his commander's car at home. But there was no budget in his days for such luxuries in Jerusalem.

He fished Madden's card out of his wallet.

"That's out of my jurisdiction, goddammit," Madden swore, after Cohen described the situation. "That's Sherman Oaks."

"I don't know anything about your jurisdictions," Cohen said quietly. "But if the case leads somewhere, we have to follow. No?"

"Tell it to me again," Madden demanded.

Cohen repeated his description of the cream-colored van with the graffiti on the back door. He took the blame for the van's accident, saying he misjudged the driver's capabilities, as well as the van's. "But this was not an accident. And it was not random violence. They knew who I was."

Sirens began to echo up and down the canyon.

"They'll be wanting to talk with you," Madden finally said, "that's for sure."

"I won't have anything to say except what I've told you. Max Broder did not commit suicide," Cohen insisted. He started the car and drove one curve up the hill, to a vantage point over the burning wreck in the canyon. By the time he was parked, two fire engines and a police patrol car pulled into the turn where he had been standing a few minutes before.

Cohen could hear Madden cursing at the sirens. "Shit, shit, shit," Madden sizzled. "Wait for me. I'll be there in fifteen, twenty minutes."

Cohen smirked at the dead receiver, remembering how he had hung up on Madden at the airport, and carefully replaced it with a click into its plastic case.

A helicopter was moving slowly up the ravine. He pulled open the car door and walked across the road to stand at the edge of the bluff. It was a long way down. The helicopter veered from sight, its whooping slices of air diminishing gradually as it headed toward the brush fire growing around the burning van below. There was a brief gentle breeze, as if the helicopter had a wake. But it lasted only a minute. He could see gray streaks of smoke floating lazily up the ravine two curves away along the descending ridgeline. It looked like a huge flying insect dropping molten silver into the ravine.

It was twenty minutes before Madden's siren reached the turn below. Half a dozen fire hoses were spraying water from the two engines, making a sparkling light show of rainbows in the ravine. The fire made a black tear in the golden yellow of the dried landscape. The van was a twisted heap of black metal issuing clouds of steam from wherever the water hit it. Cohen watched from the bluff overhead as the detective got out of his car and spoke with the uniformed cops from the patrol car. Then he joined Cohen on the bluff.

Cohen displayed the Jaguar's smashed rear bumper, and Madden asked him to go through the story of the van once again. "They were shouting anti-Semitic slogans at me. They were bald. Shaven-heads, yes?" Cohen asked. He had only read about such people.

"Skinheads," Madden said. "They usually don't come so far north. Mostly they stick down to their territory. Torrance, Huntington, San Pedro, that's their turf. But we get them sometimes."

"They were very specifically chasing me," Cohen claimed.

"Kids are always racing up and down these roads," Madden said.

"But in sports cars perhaps, or their parents' cars," Cohen guessed. "Not delivery vehicles. And they don't follow someone from all the way over there," he added, pointing toward Mulholland—and by implication, Broder's house—far to the east.

"Maybe it was a coincidence," Madden said.

"No," Cohen said emphatically. "They were waiting for me. No coincidence. Even a paranoid can have enemies," he added wryly.

Madden sighed. "Did you get a license plate number?" he asked.

Cohen recited it from memory. Madden nodded and reached into his jacket pocket. Cohen thought he was going to pull out a notebook, but instead it was a new cigar. Madden unraveled the plastic sheath and used a wooden kitchen match to pierce the end of the cigar. He scraped a fingernail over the head of the match, and it burst into flame.

The cigar lighted, he eyed Cohen.

"Trace the owner of the van," Cohen demanded.

Madden puffed on his cigar.

"They were trying to frighten me. Maybe kill me," Cohen said quietly. "I want to know why."

Madden spat a piece of tobacco from his tongue and studied the end of the cigar. He blew softly at the ash, making it glimmer red, and then he seemed to make a decision. He walked around the Jaguar again, studied the rear end, and looked at Cohen.

"What was that license number?" Madden asked, as he walked to his car.

Cohen gave him the number again, and Madden plucked the

microphone from his dashboard. Less than a minute later, they had the answer. The van was registered to a thirty-year-old Torrance man named Barry Lineker.

"He have a sheet?" Madden asked the microphone, and the pleasant woman's voice on the loudspeaker asked for a minute, then reported a fifteen-year criminal career involving mostly assault, disorderly and drunken conduct, vandalism, and stolen goods. Another minute went by, and she reported that Lineker had been in jail for a total of nine years during the last fifteen.

Cohen waited at the car's side, watching the firefighters in the distance, listening to the report. Half a dozen water cannons were spraying the car and a radius of nearly a hundred meters around it.

"The Torrance cops will look into it," Madden said, hanging up the microphone. "They learn something, they'll tell me. I learn something, I'll decide whether to let you know."

"This matter of jursidiction," Cohen asked, "it means you cannot go wherever your investigation leads?"

"It means things are much more complicated than they might seem to you," Madden admitted. "And I can't afford complication now. No, sir. And neither can you. You've been here barely two days, and three people are dead. The brass is already pissed off about what Goldie Stein said about you. When they learn you had something to do with this, they're going to want blood. They don't like interfering foreigners."

"There are four people dead. You forgot Broder," Cohen said softly.

"Listen here," Madden shot back. "You're lucky I didn't see Goldie Stein's column yesterday, before I saw you. If I had, I think I would have dragged you downtown." He started the car, pulling the automatic shift into gear. His cigar was ventilating thick blue smoke.

"You don't believe there's a connection?" Cohen asked.

"What the hell are you talking about? Between your friend and those three? What connection?" Madden jerked his thumb over his shoulder to indicate the destroyed van. "You got to be kidding."

Cohen wasn't kidding. But he was tired of the argument. The effort had weakened him, and he still had much to do. "You *will* let me know what you learn from the Torrance police," Cohen said.

"You're not my fucking boss!" Madden hissed.

"Please," Cohen said, even softer.

"That really hurt, didn't it?" Madden asked with a sardonic grin.

"No more than believing me must hurt you," Cohen said grimly.

"Tell me something," Madden asked through the window. "Where were you going when they followed you?"

Cohen looked out past the spuming smoke and steam from the burning car and surrounding brush, to the distance southeast, where the sky was almost yellow from the desert dust and the city's gases. He scanned westward, where he could see the difference in sky color over the ocean and over the land, and discern the two blues of water and sky at the horizon.

But there was too much haze over the city to see the details, and when he finally made out two marinas, he couldn't tell which might be the one south of the pier that he remembered from the limousine ride back from the funeral. "I've never seen an ocean," Cohen said to Madden.

The American shook his head with dismay, and for the second time that day gunned his engine, leaving Cohen alone in the swirling dust.

· · ·

Sunsets, he knew, were the ephemeral fingerprints of each passing day on the turning globe that hurtled around a spinning sun.
No two were ever the same. Especially over a westward sea's wide
horizon. The first sunset over the sea that he could remember
clearly was the first night on the week-long voyage across the
Mediterranean. He was one of seven hundred twelve people on
board, ready to fight barehanded if necessary against the British
navy blockading Jewish refugees from reaching Palestine.

But he only learned how to contemplate sunsets more than a
decade later, when he was posted in Tel Aviv in the early 1960s,
just before the Six Day War.

So, grateful for the familiarity of the distant reddening globe
only a few fingers off the dark line of the ocean's horizon, he had
followed the maps and his nose westward, coming out to a beach-
side promenade a couple of kilometers south of the pier. He stopped
at a liquor store for a pint of cognac to fill his flask, and then
began the hike along the promenade. He couldn't help but stare
at first. Musclemen and Indians, he thought, looking around at the
crowd.

But he didn't have any time to notice details before he heard
a girl shout, "Look out!" He had stepped directly into her path,
but she swerved past, almost naked on her wheeled skates. He
stepped backward instinctively. She was skating backward, smiling,
her tongue sticking out. He realized it wasn't at him, and he turned
his head. A boy on a unicycle in obvious chase was bearing down
on him. "Tourist," the blond boy cursed under his breath as he
wobbled lightly around Cohen, who turned to see the girl give
a slight shriek and a giggle, before spinning to continue her escape.

He was certain that his caller was not going to be one of the
hundreds of young people showing off their healthy bodies on the

beach. Someone was going to approach him, someone who knew of Der Bruder and Cohen's coming, someone who would recognize him, someone as old as he. So he walked slowly, looking around carefully. At first he paid a lot of attention to the houses along the promenade. But by the time he reached the pier, he had begun to include homeless people in his perusal of anyone who looked as if they might always be at Santa Monica pier.

He quickly placed the phone booth from where the call had come. It was beside a pinball arcade; it was the machines that had provided the carnival sounds. Two Rastafarians lounged on a bench across the pier, their conga drums resting between their thighs. He waited awhile at the phone booth, but the sunset at the end of the pier was magnetic. A regatta was heading north. He measured the sun's distance from the horizon. Three fingers. In a few minutes, he thought, each passing boat would be a silhouette on the face of the sun.

A sour smell of sweat and unwashed clothing swept into his nostrils. He turned, his scowl dropping into astonishment as he recognized the sad, droopy eyes and the dented forehead of the man beside him.

"The anarchist," Cohen murmured to himself.

The hobo answered with a smile, not giving Cohen any time to remember. "Here they call me Jack," the man said cheerfully in thickly accented English. He was dressed in layers. Despite the heat, there was a once-white shirt under a once-blue sweater under a once-beige sports jacket under an old colorless trench coat. But he wore the unwashed clothes with dignity. The collars and cuffs were aligned. His face and the backs of his hands were tanned, not dirty. And above his clean-shaven face he wore an old beret, perched cockily on the back of his head. He was a head shorter than Cohen. Rosen, Jacques Rosen. Cohen remembered the name.

"Why are you—?"

"Der Bruder didn't tell you?" Rosen interrupted. His teeth were as gray as his coat.

Cohen cursed Broder in his mind. "He told me nothing," he spat. "Nothing. He told me to come, and I came. But when I got here, he was dead," Cohen said.

Rosen nodded, but he didn't seem surprised. "He told me you were coming," Rosen said. Cohen grasped the railing. Broder had never mentioned the anarchist to Cohen. But Cohen had never asked.

Rosen started searching for something in a shopping cart. It was full of plastic bags held closed with twists of rope and twine. There were pieces of copper wire rolled into neat skeins, empty bottles and at least one full of water, several unlabeled cans of food, and a large battery-run radio. It seemed to have been all stowed carefully, and Cohen could see similar treasures buried beneath the visible stuffing of the shopping cart.

"Start from the beginning," Cohen demanded. "Why are you living like this?"

Rosen looked up from the cart. His droopy eyes couldn't hide the exasperation in his expression. But then the look softened, as if the anarchist suddenly understood that Cohen's memory was gone, that Cohen was the indigent one, needing some understanding and patience.

"You remember, Avram," Rosen rasped. "Don't you?" There was an edge of disappointment in his voice.

Cohen pulled out his flask and his cigarettes. It was as much a means of gaining time as a gesture of sharing and friendship. Rosen's fingers trembled slightly as they reached for a cigarette. Cohen lit it for him.

"Yes, I remember," he told the anarchist, who, after taking a first puff, eyed the flask in Cohen's hand. Cohen unscrewed it, opened the brown paper bag with the pint bottle of cognac from the liquor store, and carefully filled the flask until it overflowed. Rosen watched silently. Finished, Cohen handed Rosen the full flask.

It was a strain whenever Cohen delved into those memories. Staring at Rosen while the beggar drank, Cohen was looking deep into his own past.

It was difficult to tell if Rosen had been one of the lucky few or one of the most unlucky. He wasn't used for the experiments in hypothermia, when prisoners were dunked into cold water and then left wrapped in wet sheets in the snow, to see how long it took for them to freeze. He wasn't used in the experiments to see how best to warm the freezing bodies. He wasn't used for tests in pain tolerance or for testing the speed of surgical practices without anesthesia. But he was used for something.

Chosen just as Broder had written and Cohen had dreamed, Rosen had disappeared. Nobody expected to see him again. But he reappeared miraculously a few weeks later, unable or unwilling to tell anyone what had happened to him. All his wit and his passion were gone. In their place was the strange dent in his forehead.

"I didn't even know you were alive," Cohen finally whispered.

Rosen smacked his lips and handed back the silver flask. "Der Bruder saved me. He brought me here. He made me go for treatment. He took care of me. Gave me jobs on his movies. But I couldn't last. You remember, don't you Avram?"

"Of course I remember, Jacques," Cohen said, but it was another lie. He hadn't thought about Jacques Rosen until the night before, falling asleep with Broder's treatment on his chest. He hadn't remembered. "Of course I remember."

"I didn't feel free," Rosen said. "That's all. I didn't feel free. . . .

"But like this?"

"Why not?" Rosen answered, his smile exposing gaps in his teeth. "The weather is good; I can find anything I need. They throw away food here. Can you imagine that? Throwing away food?"

"Reparations money—you could have reparations money, live a proper life," Cohen said.

"I wouldn't touch that money," Rosen said with emphatic bitterness. "You didn't. That's right"—Rosen responded to Cohen's surprise—"Der Bruder told me. You didn't take it. Why should I?"

"So you wouldn't have to live like this," Cohen murmured.

"I'm free," said the anarchist.

"This? This is free?" Cohen demanded.

Rosen shrugged. "What have I missed? Family? Gone. Money?" He smiled. "I never cared about owning something. "Security?" He shrugged again. "I'll be dead soon anyway," he said. "I'm sixty-two years old. I'm amazed I lasted this long."

"Why did you call me?"

"Der Bruder. He came last week. He told me, 'Young Avram is coming.' He gave me—" Rosen's face froze as it turned to the shopping cart. His small body twisted backward impossibly. He fell, his hand grabbing at his chest for air, his droopy eyes suddenly wide and horribly frightened.

The pinged ricochet of a second bullet hitting iron drove Cohen to the ground. He rolled onto his side and came out of it in a crouch, the gun drawn. Another bullet whistled past him. A fisherman was on the ground a few feet away, shouting, "Get down! Get down!"

Cohen grabbed Rosen by the trench-coat collar and, bent like a question mark, dragged the featherweight hobo to cover behind a bench. He could hear the cracks of an assault rifle as he laid Rosen down behind the concrete-and-wood bench. Blood from the ruptured chest had already begun to darken the once-blue sweater. Rosen coughed blood, trying to say something.

"Quiet, quiet," Cohen pleaded with the man. "Jacques, please, just lie quiet."

He raised his head above the bench, searching for the source of the firing. It was definitely coming from somewhere north of the pier. People were cowering in panic, running aimlessly, screaming. He yanked at the purple trouser leg of a woman standing beside the bench, paralyzed with fear and shock. "Get down, get down," he shouted, pulling her to the ground. He rolled on, reaching the edge of the pier, scanning the water. There were dozens of boats. Some were much too far away, but others were within range of a crack shot able to identify a target. He was already wondering if he had been the quarry. Or was it Jacques Rosen the anarchist whom the sniper had sought?

His eyes darted from one boat to the next, looking for something to indicate which of them might be carrying the shooter. A motorboat with a large flying deck was making a sharp turn away from land, to speed northwest. He thought he saw a platinum-haired man, holding in one hand what might have been a short fishing rod—or a long assault rifle—standing on the flying deck while with the other hand he steered the boat. Cohen tried to read the name on the stern, but it was too far to see in the quickening darkness. The firing had stopped.

There were three knots of people, gathered around three victims. Cohen ran back to Rosen, pushing aside the crowd surrounding the dying hobo. He crouched beside him, calling his name as he lifted the man's head.

"Jacques, hold on, hold on. The ambulance is coming."

"Avram?" Rosen whispered.

"What did Der Bruder want me to have?" Cohen whispered urgently.

"Davey Bee. Davey Bee knows . . ."

"Who? What does he know?"

But Rosen was gone. Cohen laid his head down gently on the pier floor. The crowd gave him no time to mourn.

"He has a gun!" a woman's voice screamed.

Cohen turned, and his shock at the death of the man was interpreted as madness. He saw it reflected in the eyes of the stranger staring at him. They thought he had been doing the shooting. He held up his hands, as if to show he was harmless, but their eyes were frozen on the gun still in his right hand.

"No, no, it wasn't me. The shooting came from a boat," he said, pointing to the water. Trying to make them remember what had happened caused him to recall something else. A platinum-haired man. At the airport.

"Freeze!" shouted a black-bearded man in a stained white apron, who came out from behind a hot dog counter, carrying a shotgun.

Cohen moved intuitively, swinging his gun directly at the cook and backing away. He aimed with two hands, his arms slightly bent at the elbows, the intent in his eyes chilling the cook's bravado.

"Call the police," Cohen ordered. "Tell them the shooting came from a boat, a boat going that way." He pointed, using a normal speaking voice. The cook's eyes moved. Cohen turned and ran.

By the time he reached the sidewalk above the pier, he had returned the gun to his waistband and was walking at a normal pace. But it was painful. His breath came in short wheezes, and his heart pounded across the top of his rib cage. He felt drained, and there was a clammy sweat on his brow. He sucked a mouthful of the liquor into his throat, listening to his heartbeat's angry thump. The drink swept aside the pain, while his mind reeled from past to present and back. His chest was aching, and as he took the second long sip from the flask, he wondered if he might have fractured a rib in the roll across the pier. He didn't want to think about any alternative reason for the pain.

He knew that whoever had sent the skinheads after him and then had Jacques Rosen killed would soon know that he wasn't among the victims on the pier. Exhaustion and hunger clamored for his attention, but he denied them both as he deliberated his next action. He had to get out of Broder's castle. But there were things there he needed. The treatment. Broder's noose.

He started the car back to the castle, with the map book open on the seat beside him, determined to make his route roundabout, his progress slow enough for every driver behind him to want to pass—and for any car following him to be spotted. Every white-haired or blond driver got double his attention. Sirens swept by in the opposite direction, but nothing appeared in his rearview mirror except Rosen's face.

He packed quickly. Everything went into his canvas bag. Before leaving, he returned to the answering machine, but there were no messages. He had a hunch. He unscrewed the telephone's handset. The bug was under the speaker. He went to the next phone he could find, in the living room. It, too, was tapped. Somewhere not too far away, a receiver had collected conversations. But that would have to wait. He was still wondering how long the bugs had been in place, when he pulled into the driveway of Goldie's apartment hotel.

The receptionist warned Goldie of his arrival. She was waiting for him at the door of her bungalow. He didn't give her time for pleasantries. Hustling past her, he tossed his bag on the living room sofa and looked around for a telephone.

The room had a console of three televisions on one side, a seating arrangement of plush furniture on the other, aimed at the monitors. There were racks of videocassettes and dozens of paperback Hollywood potboilers lined up on shelves above the televisions. A desk covered with newspapers, pads of paper, and a computer sat in the corner.

"What *is* the matter with you?" she asked. She was out of the formal wear of the funeral, back in tight jeans and a tighter shirt. She was barefoot, and he suddenly realized how short she was.

"Have you heard any news about a shooting? At the beach?"

"No-o," she said, going to the coffee table and pressing some buttons on a remote-control device. The three televisions sprang to life. She stood in front of them pressing buttons until one was showing CNN. He checked his watch. It had been barely two hours since the shooting.

The broad-mouthed announcer's face silently tried to convey a friendly sympathy. Goldie turned up the sound, and just then, the words "Sail-by Shooting" appeared on the screen and the view shifted.

"Recapping," the announcer promised, "there are three people dead and six wounded in what police are calling the sail-by shooting at Santa Monica beach. Now for a look at that amazing footage of the action made by a tourist on the scene when it happened," the announcer said.

"What the hell is going on?" Goldie asked.

"Shh," Cohen commanded.

The tourist's camera panned the length of the pier. It passed Cohen and Rosen standing at the railing.

"That's you!" Goldie shouted. But he hushed her again as the pan continued.

It lingered over Rosen's shopping cart and then zoomed at the craggy face of a fisherman a few feet away. The camera was beginning to pan farther down the railing, when it fell. The sound was terrible. But Cohen recognized the snapping crackle of gunfire.

There were screams, and the camera microphone picked up the tourist's own gasping horror. The picture on the screen was a crazy angle shot of a corner of the video arcade and a chunk of sky. But then the tourist regained control over the camera, panning again across the pier from a low angle. People were falling to the ground, frozen in openmouthed fright, clutching children to their bodies and running. Cohen recognized his own crouching run from the bench back to the railing. Although his face appeared for only a second, he was clearly recognizable. Cohen grimaced. The tourist's pictures ended suddenly, and then the announcer promised that in addition to the Santa Monica police and the Coast Guard, the FBI was investigating the "sail-by shooting."

The next report was an interview with a man identified as a small-boat owner, who worried that all boaters would be considered suspect until the shooter was caught. "Now back to Washington for an update on the President's condition," the announcer said when the boat owner's interview was done.

"Avram?" Goldie asked, turning down the sound.

He was staring at the television, wondering how long it would take for his name to start being mentioned as part of the story.

"Avram," she repeated. "Will you please tell me what's going on?"

"That man—the one I was talking with," he said. "He's dead." Cohen slumped into the sofa.

"God, you're awfully pale. Can I get you something?" she asked as she went to a bureau, where a pair of English bottles stood guard over half a dozen glasses.

He felt exhausted and wasted, though energized by the events. His voice was raw, as if he had been screaming, and his breathing was strained. He smiled wearily.

She brought him a glass of amber liquid. "It's not cognac, I'm afraid. But it's a helluva lot better than medicinal. Glenfiddich. Great Scotch. Now tell me: The tramp? He's dead? Who was he?"

"I didn't even know he was alive," Cohen said in a whisper, remembering what Ahuva had told him about his refusal to look back. For the first time, he wondered if it had all been planned by Broder as an elaborate punishment to prove to the stubborn Cohen that *nekama,* revenge, was still the reason for survival.

"I need to make some phone calls," Cohen said after a first sip and a scowl from the whiskey's burn.

"Anything, anything at all. Let me get you a doctor. You really look bad. Gray, you know what I mean?"

"No need for a doctor," he said. "I'll be fine. Please, the phone?"

"Sure, sure, over here." She went to the desk and rummaged on its surface, revealing a multiline telephone console hidden underneath a pile of papers.

He began with Madden. "The dead beggar on the pier," he said, not even identifying himself on the phone when Madden answered. "His name is Rosen, Jacques Rosen." Cohen spelled the name for Madden. "His belongings from the shopping cart. I must know what was in the cart. Everything." Cohen gave his instructions to Madden as if the sergeant had worked for years under Cohen's command.

"What were you doing there?" Madden demanded.

"He called me. He was a survivor. My friend. And Broder's."

"Your big-shot movie director had homeless friends?" Madden asked cynically.

"Rosen wasn't homeless. He just couldn't live indoors," Cohen said softly. "They did experiments on him." Madden didn't understand, but Cohen had no time for explanations. "I'm out of his house," he told the sergeant. "The skinheads. The shooting at the pier. Someone is trying to kill me."

"How'd they know you'd be there?" Madden asked.

"Broder's telephones were bugged," he said.

"By who?" Madden charged.

"I don't know," Cohen admitted. "But I left them in place. Go on up there and check."

"I'll take your word for it. But it doesn't tell me who would want to bug his phones."

"Could you put out a missing person notice on someone?" Cohen suddenly asked.

"Who?"

"Sophie Levine."

"The housekeeper?"

"Yes."

"I saw her at the funeral," Madden said matter-of-factly, making Cohen swear under his breath. "So she's not exactly missing," Madden continued.

"She hasn't been in the house since the morning after I arrived," Cohen insisted.

"What does she have to be there for? Her boss is dead Nobody to clean house for. Except you, of course," Madden added sarcastically. "Look, maybe it wasn't you this guy was shooting at. This is L.A. you know. The home of the body bag, freeway shootings. Drive-by, sail-by—what difference does it make? You have your Arab terrorists. We have our crazies."

"What about the microphones I found in the phones?" Cohen asked, eyeing Goldie. Coiled into a corner of the sofa, her feet under her, one hand propping up her head, she was watching him with curiosity. He wondered if he had done the right thing in coming to her place. But leaving Broder's house, wondering where to go, he realized that, from the start, she had not lied to him. Everyone else had lied. But she had always told what she thought was the truth.

Why would they want you dead, whoever they are? Madden was asking.

"Because I don't believe it was suicide," Cohen raged, losing his voice in a racking cough, grasping for every bit of evidence he could muster. "Listen, there's something else," he said in a tense, soft voice, trying to prove he was in control of his emotions. "I was being watched when I arrived in Los Angeles. A man with white hair. I saw him at the airport. And it was a man with white hair who was shooting from the boat."

"A white-haired man," Madden scoffed.

"Yes, white. Not old. Not blond. White. Albino. No. Not albino," he corrected himself. "White. Like the actress. . . . He tried to recall her name. "Harlow," he finally said, relieved he could remember.

There was a long silence at the end of the line. "You know, I've seen this before," Madden finally said. "Tourists come to Hollywood. See the bright lights. Maybe they're already a little disturbed before they get here. Maybe something happens to them here. Usually, it's drugs. They think all the lights are for them. As if they're the stars. But Hollywood's a funny place. It's just out of reach. You know what I mean?"

It was Cohen's turn to fall silent. Madden's humoring sounded all too familiar. More than once, Cohen had encountered in Jerusalem tourists who had fallen prey to the syndrome, the belief that the myths were real and legends alive. Pilgrims who decided they were prophets able to walk the streets naked, or messiahs ready to attack whatever embodiment of evil they finally settled upon, usually landed in one of the state hospitals until they stabilized and could be sent home. Sometimes they ended up behind bars.

"Cohen?" Madden called down the line.

But Cohen only whispered a sudden goodbye. He was paranoid, he knew. But he was not crazy. He could hear Madden calling his name again, but he put down the phone. The drink Goldie had brought him sat on the desk, and he drained it before facing her.

"You are not to tell anyone of this," he ordered.

"What? Are you kidding? This is the greatest story I've ever had, and I can't tell anyone?" She was outraged. "Bullshit."

"Goldie," he said wearily, "when it's all over, you can write whatever you want. For now, nothing. Please. For your own safety."

"What do you mean, my own safety?"

"You heard what I told the sergeant."

"But what does it have to do with me?"

Cohen was disgusted with himself, realizing he had made a mistake. He should have gone to a motel. Someplace small and anonymous, where nobody knew him. He said as much, silently, in the way he strode to his bag on the sofa.

"You're not going anywhere," she said, determined. "Not until you've seen a doctor." She got up from the sofa and went to the phone.

"No doctor," he tried to roar, but his voice broke, turning into a rasping bronchial cough that made the muscles of his chest ache. Embarrassed, he sat down weakly.

"See?" She picked up the phone. "I'm calling Anna Dichter. She's a doctor. A friend of mine."

"Please, no. I'm putting you in danger, being here. I made a mistake."

She raised an eyebrow. "How about that? You admit *you* made a mistake." Her hand paused over the number pad of the phone.

He grimaced and adjusted a pillow to support his head. "I'll just rest here for a while. But no doctor. It is very dangerous for you that anybody knows I am here."

"Dangerous?" She chortled and then suddenly changed her voice into a parody of the woman detective in the movie from the airplane. "It's my middle name."

He didn't laugh, so she stopped her playacting, raising a forlorn eyebrow that seemed to admit maybe she wasn't as courageous as she appeared.

"No doctor. Promise?" he asked.

She hesitated, biting at her lower lip, thinking. He had to smile helpfully at her once, before she agreed. He nodded, grateful, and then looked at her with one more request in his eyes.

"What?" she asked.

"If I could be alone," he asked. "I find it difficult to sleep in a room with strangers," he explained without any embarrassment. It was just partially true enough so that it could work as a lie.

"God, you don't need a doctor. You need a shrink," she said. His eyes narrowed at her.

"Kidding, just kidding," she said, collecting a pair of notebooks from her desk and going to the doorway of her bedroom. "An hour?" she asked. "Right?" she added, uncertain.

"Right," he said, relieved when she disappeared behind the door. Instead of leaning back and closing his eyes, he opened the bag and pulled out the treatment, continuing to read where he had left off.

GREAT PILES OF BELONGINGS *are growing in the huge plaza in front of the train station. There are clothing and shoes, glimmering heaps of eyeglasses, and rows of musical instruments. Money is piling up on one table, gold on another, and jewelry on a third. Treasures come pouring out of the suitcases. Vigilant kapos and greedy Germans watch while prisoners collect these valuables. But here is a slave stealing a diamond. Here is another stealing a sack of gold coins. Levine and Rosen are running back and forth between the piles, part of a team packing one of the freight cars with the weekly shipment of clothes taken from prisoners and sent back to the home front.*

It is night in the barracks. They are discussing the escape plan. Rosen and Levine are to be packed into one of the freight cars along with the prisoners' belongings. Levine is still the strongest; flexing a muscle he is ready to try it alone, but Broder says no. It's a two-man job, he commands. Avram volunteers. Broder turns him down. Cohen works in the bakery. It's not only safer than most jobs, it's important, Broder reminds Cohen, the best thief among them. For extra food.

It is daytime again. Typhus is killing prisoners as fast as the butchers.

Cohen woke shivering, sweat pouring down his back. Goldie was sitting on the floor beside the sofa, tapping at his forehead with a handkerchief.

He felt the treatment's clumsy jab at his side. It had fallen from his hands, between his torso and the back of the sofa. He sat up, deliberately shielding the treatment from her. If she had found it, he figured, she would have been reading it. He wasn't sure he wanted anyone to see it. "I'm all right," he said, sitting up knowing he needed a wash and some coffee.

"You slept badly," she said. "Talking to yourself. Tell me, what's *nikuma?* No, that's not it," she muttered, trying another pronunciation, *"Nakoma?"*

"Nekama." He sighed. "It means revenge."

Her eyes narrowed. "Well, you weren't just mumbling it."

He sat up, uncomfortable in the stickiness of the sweat-drenched shirt, embarrassed by his weakness. He knew what she meant. His head pounded. He checked his watch. It was almost midnight. She had let him sleep for almost three hours instead of the one he had intended.

"I need a shower," he said. "Some coffee. Food. If you have some aspirin?"

"No problem," she said, jumping to her feet. "Bathroom's right through there," she said, pointing across the room to the open door to her bedroom. "And believe it or not, I make a mean little espresso."

"You have a kitchen?" he asked.

"A kitchenette," she explained. "Back there." She jerked a thumb over her shoulder.

"Wonderful," he said, staring at her. "I usually have my coffee after my shower." He shot her a short grin.

She rolled her eyes and sighed dramatically. "Men." Then she headed toward the little hallway she had pointed out as the way to the kitchen.

As soon as she was gone, he leaned forward and grabbed the

treatment. Standing quickly, he stuffed the thick magazine-like manuscript into his bag and hustled to the hallway.

Ignoring the chaos of her bathroom, he cleared a small area on the floor, unpacked a clean change of clothing, and stripped for the shower.

The water stung hot, and after he soaped himself, he stood motionless under its attack. Gradually the pain turned to pleasure, and when he began to feel drowsy, he started turning the hot tap until the water was stinging cold and he could feel his breath grow short. Only then did he get out of the shower and quickly dress in the last of his clean clothes. Packing, he retrieved his flask, taking a sip before putting it in his pocket. The last thing he did before leaving the bathroom was replace the gun in his waistband and pull on the windbreaker to keep it hidden.

"Have you ever heard the name Davey Bee?" he asked, coming out of the bathroom.

She was at the table in the living room, buttering a bagel. She had ordered room service. The breads were piled in a basket, and cheeses and jams were lined up. She halted the spreading motion and looked up at him. "Why do you ask?"

"Goldie," he said, exasperated. "Please. Do you know of such a person?"

"That depends," she said.

"On what?"

"If you'll tell me why you want to see him."

"I don't even know there is such a person," he said, crossing the room to the tiny espresso cup nearly lost amid the opulence of the hotel's room service offering. "I'm asking if you know him." The coffee was hotter than it was strong. He tried not to scowl. "You obviously do. Who is he?" he asked.

"Well," she said, smacking her lips with a certain pleasure, "you've heard of Bugsy Siegel?"

"Of course," Cohen said.

"Well, Davey Burns—that's his real name—makes a living off the claim he's a distant relative of Bugsy's."

Cohen wanted to laugh, and she could see it on his face.

"This is no laughing matter," she said seriously. "He's one of the most powerful gangsters on the West Coast."

"I need to see him," Cohen said. "How do I reach him?"

She chortled. "That depends. What do you need him for?"

"Goldie," he said softly, "I need to talk with him."

"It's easy to get to see him. Talking with him is another matter." She offered him some more espresso.

He shook his head, wishing for some straight-boiled Turkish mud coffee with as much sugar as coffee. Something to give him energy. "I'll worry about talking with him," he said. "Where do I get to see him?"

"He owns a nightclub. The Dance Factory."

The name sparked a memory. Something he had seen in the house. But he couldn't remember.

She went to her desk, scattering papers until she found a manila folder. "Here," she said, tossing it on the coffee table. There were half a dozen clips from Goldie's column, in which Broder and David "Davey Bee" Burns were reported as being together, mostly at the Dance Factory, which, wrote Goldie, was one of Burns's "many business interests."

Her texts never called Burns a mobster or a criminal outright. But they hinted about Italian and Colombian friends, referred to frequent trips to Central America and to a palatial home in Las Vegas. He turned the pages slowly.

A photograph caused Cohen to look up from the folder. "He was at the funeral. The one with the braid. I thought I saw Sophie talking with him."

"Shit," Goldie snarled. "Bastard." She shook her head. "As soon as Max started hanging around with him, I knew Davey would be after her."

"When did this relationship begin?" Cohen asked.

"Sophie and Davey?" she asked.

"No, Broder and Burns," Cohen said, shuffling through the clips to the earliest one. "You have earlier stories? This one is from two years ago."

"That's when Max showed up at Davey's. He's been a star around here about five years, but Max only picked up on it a couple of years ago."

"What about this Burns and Levine?" he asked.

"You called her Levine," Goldie said, surprised. "Not Sophie. That means something."

"Did you tell her to stay away from him?" he asked, refusing to confirm her suspicions.

"Why did you call her Levine?" Goldie insisted. "You suspect her of something, don't you?"

"Please, Goldie, just answer my questions."

She looked at him glumly.

"Please," he repeated.

"Max showed up at Davey's with Sophie. She was still an innocent here, and Davey can be a real charmer, especially if you don't know what he really does for a living. Max probably made him sound romantic to her, the bastard."

"What do you mean, she was still an innocent"? he asked. There had been nothing innocent about the Sophie Levine he had met. He thought of her tongue wiping away the bead of cognac on her lip, and how she had offered him a better view of her body.

"You know, enthusiastic about everything. She thought everything was wonderful here. The simplest things made her happy," Goldie explained.

"Like what?"

"You know," Goldie insisted. "Things. I don't know. Credit cards. Shopping malls. The car. You know. America. Money?" she added, drilling it at him, finally getting to the bottom line. "Hell, anyone coming from over there is gonna think that this is heaven."

Cohen's mistake was to think out loud. "An actress in a state-owned theater makes a good salary and gets a good pension. She was allowed to travel."

Goldie burst into laughter, unable to control herself. "A good salary? Over there? Compared to this?" She waved her hand toward the window onto the garden and the entire city beyond.

"That's not what I meant," Cohen said softly.

She eyed him carefully. "You mean politics. You think this has something to do with politics," Goldie decided. "Haven't you heard?" she added sarcastically. "The KGB's passé nowadays."

"I'm trying to understand why she has disappeared," he shot back. "Why she has been avoiding me. She is behaving strangely, Goldie, and I am trying to understand this. And when she came to Max, the KGB . . ."

Goldie interrupted him. "The way you're talking makes it sound like you think she's some kind of spy."

"I don't know what she is," Cohen admitted angrily.

"She was your friend's daughter," Goldie shouted. "How can you doubt her?"

Cohen looked at the burning ember of his cigarette, realizing that he, too, had raised his voice. He didn't believe Sophie was a spy; he didn't know what to believe. All he had was that single word, "Sorry," scrawled on the piece of paper. And the codicils.

"Where is this place?" he said. "The Dance Factory."

"Wait a second. You know something you're not telling me. Something about Sophie," she said. "You're not going anywhere till you tell me what's going on."

"Please, Goldie, tell me where this place is."

"Well, if you're going, I'm coming too. This I've got to see. You and Davey Burns. God, what an item you two make."

"I'm going alone," Cohen said. "Where is it?"

"Don't be ridiculous," she said. "I'm coming with you. You want an introduction to Davey Bee. I can get it for you. Now, you wait right here, while I change into something more appropriate." She eyed his clothing and sighed. "As for your clothes, well, we can always say it's your traditional native dress," she said over her shoulder as she went to her bedroom.

Cohen immediately went to the phone, intending to ask the desk clerk for directions to the nightclub. But Goldie read his mind and called out from the bedroom. "I'm not kidding about the doorman. Dressed like that, you'd never get in. Unless you're with me," she added cheerfully.

A powerfully built, tuxedo-clad bouncer, clutching a clipboard like a high school coach, met them at the door. They were on Sunset Boulevard, in front of a wall-sized mural of a machine. Silhouettes of dancers ran along the painted conveyor belt; others seemed to be flying out of spouts the artist had drawn like mouths and ears on his almost human-faced contraption. The drawing on the wall made him remember where he had first encountered the name the Dance Factory. On a matchbook in Sophie's room.

"Miss Stein?" the bouncer asked as they approached. His tongue fought a lisp as his eyes conveyed disapproval of Cohen's sneakers, gray twill trousers, and white cotton shirt under the gray windbreaker.

"Michael!" she exclaimed. "Don't tell me you don't know who this is? That's not like you at all, Michael. Not at all. Gotta keep on your toes, Mikey." She chucked him under the chin with a combination of disapproval and encouragement, and started past him.

The blond man flushed. "I'm sorry, Miss Stein, but—"

"No buts about it, Mikey. If there's any problem, you just tell Davey that Avram Cohen wants to meet him. Tell him that from me." Goldie grinned at Cohen.

"If you could wait right here," Michael said apologetically, "I'll—"

"I'm telling you, Davey's gonna be awful surprised to hear that you didn't recognize the commander," Goldie insisted. "Max Broder's friend?" she added. "But if you insist, I suppose we can go elsewhere." She took Cohen's arm and started to pull him away.

"No, no, please, I'm sorry. Of course I recognize you, sir," the bouncer apologized to Cohen. "From the newspapers. I'm so sorry about your friend." Nervous, he tried to regain control of his lisp. "It's just that I wouldn't have expected that, well, you know, after a funeral and all . . .

"He's here on business, not pleasure," Goldie said, preempting Cohen's answer. She pinched the bouncer's cheek and led Cohen toward the purple doorway.

"Don't do that again," he grumbled.

"What?" she asked, genuinely surprised.

"Introduce me that way," he said, leaning against the door, pushing it open.

For a moment he could have believed that the sound waves from inside had somehow created a vacuum that made the door so difficult to pull open. He had used earphones to listen to music at home, so that he could play it as loud as if he were sitting in the midst of the orchestra. He had been in the stage wings in the Sultan's Pool outside the Old City walls while rock concerts tried like Joshua to bring down the walls.

But he had never been inside a room where the sound level was so high, where the bass drove so deeply into his circulation.

He could feel the rhythms of the music echo in his chest, knowing it was supposed to stir the blood.

There was a dance floor three steps below him, and to his left was a bar that ran the entire length of the wall, which was so long as to disappear into the darkness beyond his view. The room was thick with fragrances: perfumes and smoke, colognes and sweat. Goldie paused at the entrance, calculating their passage through the hall.

He felt stiff and self-conscious, aware of people noticing him, staring. But there were no whispers in this place. The sound level prevented any kind of communication except shouting. Heads turned and mouths moved as pairs of eyes studied him. There were young women in the flimsiest of dresses and young men in a variety of jackets and trousers. Other women wore torn jeans and lacy bras, while bare-chested young men writhed sweatily before them. The musclemen and Indians from the beach mingled with the androgynes and the transsexuals. Even in the semidarkness, there were people wearing sunglasses, and when a spotlight swerved over the crowd, hitting Cohen in the eyes before moving on in its crazy elliptical path, he understood why. For a moment he was blinded, and then the illumination changed to make everything on the light side of the spectrum sparkle and everything on the dark side disappear. Just as he grew used to the black light, it changed to strobes, and the broken laughter became as spasmodic as the stop-frame motions of the people. Just as he grew used to the flashing, it stopped, replaced by a twirling globe hanging above the crowd, lasers hitting it from all directions, its tiny mirrors reflecting a spectrum of pale colors onto the faces around him.

He was only a few steps inside the club. A woman wearing a satin bustier, one breast exposed, stood a few feet away, ignoring a man talking to her. She was staring at Cohen. Her tongue flicked at him and then slowly licked her red lips, and then she winked just as deliberately. Her companion turned, glared at Cohen, and grabbed the woman's arm tight.

Goldie came to Cohen's rescue, pulling him masterfully through the milling crowd to the bar. He ordered a cognac, she asked for Scotch on the rocks. Cohen paid with one of the hundred-dollar bills he had taken from Broder's safe, and Goldie raised an eyebrow. Drinks in hand, they turned their backs to the bar and looked out at the dancers. Cohen stuffed the change into his trousers pocket.

"Is Burns here?" he asked, shouting into her ear, uncertain how loud he needed to raise his voice.

She nodded.

He motioned with a hand gesture that anyone in Jerusalem would have understood to mean "where" but that only made Goldie look at him quizzically. "Where?" he shouted.

Goldie said something he couldn't hear, and he tilted his head so she could repeat it in his ear.

"Patience," she said. "He already knows you're here. Look, here comes Alvy Landy." She waved to the young actor, coming off the dance floor. Pam was at his side. Alvy leaned forward to speak into Cohen's ear. "I never would have expected to see you here," he said, his voice raised just enough to add the last bit of pressure on Cohen's eardrum and change the noise to pain. Cohen smiled weakly. Alvy leaned forward again. "I have so much I want to talk with you about. I wanted to meet you when Max picked me for the part. But he said no."

Cohen was grateful to Broder at least for that. He followed Alvy's lead and leaned foward to speak into the actor's ear. "Have you seen Sophie?"

"Somewhere over there," Alvy shouted, pulling away from Cohen to point across the dance floor to the restaurant area of the club. "You want me to try to find her?" he added.

"Like you found her at the funeral?" Pam interjected, surprising Cohen. "*I* know where she is," the tanned beauty said to him, pulling at Alvy.

He wrested his arm out of her grip. "Promise me that we'll have a chance to talk," he asked Cohen.

But Cohen only gestured with a hand to his ear that he could not imagine conducting a conversation in the noisy room. Alvy motioned that he understood, and then he took Pam's arm. Cohen watched them disappear into the dancing crowd.

"Sophie's here," he shouted into Goldie's ear. "I'm going to go look for her. If they bring her here, make her wait. I'll be right back."

She nodded, and he started away from the bar, but immediately felt a hand on his shoulder. He spun, thinking of the gun in his waistband, no longer surprised by his paranoia.

A black man, as tall as a basketball center, wearing a tailored charcoal-gray suit and silk tie, was looking down at him, crooking a finger. Wordlessly, he indicated that Cohen should follow him. They walked the length of the bar and into the darkness at the far end of the hall. When they reached a stage, where instruments were set up but no musicians or technicians were to be seen, they were met by a tiny overmuscled man with slicked-back hair and a slim mustache, guarding a door.

The weightlifter stood aside. With an almost Oriental gesture, the tall man bade Cohen to enter. There was a steep set of stairs, and a door at the top. Cohen took a step up and turned. The two bodyguards were blocking the door to Goldie. She didn't even have time to appeal to him. The weightlifter pulled the door closed.

Alone in the dimly lit stairwell, Cohen climbed slowly. The music was still loud behind him. But by the time he had reached the doorway at the top of the steps, the noise had receded. When he closed the door behind him, the music disappeared. He was in another dark corridor, lined by doorways. Only at the very end of the hall could he see light, from the bottom of a closed door. He went to it.

A huge black marble desk floated on plexiglass pillars. The oval desk was empty except for a telephone console. One wall was covered with a dozen television monitors. One row of monitors displayed sports; a second row exhibited scenes from the nightclub. A black leather sofa and a pair of matching chairs were aimed at the monitors. All the televisions were silent. Behind the desk, a cabinet ran the length of the entire room, and above its gleaming black surface, the shiny narrow slats of a venetian blind covered what Cohen assumed was a window looking down on the nightclub. The music was as dim as the lighting, which came from the ceiling and lit specific areas of the room. The walls were lacquered in black enamel, and no decorations marred the surfaces. A door opened on the far side of the room, casting a splash of bathroom light into the room.

He was shorter than Cohen had expected. His hair was pulled back into the braid. It seemed to stretch his skin backward, so that even in repose, his large face, with its high forehead, had a constant thin-lipped grin, and his nose tilted up as if he were sniffing at the air or on the lookout over the heads of people around him. He was dressed in black, his shirt buttoned to the top without a tie, his jacket over his shoulders like a cape. Cohen remembered that at the funeral, Burns had also been in black from head to toe.

Burns was wiping his hands on a towel, and only when he finished, tossing it back into the bathroom without a glance, did his right hand extend. "I was wondering when you'd turn up," he said in a voice that sounded like gears clashing. The handshake was perfunctory and surprised Cohen with its calluses.

As he took his seat behind the desk, Burns ran his eyes over the moving pictures of athletes, horses, and racing motorcycles. Kicking with his feet and using his hands on the desk as levers, he propelled the seat backward and to the side, rolling until he was halfway down the cabinet. He slid open one of the doors, rummaged, and then slid the chair back to its position behind the center of his desk.

"Here," he said, tossing a thick manila envelope, which clattered onto the desk. Looking up, Burns's eyes caught something on the monitors behind Cohen, who had remained standing. "Fucking Yanks," he mumbled. But then he was back with Cohen. "Max said you might show up for this," he said.

"Why?" Cohen's voice cracked, just above a whisper. "Why?"

"He didn't tell you?" Burns asked.

Cohen shook his head.

"Shit. That son of a bitch," the gangster snarled with no little admiration. "That guy shoulda worked for the CIA—coulda kept their secrets for them."

He twirled in the chair, twisting a rod that opened the venetian blinds, revealing the nightclub below. Cohen looked out the window. He couldn't see the bar, and in the flashing lights the crowd of dancers appeared to be a single complex organism.

"The problem is," Burns said thoughtfully, "I don't know how much I can tell you. Max said I could trust you. But Max is gone." His back was still to Cohen.

"Why didn't you approach me at the funeral?" Cohen asked. "You could have brought it to me there," he added, wondering if it would have saved Rosen's life.

"You didn't pay attention to what I said." The little man spoke didactically, turning away from the view of his nightclub to look at Cohen. "I said I was supposed to give you this package *if* you showed up. I didn't have to invite you."

"So. Here I am. What is it?" Cohen asked, stepping toward the desk and reaching for the envelope.

"My guess, a book, a tape, something like that," Burns said.

"Your guess?" Cohen said skeptically as he picked it up. He checked the seal. He looked up at Burns but didn't smile yet.

"That's his envelope. Not mine. I didn't open it."

Burns's discretion impressed Cohen. He tore open the envelope. A stick-on label in Broder's handwriting identified the tape as *The Survivor's Secrets (Part One)*. He held it up to show Burns.

"I should have figured," Burns said, shaking his head. "I can't deal with that shit anymore. Enough is enough. When my father passed away, I said enough is enough, no more of that stuff. Since I'm twenty-three I've been giving a hundred long ones a year to Gould's outfit, the Holocaust Institute. They got more than a million from me so far. But they'll only take it anonymous." He scowled. "God forbid my name should be connected to them," he added sarcastically. "But I do it. For my father's memory."

Cohen tapped the tape in his hand, thinking as he listened. "How did you meet him?" he asked.

Burns grinned at the memory. "It was just like him. He shows up one night. Not the usual customer at the Factory, if you know what I mean. Old geezer, dressed to kill, suits cut like the forties. Like in costume. That's cool. He asks for me. My man says no way." Burns grinned. But Cohen remained stone-faced. "The fucking idiot," Burns muttered to himself, before continuing. "But Max," he went on, "he just smiles and stands up, and you know, he was a big guy, so it looks like he's getting ready to fight, taking off his jacket, but elegant like, and handing it to the broad, who, it turns out later, is Sophie." Burns chuckled softly at another memory.

"What happened?" Cohen asked.

"Well, he fucking rolled up his sleeve, just enough to show the number, and said to the security man, 'Tell Heschel's son there is someone to see him.' " Burns laughed again, softly, to himself. "That's my old man. Heschel."

Cohen frowned.

"Heschel Bernstein. He came to America, he made it Harry Burns."

Cohen's face remained impassive while his mind raced down the darkest alleys of his mind, trying to put the name to a face, a face to the name. Nothing came to light. He tried not to look worried as the silence grew longer.

Burns startled him with a laugh. "You pass," Burns said. "You couldn't know him. Max met him here. Why don't you sit down?" he asked, pointing to one of the leather armchairs facing the desk. As Cohen went to the chair, Burns tapped rhythmically with his ring on the table. "I bet Goldie told you I'm related to Bugsy Siegel," he said, just as Cohen's back settled into the leather-and-chrome chair.

Cohen shrugged.

"It's not true."

Cohen raised an eyebrow.

"I never deny it in public."

Cohen nodded.

Burns smiled. "You wanta hear the best part?"

Cohen nodded again.

"My man comes up, says to me, 'Boss, you never seen anything like it—the geezer's got a phone number tattooed on his arm.' "

Burns chortled. "Fucking *goy*," he said when his laugh finally died away. "He ain't working for me no more. Anyway, I hear about the number, I say send him in. We talk. Well, mostly he talks. About my father." Burns sighed. "I had always thought he was some kind of schmuck, a muscleman aspiring to be a bagman. I didn't know shit."

Cohen wondered what a bagman was, grateful he knew nothing of Heschel Bernstein. "What did he want?" he asked, testing the new level of trust Burns had offered. "He asked you for something, didn't he?"

Burns studied Cohen's face, deliberating. "We're getting into uncharted space here," the gangster finally said. "Max said I can trust you. Hell, for all I know, you're the Jewish Jimmy Stewart or something. But now Max is dead, and I've got some interests I have to protect. Maybe I just give you the tape and you go, and that's it. I did my duty. You did yours."

Cohen looked at the cassette in his hand. "When did you get this?"

"Last week," Burns said. "He calls me, says he wants to talk. Bygones be bygones. Friends are friends. Business is business. Two different things. He needed me as a friend."

Cohen could feel his patience dwindling, and he clasped the tape slightly tighter to keep his temper under control. "You betrayed him," he whispered.

"I did what I had to do," Burns protested. "I helped him as far as I could go. But a better offer came in. That's all. I gave him some time, warned him. He was cool. He wasn't mad at me. That," he said, pointing toward the cassette in Cohen's hand, "was a final favor. Our business was over. That"—he pointed again—"was for friendship."

"What business?" Cohen asked.

"The movie business. What else?"

"You're not in the movie business."

"You'd be surprised what businesses I'm in."

Cohen kept his voice low, trying to restrain his anger. "What business did you do with him?" he rumbled.

Burns tapped at the glass again with his ring, and then he made a decision. "Epica was making trouble for him. He wanted me to make trouble back."

"And?"

"And what?"

"Did you? Make trouble for Epica?"

Burns snorted a laugh. "Yeah, I made trouble. I made trouble till it made me trouble."

"When did all this happen?" Cohen asked.

"During the past year. Since Andy Blakely came in."

"When did you betray him?" Cohen asked.

"When he started acting crazy, dangerous. If you really want to know," Burns shot back. "He was paranoid. Totally. You'd think it was him the feds wanted to get their hands on. He'd never use his home phone to talk. He only wanted to meet in the open, nobody else around. I asked, him, 'Max, what is this shit, meetings in the middle of the fuckin' desert, on the beach?' And all he does is smile and say, 'It's safe this way.'"

"Safe from what?" Cohen asked.

"That's what *I* wanted to know," Burns exclaimed. "It got to where his fucking paranoia was making me paranoid. So I asked him, 'Max, you telling me you're worried about Nazis? In America?' And you know what he says?"

"No," Cohen said.

"He just laughed—you know that laugh of his—he just laughed, and he says, 'It would be easy if it was only that. I'm talking about a ghost.' Crazy, no? That's when I figured it was time for me to rethink my position. I mean, I can dig the obsession with the flick. A guy spends his whole life planning something, he wants to do it right. Perfect. But he wanted to go to fucking war."

"Against who?" Cohen pressed. "Blakely? Who?"

Burns shrugged. "Ghosts?" he asked back.

They sat in silence for a long minute, Cohen letting his own ghosts lead him to his next question.

"Sophie," Cohen said, her name itself a question.

"What about her?" asked Burns, suspicious for the first time since Cohen entered the room.

"I have to talk to her."

"So?" Burns asked.

"She avoided me at the funeral. I saw her with you there. I understand she is here tonight."

"Maybe she's not interested in talking with you," Burns said. "Maybe you remind her of Max." There was only the slightest edge of sarcasm in the suggestion that Sophie had a good reason to avoid Cohen.

"It would be in her interest," Cohen said, dangling a generous smile.

"The will," Burns finally guessed, just as Cohen had wanted.

"Can you get her up here?" he asked Burns.

"Maybe she doesn't need the money," the mobster suggested. "Maybe I'll take care of her now."

"Don't you think it's about time she was allowed to take care of herself?" Cohen asked, testing.

Burns raised an eyebrow, swallowing once as he thought, before taking Cohen's bet. "Sure, why not?" He slapped at the telephone console on the table. "Cheryl, ask Sophie to come up, will you?" he said at the console.

"She split," a woman's disembodied voice said.

"Yeah? She say where she was going?" Burns glanced at Cohen, who moved forward on the armchair.

"I don't know," Cheryl grouched. "She left with that gossip. What's her name? Pearl? Ruby?"

"Goldie. Goldie Stein," Burns said.

"Yeah, right. Goldie Stein," the woman answered. "They split. About ten minutes ago."

"Fuck!" Burns cried, slamming his hand on the desk.

Cohen stood up, clutching the envelope and cassette.

"You sure?" Burns asked the loudspeaker one more time.

"Yeah, sure I'm sure," the woman's voice said. "I saw 'em go. Maybe they're just outside. Getting some air. You know what I mean?"

It had taken her fifteen minutes to lead him to the Dance Factory. It took him more than an hour to return to her hotel, making certain nobody was following. If he interrupted them, he thought, that would be all right. He'd finally get to confront Sophie. And if they weren't there, he'd watch Broder's movie.

He slipped down a path through the parking lot, avoiding the reception desk. He knocked once on the bungalow door. Silence. He knocked again, slightly harder, and the door swung slowly open. He peered inside, calling her name softly. Again, no answer. He drew the gun and moved gingerly through the living room. One of the consoles was on; an old black-and-white musical sang and danced silently. There was an empty bottle of pink champagne upside down in the melted water of an ice bucket on the coffee table. The ashtray held some butts of hand-rolled cigarettes. Looking without touching, listening to his breathing and an electronic melody from a distant party elsewhere in the hotel compound, he moved toward the bedroom.

He saw her legs first. They were crossed at the ankles, tied by a black velvet cord. He said her name once, softly, and took another step toward the doorway, quietly clicking off the safety on the gun in his right hand. Like a bikini in negative, the white strip of untanned skin across surprisingly taut buttocks came into view.

He was aware of the heat of his hand under the cool grip of the gun butt, feeling slightly foolish as he realized she might simply be asleep. "Goldie?" he asked, not harshly but loud enough to startle someone awake, as he took the next step into the room. His eyes darted to all the corners, seeking ambushes and possible hiding places, before he looked again at her body, on its stomach on the bed.

Her auburn hair was a dark jungle sprawled across white pillows and the leathery brown tan of her broad back. Again, he said her name once softly, a second time louder as he approached, and as he touched the soft spot between her neck and shoulder, he said it a third time, loudly, still hoping he was only waking her. But by then he knew it was hopeless.

Her body was warm, but not warm enough. He pressed for a pulse, then leaned over her, searching out her face in the darkness of hair and rumpled bedding. He dared not move the body, but he did brush aside some hair. Her face was buried in the pillows.

He checked her hands. One was curled into a tight fist. The other was spread open, her red fingernails like five drops of blood on the ivory sheets.

He shivered, mourning her lost vitality, alone in the room listening to his heartbeat and the damn air conditioner. He blamed himself, thinking that if he had told her to piss off and ignored her on the plane, she might still be alive. And he was aware that it was he who had raised doubts in her mind about Sophie, the kind of doubts Goldie would have been sure to raise with the younger woman. But ultimately, he knew it was Der Bruder's affairs, not his own, that were to blame for Goldie's death. So he went to the phone, still wanting to believe Sophie was Bernard Levine's daughter, still hoping to redeem her from his suspicions, and himself from his fears.

"This better be important," Madden snarled after the fourth ring and a fumbling with the phone.

"It is," Cohen said.

"Cohen?" Madden asked.

"Goldie's dead."

There was a long silence. Cohen did nothing to interrupt it. Finally, Madden asked, "How?"

"Strangled," Cohen said.

"Fuck."

"You'll find her in bed, at her hotel," Cohen said.

"You there now?" Madden asked.

Cohen paused before answering.

"Cohen," Madden started, threat in his voice. "You wait for me there."

"Your technicians will find my fingerprints in the room," Cohen said. "But I refuse to be considered a suspect in this matter," he added forcefully.

"So who is?" Madden demanded.

If she was Bernard Levine's daughter, he owed her the chance to explain herself. If she wasn't, he owed both himself and Broder the effort to find out why she had pretended to be Sophie. He doubted any American could understand and had no faith in Madden's abilities.

"I can't say," he finally answered Madden.

"You mean you don't know or you won't tell me?" Madden asked.

"I don't know if I can trust you," Cohen answered truthfully.

They shared a long silence on the phone, and then Madden made an offering. "I've heard something from Torrance. The driver's two buddies were also Linekers. His brothers." But now it was Madden's turn to hesitate.

"There's something else, isn't there?" Cohen asked.

"When I see you."

Cohen wondered if Madden was trying to get him to agree to anything as long as he stayed still. He could hear a distant siren. "You're not going to see me if you're going to arrest me," Cohen said.

"Don't be silly," Madden said. "Nobody's going to arrest you."

Cohen was hearing too much sweetness in Madden's voice. He worried that the siren might be the inner echo of his own fears. Madden was humoring him, and that made it doubly difficult for him to trust the American. "How long will it take for you to get here?" Cohen finally asked.

He heard Madden let out a lungful of air before answering, "Twenty minutes."

"I will wait twenty minutes. No more. If you are not here by then, I will leave." He hung up on the spluttering American.

Returning to the living room, he began his own search with a memory of Sophie. He dug inside his canvas bag looking for a pair of surgical gloves he had found in her bathroom. He reached deep past his laundry, finding the gloves, and then freezing. The treatment. He flipped over the bag, dumping everything onto the sofa. The manuscript was missing.

He felt suddenly dizzy and sat down heavily beside the jumble of all he had collected. He looked forlornly at the pile of clothing, magazines, cigarette cartons, and the shiny box with the duty-free cognac he had planned to drink with Der Bruder. The noose, too, was missing. He blinked back his frustration, the details of the room blurring in front of his eyes. But he had no choice. He had to start with the tiniest of details, the simplest of all facts. He returned to Goldie's bedroom, muttering to himself as he pulled on the gloves, knowing that they would be a useless precaution.

His prints were already all over the suite. His mind strained, trying to understand. If she was intelligent enough to pretend to be Sophie Levine, he thought, surely she was intelligent enough not to act so obviously suspicious. So she really was Sophie. But if she was truly Sophie, why was she avoiding him?

He thought bitterly about Max Broder as he attacked the night table, a battlefield of cosmetics and lotions. The dresser drawers were an archive of frilly fabrics. The closet could have belonged to a married couple: both men's and women's clothes were draped from hangers. But it smelled only of Goldie's perfume. The bathroom was just as he remembered it.

He decided that the living room, with its shelves and desk and coffee table, littered with artifices of pleasure, was more likely to reveal something. He started at the desk. The jumble of papers and computer diskettes, newspapers and magazines, appeared as it had when he left with her a few hours before.

She had two index files of telephone numbers. He strummed the cards, wondering whose numbers to take. He paused at Alvy Landy's name. The boy's seeming familiarity with Sophie intrigued him, and though he had yet to fulfill his promises, twice the young actor had offered help. More, twice the actor had beseeched him for a private interview. Perhaps there was something to learn from the youth, after all, Cohen thought, copying down his number in the yellow notebook.

From there he went to the coffee table. There were two different lipstick colors on the cigarettes. Delicately, he picked up the two glasses and looked for possible prints. He put them down and leaned back in the sofa, looking around the room.

A pair of brass candlesticks sat high on a bookshelf. There had been a similar pair in his young wife's dowry. She lit them on holiday evenings and Friday nights during the single year they were married. She had not been religious but had liked the ritual, and after her death, the candlesticks had remained unused, even by Ahuva.

He had to stretch to reach the yellowing envelope standing between the candlesticks on the top shelf. He plucked it out and carefully removed a flimsy piece of paper. The handwriting was almost childish, as if the writer was not used to putting anything on paper. There were only a few lines.

Please Goldie, forgive my silence. It was my weapon to defend you and protect you. It hurt me more than it hurt you. Believe me. Please.

It was signed *Papa.*

Cohen took control of the sorrow he felt rising inside him. It was a sorrow for his own regrets as well as Goldie's father's, and it made him think of Goldie with even more pity. The letter fell to his lap as he wondered what would have been if his wife had lived, if the baby had been born and had grown up to ask about the camps. He wondered if he would have had the strength to tell his child, or, worse, the strength to remain silent.

The crunching of gravel from the open front door silenced the pitiful letter's reproach. Instinctively, he shoved the candlesticks and the letter into his bag in one swooping motion. He had the feeling that they were Goldie's legacy to him, a private compensation. They spoke softer than the demands of Broder's last will. But he promised himself that if there was any indication that the letter was meaningful to the case, he would use it. Otherwise, it would remain her secret. He stood up.

The American eyed the surgical gloves on Cohen's hands. "Shit," he said.

Cohen peeled off the gloves. "Habit," he said, shrugging unabashedly. "They were useless," he added. "I was here this afternoon. My fingerprints are probably all over the room. But there will probably be others as well." He ached for a cigarette but knew it would have to wait.

Madden looked around the living room. "Where is it?"

Cohen led him to the bedroom, pausing in the doorway. Madden entered first, going directly to the body. He didn't touch it. He scanned the body, took a cursory look around the room, his eyes ending at Cohen. "All right," he said. "You get out of here. There's a bar on Santa Monica, two blocks past the Mormon Temple. It's called the Parrot. Think you can find it?"

"I can find it."

"Take a right when you come out the driveway, get onto Santa Monica, and it's not far," Madden ordered.

Fifteen minutes later, Cohen was sitting at the bar. The only other people were a bartender and a heavily made-up woman in her late thirties or early forties, wearing a tall bouffant hairdo and sitting at a corner table with a man dressed in cook's clothing.

Cohen asked for coffee, and the bartender scowled at him. "Minimum ten bucks," he said.

"Ten dollars for coffee seems a lot," Cohen said.

"Cover charge. For the show," the bartender said.

Cohen looked around. The cook was holding the woman's hand, but she was staring into space, ignoring him.

"What show?"

"Hey, Katy, what time you go on?"

The woman looked around the room, scowled at him, and then offered the cook a more tender glance.

"She goes on. Later. Cover charge now," the bartender said.

"How much is a cognac?" Cohen asked.

"Three bucks," the bartender said.

"A double. And coffee," said Cohen.

By the time Madden showed up, the cognac was gone and a second cup of coffee was in front of Cohen. The policeman greeted Katy and the bartender by name. The cook scowled, and the stripper didn't seem happy to see Madden. But the bartender set up a shot of whiskey without Madden's asking for it.

"I told them I got an anonymous tip," Madden said softly to Cohen as the bartender went down to the cash register.

"But you told them it was connected to Broder's death, no?" Cohen demanded.

Madden buried his head in his hands. "What are you doing here?" he asked.

"What do you mean?" Cohen asked.

"Listen very carefully," Madden said. "The only thing right now between you and an airplane back to Israel is me. And that's the better offer. There are some who wanted you picked up after the skinheads. And the pier? Don't ask. Now this. When they find out about you being in Goldie's room, I don't want to think about what they'll do. You're going to become a diplomatic incident if this keeps up. So if you want me to keep helping you, I need you to help me. What the fuck is this all about?"

Cohen tipped a last drop of cognac into his mouth. A ghost, Burns had quoted Broder as saying. Not a Nazi; a ghost. Blakely was also on his mind, and he couldn't shake away the memory of Sophie's hot breath on his face. He stared sorrowfully at the American policeman. Ghosts laughed in his mind. He needed sleep. But he needed to see the movie. He was tempted to say that he was leaving the country, going home, forgetting all of it. He couldn't bring himself to give Sophie Levine's name to Madden. Not unless it was absolutely necessary. He wanted to find her first.

"Jacques Rosen," he said. "The dead beggar on the pier," he explained wearily, angry at Madden's ignorance of the name. "I think he was the target of the shooting. I know he had something for me. He said so before he died. Whoever is handling those shootings has his shopping cart. I believe there is a videocassette for me," Cohen said. "A message to me from Broder."

Madden stared at him. "You believe," he finally said incredulously. "You know," he added with a biting thoughtfulness, "come to think of it, that's all I've heard from you since you showed up. You believe your friend couldn't commit suicide. You believe those skinheads were trying to kill you. You believe a bum you meet on a pier. Jeezus," he said.

"Get me the cassette. And the skinheads—you said you had something."

"They hung around a storefront neo-Nazi office in Torrance," Madden admitted.

"Where is this Torrance?" Cohen pulled his notebook out of a pocket.

"You're not going down there," Madden spluttered.

Cohen studied Madden's face before answering. "They tried to kill me."

"All right. *Maybe* they tried to kill you. But it's over. Let the Torrance cops do their job. They'll pick up Dugan. He's the local führer down there. They'll ask him. They learn something, they'll let me know."

"Tell them to ask about Max Broder," Cohen ordered.

"They know how to do their job," Madden snarled.

Cohen considered asking if the Torrance police knew how to do their job the way Madden had been doing his job. But he had one more request. He knew it would be the most dangerous for Madden, so he brought it out like artillery, a threat that would hang over Madden's head. "Andrew Blakely," he said.

"Fuck you," Madden whispered softly. But then he slapped the heavy wooden bar so the whiskey jiggled in his glass. The bartender looked up, shared a look with the stripper, then went back to his polishing. "That does it," Madden hissed. "He's the goddamned head of a fucking studio. Your friend had business relations with him. It went bad. That's no fucking reason to investigate a studio president. Not in this city. Because I'm gonna tell you something you might not want to hear. Goldie got it because she went a little too far playing one of her games. She had quite a rep in this town, you know. Maybe whoever did her had nothing to do with Broder. Nothing at all. And you know what? Your friend the hobo. An innocent bystander. That's all. The creeps from Torrance. Creeps, that's all. So don't give me this Blakely shit, this conspiracy crap. Your friend committed suicide. Goldie got it because she was bound to catch it. And all the rest—coincidence, that's all. Coincidence."

Cohen's face was an impassive granite wall as he waited for Madden to finish the speech. "You don't believe that, do you?" he finally asked. It was his turn to be patronizing.

But Madden only smirked at him. "I thought you were some kind of ace," he said cynically. "You people are supposed to be smart. But the newspapers are right for once. You overreact. Seems to me you've had enemies so long you can't even see your friends anymore. I'm trying to help you."

Cohen slid off his barstool. He was too tired for arguments. "Tell me," he asked, finding a twenty-dollar bill in his wallet and putting it on the bar. "How much longer do you have?" He could sense Madden tensing, and he suddenly felt like Goldie. It panged him, so he added, "Don't worry, Mike," in a paternal tone. "You're one of the lucky ones. You get to see it coming. And I understand. You don't want trouble. I'm trouble. So how much longer do you have? A month? More? Less? I bet less than a month. I bet two weeks."

"Twelve days," Madden confessed, almost contrite.

"Well," said Cohen, "I hope this is all over before then." He bent down to pick up his bag. "What will you be doing thirteen days from now?" he asked in a friendly tone as he stood up.

"First you tell me you're not going to Torrance," Madden said, trying to regain his authority.

"Listen to me, Mike Madden." Cohen bent over so none of the other people at the bar could see him speaking. "There are things I can do that you can't. Here, I am nobody. And you? You are a cop on the verge of retirement. You can't afford to do the things I can do. And I can tell you this: There are things you don't want to know."

With that, he marched out of the bar, stretching as he blinked into the rising dawn's sunlight after the door closed on Madden's laugh behind him. Leaving everything behind, he headed due west in the Jaguar, ignoring road maps and street signs, ignoring everything except his instinct to go to the west, where the patient ocean waited without judgment.

The motel's red neon sign winked pale triple X's. But Cohen was thinking only about the ocean. He listened for the surf as the pockmarked clerk, with his open flowered shirt revealing a hollow chest, gave him two keys and change from another of Broder's hundred-dollar bills. One key was for the room, the other for the lock on the video player.

"Don't you want to pick out a flick?" the clerk asked, shoving a catalogue on the counter in front of Cohen.

"I brought my own," said Cohen. The clerk raised an eyebrow, peered over Cohen's shoulder to look for a passenger in the Jaguar, and, seeing none, shrugged.

Cohen parked by the room at the end of the lot, dropped off his bag in the room, and walked the two blocks to the ocean. There was an illusion of wind created by the sound of the surf. It was low tide, but the waves were huge, bigger than any Mediterranean surf along Israel's coastline. The nearest person was more than a kilometer south.

Cohen began unbuttoning his shirt halfway across the sand. By the water's edge he took off the rest of his clothes, leaving them in a pile on the dry sand. He ran into a wall of surf and plunged over it, aiming his body to the undercurrent, and then rose out of the shocking chill to turn onto his back after breaking through to the surface. Fast, he backstroked a dozen meters and then stopped suddenly, catching his own wake and treading water to look at the view. The rising sun's glare made it impossible for him to see more than haloed outlines of the skyline. To the south, the curve of the coastline and the bits of city beyond were visible. He crawled and breast-stroked until the memories were as vague as the surf, until the smells he remembered were washed from his system. He swam until his breath came fast and heavy, then he caught a wave that carried him inland, and he found himself on his hands, pulling his body to the knee-deep water, where a wave pushed him to shore.

He used a shirt from his bag as a towel and dried off quickly. While he was in the water, some surfers had gathered about two hundred meters to his left. A man was walking a pair of dogs just as far to his right. The pier was a kilometer north, high above the water. For a moment he was naked on the beach, and then he hopped into his trousers.

The trudge through the sand exhausted him.

On a bench near a pay phone at the end of a commercial street parallel to the boulevard, he pulled out his flask and took a long sip, trying to decide whether he wanted to eat first or sleep, but knowing what he really had to do. Disgusted with his own procrastination, he held up his face to the warming sun, letting it bathe him with its light, thinking, trying to order the information and organize the tasks in his mind. He sat that way for a long time, until he was ready.

It was work, he thought, as he put the cassette into the machine. "Separate feelings from observations," he said aloud in his most didactic tone, sitting on the edge of the bed. But as he lit the cigarette, listening to the rising pitch of the whining tape rewinding on the player, he knew that sometimes feelings, too, needed to be observed.

There was the rough click of the tape stopping, the whir of the machinery, and then, just as he had read in the first pages of the treatment, the movie began with the hanging epidemic.

Broder had all the wise and inspirational dialogue, and was portrayed as an unflawed leader. Young Avram was clever and fast on his feet, learning quickly how to be fawning toward the kapos, invisibly obedient toward the Germans, and helpful to whomever he could. This is not the way it was, Cohen snorted within five minutes. There were even stranger turns of the truth. Levine was played wild-eyed, his democratic socialism turned into Stalinism. In a barracks scene, Levine's actor was given a speech promising a better world under the hammer and sickle, which would come out of the east to rescue them. And there was Alvy Landy, listening eagerly to the pompous political poetry. By the time Rosen was introduced as the most clever of them all—the first in his shipment to grasp the rules of survival—Cohen realized that everyone in the movie was inhuman.

Manheim and his doctors, of course, all the butchers and their helpers, were portrayed with their manias as polished as their boots, their perversions as distorted as the eyes behind their spectacle lenses. But the slaves, too, were presented as beyond humanity, almost godlike in their religious piety or ideological purity. Even the criminals, murderers, and rapists were somehow elevated to more mythic levels of being, in which their ability to survive not only justified their past crimes but cleansed them as well.

There was no guilt in Broder's tale, no fatal compromises. All but the masters were given a moment alone in which to cry, each was shown wiping away tears as if he would never cry again.

Cohen watched with equal measures of fascination and revulsion, hating each and every scene. As far as he was concerned, Broder's magnum opus was a disaster.

The movie went on, sometimes broken by snippets announcing a code number of film that should yet be inserted. Cohen fumbled with the pause button at each one, making a note in case he needed to return to the cutting room to look for the missing segment. It was work, he kept telling himself, trying to concentrate on the film instead of his own memories.

Ever systematic, Broder helped. With the characters established, the director had turned to the routine of work and survival for each one. Cohen watched scenes of bodies shoveled into the crematoriums and scenes of the ashes being shoveled out. There were shots of insects and maggots in soup, bread crawling with worms, and a fight to the death over a potato. There were roll calls and killings. There was the constant head-down running, faces constantly averted lest a wound or scar mark the slave for execution. Cohen watched through a haze, fighting off memories far worse than anything Broder could show. By the time Broder was ready to tell the tale of the escape plan, Cohen had his emotions under control. He knew the ending.

But Max Broder was a professional, Cohen admitted to himself, as the scenes of the secret effort built up to the horrible disappointment of failure. More anecdotes followed. Slave doctors worked against typhus, while the German doctors conducted their crazed experiments in hyperthermia. Rosen's miraculous return in body if not spirit was explained with a melodramatic silence in which the horror was evoked by his vacant eyes. Then came Der Bruder's decision that they should organize a revolt. But the revolt never happened.

The Americans showed up first. There was a wide view of the camp in a state of chaos, which at first appeared to be shot in slow motion. Two American tanks were parked just inside the main gate. But the pace was set by the walking dead, while the Americans stood paralyzed by the sights around them. The shot narrowed in on the main administration building, a red-brick factory house that had served as the backdrop to the gallows on the center stage of the parade ground, which earlier was seen as the site of roll calls in front of hanging bodies. Smoke poured from a window on the second floor, and below, in the foreground, an American was trying half-heartedly to stop four or five slaves from weakly beating a kapo.

The camera zoomed through the main arch of the administration building, across the parade grounds, until it reached the faces of Max and Bernard, who were walking slowly toward young Avram. Alvy Landy stood in front of a barracks, watching a weeping American medic.

Cohen pulled at the sheets of the bed, wrapping them around him in the air-conditioned cold of the motel room, in unconscious replication of Alvy Landy, who wore a U.S. Army blanket like a shawl over his shoulders. Cohen watched the young actor watching Levine and Broder approach, and just as Alvy was about to speak, Cohen did it for him, like Goldie in the airplane. "Manheim?" he asked aloud in the lonely motel room, watching Alvy Landy say the same thing on the television screen. Bernard shook his head.

"Gone," said Broder, and then the screen faded on the three skeletal men exchanging piercing stares.

Cohen thought the movie was over, and stood up. But suddenly there was a brightness on the screen. For a second it illuminated even the farthest corner in the darkened motel room, making Cohen blink in the unexpected light.

The camera panned down out of the bright sun to Broder and Cohen, alone at the gate to the camp. Tracking from afar, the camera moved up behind an American soldier with his camera, and then it zoomed over him until it froze on Broder, his arm around Cohen's shoulder, pointing into the distance. The screen went dark, the caption *End of Part One* appeared briefly in white, and the electric snow of static filled the lonely motel room with a sickly light.

A CHILD IS PLAYING with a ball in the front yard of a farmhouse. Behind the building is a snow-covered meadow, a thick-trunked oak tree growing out of the white center. The child stops kicking the ball as a dark car pulls up in front of the house. Three faceless men get out. They are dressed as businessmen, wearing woolen overcoats and hats pulled down over their foreheads. But there is no sun from which to shield their eyes. It is cold, and gray skies foretell more snow. One man reaches down for the ball and, tossing it gently up and down in the air as he speaks, asks the boy about his father.

The ball rolls to a stop under a first-floor picture window. The child's face appears in the window, looking in. All three men are in the front room. A fourth, the boy's father, is on his knees. He is wearing thick spectacles, which give his eyes a maddened look. One of the visitors notices the child peering through the window. He goes to the curtain and pulls it shut.

"Now tell us. Where is he?" the man says as he turns back to the kneeling Nazi. But the weeping man is defiant. It's Cohen's voice asking now, "Where is he?" There is the sound of a child calling for Papa. All four men face the child, who stands at the doorway of the parlor.

Broder goes to the boy. The Nazi shakes his head. "Please, don't hurt my boy. Please. He is innocent." Broder's laugh saws through the air. The boy starts to cry, and it turns into the sound of car tires squealing.

The three men are in the car. The two men in front are in a celebratory mood, laughing.

Cohen opened his eyes, aware he was waking up to avoid what would come next. He had looked out the back window of the car, and the image of the father and the son, hanging by their necks from ropes tied around the branches of the tree out in the meadow, had remained in his mind forever.

He was in a large bed in the gabled upstairs guest room of Alvy Landy's beachfront house in Venice. At the end of the room was a set of sliding doors, open to the sky. Cohen's heartbeat returned to a more normal pace. He lay back, remembering. He had stopped at a pay phone, to try Barbara Darnaby's telephone numbers. One answering machine had her voice. The second was a secretary's, announcing that messages could be left. Alvy Landy, he had thought, Alvy Landy might have a copy of the movie. Alvy Landy would help him find Sophie, he decided, hoping he wasn't grasping at the wind.

An hour later, he had crawled into the bed, hoping that Landy would find Sophie while he slept, knowing he'd have to rely on Madden for Rosen's cassette, or on Darnaby for the studio's, to see the second half of the movie. Alvy had neither part of it.

He checked his watch. It was just past noon. Four hours had passed since he saw Part One. He had been in the city less than a hundred hours. His dream, he knew, would have to be in Part Two, where Broder must have told the secrets that all three had vowed would never be told.

Though he had eaten a sandwich in Alvy's kitchen before going to sleep, his stomach was rumbling. He stood up, shocked by his dizziness, and lurched to the bathroom, his morning cough turning into dry heaves that made his ribs ache. A hot shower helped. Through a porthole-like window he looked out onto the beach as he washed, watching the volleyball players and the skaters. A homeless person—it was impossible to tell if it was a man or a woman—was walking slowly down the Strand, pushing a shopping cart. He thought of Rosen, as the shower stung his back. When he felt strong enough, he slowly turned the water to cold, until finally his breathing became short and his blood was rushing.

Flushed, he dried off and pulled the towel around his waist, heading through the bedroom and down the stairs to the main floor of the house, where he remembered Alvy had thrown his clothes into a washer built into the kitchen cabinets.

The living room was a sprawl of bamboo furniture and pillows on the floor. Sliding doors opened onto a miniature wooden-walled yard. A small dining room table was set for three. He went into the kitchen and was about to open the washing machine, when a woman's voice from behind startled him.

"You finally woke up," she said.

He spun, fear in his eyes. His thoughts went to the gun, which he had stored in the bag sitting upstairs in the bedroom Alvy had provided. Looking at her made him feel foolish and old.

She was dressed in a bikini bottom and an unbuttoned blouse. He had to fight his eyes off her breasts. She smiled and tied the blouse tails into a tight bra. "I didn't mean to surprise you," she said. "I'm Pam, Alvy's friend? Maybe you remember me?" she asked, unsure.

"Of course," he said. "My clothes," he added, embarrassed. "Alvy put them in the washer."

"*And* he ironed your shirts," she said cheerfully, pointing to a chair in the corner as she came into the kitchen. His trousers were folded neatly, and the shirts wer piled on top.

Cohen hiked the towel and went to the clothes, stepping into the corridor out of her view, to pull on a pair of trousers and a shirt. "He'd never do that for me," she called out to him. "He really thinks you're something special, you know? It's like he's your fan."

"Where is he?" Cohen asked, as he returned to the main room.

"On a supply run," she said, absentmindedly gazing at him.

"Excuse me?' he asked.

"I was just wondering," she said dreamily, "if Alvy is going to look like you when he gets to your age. Course, the real question is whether I'm going to still be with him by the time he gets as old as you." She made a sudden dancer's pirouette across three meters of open living room, ending the move with a slow raising and lowering of her left leg. She faced him, and seeing something cross his face, she added brightly, "I don't mean you're decrepit or something," she said. It was honestly apologetic. "In fact"— she raised her leg again and watched her foot rap the air three times—"Alvy and me watched that tourist's tape over and over again. You were amazing."

Cohen couldn't tell if she was playing with herself or him. But he was enjoying her show-and-tell. "He thinks you're so cool," she was saying, as she bent backward into a handstand to walk upside down across the room to him. "But hey," she said, jumping to her feet. "I'm doing all the talking. You're the one with the questions."

"That's all right," he said. But before he could ask her anything about Sophie, the front door slammed. "Avram!" Alvy Landy was calling out as he entered. "Wake up!"

"We're in here," Pam shouted back. But she kept her quizzical eyes on Cohen.

Alvy came in carrying two large brown paper shopping bags. But there was no joy on his face. He dropped the bags on the counter and looked wild-eyed at Cohen. "Have you heard?" he asked. "Goldie Stein's dead."

"What are you talking about?" Pam asked. "We saw her just last night."

"It's true," Alvy said. He hurried to the television set. "I heard it on the car radio just now. They're calling it murder." He pressed angrily at the buttons of the remote-control unit, searching for a news station, stopping at the first announcer. He turned up the sound. She was talking about Wall Street. He cursed.

"Here, give me that," Pam said, reaching out for the remote-control device. Alvy handed it to her without question—indeed, as if it were why she was there—and went to a wicker chair while she started scanning the channels.

Cohen watched the back of Alvy's head as well as the television, wondering if the actor was clever enough to have filled in the missing pieces that Cohen had carefully left out of his story when he arrived.

He didn't have to wait long. Alvy turned slowly in his chair. "You knew," he said to Cohen. "You knew when you called me this morning," he said, standing up. Pam turned away from the screen.

Cohen nodded. "Did you locate Sophie?" he asked Alvy.

"Did you do it?" the actor whispered.

Cohen shook his head. "I discovered the body."

Alvy considered the information, while Pam merely stared at Cohen.

"How?" Alvy finally asked. "The radio says there were signs of violence."

Cohen thought of the sheets on Goldie's bed. They had been still damp from sweat, and for a moment he confused the salty ocean smell at the beach house with his memory of the musky smell in the bungalow bedroom.

"How'd he do it?" Alvy asked. He didn't notice Cohen's wince at Alvy's assumption that a man had murdered Goldie. "A gun?

Strangled? How? A rope? A cord?" A glint appeared in Alvy's eye. "Bare-handed?"

"Alvy!" Pam moaned, burying her head in the sofa cushions.

Cohen smirked at Alvy. "With a pillow," he said, understanding all too well the boy's curiosity, frightened by his recognition of himself in it.

"A pillow," Alvy said to himself, trying out the idea. "Like smothered?"

Cohen nodded. "Did you find Sophie?"

"Yeah. Just like you predicted. She's with Davey Burns. At least she was a couple of hours ago." Alvy flopped into an armchair facing Cohen, staring intensely at the detective. "You think it's all connected to Max's death?" he finally asked.

"Do *you* see a connection?" Cohen asked.

Pam interrupted. "Sophie left the club with Goldie," she said, almost to herself. "Remember?" she asked Alvy, louder. "You found her and brought her to Goldie, and then I wanted to dance, and—"

"Pam, will you please be quiet for a minute," Alvy snapped at her. But he expropriated her thought. "They were gone. That's right," he said, unable to conceal his excitement. "*That's* why you're looking for her," he said. "You think *she* killed Goldie. But why? They got it on together. Why would Sophie kill her?"

"I wish you'd woken me when you found her." Cohen sighed, going to a barstool at the kitchen counter.

Alvy looked grimly at Pam. "I tried to wake you," she confessed. "You were really out of it."

She was trying to place some of the blame on Cohen. But he had other worries.

"I was talking?" Cohen asked.

"I thought it was German," Pam said. "But Alvy said it was Jewish."

"Hebrew," Alvy snapped at her, and then, glancing once at Cohen, he added, "And not Jewish—Yiddish."

Cohen had not been lying when he said he was uncomfortable sleeping in a room with a stranger. He knew he spoke aloud sometimes in dreams. His voice sometimes woke him. But nobody else knew it. Until this week. Except Ahuva, of course. But she never asked. Sometimes she, too, woke up to save herself from a nightmare.

Cohen put his hand down carefully on the kitchen counter, trying to refocus. "Does Sophie know I'm with you?" he asked.

"No, of course not. You said not to tell her," Alvy said. "I just called Davey. Told him I had a good time last night, said I wanted to try out my new car on a drive up north, just like you suggested, maybe stop by his place later on. That's when I asked him if Sophie was there. He wanted to know why I wanted to know."

"And you said?" Cohen prompted the actor.

Alvy grinned. "That if Sophie was around, I'd bring Pam. Davey doesn't like it if you bring someone over and he doesn't have someone too. You know what I mean?"

"He's a pig," Pam interrupted. "And she's a freak," she added bitterly, making Cohen glance at her.

"Don't pay any attention to her," Alvy said. "She's never liked Sophie. Anyway, they're gonna be there all day. Davey said she wanted to do some surfing this afternoon. She's amazing on a board."

"See what I mean?" Pam complained. "This guy dies, and, like, he was her rescuer, right? That's the story, right? So now you'd think she was celebrating or something. Partying, surfing. You know what I mean?" She was pleading with Cohen to understand.

"I know exactly what you mean," Cohen said quietly.

"I think it's kind of cool the way she's handling it," Alvy said, ever enthusiastic to pursue another idea. "Like showing life goes on—the real *nekama*," he added, with a proud smile at Cohen, "the one you tried to tell the brothers about."

"It was different then," said Pam. "Avram made a breakthrough to a different plane. She's not doing that at all. If you ask me, she's flaunting it."

They were like two children competing for their teacher's praise at their understanding of the lesson. But unlike a schoolteacher, Cohen didn't have any answers. "Did Davey say anything about Goldie?" he asked.

Alvy shook his head. "I told you, I only heard about it on the radio just now."

"Nothing about Sophie leaving with Goldie last night?" Cohen demanded.

Alvy studied Cohen's face for a second, trying to understand the question. "Oh, I see what you mean," he finally said. "No, he's cool. Someone wants to go both ways, that's their business. Isn't that right, Pam? He didn't even mention it."

Cohen remembered a different expression on Davey's face the night before. He rubbed at his brow, thinking. "So they are there?" he asked. "You are sure?"

"Yup," Alvy said, pushing himself up from the chair and going to the counter. He reached for his car keys. "You ready?"

"Alvy, are you sure you should be getting involved in this?" Pam said. "I mean, we're talking about Davey Bee. If he thinks that you're fucking around with him, you know what he can do. And you know he's crazy about her. If he thinks she's in trouble, he'll try to protect her."

Alvy looked back at Cohen, his expression changing from an attempt to share some secret fearless macho code to the expectation of reassurance.

But Cohen disappointed the actor. "There's no need for you to get involved," he told Alvy.

"All you want to do is talk with her, right?" Alvy asked. "What could be such a problem about that?"

"It's Davey Bee," Pam protested again.

"You know," Alvy said, ignoring the girl, "there's this great part for a rookie detective. There's talk about getting Redford as the old-timer who teaches me the ropes. But I got someone better," he said to Pam, who had turned her back on both of them and was angrily tapping one foot. "You," he added, pointing at Cohen.

Cohen had negotiated with politicians and rabbis, with angry demonstrators and coolheaded crooks. But he had never dealt with a twenty-year-old Oscar candidate.

"I'll drive you," Alvy suggested.

"Just give me the directions," Cohen insisted.

"I don't go, you don't get the address," Alvy shot back. "Besides, you'll never find it. The people who live on that street took down the signposts a long time ago to prevent people from doing just what you want to do—dropping in unannounced. You want, I'll take you. You don't want, well, it's your decision," and with that, Alvy started for the door to the yard.

Whether he was acting or not was irrelevant, Cohen realized. "You can drive me," he said. "But you stay outside."

"I come in."

"But silent. Not a word."

"Deal," Alvy said, putting out his hand.

"If he goes, I go," Pam interjected, making Alvy freeze and Cohen turn to her. She stared at Cohen defiantly, as if she knew he was thinking that if he had a choice, he'd much rather use her than the actor as a guide. Alvy's eyes also conveyed anxious anticipation of Cohen's decision.

"We'll discuss it over dinner," Cohen finally said.

· · ·

Alvy drove slowly along the street. "That's the house," he said, pointing to a high stucco wall. Cohen saw the glint of broken glass embedded in the top. The car glided past a thick wooden door set into the wall. "And that's Sophie's car." Alvy nodded toward a yellow vintage Mustang parked in front of the house. "So? How do we do it? Scale the wall? We can get in from the beach, if you can handle the alarms."

Pam snorted. "We can just ring the bell," she said from the back seat. Cohen smiled.

The basketball player from the nightclub opened the door. He was wearing a three-piece suit. Cohen noticed the jacket's tailored camouflage of a shoulder holster. The bodyguard blinked, gazed quickly at Alvy and Pam, and looked at Cohen with curiosity.

"Davey invited us," Alvy said to the giant, and stepped forward.

But the bodyguard did not move out of the doorframe.

"It's all right," Alvy said, smiling embarrassed at Cohen. "Davey invited us."

The bodyguard finally raised a finger, silently telling them to wait. Backing away, he started to close the door on them. "We'll wait inside," Cohen said, stepping forward. Alvy and Pam shuffled forward too.

The big man stared down at them impassively, not forcing the door shut but not giving up. Cohen sighed but didn't back down. His foot was in the door. The gun was in his waistband. His eyes showed all the origins of their weariness.

In his peripheral vision, he saw just beyond the bodyguard a wooden flight of stairs, leading up to the flat roof of the two-story building. Davey Burns was standing on the roof, peering down the stairwell at the tableau. He was wearing an open gray robe that stopped at midthigh. Cohen had the feeling that Davey was demonstratively naked under the short toga.

"Davey, I'm too old for games," Cohen grumbled, not taking his eyes off the bodyguard.

"This isn't a game," Davey said. But he tied the belt of his robe.

"I know," Cohen said, slowly putting his hand behind his back. The bodyguard tensed.

"I'm saving you the trouble," Cohen said, slowly bringing out the gun, dangling it on his forefinger. He glanced at Alvy, who wasn't able to hide his disappointment. Pam raised an eyebrow, but Cohen mouthed "Don't worry" behind the bodyguard's back.

"Let 'em up, Henry," Burns said from the roof, and stepped out of view.

Henry held out his hand, smiling broadly at Cohen, who deposited the gun in the guard's broad hand. "Don't lose it," Cohen mumbled as he walked past Henry. "I want it back on my way out." Alvy snorted a laugh behind him, as Cohen started up the stairs.

Burns was sitting on the edge of a chaise, his back to them. He was tapping at the keyboard of a laptop computer, a cellular phone propped on his shoulder to his ear, as he recited four-digit numbers in tens. "Forty-seven twenty-three, ninety-two eighty-six, nineteen twenty-nine," he said, typing out each number with a quick hand on the keypad. "That it?" he asked. "Okay. Thanks." He let the phone slip to his lap, but instead of turning to them, he continued tapping at the keys on the computer, saying, "Sit down, you guys. I'll be right with you." He didn't take his eyes off the computer screen but pointed toward the deck chairs behind him.

Alvy took one, and Pam another. From the roof, across the

broad field of sand, Cohen could see a raven-haired woman in a white bathing suit standing in shallow surf, her back to the house, a surfboard in her hands. He went to the railing, past Davey. The woman flopped onto the board and started paddling her way past the breaking waves.

"She's been out there all day," Davey said to Cohen's back. "You know, if she had grown up here, 'stead of that dump, she could have been a great surfer. A champion. Amazing body on that girl. A real athlete."

Cohen turned to face him. Davey was leaning back in the chaise. "Something to drink?" he offered, pointing to a tequila bottle. "No, wait—I'm told you prefer grape. Some cognac?" Davey's grin mocked him.

Cohen shook his head, engaged in watching Sophie paddle out to just beyond the point where the waves rolled into surf. She was sitting on the board, looking over her shoulder toward the ocean. As far as he could tell, she hadn't seen him yet. A swell lifted her on the board, and then she dropped momentarily out of sight before rising on the next wave.

Suddenly she lay down on the board and started paddling with her hands toward the beach. A wave Cohen had not noticed came from behind her, lifting her in the same rhythm that she used to rise onto her feet. The wave was three times her height, and she rode it with élan, cutting across its steep surface as it built into a deep turquoise wall topped by a crown of froth. It curled over onto itself, and she disappeared in the tube.

Cohen clenched the railing. "See what I mean?" Davey said. He had taken up a position beside Cohen. "She only learned how to do that this summer. A real talent," Burns added.

Sophie's board flew into the air, and Cohen tensed. "Don't worry," Burns insisted. "She knows what she's doing. See?" He pointed. The girl was standing in the waist-high foam of the surf.

She ran strongly through the water to the board, grabbed it up, and immediately began paddling back out to sea.

She seems possessed, Cohen thought.

"What did she do? Go back to the club after Goldie?" Cohen asked. "Make you her alibi?"

"Who said she was at Goldie's?" Davey shot back. "What the hell makes you so sure?"

"They left the club together last night," said Cohen.

"So?" Davey said, "What does that prove? They're friends."

"Goldie's dead," Cohen said. "Sophie was the last person seen with her."

"That doesn't mean shit," Davey protested angrily. But before Cohen could respond, the mobster changed his tone. "Listen, I understand. Your friend does himself in. We all know why, right? And you're a stranger here. A little confused. Look, she's not going anywhere. Sit down; we can talk about this. Come on," he said, putting as much friendliness as he could muster into his voice. He put his hand on Cohen's shoulder. Cohen twitched it off. "Chill out, man," Burns said. "Just chill out." He pushed himself off the railing and went back to his chaise.

Cohen sighed heavily. Sophie was standing in the water, looking toward the house. He realized that if he could recognize her from the distance, she could recognize him. Burns was right, he knew. She had no place to hide from him on the beach. Nonetheless, he stepped back into the center of the porch, out of her view, thinking of it as a precaution, like the gloves he wore in Goldie's apartment while he searched. Burns was on his chaise. Henry stood in the background. Alvy and Pam remained silent, both studying Cohen.

"I have to talk with her about Broder," he said softly.

"You want to frame her for Goldie's murder, that's what you want," Burns charged angrily. Then he smiled. "Cuz right now, you're the cops' prime suspect. Don't give me that look. I got my sources. They want to question you about Goldie. I could call 'em right now and tell 'em you're here. Fuck." He chuckled. "I bet I could make a deal. I give 'em you, they lay off something they've been bothering me about."

"You're wrong, Davey. All I want to know is the truth," Cohen said.

"The truth? What the fuck does the truth matter in this? Someone iced Goldie Stein. A lot of people might have wanted to do that. Sophie was seen with her last night, so everyone is saying she's responsible. Well, she isn't. You got that?" he asserted. "She isn't," he repeated, as if trying to convince himself as well as Cohen. "Not my Sophie."

"Maybe," Cohen said softly. He stepped back toward the railing, looking for her. The sun was sitting on the water at the horizon. She was paddling back out for another wave, so far away now that he could recognize her only by her long black hair and the white suit she was wearing. "But what if she isn't your Sophie?" Cohen suggested.

Burns looked confused. "Of course she's mine."

"But what if she isn't who she says she is?"

"What the fuck are you talking about?" Burns sat up on the chaise, leaning forward.

"You mean she's not really Bernard's daughter?" Pam asked, astonished.

"Max wasn't sure," Cohen said.

"He never said anything to me," Alvy said.

"He wasn't sure," Cohen repeated.

"He introduced me to her, for crissake," Burns complained. "He said she's the daughter of an old friend. One of *your* old friends, as a matter of fact. What the hell are you talking about, she's not Sophie?"

"She hasn't exactly been in mourning," Cohen pointed out.

Pam nodded vigorously. "What did I tell you?" she said to Alvy, who hissed at her to shut up.

"She was supposed to have been so adoring of him," Cohen went on. "Nightclubs, surfing? This is not mourning." He was unable any longer to hide his disgust.

"She's with her friends," Burns protested. "A person you love dies, you want to be with other people you love."

"Max's will raises some doubts about her identity," Cohen said.

"Which raises some doubts about who she really loves," Pam said, looking triumphantly at Alvy. He hissed at her again and kept his eyes on Davey Bee.

But Burns was staring at Cohen.

"I'm just trying to find out the truth," Cohen said.

"That's crazy," Burns finally said, smiling as if it was all a joke. "If you believe that, you're as crazy as Max. Can you believe this?" he said, grinning at Henry the bodyguard. Henry smiled back obediently. "Next thing, you'll be blaming her for Max," Burns said sardonically, "and that's bullshit too."

"I just have to talk with her," Cohen said, not yet ready to admit the possibility that she might be considered a suspect in Broder's death.

"If she's as innocent as you make her out to be," Pam said to the mobster, "why is she running away from Avram?"

"Yeah, Davey? How come?" Alvy asked, his curiosity breaking through the timidity.

"What the fuck are *they* doing here?" Burns asked Cohen angrily, pointing to the actor and his girlfriend.

"Just being friendly. That's all. You know, helping me out," Cohen said. "The way I thought you were going to help me out," he added, making certain that Burns heard the disappointment in his voice.

"I told you what I know!" Burns insisted. "The guy was going crazy. She needed an alternative. Someone she could trust. She came to me. She trusts me."

The memory of Sophie's breathy "Trust no one" rushed through Cohen's mind. He didn't know whether to laugh or cry. He looked out to the surf. The sun was halfway gone, a red dome sitting on the horizon. Her silhouette seemed drawn on its darkening surface as she sat on her board beyond the surf, waiting for a good wave. "Isn't it getting dark for her to still be out there?" Cohen asked, looking up at the purpling sky. To the east, a sliver of moon appeared above the steep hills.

"You see other surfers?" Burns asked from the chaise. Pam stood up to gaze out to the ocean. Alvy pulled at her to sit down.

Cohen looked to his right and left. There were other surfers on the beach, though far fewer than there had been only a few minutes before. Beyond the swells, a few pleasure boats roamed.

"Yes."

"She's fine," said Burns, satisfied.

"You still haven't answered his question," Pam demanded. "What does she have to hide?"

"Alvy, shut the bitch up," Burns snapped angrily.

"Pam?" Alvy whined slightly.

"Avram?" she called, looking for Cohen's defense.

But he was watching Sophie paddle toward a large wave that was rising fast and high. Just as she reached it, she turned so the wave lifted her and the board high above the horizon. For a long moment, her full body was silhouetted across the sun, and then she began the run down the wall of water. He gripped the railing. It was a huge wave, the largest he had seen so far, easily four or five times her height.

"Avram?" Pam repeated, now merely trying to get his attention.

Cohen was hypnotized by the wave and Sophie's dance on the board, which took her up to the highest level of the curling peak.

He held his breath as she began a long descent across the face of the wave, disappearing into the tube. His eyes traveled across her invisible path, watching for the surfboard's leap that would carry her long body onto the foam of the crashing surf. Burns must have sensed his tension, for he joined Cohen again at the railing, Alvy and Pam in tow.

"Where is she?" Alvy asked.

"She should have come out right about there," Cohen said, pointing southwest of the house.

"I don't see her," Burns said.

"Neither do I," said Pam.

The sun was almost gone. The sky was going quickly from blue to purple. The surf from the wave she had caught was long gone. New waves kept coming in. No dark-haired nymph appeared magically from the white foam of water.

"Henry?" Burns called out. The tall black man joined them at the railing, passing a pair of binoculars to Burns.

Cohen snorted. "I'm going down there," he said.

The others followed as he ran clumsily across the sand. They spread out across the waterline.

Burns was the first to start shouting. "Sophie? Sophie?" he called out from Cohen's left. To Cohen's right, Alvy and Pam took up the chant.

Henry broke the rhythm. "Her board," he shouted, making sure he kept his shoes dry as he danced where the water kissed the sand.

The pale-yellow board was floating on the white foam of the surf. Cohen ran into the water as if it would cleanse him of all the guilt for all the deaths he had brought to Los Angeles.

· · ·

Jeeps sprayed the water with klieg lights, and a helicopter floated noisily overhead, its projector lamps sweeping the beach. Figures darted back and forth through bright spots of light and then disappeared into the darkness.

Davey raved and ranted, running back and forth between the beach and his house, demanding more searchers, screaming bloody murder when the FBI agents who kept his house under surveillance used the opportunity for a look around it.

Alvy's lawyer and his agent showed up to extricate the actor and his girlfriend. He smiled weakly at Cohen as they escorted him out. For what seemed to Cohen the hundredth time since they had found the surfboard, Pam apologized to him for calling the German girl "a freak."

Cohen used Madden's name, waiting half an hour on the roof, under a bored deputy sheriff's supervision, until the Beverly Hills detective appeared.

Only when they were out on the street, standing alongside Sophie's Mustang, did Cohen begin.

Madden listened patiently, almost as if he was humoring Cohen. But when Cohen reached his reasons to suspect Sophie's identity, Madden lost his temper.

"What the fuck's that supposed to mean?" he demanded.

They were standing beside Sophie's car. The hot night air under the streetlamps made Madden's sweaty face gleam as if it had been oiled. Cohen's trousers were still rudely damp, gritty with sand.

"What do you know about her?" Cohen asked.

"What's-her-name? Fine? The lawyer? She said she was the daughter of some long-lost friend of Broder's."

"And mine," Cohen added.

"Right," Madden apologized. "So?"

"The will raises doubts. About her identity," Cohen said. "Fine checked her out and came up with nothing, but Broder left the question in his will."

"Why didn't she tell me anything about that?" Madden demanded.

"She said Broder told her it was a joke."

"Some joke," Madden moaned. "I'd hate to hear the punch line."

"The punch line?" Cohen was unfamiliar with the term.

"You know, the point of the joke."

"He wanted me to prove he still had power over me," Cohen said softly. "He wanted me to do something for him."

"Some friend," Madden said. "What did he want you to do?"

"Prove her identity," Cohen confessed.

"Jeezus," Madden moaned again. "Why didn't you tell me this before?" he asked.

"I wasn't sure," Cohen said. "I didn't want to make allegations I couldn't prove."

"You can prove it now?"

"I don't know. Maybe. I need your help."

"Shit," Madden said.

"Interpol," Cohen said. "They should contact the Germans, look into the Stasi files, find out what they have about Bernard, his family."

"Why didn't Phyllis Fine take care of this when she checked her out?" Madden demanded.

Cohen scowled. "History," he said.

"What the fuck is that supposed to mean?"

"The wall," Cohen said.

"What?" asked Madden, still not understanding.

"The girl came when there were still two Germanys. The lawyer had nothing from East Germany. No access to such files. But they are available now."

"Do you have anything to go on? A passport?"

Cohen nodded. "I didn't find anything in Broder's house, but while I waited for the police to arrive, Davey showed me her things. There's an old East German passport." He recited the number from memory to Madden.

"You still haven't told me what you were doing here," Madden said, looking up from his notebook, where he had penned the number Cohen recited.

"Broder was friends with Davey. Davey had eyes for Sophie. I had to talk with him, especially after last night." He took a breath before going on. "Sophie was the last person with Goldie last night."

"Fuck. Fuck, fuck, fuck." Madden slammed the hood of the car with his fist. "You knew that. Last night you knew that," he guessed. "You didn't tell me."

"You haven't seemed very interested in anything I have told you," Cohen shot back, but then added an apology. "I didn't want to make any allegations until I was certain."

"So what makes you so sure now?"

"I think Goldie knew about my suspicions," Cohen confessed. "It was my fault. I let it slip," he added.

Madden exhaled a thick cloud of smoke over Cohen's head. "If she was trying to hide something, the last person she'd want to know would be Goldie," Madden admitted.

"Exactly," Cohen said, relieved Madden was beginning to understand.

"I got another problem for you," Madden said. "Your buddy from the pier—what was his name?"

"Rosen. Jacques Rosen," Cohen said.

"Yeah. Rosen. I got some bad news for you." He took another puff on the cigar. "No videocassette. No such thing. Not in what they found."

The news stunned Cohen. "Someone took it," he muttered. "Someone on the pier. I'm sure of it."

"Sure. And the million bucks in cash he was hiding too," Madden said sarcastically.

"I want to see what he had in the cart," Cohen insisted. "He was reaching for something to give me when he was shot. There must be something there."

"Well, I figured you'd say that," said Madden. He pulled a folded piece of paper out of his inside jacket pocket and handed it to Cohen. It was in handwriting, and in the bad light of the streetlamps, difficult for Cohen to read.

"Gimme that," Madden said, grabbing back the list. "I copied everything down." He read aloud in a monotonous tone. There were two shirts, one pair of trousers, three varying lengths of copper tubing, a battery-run radio, two plastic containers of mineral water, a dozen cans of tuna fish, three irregular-shaped sheets of plastic, two blankets, six pencils, and two dozen glass returnable bottles.

Cohen shook his head in disbelief. He had expected a videocassette. But lacking a tape, he would have expected something else. A letter. A document. Something Broder needed to hide, knowing that only Cohen would seek it out and only Cohen would understand its meaning. There was no other explanation.

Madden read the expression on his face. "I guess you really were counting on finding something," he said. "Sorry."

Cohen answered with a humorless smile. He checked his watch. "It's going to be morning soon in Germany. Interpol could make their request now, and we could have an answer as soon as tomorrow night."

Only after Cohen said "Please" did Madden look up from the tip of his cigar, which he had been blowing softly to make the ember burn bright beneath the long ash. "Thanks," Madden said.

"I'm sorry," Cohen added. It was strained, but sincere, and made Madden's thin lips rise into a slight smile that said the apology was accepted, though it wasn't expected.

It happened in the hotel room's shower, and Cohen knew he was lucky for that. He had just begun lowering the hot-water level, the water stinging his face turning lukewarm, when the pressure began.

It squeezed down on his chest. His lungs refused to expand with air. He concentrated, forcing himself not to panic. He watched his left hand's grasp on the handle loosen. The pressure evened out, a constant weight. Like a wire charged with hot electricity, a sharp pain pierced the length of his right arm as he tried to close his grip on the hot-water handle. The pain rode across his shoulder, disappearing in the pressure on his chest.

He focused on the water drumming at his scalp, and while he watched the second hand of his watch move slowly up from the six to the twelve, he concentrated on not falling. The pressure began to ease. Testily, he tried closing his hand. The hot wire was gone. He took a short breath and knew the worst was over.

Slowly he turned, pushed the shower curtain aside, and stepped out. He didn't even try to dry off. He went to the bed. Car sounds from the street wafted in with the heat through the open window. But he was freezing cold.

He lay down, pulling weakly at the bedspread until it covered his torso, and then closed his eyes, sleep sweeping over him like a rising tide's surf onto dry sand. His last thoughts were of Ahuva, but he expected dreams about the doctors at Hadassah Hospital, shaking their heads at his cigarettes as they watched him recuperate from the wound in his belly.

Instead, he woke to sunlight flooding the room. For a moment he was afraid to move, lest he discover the pressure was still on his chest, the pain was still in his lungs, the hot electrical wire was yet loose in his arm. He realized he had slept without dreams, without nightmares shaking him awake.

He was still wrapped mummylike in the spread, hands across his chest. Taking a breath, he forced it to go deeper, testing the limits of his lungs until he had the familiar bronchial morning cough he knew so well after long nights of too many cigarettes. He rolled over to free himself of the bedspread and sat up, checking the time. He had slept almost twelve hours. The bedding smelled of a summer fever; sweat had dried itchy in his armpits. He knew what Ahuva and the doctors would say. But it was his life. And he still had it.

Half an hour later, he was sipping room-service coffee, with a splash of cognac from his flask, on a balcony with a view that went far beyond the courtyard palms of the hotel. Below, there was the splashing of a lone midday swimmer. But he looked across the compound at the sprawling city. The red tiles of some of the rooftops had a strange familiarity, but instead of limestone, whether soot-covered or gleaming white, here the buildings were wood and stucco, or steel and concrete. The foliage was the same as in Tel Aviv too, he noticed: jacaranda, ficus, and cultivated cactus. He couldn't smell the ocean, but he could sense its presence, larger than anything he had ever felt, making him feel his loneliness even more deeply.

Newspapers were spread out across the room, CNN was playing on the television. He still knew far more than the press about what had been happening.

"We're a different nation," he had said in the car after a long stretch of silence while Madden drove north back to Alvy's house.

"What? Jews?" Madden asked, startled by the comment in the night.

"Policemen," Cohen said, thinking of Sasson and Halil, the Jewish-Arab team number 72. "That's why I thought of you when they let me use the phone at Davey's."

"You were fucking lucky. You're lucky those guys don't work Hollywood. If they did, they would have recognized you. And get a load of this: You know why the feds missed you at the Dance Factory? A car accident. Talk about luck," Madden mused. "A guy shows up half an hour late because of a drunk driver. Bam, you're in and out. Talk about luck," he repeated.

"I don't want you to get in trouble, Mike," Cohen tried. "I appreciate your help."

"Fuck appreciation. Just stay out of trouble," Madden had said. But if anything, Cohen could see only trouble ahead. He knew that as far as Madden was concerned, Cohen's luck was the "luck of the loony." Cohen had heard the American mutter it to himself under his breath as he drove, while Cohen dozed off and on during the highway drive.

At Alvy's, Pam had wordlessly passed Cohen's canvas bag to him at the door. One of Alvy's lawyers stared glumly from the hallway behind her. Alvy had gone into shock on the beach at Burns's house, and Cohen hoped the actor's handlers were helping the boy. He decided Pam could take care of herself.

He had told Madden that he'd be going back to Broder's house. But it had been a lie, told to protect everyone. He had come to California expecting Broder's guidance, but all he had as a guide was the little yellow notebook, its names, phrases, and numbers all carefully condensed abstractions of the anecdotes that added up to a private poetry only he could understand as he read. It was a personal matter he was on, not a case for prosecution. Madden thought he was crazy. Cohen knew he wasn't. He looked through the notebook, searching for a thread to pull, something that would unravel all the knots.

When he came to Barbara Darnaby's card,, he reached for the phone. A haughty secretary put him through right away. "I'm so glad you got my message," Darnaby began.

"What message," he asked.

She sighed. "I"ve been leaving you messages for two days on Max's machine. I'm afraid there's been a terrible balls-up. About seeing the movie."

"I've already seen the first part," he said, knowing it would surprise her. "The second part? In the field?" he asked, before she could ask her question. "I'd like to see it, and please, also, is there a third section?"

There was a long silence.

"Miss Darnaby?" he asked, wondering if there was a problem on the line.

"He made a copy," she said to herself, adding, "that cheeky bastard," in the same astonished whisper. Then, as if remembering Cohen was on the line, she demanded, "Where did you get it?"

"It doesn't matter. I have some questions, and—"

"It certainly does matter," she complained, properly officious. "The film is the property of Epica Studios. Please do try to understand," she pleaded, and he scowled at the phone in his hand, at one more Hollywood person speaking to him as if he were an idiot. "If there's a bootleg copy of the film, it could be a serious violation of his contract with Epica. There could be criminal as well as civil complaints."

Cohen almost laughed. He could feel his fury building up like one of the waves Sophie had been riding, and he fought to restrain it. "Yes. Contracts are important," he finally murmured. "But so are lives. People are dying. I want to know why. I think it has to do with this movie."

"Well, the last thing you want to do is tell people that," she exclaimed. "That is, if you want the movie shown," she added as an afterthought. "Besides, what could Goldie Stein's death possibly have to do with the movie? From what I've heard, she went looking for one too many Ms. Goodbars."

Cohen could only guess at what she meant, and he still had other questions he wanted answered before his temper took over and he lost all access to her. "I understand there is a list of people who have seen the movie," he said carefully.

"Yes," she said hesitantly.

"I need to see that list," Cohen insisted.

"And I need to get legal approval. Frankly, the existence of a bootleg is not going to make it any easier."

There was a silence while she waited for him to answer. He surprised her with his next question.

"Tell me about Sophie Levine."

"Sophie? What does Sophie have to do with this?" she asked.

There was something in her tone that made Cohen realize something, and he prompted her with the idea. "You don't like her," he guessed. "In fact, none of the women I've met here seemed to like her very much," he baited her.

"I'm not surprised," she said. "She was too . . . too—I don't know—easy. Accommodating. Yes, that's right, accommodating. She never complained. She did everything for him. Whatever he wanted. I don't know if you know this, commander, but there was something monstrous about your friend." She paused. "Especially when it came to women." Now she was fishing for his response. Cohen's silence made her continue. "He was charming and brilliant, and maybe even a genius. And he played the rescuing knight for his Sophie. But he made her pay for it."

"I thought . . ."

"I know, I know. You thought I slept with him. I know everybody's saying that. But it's not true. I worked for him. That's all. Oh, he wanted me. He wanted every woman who came into his life. He got a lot of them too. But not me. Never. Especially after I saw what he did to her. And she accepted it. When she came to him, he should have treated her like a daughter, like a niece. She was Bernard Levine's child. And we both know what that meant to Max."

"Why did you go over to Blakely?" he asked. "Max must have felt betrayed."

"That's not true. Not at all," she protested. "I know that's what Goldie was saying, but it's not true."

"Please, you have to explain this to me," Cohen asked.

"It's really very simple. I worked for Max. Officially I was an associate producer. Actually I handled all the production administration. Now I do the same thing for Andy Blakely, except instead of one movie, I'm overseeing twelve. Andy simply offered me a better deal," she said.

"The week before Max Broder died?" Cohen asked.

"It was *Max* who decided that *The Survivor's Secrets* was his last movie. He didn't have any more work for me, even if it was going to be distributed. I came a long way to be in this industry. My job with Max was over. That's all. It had nothing to do with the movie, or whether Max was obsessed or not." She plunged on, before he could ask the question. "I know about all the talk, how people are saying that I left Max and went to work for Andy, as if it had anything to do with their dispute. It didn't. Max and I made our peace before I left. He wasn't happy about it, but he accepted it. Even *he* knew that it was a clever move for me," she said, adding, "I'm sure you will find something about it in the computer."

Cohen listened carefully, as much to the tone as to the content. She was persuasive, a professional talker. Long before the movie,

Der Bruder had been obsessive about loyalty. Cohen was ready to believe her explanation of the move from Broder to Blakely. He wasn't prepared to forgive her abandonment of Broder at a time of crisis.

"I need to see the second part of his movie," Cohen said.

"This friend? Didn't he have the second part?" she asked, her curiosity tinged with worry.

"No," he admitted.

"I can't make any promises," she said. "But I'll see what I can do. I do understand why it's important to you. I will have a word with the legal department. Maybe I can convince them it would be all right. A private screening. But they're going to be very upset about that bootlegged copy."

"Please," he asked. "Talk with Andrew Blakely about it."

"I assure you, commander, that I keep him informed. But I must also tell you that this whole matter of Max's movie is really a very minor concern of Andy's. He deals with the larger picture of the studio, you see."

"I understand," Cohen said. But his instinct told him Blakely had more than a passing interest in the film.

"Ring me this evening," she said. "I promise I'll have an answer for you about seeing the second half. Now I really—"

"One last question," he breathed urgently into the phone. "When exactly did Sophie come to Los Angeles?"

"When did she come to Los Angeles? Or when did Max meet her?" Darnaby asked.

"When did *you* first meet her?"

"I'll tell you exactly when. We were in Naples, for the scenes where you—I mean where young Avram leaves the *nokmim,*" she said, using the Hebrew word.

But while she continued with the anecdote of Broder's arrival with the mysterious German girl at the hotel in Naples, he damned himself for not forcing himself to read the treatment all the way through when he had it in his hands, as if he were back in his office, alone at night, reading through an entire file of a three-year investigation. And what happened to Broder's self-discipline? he wondered, as he accused himself of losing his own.

"There's no doubt about it. She was something special," Darnaby said about Sophie. "Max asked for something, and she was there with it, or found out quick enough who could get it. And she never got in the way, I have to give her credit for that. You know what someone called her? 'His custom-made refugee,' and they were right. She was one of the DDR's well-fed youths. She certainly knew a good thing when she saw it. Here she is, Bernard Levine's daughter, and Max walks into her life. At that festival."

"I'm told she played an athlete in a movie."

"She gave it all up for him," Darnaby said. "He could have opened all the doors for her, but she preferred to take care of him."

"When were you in Naples?" he asked.

"Nineteen eighty-nine," she said.

"When"—he sighed—"in eighty-nine?"

"Autumn," Darnaby said. "Now really, I have to run."

"The exact date, Miss Darnaby," he asked, "if you would be so kind."

"If you must know, it was October first, nineteen eighty-nine," she said. "Is it so important?" she asked. "Commander?"

But Cohen was staring into the distance, trying to understand. When Barbara Darnaby began her description of Sophie, he had still been contemplating the meaning of Broder's use of the term *nokmim*. But now he faced a much more immediate despair.

A week after Broder started making the movie about the *nokmim*, Gorbachev had gone to East Berlin, to tell Erich Honecker that it was all over. A month after Sophie appeared in Broder's life, the teenagers were dancing on the graffiti-covered wall. If he had been religious, he thought, he would have thanked God that he had asked Madden to requisition Interpol for the Stasi files. For now, he had to be patient about Sophie, he decided, looking out from the balcony to the edge of ocean just past a wide billboard advertising a trip to Hawaii.

The hint of the expanse made him realize that while he had to be more careful than ever, he also needed to start weaving a net of his own. If what he suspected was true, he needed proof. For that he needed information. He looked down at his notebook.

I'm always at Santa Monica pier. I look forward to seeing you again, it said in his carefully drawn English lettering. He tapped at the word *always* and decided he had nothing to lose.

Four of the people ignored his very existence, a fifth snarled at him angrily. The sixth interpreted Cohen's efforts as an opportunity to tell a life story about losing a job and a family, but he did not know Jacques Rosen.

It all exhausted Cohen. They were like broken DPs, refugees in their own land, homeless and hungry amid the luxury that had been assailing Cohen with its temptations and offerings ever since his arrival in the country. He wondered what would be more difficult—to wander as he did, burned to the core in a land where everyone had been ravaged, or to scavenge amid such wealth, the riches just beyond reach behind the glass windows.

He sought a seat on a park bench, longing for simplicity and the truth instead of the artful representations he saw in the shops along the street where he had parked. Roller skaters tried dazzling him, rappers wanted to blow his mind. Everyone around him seemed luxuriously healthy—except, of course, the beggars—yet everyone seemed cold, each smile no more than a show.

He suddenly realized that few of the smiles he had been offered since his arrival carried much warmth. Politeness was all. He remembered poignantly Goldie's reprimand of his manners, then he took a sip from his flask and raised his face to the sun.

He spent three precious hours on the walk at the beach, trying to find someone who might have been a likely acquaintance of Rosen's, while constantly watching his back for followers.

He learned that people feared strangers in this place. They believed it took courage to get involved. Nobody knew anything about Jacques Rosen, though "Jack, who died in the shooting" was known by a busboy at an ice cream parlor. "He liked cherry vanilla," the Moroccan-looking boy had said. But he knew nothing more of the "homeless guy who got it," as he conveyed Cohen's query to the soda jerk, who had also just shaken his head at Cohen's hopeful smile.

"I *thought* it was you," said a woman's voice in front of him.

Startled, Cohen opened his eyes. He was looking into the red, runny eyes of a narrow-faced and ageless woman. She was wearing a wool cap that covered all but a few stray strands of her hair, streaked gray. Her only concession to the heat was that her mud-colored overcoat hung open as she leaned over him, revealing other layers of faded pastels.

He leaned away from the draft of her sour breath. "Pardon me?" he said.

"You're Jack's friend," the woman said, tilting her head, birdlike, and studying his face. "You know—Jack. The Jew?"

She was stooped, almost hunched, but it was difficult to tell if it was the weight of the clothing she was wearing or merely the weight of her own suffering that made her stand bent, her head borne on a spindly neck that gave her the look of a carrion bird.

"You a Jew too?" the woman asked, but she didn't wait for an answer as she continued. "I'm Lucy," she added. "I'm not Jewish. But we were friends. Jack and me. Don't worry," she said, reading the expression on his face. "I was on the pier. When Jack got it. I saw you. And that night, I was over on Wilshire, and there's this TV store, they got a bunch of sets in the window and I watch TV there sometimes, and there was Jack and you. Right there. The camera missed me," she said, slightly sorrowful. "I was on the other side." She spoke matter-of-factly. "Can I have a sip of that stuff you got there?" she asked.

Cohen realized he was still holding the flask. He offered it to her. She took it with two hands, as if to make sure of preserving its treasure, and lifted it slowly to her mouth. The cap was on. She smiled apologetically at her own foolishness and then tried to unscrew it.

"Let me, please," Cohen offered, taking the flask from her hands. "Sit down," he added, uncapping the flask and handing it back to her.

"Thanks," she said, pleased with his attention. She sniffed at it, beamed at him, and then poured a splash into her mouth without letting the rim touch her lips. "I didn't want you to think you'll catch any germs," she said as she handed it back. "Rémy?" she asked.

"Martell." He smiled.

"Well?" she asked.

"Well what?" he answered.

"Isn't that a coincidence," she said. "You and me meeting like this," she added. "Poor Jack." She pulled a folded handkerchief from a pocket of the overcoat she was wearing and blew her nose. "Course, he's probably looking down on us both now and laughing. But what are you gonna do?" she asked fatalistically, turning sad. "Cosmic coincidences."

Cohen knew it wasn't a coincidence. He had smiled at everyone, tried to catch eyes wherever he could. He couldn't roller-skate or chant rap, but he knew how to draw attention, just as he knew how to withdraw into the invisible cover any crowd offers. He had walked the area hoping for just this. He wondered if she had the tape.

"So you saw everything that happened," he said.

She nodded, and proudly told her version. "Maniac in a boat," she summed up. "Jack went through all that shit over there in Europe, to get it from some rich asshole playing with himself on a boat. Now, that was some cosmic coincidence." She used the back of her hand to wipe at her face.

He wondered if she had cried, and asked if she had talked to the police. She eyed him suspiciously.

"Jack's belongings?" he finally pried. "He had something for me. Maybe he told you about it."

She smiled knowingly. "He told me it was special," she said with self-satisfied knowledge.

"Of course," Cohen said, reaching into his pocket, fumbling for a single bill. It was a fifty. "Here," he said, offering her the money. "You have it?"

"He wouldn't tell me what it was, of course," she said. "The package, I mean."

Cohen pulled another stray bill from his pocket. It was a twenty. He offered it to her. Disappointment crossed her face. He fumbled again, and this time produced a hundred-dollar bill. But he held it as bait, rather than give it to her. "Where is it?" he asked, keeping it out of her reach.

She folded her arms over her chest and looked across the street.

"Lucy, please."

"He told me it was important. Said it wasn't supposed to fall into the wrong hands," she said, lowering her voice but emphasizing the words. "If you know what I mean."

"I was his friend. You said so yourself," Cohen said.

"And so was I." She reached for the flask.

He unscrewed the cap and offered it to her. "You're right," he said while she drank. He traded the hundred-dollar bill for the flask.

Tears welled in her eyes. "I wasn't always like this, you know," she said.

"None of us were," he said gently.

She wiped at her tears with the back of her hand. "You know, I haven't eaten since yesterday. Why don't you and me go get something to eat?"

Cohen got up quickly, feeling better. "Come," he said, pulling at her arm, and nodding toward the restaurant on the pier. She shook her head. "We ain't exactly their cup of tea in there," she said. "People like me. 'Sides, I was thinking along the lines of ice cream."

She nodded at an ice cream stand a few doors down from the restaurant. It wasn't the same one he had been in an hour before. Cohen smiled at her.

"I'm buying," she said with a gallant smile, holding up the money he had given her.

"Thank you," he said, getting up and starting for the stand.

"Wait," she said behind him.

He turned. She primped at her hair, making sure it was tucked into her woolen cap, and then started dabbing a gray handkerchief at her tongue to use to wipe her face clean. "How do I look?" she asked.

"Fine," he said. "Do you like cherry vanilla?" he asked.

"Jack's favorite," she said, smiling as she stood up with her large plastic bag. It seemed stuffed with more plastic bags. Cohen held out his hand to carry it for her, and she eyed him suspiciously. "But I prefer almonds in peach," she warned him. He smiled, holding out his arm to support her.

She walked slowly. Her feet were swollen in her sneakers, and he wondered when she had last removed them. A skater cursed them as he flew past, and Cohen cursed back in Hebrew, a natural reflex that pleased him, though when she eyed him with a quizzical grin, it embarrassed him. By the time she was on her third almond-and-peach cone, and he had decided he still liked chocolate and vanilla best, he had called Phyllis Fine.

The cassette in his hand, he told the lawyer to send a car for Lucy. "Get her cleaned up. And hide her," Cohen ordered.

"Excuse me?" Fine said, startled.

"As of now," he amplified, "you're my lawyer in case anything goes wrong. Just do it. I'll explain later. Your office can bill the Broder estate," he said. "But, Miss Fine?"

"Phyllis," she corrected him. "Yes, what is it?"

"From now on, everything between us is privileged conversation. Attorney and client. You are not to say a word of this to anyone."

"I know my responsibilities," she said, offended. "One of them requires that I tell you that I understand you have begun those inquiries about Sophie Levine. That sergeant. Madden? He just got off the phone. He said you told him about my inquiries, and wanted to get photocopies of whatever we had in the file."

"I hope you gave them to him," Cohen said.

"Officially, he needs a warrant for such a request," she warned Cohen.

"Call him back," he ordered. "Give him the file."

"Are you sure?" she asked.

"Yes."

"Might I ask if you have learned something further about Sophie?" she asked.

"All I can tell you right now is that she is missing," Cohen said, suddenly worried. "I promise you, as soon as I know something certain, I will let you know. In person," he added. Some things were not for the phone, he was thinking as he hung up.

It was Broder's idea to poison the Munich water reservoirs. Levine had immediately embraced the idea. Cohen said he didn't know. But that came later.

Part Two of *The Survivor's Secrets* opened in a Munich restaurant. Broder and Cohen were in the city to meet up with a group of Jews coming out of the liberated camps in Poland. Levine was with them, on his way to Berlin, with dreams of a workers' state. By chance, in the same restaurant that night, a middle-aged German man had an argument with a waiter. The loud voices coming from behind him irritated Levine, and he lifted his head out of their conversation to see what the noise was all about.

Pale, he looked back at Broder and Cohen. "That's Witten," he said. "Henryk Witten. From the third *Lager*. You know," Levine insisted, "the lieutenant."

Cohen looked over discreetly. His eyes started to widen, and he quickly lowered his head, nodding.

Broder didn't look up. Instead, he smiled to himself and asked, "Is he alone?"

There is the sound of car tires squealing. Levine's driving, Broder's laughing. Cohen is packing guns into sacks for disposal. A gang on the getaway.

Cohen sat on the edge of his bed, staring at the movie. The first part had offended him for its rhetorical heroism. The second part had turned his life into a cheap thriller, full of car chases, shootouts, and ambushes of unsuspecting victims.

After the first assassination, it became easy. Contacts in the British army's Jewish Brigade, made up of volunteers from Palestine, gave them access to the kinds of documents they could use to travel across occupied Germany, seeking out the whereabouts of Nazis still uncaptured by the Allies.

Transport, uniforms—it was all simple once they had the routine down. Some they strangled, some they shot. Often they made it look like suicide. That was when they wanted to cover their tracks, to prevent escapes of other Nazis in the area.

Cohen kept putting off plans to get on one of the freighters carrying illegal immigrants to British-occupied Palestine. Levine pressed occasionally for them to head east, but he, too, was thrilled by the act of revenge. And Broder had always been good as their leader, directing them with skill as he plotted approaches and assigned tasks.

So Cohen watched the movie, hating the memories, knowing he was waiting for what came back to him in his nightmares. The day they killed the child along with his father. For Cohen, it was the beginning of the end of the *nokmim*.

It began just as he had always remembered it in his dreams.

The doctor and his child are standing side by side, a rope around each of their necks. Broder is doing the questioning. "Your last chance," Broder says. "Where is he?"

The doctor studies their faces. "He got away. As a Jew," he finally says. "He had a number put on his arm."

Levine strikes the doctor across his face. A drop of blood hits the white snow. The child's eyes watch everything, silently.

"Liar," Levine shouts.

"No, no, it's true, you must believe me. On my boy's life, I tell you it's true. . . . He got away."

That's not what happened, Cohen thought, gripping the edge of the bed. Manheim had escaped in advance of the Americans. He was captured a few days later. But Broder's movie was saying that Manheim had survived. This was the message the director had left behind for Cohen.

Shocked, Cohen watched the movie continue with its tale of revenge meted out in all the different ways they could muster, until the end, the parting on the dock at Naples. Cohen was done with the *nokmim*. The fight for the state had begun in Palestine. He was done with revenge.

He watched, remembering well the foggy night on the docks. Hundreds of refugees were being shepherded onto a rusting leaky freighter that would try to run the British blockade. Broder had come to the port to seek Cohen out, to make one last effort to keep the *nokmim* together.

Cohen watched the TV screen as if he were watching his own dreams.

"Was it Arabs who made you a slave?" Broder had asked Cohen sarcastically. "Or was it Germans? Besides," he added cynically, pointing at the old, rusted freighter. Dark water was spilling from its bilges. "First you'll have to get past the British. You'll end up in one of *their* camps. In Cyprus. Or Africa. What good will that do?"

"And what good will all this killing do? What good will poisoning a million Germans do?" Cohen hissed back.

"It will make them feel what we feel," Broder said. "Make them know what we know."

"Will it bring anyone back? Will it save anyone?" Cohen demanded. "Why not kill six million, ten million. We'll be like them. Ten of them for one of us."

Cohen watched Alvy's eyes narrow on the screen. "Revenge won't save anyone," the young actor whispered intensely.

"Us," Broder whispered back. "Us, Avram. It will save us."

"I must go," Alvy said in the movie. "I'm sorry, my brother, but I must go. I beg you. Please. Stop the killing. Start thinking of life. Not death." With that, Alvy crossed the dock, leaving Der Bruder and the *nokmim* behind.

But Der Bruder had something more to say, something that he could never have said on the dock in Naples.

While Alvy Landy climbed the ramp to the dangerously over-crowded deck of the ship, the actor playing Broder, his profile a silhouette against the ungainly prow of the boat, spoke. His voice was a harsh, threatening whisper.

"You think you're going to a new life, putting it all behind you. But I promise you, Avram, you won't be able to forget." The profile turns to face the camera directly, and Max Broder continues. "If someday, ten years from now, twenty, even forty years from now, your path crosses with Karl Manheim's, don't tell me you won't do what we did that first night, to the first butcher we caught. Because whether he's a beggar or a baron, he'll still be a butcher, Avram, and don't tell me you won't want to kill him. Don't tell me that, Avram. I won't believe you."

The screen faded, and a caption appeared, saying, "Insert epilogue here." Cohen sat frozen on the edge of the motel bed, only moving when the screen went white with the snow of unrecorded tape. He had searched for the loophole Broder left behind instead of a suicide note, and found it in the movie.

He leafed through his notebook quickly, almost tearing pages as he sought Rabbi Gould's number.

"Commander," Gould said effusively, getting on the phone. "I'm so glad you called. I've been leaving you mesasges at Max's house.

The benefit. I wanted to remind you about it. And to let you know that—"

"HEI? The institute, it investigates the whereabouts of Nazis?" Cohen broke in.

"It's our specialty," Gould said proudly. "We helped get Demjanjuk. Now we're working on a Croat, a former police commander. He's been living in Phoenix for the last thirty years. We found that bastard. He used to like using dogs on people. We were on the Waldheim case, and the second in command at the Saloniki transport. That butcher sent three hundred thousand Jews to Auschwitz in less than three months. We found him in—"

"Did you ever hear of a camp officer named Karl Manheim?" Cohen interrupted. "Dachau?"

"Of course. Max was very interested in his case," Gould said. "And?"

"Well, I suppose I could look up the files," Gould said. "But if I remember correctly, the bastard got away. The Americans had him, but he got away."

"How?" Cohen asked.

"The rumor is that he had a number tattooed on his arm. Got away as a Jew. There's never been a trace of him since."

"When did Max first mention it to you?" Cohen asked.

"Let me think," Gould said. "Maybe two, two and a half years ago."

Cohen rubbed a hand over his brow, not knowing if he should feel relieved or frightened as he saw another piece of the puzzle fitting into its proper place. There were still gaps in the map he was drawing in his mind. But the outline was taking shape, the questions could become more focused.

"Commander," Gould said, breaking into Cohen's thoughts. "While I have you on the phone, I thought you'd like to know that I got a call from Andrew Blakely's office. We're getting the movie for the benefit, after all. Well, the first half, at least. They said the second is not in final-cut version yet."

"So you'll be showing it?"

"Of course," Gould said. "It's perfect for the evening. We even have permission to auction it, as part of the fund-raising portion of the evening. The cassette, I mean, not the distribution rights, of course. Considering the circumstances, with Max's death and all, the symbolic value of the tape is enormous. We've decided to use the proceeds to establish a chair in Max's name, for the study of the Holocaust in film."

"Very nice," Cohen said politely. He was less interested in fund raising than he was in the change in Epica policy regarding the movie.

He wished he were a chemist, able to put it all in a bottle and shake it or heat it or mix it so that everything flowed together into one clear fluid that he could see through and understand.

"Anyway," Gould was saying, "you can imagine, the way you didn't make an appearance at the *shiva,* especially after that business with the Kaddish. Leo is very worried about whether you'll be—"

"You want to know if I intend to go to this affair?" Cohen said, easily guessing Hirsh's concern.

"Well, yes," Gould said hesitantly. "And sit at the head table? If you need a tuxedo, I'm sure arrangements can be made. It would be so helpful, you see. For the fund raiser. To have you there."

But Cohen was thinking about ghosts. He promised to attend the banquet and hung up the phone, wondering if there was a connection between Sophie Levine's appearance in Broder's life and the filmmaker's discovery that Manheim had survived. The skinheads, too, suddenly became much more serious than a bunch of punks in over their heads. He sighed, picking up the phone again.

"Mike," he said, when Madden finally answered the phone. "I have a movie I want you to see."

"What I don't understand is why he didn't just tell you. Call you up and say, 'Listen, old buddy, I think I've found Manheim.' " Madden was pacing Cohen's hotel room, too excited by what he had just seen to sit down.

"He knew why," Cohen mumbled to himself.

"What's that?" Madden asked, halting in his tracks halfway across the room.

"I said, he knew why he couldn't tell me."

"Why?"

"I would have said I wasn't interested."

"What?!" Madden asked, putting down the bathroom glass of cognac Cohen had poured out for him as soon as the movie was over. "What do you mean, you wouldn't have been interested?"

"I would have told him what I told him then. Enough is enough. I would have said the world has changed. The war is over."

"Yeah, right," Madden said, disbelieving. "Bullshit."

"That's what I would have said," Cohen said softly, getting up from the armchair where he had sat watching the movie for the second time, and going to the night table, where a bottle of Martell was open and waiting. "That's the truth. Even now I am acting because of what happened this week, not something that happened a half century ago," Cohen said simply. "The past is only a clue for me in this." He filled half his glass with the cognac and took a long sip before going back to the chair.

Madden fell silent, studying his cigar and then taking a deep puff, which he chased with a long quaff of the liquor. "But he got you in the end anyway, didn't he? He's making you look for this Manheim fucker." He smirked at a thought. "It's just like he got that suit Blakely. The movie's gonna come out, after all. You gotta hand it to the guy," the American policeman said admiringly of Broder. "He got what he wanted."

Cohen nodded sadly. "He usually did," he said.

"All right. So now, where is he?" Madden asked.

Cohen shook his head. "I don't know. Not yet."

"What's your plan? How do we find him?"

"You are going to help me?" Cohen asked. "You believe me now?"

"That depends."

"On what?"

"What are you going to do when you find him?" Madden asked.

"*If* I find him. *If* he is really alive."

"All right," Madden conceded. "If you find him."

"I don't know," Cohen admitted.

"What about knock-emma?" Madden asked, mispronouncing *nekama,* the word Broder had used throughout the movie.

Cohen shook his head. "It is over." But he knew he wasn't sure, and couldn't be until he faced his past, the confrontation that first Broder's death, and now Broder's message, were forcing him to make.

He had held it at arm's length, like a farsighted reader, examining it in his dreams lest it intrude on his life. Seeing the movie had made him understand that it wasn't merely his weakness that had enabled Broder to entice him to Los Angeles. He had wanted to believe he had drawn limits, that he was done with fatal compromises. That's what leaving the *nokmim* had been all about for him. No more innocent victims at his hand—if he could avoid it. But even while he explained to Madden that Broder "wanted revenge, not justice," he knew that the origin of his own survival was in Broder's promise for a cleansing revenge.

"So what do you want?" Madden asked.

Cohen gave it some thought before answering. "To find out if

Max Broder committed suicide," he said, holding up a finger, counting. "To find Jacques Rosen's killer." He added a second finger. "To find out who Sophie Levine really is," he said, the third finger in the air. "But what about you, Mike?" he asked. "Maybe it's too risky for you to get too involved now."

"Are you kidding?" Madden exclaimed. "Twenty years I've been baby-sitting for rich fucks who think that because they're in the movies, their lives are just like the movies. Twenty years I've been chasing down the scum, picking up after the assholes. Finally, I get a chance to go after a real bad guy, and you're telling me it's too risky?" He snorted in astonishment that Cohen could doubt him. "I was watching you guys, the knock-mim, and all I could think was, Jeez, that's the way it should be done."

"No, Mike. No."

"Don't get me wrong. I'm an American. I believe in due process. But sometimes, when you know what the fucker's done, and you can't touch him? 'Cause he's protected? I gotta admit, I envied you."

Cohen shook his head sadly. He had not been able to convince Madden, but the movie had. And perhaps too well. He worried that Madden's enthusiasm for the hunt would endanger them both.

"I'll tell you something else," Madden suddenly added. "I don't know why Blakely's got such a hair up his ass about it. I think it's a great flick. And seeing it with you?" Madden said. "That was great. I'll always remember that. I'm telling you, no reason this flick can't do well. Especially the second part, the knock-mim part," he said.

"Just remember that we are not *nokmim*," Cohen said.

Madden drove around the dingy block twice in Cohen's rented sedan before Cohen was satisfied with their surveillance position,

a few doors down from the storefront headquarters of the Douglas
Davis Brigade Headquarters, a hangout for "Aryan Nation members
and various other forms of scumbags," as Madden said.

According to Madden's information, Davis was a hometown
boy who had "made good in the eyes of brigade members." He
had been killed fighting for Ian Smith as an eight-thousand-dollar-
a-month mercenary in Rhodesia, twenty years before.

"There's the local führer," Madden mocked, nodding toward a
balding redheaded man in a brown uniform, leading three followers
down the sidewalk. "Dugan."

The uniform was distinguished by thick bandoliers crisscrossed
with leather belts. Cohen guessed him to be in his mid-forties.
The three other brownshirts were much younger. Dugan had the
keys. The chains on the shuttered doors rattled, and a pair of
skinheads stepped out of a doorway a few shops down from the
Aryan Nation's storefront office and approached the brownshirts.

"Why are they not in uniforms?" asked Cohen. "Nazis love
uniforms."

"They're street punks," Madden said cynically. "They get into
it in the joint. Whites against the blacks. The skinheads are muscle,
to scare people. Compared to them, the brownshirts are intellec-
tuals. Dugan's a pharmacist," Madden added, as if to put it all
into perspective for Cohen.

"The SS would have had them all arrested," Cohen mocked, as
he watched the group arrive in twos and threes. "No pride in
their appearance."

"Let me have one of the doughnuts," Madden said. Cohen pulled
one out for the American, and they settled down in the car seat
with coffee in paper cups to wait for their opportunity.

Altogether, fourteen people were attending the meeting. They
straggled out an hour later. Madden adjusted his seat as the skinheads appeared in the doorway.

"No," Cohen said, "we wait for Dugan," and he explained what he wanted to do.

Dugan was the last to leave, with his three followers in the brownshirt uniforms. While Dugan locked up, the three went to wait beneath a streetlamp at the end of the sidewalk.

"They're making it easier for us," Cohen said. "You ready?"

"You sure you can handle him?" Madden asked.

Cohen shot Madden a grin. "How do they say it in the movies? Action!" he exclaimed, his eyes alight.

Madden gunned the car and pulled it up deftly at the curb so that Cohen emerged directly alongside Dugan, grabbing him from behind.

"Cops," one of the brownshirts at the corner shouted.

"No," said Cohen, aiming his gun at the brownshirts. "Jews." He smiled grimly, and the first one started to run. The others followed quickly when Cohen raised the gun to take aim. Dugan was frozen with fear, making it easy for Cohen to hustle him into the back seat. Only when Madden started driving away did Dugan speak.

"What do you people think you're doing?" he howled.

"Quiet!" Cohen commanded only once, jabbing the gun into Dugan's belly with a short, sharp thrust, silencing the man.

Madden wheeled out of the district, up onto the hump of the Palos Verdes peninsula, and then along the coast until they reached a dark dirt road that led to a clifftop spot overlooking the ocean. Madden turned off the car lights, and Cohen realized how secluded a place the American had found.

The only light was the moon, but clouds racing above the ocean played hide-and-seek with the pale silver light in the sky. Far beyond, Catalina Island's lights glowed vaguely on the horizon.

"It's very simple," Cohen said, opening the door. "You tell me why those skinheads—what were their names? Lineker? the brothers—why did they chase me? What were they trying to do? And I'll let you live." He pulled Dugan out of the car.

But Dugan remained silently defiant, staring back at Cohen as the Jerusalemite pushed him away from the car.

"That's not a good idea," Cohen said, shaking his head. "Much better you should tell me what you know." There was genuine disappointment in his voice. "I don't care about you or about your group. You don't frighten me; you don't even make me sick. But if you don't cooperate, well, that's something else. That might make me angry. You see, I knew real Nazis, not people like you, playing at it. I learned a lot from them."

Dugan's eyes flickered toward the car. Madden was getting out of the driver's seat, a gun in his hand.

"Quite a lot, actually," Cohen said. He was speaking in almost a whisper. But in the seclusion of the place, the only other sound was made by the distant crashing waves far below.

"I can show you some tricks," Cohen continued. "Perhaps you are interested?" He waved his gun, backing Dugan up three steps toward the edge of the steep cliff.

"You!" Dugan shouted to Madden, trying to sound confident. "What's he talking about?"

"He's the expert," Madden shouted back. "Ask him. My guess is that he's not kidding around. And I know for a fact that he knows exactly what he's talking about."

Cohen jabbed with the gun at Dugan's belly. "Back up," he ordered.

"You're kidding, right?" Dugan asked. There was a glimmer of sweat on his brow.

"No, not at all," Cohen said calmly. His voice sounded to him like a stranger's. He had the feeling he was watching himself do all these things and had no way to stop it. "Do it now," he ordered.

Dugan obeyed.

"Turn around," Cohen commanded.

Dugan did not move.

"Turn," Cohen repeated, and for the first time cocked the gun.

Dugan inhaled sharply and turned, gasping again. He was half a pace from the edge of the cliff.

"Kneel down," Cohen ordered, putting his hand on Dugan's shoulder and pressing, as if he were teaching a dog to sit. He could feel Dugan trembling under his hand. "It really will make it easier for all of us," Cohen said softly, "if you do as I say. I want you to notice that I am doing this exactly the way your heroes used to do it. So there will be no misunderstanding. Now, do you understand me?" He tapped the gun very lightly against the side of Dugan's head.

Dugan sank to his knees, shaking.

"Now, as I said," Cohen continued in the same calm voice, "it's very simple. You tell me why they chased me, and I'll let you go home. If you don't tell me, well . . ." Cohen leaned forward, peering over Dugan to the churning waters, and then stepped back, the gun pressed into Dugan's neck.

But the shot wasn't his. Instinctively, Cohen leapt aside, into the darkness beyond the headlight beams that illuminated the kneeling man at the edge of the cliff. "Avram!" Madden cried, as Dugan fell over, a crumpled pile.

Another shot screamed by Cohen's head, and he crawled toward the dark cover behind the car.

A spurt of bullets kicked up dirt in front of the car headlights. All Cohen could hear was his breathing and the slaps of an automatic rifle. He rolled out of the yellow spread of light made by the headlights and into safety behind the car. It jerked with the bullets ripping into the sheet metal. Gradually he began to hear other sounds. The crashing waves below. He could see Madden, who had taken cover behind a rear wheel. The American was shouting at him.

"Quiet, Mike," Cohen commanded.

"Are you all right?" Madden asked. "Hurt?"

"No," Cohen wheezed back, leaning against the front tire. The shooting had stopped.

They exchanged glances, and as if they had been a team for years, they nodded to each other and grinned. For a second, Cohen had the memory of the movie in the airplane, the team of assassins moving silently in for the kill. "One, two, three, *now*," he whispered aloud, and then leaned around the front tire and took aim, scanning the scene.

Dugan appeared dead. There was a thick, dark stand of woods beyond the car lights. Cohen strained his eyes, seeking something human in the darkness. He saw a glimmer of white and a face. A stream of bullets raced past Cohen's head. He fired once, before rolling back behind the car.

A burst rattled the far end of the car. Then there was an awful hush, into which a wave below crashed with a violent slap, raising a gust of spray that flared in front of the car lights at the cliff's edge.

The telltale clicks of a metal ammo clip being removed from a rifle made them exchange glances again. Cohen wondered if his breath would last long enough for the effort.

He broke out of his hiding place and rolled across the ground, grasping his gun, and he spotted the platinum-haired man at the edge of the clearing.

"Halt!" Cohen shouted.

"Police," Madden cried out.

But the man stepped backward, into the darkness. Cohen let off a shot. Again, the ocean sounds camouflaged all others until the assassin's bullets whipped about the car, blasting the front tires and then the rear. The car sank onto its axles, making better cover for Cohen and Madden.

"Who is he?"

"The man with white hair," Cohen gasped. "I told you. The shooter. At the pier."

"Nobody followed us," Madden insisted.

"He wasn't following us," Cohen deduced. "He was after Dugan. Silencing Dugan was his mission. Then me." It was a guess, Cohen knew, but it was the only explanation he could find. "He was good at his job," he added. "But not very good."

"This isn't good?" Madden asked, incredulous.

Cohen shook his head like a disappointed teacher. "If he was good, we wouldn't be alive to shoot back at him. Listen. We must take him alive," he said. "He has answers."

Another half magazine of bullets crashed into the car. "First let's make sure *we* get out alive," Madden moaned.

Footsteps pounded beyond, away from Cohen's end of the car. Cohen swung the gun upward, over Madden's head, standing and propping his weapon on the car roof. The killer was just beyond the front of the car, his rifle aimed at Madden.

Instinct made Cohen fire three quick shots. The first struck the cocked rifle at the shooter's eye, the second hit him in the shoulder, and the third in the chest. Cohen was cursing himself even before he heard the dull thud and the clatter of the rifle. He became aware of the sound of his own breathing and the sound of the ocean, and then all became silence. Cohen sat down slowly in the dust, suddenly exhausted, his eyes closed to the glare of the car's angry headlights, as he listened to a quiet that seemed suddenly inexplicable after all the shooting.

Madden broke the hush, but Cohen didn't even hear him at

first. "Avram, you okay?" he was asking. Cohen opened his eyes. Madden was standing above him, the shooter's rifle in one hand, the other hand extended to help Cohen up. "You okay?" Madden repeated.

Cohen blinked. His heart was still thumping. He sat up, leaning against the car. "Is he . . . ?"

"You're a good shot," Madden said, nodding. "Thanks."

Cohen closed his eyes again.

"You hit?" Madden worried over him.

"No. But please. A minute. To rest." Cohen was as embarrassed as he was frightened, as awed as he was terrified by what he had done. Killing had always done that to him, even when he was a *nokame*.

"All right. I'm gonna look around. Be right back." Madden disappeared from view.

Dugan's crumpled body was a few feet away, in the unblinking light of the car headlights. Cohen turned to his left. The ribbing on the soles of the dead man's sneakers smiled stupidly at him. He heaved himself painfully to his feet and went to the man lying in the dust of the clearing. Grunting with the effort, he rolled the body over. The man's eyes were open. Ice-blue eyes. Like Sophie's. Like Levine's. Like Manheim's, he suddenly thought.

Madden interrupted his thoughts from behind. "His car's back there," the policeman said, pointing into the darkness of the dirt road that had led to the cliff overlooking the cove. "His name's Roland Berger. California driving license. But get this," Madden added excitedly. "The car registration says it belongs to Epica."

"Blakely," Cohen said reflexively.

"Yeah, Blakely," said Madden.

They both fell silent, considering the implications of the discovery.

"Blakely's a whole different ball game," Madden finally said.

"I know," said Cohen, although he was hearing the expression for the first time.

"You can't try the same thing with Blakely," Madden added, just to make sure Cohen understood.

Cohen nodded, thinking of a solution to the problem. "But I could be a sound thief for you," he suggested.

"Sound thief?"

"I'll get him to talk. Wear a microphone. A tape recorder."

"No violence? No threats?" Madden asked.

Cohen ignored the question, as if it was beneath him. "Can you get a miniature microphone? A transmitter to a listening post? You'd get it all on tape. I'd be inside, talking with him. You'd be outside listening."

"It would be useless in court," said Madden.

Cohen sighed. Madden still didn't understand. "I'm not doing this for the courts. I'm doing it for myself. But I need you as my witness."

"Goddammit," Madden snarled in frustration. "Don't you think I know that. But don't you understand? There won't be any prosecution if you're not careful. *You* could end up in fucking court. I can't keep protecting you forever." His voice had risen into the same kind of shouting he had used on Cohen the first days in Los Angeles. But he suddenly seemed to realize that and lowered his tone. "Look, I'm on your side."

"You thought I was crazy."

"All right, all right, I thought you were crazy," Madden admitted.

"A movie convinced you," Cohen said, as if it was folly.

"You convinced me."

"With a movie," Cohen muttered.

"Are you trying to talk me out of it?" Madden demanded.

"No," said Cohen grimly. "But now, before this goes any further, I must know why you agreed."

"I told you, to get that guy Manheim. Oh, shit!" he exclaimed. "I just thought of something."

"What?" Cohen asked.

"What if Blakely's Manheim?"

"He's not," Cohen said confidently.

"How can you be so sure?" asked Madden.

"Because of what Broder said. I'll recognize him when I see him."

"See, the movie convinced you too."

Cohen looked down again at the dead assassin. Madden was right.

"But if Blakely's not Manheim, why an Epica car?" Madden asked.

"That's what I want to ask Mr. Blakely."

"We're gonna have to call the locals," Madden said, adding cynically. "They're gonna just *love* this."

"Mike," Cohen said, a plea in his voice. "For the first time, I am ahead of them."

"Ahead of who? That's what I'd like to know."

"I cannot let investigators who know nothing of this get in the way," Cohen insisted.

"I gotta extricate you again, is that it?" Madden asked wearily. Cohen nodded.

The American scratched at his head, then pulled out a cigar, absentmindedly lighting it as he looked at the two bodies. "I bet you want it kept out of the papers too," he said.

"At least for a day," Cohen admitted.

"I'm beginning to wish you never showed me the movie," Madden said.

Cohen froze.

"Kidding, I'm only kidding." Madden smiled. "C'mon, we'll use his car. This one's a piece of shit," he said, kicking at the bullet-riddled rental car. "I'll make some phone calls."

Cohen dozed on and off as Madden cruised in the center lane, expertly stitching paths ten miles an hour faster than the other cars on the road.

They passed a long convertible. Through half-open eyes, Cohen watched the pretty young couple in the front seat. The girl's hair whipped around in the wind, the boy had his arm over her shoulder. For the three seconds it took for the car to fade behind, he had a flashing memory of one of Max's early movies. It was a western, Cohen had always thought, even though there were cars and motorcycles instead of horses. And there had been an innocent couple driving just that way.

"I give people what they want so they will give me what I want," Broder had once said, explaining himself. He believed in happy endings, Cohen thought. But it had nothing to do with altruism or commercialism. It was the stark truth of Broder's method.

"And what happens when there is a conflict?" Cohen had asked. "Between what you want and they want?"

Broder had just smiled. "You don't understand: there is always a conflict," he said.

The road ahead was wide and well lit, and to each side the city's lights spread out endlessly shallow into the dark. He longed for a tower from which to look down, a reference point from which to work. He had arrived helpless in the city, without any immunity to the people or places, a stranger to everything. He had expected Der Bruder's guidance, not his secrets.

He glanced at Madden, grateful for his company, wondering how much the man reallly understood, knowing there would yet be passages that, through no fault of his own, the American could not traverse, because he could never understand. "Thanks," he said softly to Madden, and then closed his eyes again, letting the dreamless sleep wash over him.

Only when Madden pulled up in front of the West Hollywood house did he wake up the soundly sleeping Cohen.

"We're here," Madden announced.

"Berger's house?" Cohen asked, stretching and feeling new aches in his body.

"That's the place," Madden said, pointing to the single-story house.

Cohen sought the car-door handle.

"Listen," Madden said. "About what happened. Back there. I've got something I've got to ask you."

"What?"

"Would you have done it?" Madden asked, and then, embarrassed by the question and Cohen's silence, he added, "I mean, I wouldn't blame you, I suppose. A Jew, a survivor, and all, and having to deal face-to-face with scum like that. But he wasn't Manheim. You know what I mean? It's not as if he did the kind of stuff that motherfucker——"

"Would you have done what you were going to do?" Cohen interrupted.

"What?"

"Shoot me, to stop me from shooting Dugan?"

"Probably," Madden said cheerfully. "But I didn't think you were going to do it."

"Dugan did," Cohen said in a subdued voice. "You know, I once fired two of my boys for doing the same thing to a pair of rapists." He patted for a cigarette but then decided to give his lungs a rest. "Maybe it's because everything is strange to me here," he admitted, unhappy with the feeling. "I am a stranger to this place. It has made me a stranger to myself." He squirmed in the seat to reach into his pocket for the flask, offering it to Madden. "It does not feel good," he added, as Madden took it.

"Truth is, I was enjoying myself," Madden said. He poured some cognac into his mouth. "Thanks for making me an honorary Jew back there. I liked that." He laughed.

But Cohen didn't laugh. He fought his way out of his sorrows for himself and all the victims of Broder's secrets, wishing he had never shown Madden the movie, had never seen it himself. He opened the door and stepped onto the sidewalk, stretching his aching muscles and then walking up the flagstone path to the front door.

The only thing of significance they found was an Austrian passport. The photo was black and white, turning the icy blue eyes Cohen remembered into a sharp white with a slight blur of dark pupils. Cohen found it in the single suitcase stashed under the bed in the sparsely furnished house. He brought it to Madden, in the front room making his calls.

"Well, at least it's the same name as the driver's license," Madden harrumphed, handing it back to Cohen. "I don't think I could take another fake identity on this case. A Nazi hiding as a Jew. I still can't get over that."

"Interpol? Twenty-four hours?" Cohen asked.

"They've already sent the fax," Madden said. "Extreme urgency. That's what I told 'em."

"Call them back," Cohen said, handing over the passport. "Have them ask about this one too."

"You remember when they had bells on the telexes?" Madden asked as he dialed, grinning at Cohen. "In the old days, we would have said, 'Send it out with bells.' "

"You're not so old," Cohen mocked him.

"Look who's talking," Madden shot back. "No, not you, darling," Madden purred into the phone. "Yeah, it's me again. No, not about Sophie Levine. Someone else. From Austria. Yeah, yeah, I know you need paper on it. But it's the same case. Appendix it. I'll send you a memo tomorrow. Promise. Here's the name, and I have a passport number. Right. Austrian. Ready?" He grinned at Cohen, who had a thought, and signaled Madden.

"Hold on a sec," Madden said to the phone, holding his hand over the mouthpiece.

"Ask her to send it to Germany *and* Austria," Cohen said. His thoughts were on Berger's icy blue eyes, and tumbled back all the way to the little boy hanging beside his father from the branches of the tree. For a second, a crazy theory that Berger was Manheim's son, trying to protect his father, invaded Cohen's mind. But he said nothing of this to Madden, who was promising to call back in a few hours to find out if anything had come in.

"You look exhausted," Madden said, hanging up.

Cohen checked his watch. It was halfway between midnight and dawn. "A little," Cohen admitted. "I could use some good coffee. Or some sleep." But he couldn't sleep. Not yet. His mind was racing. He had to take it a little easier for a while, if he didn't want to end up in the hands of the doctors again. He rubbed absentmindedly at the scar on his belly. "I choose sleep," he said.

As Madden started the car, Cohen decided he'd call Phyllis Fine, to tell her to be ready—just in case—to handle any problems Madden might have with his bureaucracy as a result of helping Cohen's investigation. Like Jacques Rosen's friend Lucy, Madden was a potential victim of Broder's conceits.

"Listen, Mike," he said as the car began moving forward. "I'm sorry if sometimes I treat you like a driver."

"Forget it," Madden said. "Call it professional courtesy."

But Cohen had already decided to consider it friendship.

BY A QUARTER TO ELEVEN, Cohen was in an electric cart driven
by Barbara Darnaby, rolling through the sprawling Epica grounds.

"What do you know about Epica?" she asked, as they glided
into a large plaza bounded by tall hangars. Doors the height of
small houses and the width of semitrailer trucks faced onto the
plaza.

"Nothing," he admitted. "Except that Andy Blakely's in charge
and some people seem to believe he's ruining the Epica tradition.
Whatever that is."

"There's no tradition if there's no studio," Darnaby said. "All
Andy's trying to do is save the studio."

"If it is losing money, why did Oceanic buy it?" Cohen
asked.

"For that," she said, pointing to a low-slung building framed
by an emerald lawn. "The archives. There are more than a hundred
Oscar winners in there, more than seven thousand movies in all.
In the long run, it's worth a lot of money. Get it?" she asked.
" 'Oceanic works for the long run'? Their corporate slogan? You
know, the ads?"

"Ahh," Cohen said. "We don't get much of their advertising
in Israel."

"That's funny," she said. "I thought Laszlo Katz was heavily
involved over there."

"There are two kinds of rich Jews in this world." Cohen sighed.

"Jews who care about Israel, I mean. Those who give and those who invest. He's one of the givers."

"It sounds like you'd prefer investment to charity," she said.

He nodded, but he was thinking of another question. "Max owned shares in Epica," he began.

"Yes, I know."

"Was he under pressure to sell?"

"What do you mean, pressure?" she asked suspiciously.

"You tell me," Cohen answered.

She pursed her lips, thinking. "Truth is, he tried pressuring Andy. He offered to trade his shares for Epica's relinquishment of the rights to the movie. But Andy couldn't make the deal. The movie cost fourteen five to make. Max's shares were only worth half that, tops."

She paused at a T intersection in the lot. To his left were more hangars. To his right was a campus of brick and wood colonial-style buildings. Four men in outer-space-alien costumes waddled past them, carrying headpieces under their arms. Cohen snorted. "It looks more realistic in the movies."

"That's what it's all about," she said, pleased. "Over there," she added, pointing toward a distant hangar, "we're making a—"

"You said you had the list for me," he said, interrupting her.

"I thought we'd look in at the new animation studios," she said, stopping the cart with a disappointed look on her face. "It's really amazing what they—"

"Miss Darnaby, please."

"Barbara," she said, offended.

"Fine, Barbara. Right now the list is more important to me," he said. "I will have questions, you see. About the people. And I would like to have that done by the time I meet Mr. Blakely."

"What kind of questions?" she asked suspiciously. But the cart jerked forward, and she took a sharp left and then a right through a half block of an English village and then onto a street lined by wooden New York brownstones.

They came out into a small plaza bordered by red-brick buildings. She swept into a parking space alongside four other carts.

He waited until she had stopped before he answered. "Their ages, for example."

"Interesting," she admitted. "Whatever do you expect to discover?"

"A ghost, Miss Darnaby." He smiled at her with equal politeness.

Her office in the one-story classical revival building reminded him of Broder's study. There was a large old wooden desk and leather chairs. But one wall was a floor-to-ceiling multicolored grid of palm-sized rectangles. On close inspection, he saw that the color coding referred to movies in production, each rectangle another stage in the process. There were at least a dozen different colors.

"The list," she said, slapping a blue folder onto her desk. "Essentially, this is a list of everyone on the production," she explained. "Max allowed everyone on set into rushes. Not everyone saw every rush, obviously. So I marked those people whose positions required their daily attendance and those who had their own copies of the script, rather than their subordinates, and of course processing people. Labs, cutters, editors. You'll find a key on the inside flap of the folder. All together there are eighty-seven people I've marked who actually saw a full version, even if it was a very rough cut. Some only saw it because they attended rushes, which means they didn't necessarily see it in sequence. I've also separated them into two lists: people who had been on both shootings—in Oregon for the camp and Europe for the avengers—and those who were only in one or the other." It was obvious she loved her work. She picked up the folder and held it out to him as if it were an offering. But he didn't take it.

"First of all," he said, "I need to know all those over the age of sixty. And all those of European origin," he said.

She raised an eyebrow, obviously astonished at his request, but before she could say anything, he added, "And anyone with blue eyes."

It was on the spur of the moment that he added that category, a wilder guess than the others, but he couldn't shake the memory of Roland Berger's lifeless orbs and Karl Manheim's daggerlike eyes. It was the kind of detail that Nissim Levy, his former assistant in Jerusalem, might have made into a much bigger question. Now, in Los Angeles, propelled by paranoia, Cohen perceived the co-incidence of the eyes as larger than it would have seemed at home in Jerusalem. But he had to try everything. Barbara Darnaby's own brown eyes weren't smiling as she studied his face.

"Miss Darnaby," he said. "I realize Max was not your favorite person. I can understand this. I don't blame you. Sometimes it is very difficult to explain one's friends," he said. "But you worked for him so closely on this film. You yourself said he taught you so much." He looked around the room. "I can see his influence," he added. "So if you could think of him as a former teacher, one whom you remember not with fondness maybe, but with admiration for what he taught, it might make it easier for you. We'll start with the eighty-seven. Please."

"Perhaps if you told me why you needed this information . . ."

"Miss Darnaby," he began.

"Barbara," she insisted. "You make it sound like I'm some kind of suspect," she added nervously.

He apologized and started again. "It is possible," he said, "that someone from a long time ago——"

"I'm not a child," she interrupted. "Please."

"I'm looking for a killer," he shot back, tired and angry. "My methods may not be what you see in your Hollywood movies. But they are the only ones I know. I am sorry if you are offended. I told you, I am truly grateful for your assistance."

"In your inquiries," she said sarcastically.

"Yes," he said seriously. "May we begin?"

For a moment, he thought she was about to ask him to leave. Her face flushed and she tapped an erratic rhythm on the table with the eraser end of a pencil. But then she sighed, opened the file to the first page, and announced that the names were in alphabetical order.

"Stephen Aronson, a sound engineer," she read. "He's in his mid twenties." She watched for his reaction.

"Next," said Cohen.

She looked down at the folder and back at him. The reddening of her face deepened.

"Please," he said, "go on."

"Andrew Blakely," she practically whispered.

He waited.

"He's sixty-four," she said, exasperated.

"I thought he was older," Cohen said matter-of-factly.

She smiled hesitantly. "Don't tell him that. He thinks he doesn't look a day over fifty-five."

Cohen didn't smile back. "He is American?"

"Yes," she said softly.

"You are sure?"

"I have the *Who's Who* right up there on the bookshelf," she said, pointing to one of the shelves. "Andy Blakely the First was in railroads. He made the money. The Second went into the diplomatic service. He thought he owed the country something for all the money his father stole. Andy seems to have taken after his grandfather. Yes, they were all Americans."

"Next," he said.

"Toni Carroll. Alex Corn. Donna Danforth. Henry DiMaggio. He's from Europe," she said, hopefully, but then ran her finger across the page and added with disappointment, "He's thirty-three."

"Too young," Cohen said, fingering the button of the Walkman tape recorder in his jacket pocket. He had cut a hole on the inside of the jacket, slipping the tiny microphone wire through it and taping it out of sight under his shirt.

He paced the room in thought as she droned on. But he didn't turn on the microphone yet. It was waiting for Blakely.

Maybe Darnaby's list was as unimportant as the recording of the conversation he would have with Blakely. Or maybe both would turn out to be important. He wouldn't know until he tried. He had spent so many years, he thought as she read on, turning over rocks that hid nothing, looking for the one where the scorpion slept. Maybe, he thought, by the time he was finished with Blakely, word would have come in from Interpol about Sophie or Berger. Something had to break open. Anything.

"You didn't mention Roland Berger," he said, when she reached the final name. There were people old enough, but not from Europe. Others were European but hardly old enough to be Manheim. If Manheim was indeed alive.

"You never said anything about our security people," she griped. "You said you wanted the people involved with the production."

"How long has he been working here?"

"Six, seven months."

"Why was he hired?" Cohen asked.

"You'll really have to ask Andy about that," she said. "In fact," she added, checking her watch, "we'd better go. Andy's expecting us. And it's very bad form to keep him waiting."

He expected her to take him down the hall to where he had seen two secretaries—one gray-haired and matronly, the other looking like a model advertising business suits for women—guarding the door Darnaby said led to Blakely's office.

Instead, they returned to the electric cart, for a two-block ride into a street of smaller versions of the building they had just left.

"Oh, my Lord," she mumbled as they turned into a small parking lot. Cohen looked around nervously, but all he saw was the distant façade of a western town, and a billboard painted with a perfect sky and a pair of cumulus clouds.

"What is it?' he asked nervously.

"They've already taken down the sign with Max's name. For his parking slot."

His eyes followed hers. "And put up yours?" he asked, pointing.

"That's from last week," she admitted softly, but she translated her embarrassment into an angry stride to the front door. "Andy's in here," she said, waiting for him at the smoked-glass door.

She pushed it open to a chilly dining room, as well appointed as the best French restaurant he knew in Jerusalem. Thick red and white linen covered round tables. Crystal and silver glittered. There were no more than a dozen tables. Blakely was alone at the corner table at the far end. He was reading a document, a pair of half-spectacles perched at the end of his nose.

Cohen passed a table where Leo Hirsh was eating with two other men dressed in three-piece suits. Hirsh almost choked on a fat forkful of spaghetti when Cohen said softly, "Hello, Leo," but didn't stop to chat. As he approached Blakely, Cohen was aware that the low chatter had evaporated into a hush behind him.

Blakely looked up from the document, peering at Cohen over

the rimless lenses. His chilly smile at the end of the still, silent gauntlet of staring younger versions of the corporate chieftain made Cohen finally flick on the switch in his windbreaker pocket, before reaching for Blakely's extended hand.

"I must say," Blakely began, "I was intrigued when Barbara said you wanted to talk." He signaled the waiters, and the whispering at the other tables resumed.

"I told you at the funeral I have questions," Cohen reminded him.

"I'm sure you do," Blakely said. He toppled a white linen napkin and flapped it in the air to open it. His smile represented dental bills bigger than Cohen's annual pension. Blakely looked up at Cohen, expectant. But before Cohen could begin, three waiters descended on the table, bringing three large plates with small portions. Cohen waited for them to back way before he spoke.

"Does the name Karl Manheim mean anything to you?" he asked.

The executive's dark-green eyes turned chilly at Cohen's question. At least Cohen knew for sure that Blakely wasn't Manheim. "I see," Blakely said. "Perhaps I was wrong. Perhaps this *is* a matter for lawyers."

"That means you know him?" Cohen asked.

"It means that it seems to me you'll do better to ask me if Max's movie means anything to me." Blakely easily read the shock on Cohen's face. "Please, there's no reason for you to take it personally. You see this?" he said, pointing at the thick yellow folder containing the document he had been reading. "It's a seventy-million-dollar budget for a project. Frankly, Max's problems with his film really were a very small aspect of my concerns."

"Again, I ask you: Karl Manheim?"

"I know, I know," Blakely said wearily "He was a Nazi. A

horrible man. What was it Max used to call them? Butchers. That's right. Butchers. And he got away. I saw the movie, Mr. Cohen. I know the story."

"People have died." Cohen reprimanded him softly.

"I am not a heartless man, Mr. Cohen," Blakely protested. "But I cannot let the sentiments of someone's private past intrude on my business decisions."

"I'm not talking about the past," Cohen hissed. "I'm talking about this week."

"Ah, yes, Goldie," Blakely said haughtily.

"Yes. Goldie. And Jacques Rosen. And even Dugan and his skinheads."

"What *are* you talking about?" Blakely asked, perturbed by Cohen's anger.

"Roland Berger," Cohen said. He realized suddenly that Blakely might not yet have heard about Berger's death.

Blakely's fork paused slightly. "What about him?" Blakely asked.

"When did he come to work for you?"

"We brought him in six months ago. I'll tell you the truth. When this unfortunate business with Max began, he—ah, Max— used some, shall we say, contacts of his own to put pressure on me. I was not going to stand for those kinds of tactics. I fought back."

"Davey Burns told me about that," Cohen snapped back. " 'Fire with fire,' Davey said."

"Yes, you could say so," Blakely said tentatively.

"Until you managed to put out Max's flame," Cohen charged.

"That's ridiculous," Blakely spluttered.

"I can understand bugging Max's house," Cohen said softly. "But why did the anarchist have to die?"

Blakely's fork stopped midway to his mouth. "Pardon me?" he asked. "Bugs? The anarchist?"

"Jacques Rosen. A friend of mine. And Max's. Why did Berger kill him?"

Blakely put down his fork. "I assure you, sir, I have no idea what you are talking about. I asked Roland to keep an eye on Max. In fact, that bootlegged tape you saw is proof of why I needed Roland," Blakely said with self-righteous resentment. "I took on Roland to make sure just that sort of thing didn't happen. I've already talked with him about it. And when that gangster started making trouble in the theaters, Roland hired guards. He's a security expert—quite proficient, actually. But I have absolutely no idea what you are talking about when you speak of anarchists." He smiled at Darnaby. "I thought anarchists went out in the sixties."

"This is not a joke," Cohen said in a low, rumbling voice.

"He was the homeless person. On the pier," Darnaby gently prompted Blakely. "The sail-by shooting. One of the victims. And a character in the movie."

"Shut up," Cohen ordered, shocking her. He turned to Blakely. "He was a friend of mine. And Broder's. And your man Berger shot him."

"I did hear about your heroics on the pier, commander," Blakely said wearily.

"Berger?" Cohen asked, staring at Blakely. "You hired him?"

"I told you I did."

"He's dead."

"What do you mean, Roland's dead?" Blakely asked in a hushed voice.

"Someone shot back," Cohen snapped. Ignoring Blakely's shock, he plunged on. "Where did you find him?" Though his voice was firm, it was so low as to be heard only by Blakely and Darnaby.

Nonetheless, waiting for Blakely's answer, he was aware of the eyes of the other diners upon him. Leo Hirsh's table was silent, staring.

"I know nothing of this," Blakely protested. "Nothing at all. Barbara?"

She shook her head. "There was nothing in the newspapers. The police haven't called."

Blakely eyed Cohen suspiciously. "*You* were a suspect, I thought, in that tragic business with Goldie. I hope you didn't get out of that by offering to make *me* a suspect."

"Where did you find him?" Cohen persisted. "He has an Austrian passport. Europe? Here?"

"If you must know, he came over from OSDS; a loaner, so to speak."

"OSDS?" Cohen asked.

"OSDS," Blakely repeated. "Oceanic Security and Defense Systems. It's a subsidiary."

"Of Oceanic," Cohen asked, wanting to be sure.

"Yes, yes, Oceanic," Blakely said, exasperated.

But Cohen didn't remove his expectant stare from Blakely's face.

The executive sighed, taking off his glasses. "I had to report to my board about my cutbacks. Max's film came up; Davey Burns's name was mentioned. It was suggested I make use of the company's internal resources. Voilà! Roland Berger."

"Who made the suggestion?" Cohen asked.

"Who gave you the tape?" Blakely shot back.

Cohen thought quickly. "Maybe Berger wasn't your fault," he said softly. "After all, he wasn't your man."

It was like a blowtorch on Blakely's icy glare.

But Barbara spoke for him. "What do you mean?" she asked.

It was Blakely's turn to snap "Shut up" at her. She shifted

uncomfortably in the chair and then poured some sparkling water into a wineglass. Blakely turned to her. "I'm sorry, darling, I didn't mean to snap." He checked his watch and then picked up the yellow file with the seventy-million-dollar budget. "Could you do me a favor. This has to be read for typographical errors. I spotted three. And it has to go out to Tokyo this afternoon." He didn't say please.

"If that's what you want, Andy," she said softly. Beyond her, Cohen could see Hirsh's eyes alight with curiosity. Cohen looked back at Blakely, noticing his perfunctory grin at the woman.

She stood up, draining her wineglass. "Until tomorrow, commander," she said, bidding him farewell.

"Tomorrow?" he asked.

"The HEI benefit, of course. It's tomorrow night. I may no longer work for Max, but I do support the cause."

Cohen nodded, wondering what cause she meant. Gould's? Der Bruder's? The cause of the politicians who wanted to keep people frightened? The victims'? The survivors'? Whose cause? Cohen wondered as he promised that he, too, would be at the benefit, at Laszlo Katz's estate.

"What do you know about Laszlo Katz?" Blakely finally asked after she had gone through the smoked glass.

Cohen shrugged. "What everybody knows, I suppose. Big businessman. Philanthropist. Mr. Europe."

"Yes, he's quite the visionary. He talked about a United States of Europe before anyone else. He was doing business in Japan in the fifties. But you've never met him, of course."

Cohen shook his head. "No. But he's given a lot in Israel. Hospitals. Research institutes."

"He's a survivor too, you know."

"Yes," Cohen admitted.

"You know, I really didn't think about that very much. I mean, I understood Laszlo's vision. But I never really appreciated how much of it was a result of his experiences. In the Holocaust. Until I met Max. Laszlo and Broder, they seemed at first to have so little in common. Laszlo with his global vision of a new world, Broder with his hedonism and his obsessions about the past. But then I realized that they shared something very profound. Now I see you share it too."

It startled Cohen, and Blakely noticed.

"Please, don't misunderstand me," the executive asked. "I am certainly not an anti-Semite, no matter what Max Broder might have told you."

"He told me nothing," Cohen said.

"Yes, well, if you say so." Blakely smiled, disbelieving. "In any case. There's something compulsive, obsessive, in your methods. I noticed that. About Broder. Laszlo. Even you. The way you have not accepted suicide as the reason for Max's death, standing alone against everyone. That's a real strength. Obsession. Believe me." He glanced around the room at the other executives. "I envy it," he said wistfully, and then icily looked back at Cohen, "if the obsession is for the right thing."

"What are you trying to tell me?" Cohen asked in a hushed voice.

"I told you Laszlo gave me a complete mandate. That's absolutely true. He thinks on a global scale. Truly. And perhaps the best thing about him is that he conveys trust. When he delegates, it is with complete authority. But I have seen him become obsessed. Before he brought me to Epica, I worked with him on another project. You know he was one of the first to see the opportunity in *glasnost*. He had us tramping through the snow, he practically had me walk across the length of Siberia. But he was right," Blakely added, changing his tone from concern to admiration. "Oceanic got the franchise. He introduced me to Gorbachev," Blakely concluded proudly.

"Goldie told me that Katz was a strong backer of Broder's movie. Everyone says so," Cohen said, confused.

"Precisely my point," Blakely said sincerely. "He wanted everything to be perfect. In fact, I wouldn't be surprised if that's why he wanted Roland to pay particular attention to it. But you've seen it—at least the first half. You tell me, honestly: Who will want to see it? Our generation doesn't go to the movies, Mr. Cohen. Times have changed. Tastes change. Interests change. People want their issues clear-cut and clean. And a plot to murder a million Germans!" He snorted. "How do you think that would go over in German theaters? How do you think that would go over *here?* My job is to make sure that Epica is done making movies that nobody goes to see."

"The plot failed," Cohen objected.

"Don't you see." Blakely laughed. "That makes it even worse for us. No climax. I'm sorry, commander, the movie didn't work. Not the way we thought it should. I think, more than anyone, Laszlo was disappointed. Of course, as I told you at the funeral, maybe now it can be recut, issued in a small release. The publicity was helpful—"

"Katz has seen it?" Cohen asked, astonished.

"Of course."

"Barbara gave me a list. His name was not mentioned."

"I should hope not," Blakely said. "He surely should be above any suspicion in your mind. No. It's obvious to me what happened—if Roland is indeed involved in those crimes you mentioned. He was a very thorough man. Very thorough. Very gung-ho. He once told me that he went into private business because the Austrian army offered him no opportunity for action.

"You know," he added thoughtfully, as if realizing it for the first time, "Roland had the same kind of perseverance I was talking about before. So it's obvious," Blakely said, satisfied with his theory, "Berger was carried away. I always thought he was a little too dazzled by working in Hollywood. He turned a simple assignment into a disaster. Laszlo is going to be terribly distressed about this. I know I am. But frankly, Mr. Cohen, it's really a very minor concern of mine. In the long run, if you know what I mean."

"That is an understatement," Cohen said quietly. He pushed back from the table and stood up.

"You didn't touch any of your food," Blakely complained with surprise.

"I'm not hungry," Cohen said. It was a lie. But he realized he had work yet to do. He hoped the Interpol message from Germany had come through. "Thank you, Mr. Blakely," he said, starting to turn. But he paused in midturn, with one more question.

"Yes?" Blakely asked.

"Why did you change your mind about letting the movie be shown at the benefit?"

"How did you know?" Blakely asked, surprised.

"The rabbi. Gould. He told me."

"Actually, it was Laszlo's idea," Blakely said.

"To show only the first part?"

"Well, it's such a long movie, and the second part is only in rough-cut form. The ending is still problematic."

Cohen snorted. He wondered if Blakely knew exactly how problematic. "Thank you," he said, and started out of the dining room.

"Cohen?" Blakely called out to him, and the chatter, which had resumed with Darnaby's departure, collapsed into silence.

Cohen turned.

"I hope you will be careful about future accusations. A man's reputation is only as good as his name. Your obsession with the past, I can understand it. But you mustn't let it cloud your judgment. What was it I read a few weeks ago? That maybe that fellow—the Ukrainian? the one on trial in your country?—they say that maybe he really wasn't Ivan the Terrible." Blakely pursed his lips into a calculated smile.

"Have a nice day, Mr. Blakely," Cohen said, refusing to take the bait. He shot the executive a humorless grin and turned, leaving the room quickly, barely aware of Hirsh clambering to his feet as he passed.

Outside, the hot sun quickly raised sweat under the windbreaker. He was ordering his priorities in his mind, striding angrily by foot away from the dining hall, when he heard Hirsh's voice calling his name. He paused to wait for the fat man to catch up.

"What the hell was that all about? Ivan the Terrible? My God!" Hirsh bawled. "What did Andy mean by that?"

Cohen was disgusted. With himself and Broder, with Hirsh and Blakely. He looked up at the sun, and then off to the open skies above the ocean to the west. "He thought he meant that mistakes can be made," Cohen said.

"What did you tell him?" Hirsh asked, worried.

"Have you ever met Laszlo Katz?" Cohen asked.

The question caught Hirsh completely off guard. He shook his head and smiled abashedly. "I may be on the board at Epica. By Laszlo Katz's standards, that does not make me one of the elect."

"Did Max ever meet him?"

"You know, I really don't know," Hirsh confessed again. "Maybe. I remember right after Oceanic bought the studio. Max was pleased. He said that with Katz in charge, the film could really take off. Poor Max. It didn't take long for him to find out he was wrong."

"When exactly did Oceanic buy the studio?" Cohen asked.

"Three years ago next month," Hirsh said.

Cohen smiled. Another piece had fallen into place. Timing, he thought, as he drove out of the studio. Everything is in the timing.

E I G H T

He is in the passenger seat of a car in Jerusalem. He looks to the driver, expecting to see Nissim Levy, but sitting behind the wheel of the police car is the young actor who played Max Broder in the movie.

He looks away, to the shoppers on Jaffa Road. But then he realizes something is wrong. "You're not supposed to be . . ." he starts to say, turning back.

It is now Max Broder himself, laughing as he talks and drives. "You always had to do the right thing," Broder is saying. "You wanted to arrest an old man for killing that beggar, that butcher's dog kapo he found here."

Cohen looks away, through the windshield of the police car. They are heading down the hill toward Zion Square. It is the day of the refrigerator bomb. He sees his young wife in the crowd. He recognizes her gait, its easy sway and life-giving bounce. Der Bruder, beside him, is calling to him, but he shouts her name. He sees the refrigerator ahead. He shouts her name again, and she turns to face him. It is Manheim. His eyes are like the ends of broken icicles, aimed at Cohen.

He woke to avoid the explosion, grabbing the sheets around him like a soldier digging for cover in an artillery barrage. But gradually the realization that he was in the guest room at Broder's house, not in a bloody street in Jerusalem, penetrated his consciousness.

Slowly he got off the bed and went to the bathroom, taking a long, deliberate shower, as if he could wash away the memories as well as the sweat. Dressed, he made himself a cup of coffee and then worked his way through the house, removing every one of the remaining wiretaps on the telephones. He finished in Broder's bedroom.

Only then did he try Ahuva again. It was Saturday evening in Jerusalem. Maybe she was visiting friends, he thought, as he hung up after half a dozen rings.

He studied the dial, thinking. He could call Benny Lassman, a reporter he knew and trusted. He tried to remember his number, swearing he would never leave home again without his Jerusalem phone book. He tried three permutations of the number before catching the reporter on his way out the door to the office.

An hour later, Lassman called back with the answer to one of Cohen's questions. Laszlo Katz had his name all over the place in Israel, but nowhere in the newspaper archives was anything ever reported about a Katz visit to Israel. Lassman had learned nothing about Judge Ahuva Meyerson's whereabouts.

Madden's call came a few minutes later. "I've got bad news," he began.

"What?"

"Someone got there before us," Madden said. "Interpol can't help us with Bernard Levine. Or his family."

"Why not?"

"The fax says all inquiries regarding Bernard Levine are supposed to be directed to something called the BND. What's that?"

"The Bundesnachtrichtdendienst," said Cohen.

"If you say so," Madden said. "What's that?"

"Their federal intelligence agency."

"Shit," Madden said.

"Yes," Cohen said, rubbing his forehead. "What about Berger?"

"He was easy. Top-rated in the Austrian army. They sent him to Namibia, UN peacekeeping force. But at the end of the tour, he quit. Stayed in Africa as a merc. Suspected to have worked both sides of the civil war."

"Anything on when he started working for OSDS?"

"Nothing," Madden said. "So," he added, "we going after Katz tonight?"

Cohen had wondered how to break the news to Madden. He decided on a diplomatic tactic. "How many more days do you have now? A week? A mistake now, and——"

"You aren't going in to that guy alone," Madden growled.

"Mike, please. Understand me. This is my business. It is between Katz and me."

"And Manheim," Madden said. "Don't forget that mother-fucker."

"I haven't forgotten," Cohen said softly.

"Sorry, sorry, I didn't mean it that way. Look, you want it just you against him, you got to realize he's gonna have his own security there. It won't be just you and him. It'll be you and him and all his pals. You're gonna need a buddy there."

"Perhaps," Cohen said. "Let me think about it."

"All right, all right. But just don't forget. A lot of people have gotten killed for this," Madden said.

"I haven't forgotten," Cohen said.

"I didn't think so," Madden said gently, hanging up.

Cohen looked away from the phone. "It wasn't my fault," he said to the dancing girls in the drawings on the wall. The girls remained frozen in their silent grace. "It wasn't my fault," he said louder. His voice carried throughout the second floor of the house. "It wasn't my fault!" He shouted this time, his eyes closed, his head tilted back to let out all the pain. "You bastard!" he cried out at Broder. "It wasn't my fault."

Young Avram and Max are hiding by a set of train tracks. There is a short stretch of tracks, a hundred meters of no-man's-land beside a sheer mountain wall. To their right is the German border crossing. To the left is the Swiss border. There's a train stopped at the crossing. They watch the German police and soldiers get off, one by one, and then the train starts forward, moving slowly enough for them to grab hold of a rail, a step, anything that will carry them to freedom. Everything goes smoothly. Broder leaps first, grabbing a railing and slinging his arm through it, turning back for Avram. But there is a rock on a wooden tie. Cohen notices it too late. He stumbles, calling out Max's name.

Cohen woke just before Broder was going to jump off the train and run back to him, before the sirens began at the German border crossing behind them, before they raised their arms in surrender, before the German officer's admiration for their pluck saved their lives because instead of shooting them on the spot, he decided to send them back to headquarters. From there, it was only a day's trip to the camp, on a very different train.

It was late afternoon. He tried calling Ahuva one more time, but the phone rang until it automatically turned into a louder busy signal. He showered and shaved and then dressed, at one point calling Hirsh to ask if the tuxedo was absolutely necessary.

"Oh, God," Hirsh moaned, begging Cohen not to ruin the evening. "And be ready in an hour," Hirsh said. "It's an hour and a half drive in good traffic. Tonight? Who knows?"

"So many people will be going?" Cohen asked, suddenly feeling the way he had the first night, when it seemed he had lost his grip on reality, not knowing what questions to ask for lack of any information, uncertain whether he, or the world, had gone crazy. But at least now he was aware that he had arrived, without an immune system to protect him, unable to distinguish truth and illusion, between reality and the image Hollywood projected. Now, knowing the reason for his weakness, he felt strong.

"Haven't you heard?" Hirsh asked, genuinely concerned. "They're saying there's one hell of a storm coming in. Real freak weather we're having this year. First this heat wave. Now this rainstorm. Really freaky weather."

So Cohen started putting on the tuxedo he had bought after leaving the movie studio. The saleswoman had been perturbed when, after Cohen picked out a simple black suit, he asked for one a size larger. "It really should be worn snugly," the woman had said.

At eight o'clock that night, half an hour past the official time for the start of the reception, the ponytailed chauffeur drove Cohen into the Laszlo Katz estate, on a private peninsula off Highway 101 just south of Santa Barbara.

Gould was at the head of the reception line. He filled his first function in Cohen's plan just as Cohen had expected, by welcoming him extravagantly. Gould's bass carried the name Avram Cohen loudly through the lobby. Cohen then put the second part of his plan into motion by asking Gould how the video would be shown.

"They're setting up a large-screen projection in the ballroom," Gould said confidentially. "Don't ask. Everything was planned for the garden, but we decided not to take any chances with the weather. Look, there's Jeremy." He waved.

But Cohen didn't look. There was someone else he wanted to meet. "Our host?" he asked. "Mr. Katz?"

"Laszlo?" Gould said, surprised. "He's upstairs, of course."

"Will he be coming down?"

"No. He never actually attends. His health, you know."

"You *have* met him?" Cohen asked.

"Yes, yes, of course," Gould said impatiently.

"What is he like?" Cohen prodded.

"A most spiritual man," the rabbi said, but he was already looking for arriving guests beyond Cohen. "Why don't you get yourself something to drink, Avram?" Gould indicated the entrance to the ballroom with his head as he waved to a party of evening-gowned ladies.

Cohen moved on, seeking Madden. He had tried once more before the limo arrived to explain to Madden that he was being reckless with his pension. He even considered creating a trust fund from Broder's money from which Madden could draw a retainer for life, if the events of the evening turned into disaster for the American. But Madden insisted he had a right to be there.

"In that case," Cohen had finally conceded, "it will be best if I arrive alone. I think it will also be best if we are not seen conspicuously together. You will say you have come because of your investigation into Roland Berger's death. But please, leave Katz to me. For your own sake."

Two technicians were busy with the large-screen projection equipment, while around them the growing crowd milled and knotted with greetings among friends and acquaintances. Just like the funeral, Cohen thought, as he made his way around the edges of the crowd, edging toward the cassette sitting on top of the player on a table in the corner that had been set aside for the technical equipment.

He had stuffed the cassette of the *nokmim* under his tuxedo jacket, between his left biceps and his chest. Trying to look like an aficionado of the audiovisual equipment, he glanced around once to see if he was being watched and, in a quick motion, switched the cassettes. Then he quickly backed away from the machinery, moving into the edge of the crowd before striking out for the center of the ballroom.

It was bigger than a Jerusalem wedding hall. Cohen guessed

there might be as many as a hundred tables in the room, each table set for ten people. He moved into the foreign territory of bright, too-perfect smiles on faces made taut by plastic surgery, extravagant fashions bespeaking tasteless wealth, high-pitched voices disseminating insincere greetings, and narrow-eyed glances between transactors of covert business deals, as others focused on their hairstyles or golf handicaps.

Leo Hirsh was handshaking his way through a large circle of people heading toward Cohen. "Avram," he exclaimed effusively as he approached. "I see you got the tux right," he said, looking Cohen up and down. "I never would have believed it. You, in a tux." He grinned and then looked around. "So? Who do you want to meet first?" He clasped his hands, considering the crowd like a connoisseur about to make a choice recommendation. "Look, there's Vicki. I don't know what the hell you said to her, but listen, thanks again. Getting her to go to Max's funeral . . . I know it sounds crazy, but it, like, gave her new hope. You know what I mean?"

Cohen felt strangely elated, almost euphoric, and he surprised Hirsh with flattery. "I thought you were responsible for that, Leo," he said.

Hirsh beamed.

"Is it true our host never attends social affairs?" Cohen asked.

"Well, he's here. That's for sure. He's probably upstairs right now. But you're right. He never appears in crowds. Man talks to presidents, and he can't handle a little pressing of the flesh," Hirsh said. "He is not a mingler, if you know what I mean." The producer's purple bow tie bobbed with each word. He leaned slightly forward, to convey something more confidential. "They say that sometimes he watches. From behind one of these mirrors." He nodded toward a glittering reflection of the room, which faced another mirror on the other side, multiplying each other infinite times. "It's a rumor, of course," Hirsh added. "But who knows?"

Vicki Strong approached, smiling wryly at Cohen. "You've been busy," she said in the hoarse half-whisper. "That business in Santa Monica. On the pier. Extraordinary." She looked far better than she had only a few days before, and he wondered if the disease, like cancers he had seen on dying friends, had gone into one of the mysterious remissions that give so much work to holy men and their hucksters. But as he studied her face, he realized that it was makeup, not miracles, that had changed her.

"I think you are the remarkable one," Cohen said sincerely to her, making it her turn to blush.

"Wow," Hirsh exclaimed, beaming like a teenager at them both.

"Ladies and gentlemen." Gould's amplified voice cut through the rumble of chatter. "As we all know, a great friend of the institute is no longer with us. Max Broder."

There was a scattering of applause, and Gould encouraged it with open upraised palms, until it reached a crescendo and he lowered his hands to call for silence. "But we have something from him that will live longer than us all, something that tonight we are proud to be able to share with all of you." Gould paused for dramatic emphasis. "His movie. So if you'll please find your seats, we can get started."

When Cohen didn't respond to Gould's request, neither did Vicki Strong. "I made my own recording of that tourist's tape of the scene on the pier," she whispered to him. "And I watched it over and over. How you ran across the pier. It was so exciting," she said, her eyes glittering, "because it wasn't the movies. It was real life, and you weren't acting, you were really doing it. You really have to tell me all about it." She took his arm.

"I wish it had been the movies"—he smiled at her—"just as I wish what we are going to see now had only been a movie."

The comment sobered the actress but did not release him from her grasp.

"Aren't you going to sit down?" Vicki asked.

"I have already seen it," Cohen said.

"So have I," said Hirsh, "but—"

"I *am* interested in seeing the reactions of the audience," Cohen quickly added. "I'd like to watch from the side."

"I can dig that," Hirsh said.

The actress interpreted for him. "He means that he understands. I hope you'll pay attention to *my* reactions," she flirted before floating away into the milling crowd.

"Leo," Cohen said, before Hirsh could get away.

"Yes?"

"Blakely? Is he here?"

"He's one of the elect," Hirsh said sarcastically, raising his eyebrows and glancing upward.

Cohen crossed the room to stand a few feet from Madden, who was at the long white-clothed bar, using a pocket knife to slice pieces of an apple he had taken from a fruit and flower arrangement.

"I made the switch," Cohen whispered out of the side of his mouth. "I'll wait for the movie to begin before I go upstairs."

"Okay," said Madden. "I'll keep you covered."

"Only that," Cohen warned, and then left Madden, going to the back of the room. The audience was settling down, and Gould again mounted the podium, his back to the full-sized movie screen set up behind him. The speech was short, introducing the film and announcing that afterward there would be a few speeches. "And then the bidding begins," Gould summed up. "The video-cassette, for private viewings only—no pay-for-play distribution rights on this deal," he said, winning a laugh, "will be auctioned to the highest bidder, as a symbol of our commitment to the values Max Broder stood for."

Cohen wondered how many of the people in the room believed in Broder's values. He was trying to decide between almost all or almost none, when the lights dimmed. Then Blakely came in from the doorway to the foyer, going to a seat at the end of the head table. Even in the semidarkness, Cohen could see that Blakely didn't look happy.

Servants were beginning to close the doors, forcing stragglers in from the foyer. Cohen squeezed out of the ballroom just as the last of them came in. He asked a white-gloved butler where to find a toilet. The servant pointed to the left of the flight of stairs that entered the foyer from above.

Cohen heard the opening notes of the musical theme for the second part of the movie. Broder had a few bars of the traditional Kaddish melody arranged symphonically as the musical theme for the movie, and it echoed through the foyer like a mourner's wail at a cemetery, once again making Cohen shiver.

A servant bustled past him, and again Cohen used the excuse of searching for a bathroom as he edged toward the stairs. The servant's clicking shoes disappeared, and Cohen took the carpeted marble steps three at a time, until he was in the wide corridor of the second floor.

A dozen doors faced onto the corridor in each direction. Between them were half-oval tables with flowers. Someone had chosen Escher's optical illusions—fish turning into birds and staircases leading nowhere—for the walls. Cohen glanced closer at one of the glass-covered drawings. They were originals.

He began his search, fixing in his mind his position in the house. The ballroom below was to his right. He took a deep breath before trying the handle of the first door. It opened to an apparently unused bedroom. The second and third, also, were unused guest rooms.

But the fourth room was different. As his eyes adjusted to the darkness, he realized he was in a library, as big as all three bedrooms combined. An open door at the far end displayed the first signs of life he had seen on the second floor. He could see part of an extra-large television monitor. He walked quietly toward the flickering images. As he drew nearer, he realized that it was showing the movie that was playing downstairs. It was the restaurant scene in which the three *nokmim* recognize Witten.

He froze, aware of a presence behind him, then he spun, gun drawn, his fingers hot on the cool steel.

"What are you doing here?" he whispered.

"Keeping an eye on you," Madden responded.

"I'm going in there." Cohen gestured toward the monitor. "You stay here."

Cohen took a breath, holding out his gun with cocked elbows. He exhaled a little more than halfway, and then moved into the room in one fluid motion that covered every corner in a single sweep.

Half a dozen computer monitors glowed in the semidarkness. But the old man behind the desk was staring at the large television screen playing the second half of *The Survivor's Secrets*.

Cohen kept his eyes on the man, hearing the sound of car tires squealing.

Levine is driving, Broder is laughing, Cohen is packing guns into sacks for disposal.

"Was it worth it, Avram Cohen? Asking your questions?" the old man said, not even looking at Cohen. "Tell me the truth, if you want me to answer any of your questions."

If it was Manheim, he had changed. His voice was still raspy, with the familiar odd high pitch. But it was softer, the sarcasm replaced by sorrow.

And his eyes. They reminded Cohen of Dayan's. One was worn red by years of strain and tears. The other was a scar sewn into an empty socket, a dark hole of closed skin.

Cohen tightened his grip on the gun, disarmed by the old man's question, confused by his near-blindness. "I needed to know the truth," Cohen said. "I had no choice."

The man rubbed at his good eye until it glistened with tears, and then he passed his hand over the desk, feeling blindly for a pair of glasses. Three different pairs lay on the table, alongside a forsaken eye patch that lay stricken across the gold-on-black cover page of the treatment of *The Survivor's Secrets* stolen from Cohen's canvas bag at Goldie's. Beside it was another crumpled piece of cloth. It took Cohen a second to realize that it was a black silk yarmulke. It was sitting on the plastic bag with Broder's noose.

The old man carefully placed a pair of rimless spectacles on his face. He blinked, and the good eye focused, peering curiously at Cohen, while his mouth twitched into a crooked smile.

"I see you have a question," he said. But he didn't wait for Cohen to ask it. "You know," he said, "after I learned from Max's film that you all called each other brothers, something occurred to me. We were all brothers there, in that place. Especially those of us who survived."

"You're mad," Cohen whispered.

"Pardon?" the man asked. "A chair? I'm terribly sorry. Of course. Please, behind you." He put his hands together in front of him like a magistrate waiting for the defendant to calm down.

Cohen shot a glance behind him. An upholstered tall-backed rocking chair invited him, as if it had always been there, waiting for him. But the slight whir of an electric motor made him spin back, nervous, his gun aimed at the noise.

A wheelchair was carrying the old man out from behind the desk. A blanket hung like a checkered wool curtain over the stubs of his legs, truncated above the knees.

Cohen took a step backward out of the instinct of shock, falling into the chair just as he noticed the old man's gun. It was in his left hand, while the right controlled the wheelchair's joystick.

"I'm going to tell you something I've never told anyone," the old man said, leaning forward, "but first I would appreciate it if you poured me a drink." He motioned to the table at Cohen's side.

There was a simple glass decanter and two pear-shaped crystal glasses with slender stems. "Take one for yourself too. It's your favorite," the old man said.

Cohen didn't let go of his gun or take an eye off the old man. But he shifted in his seat to pour the drink. He handed it over and sat back, waiting.

"What about yours?" the old man asked.

"First you tell me your secret," Cohen said. "The one thing you've never told anyone before," he added, without any effort to hide his sarcasm.

"I should have told Broder," the crippled man admitted, taking the glass from Cohen. "But it was too late when I thought about it. He was dead by then."

"How?" Cohen asked. "How did he die?"

"You see," the old man said, ignoring Cohen's question. "Of all the scars, all the wounds my body has suffered, the one I cherish most, the one that taught me most, is my circumcision. It was my first real step toward true survival. A number wasn't enough, I learned. I really had to become a Jew."

Cohen could hear his heart beating. His first instinct returned. He wanted to say "You're mad" again. But he realized that he still wasn't sure the old man was Manheim.

There was a similarity to the bone structure, but the face had changed shape as the result of whatever disaster had taken the man's eye. The smile only emphasized the skull-like quality of the face, the skin like transparent parchment, shiny and delicately drawn over the bone. Cohen could see a vein that rose from just above the bridge of the man's nose high onto the forehead. He shoved and pushed at the fears climbing up from the dark places where he had long ago sent them to hide.

Cohen sought time, pouring himself a glass of the cognac, keeping his gun in one hand as he poured with the other. Broder had said he would recognize Manheim. A beggar or a baron, the movie had said. The crippled man in front of Cohen had the body of a Jerusalem beggar.

"Does it matter," the man said, as if reading Cohen's mind, "if I am Laszlo Katz?" And then, with an off-center grin and a flurried tick below his missing eye, which changed the pattern of wrinkles around the empty hole, his voice changed slightly from rasp to whisper: "Or I am Karl Manheim?"

It was as if he had two different faces, two different voices. Cohen's fear crawled higher into his craw, until he knew what to say, intuitively repelling his anxiety. "Or if you are mad," he finally said, his voice cracking in the chasm between his fear and the determination to settle the matter once and for all.

"If by mad you mean there are two different people inside one body, then yes, I am most definitely mad," the old man said matter-of-factly. "For forty years Laszlo had Manheim under control. Buried away." He spoke as if he were a third person, neither Katz nor Manheim, as he spoke of himself. "I thought it would go on forever, I suppose. Even after the wall came down in Berlin, I thought it could go on."

"Did he commit suicide?" Cohen thundered, each word rising

from a deeper place within, until he was leaning forward in the chair, the gun aimed directly at the old man's good eye.

"They used him like they used me," the old man said softly. "I know that now." Again Cohen had the feeling that there was something almost magisterial about the man in the pitiable body.

Cohen struggled against the feeling that he was being hypnotized, caught in a trance woven by the extraordinary will power exerted by the crippled man.

The crazed confession continued. "None of it was supposed to happen this way," the old man admitted. "The wall coming down. That was the first surprise. Even to me. And who better than I should have known what was happening on both sides of the wall?" But he wasn't asking Cohen to provide an answer. "In any case," the old man continued, "you surely must understand by now that if you had not investigated your brother's death, several people would still be alive right now."

Confused by the first part of the old man's answer, Cohen was shaken by the second part.

"How long did he know about you? How did he find out?" he asked softly, leaning deliberately back in the chair as he exerted his own will to resist his body's demand to reach out and strangle the old man into silence.

"I see," the old man said, nodding. "You want to know if you could have prevented it," he said. "Prevented what? The movie? The revelation? The death? Let me redeem you, Avram. When Max Broder first asked you to quit the police and help him make the movie, he didn't know."

"Sophie," Cohen murmured to himself, picking up that piece of the puzzle.

"He never would have found out if the wall didn't come down," the old man said bitterly. "As long as Germany was divided, he never would have known. Never. You figured that out, didn't you?"

"Yes," Cohen said softly.

"Some people think the Stasi was worse than the SS," the old man said thoughtfully. "How little they know," he added sorrowfully, as if the misconception pained him. "But I can tell you one thing, from personal experience. They were no less mad."

"They sent Sophie against *you,* not Broder," Cohen finally could deduce.

"Against us both," the old man said, correcting Cohen. But before the Jerusalemite could ask anything else, the other added, "But she made a terrible mistake."

"Killing Goldie?" Cohen asked.

Instead of an answer for Cohen, the old man had a question. "What do you think I do?"

"Business," Cohen said. "Buy cheap. Sell dear. Business."

"Yes, but what do I sell? What do I buy?" Katz answered patiently.

"Things," Cohen spluttered, wondering if it was a trick question. "Movie studios. People."

But his answer disappointed the old man. The expression on the face began to change again, with an anguish-ridden tic. Cohen felt apprehension pushing his fear ahead. He looked around the room for a clue. The television monitors were showing the three *nokmim* in a meeting with a Jewish Brigade intelligence officer. Cohen continued his survey of the room. The computer terminals. The phones. The fax machines.

"Information," Cohen said, forcing himself to keep out of his voice the feeling of panic that had driven him to the answer.

"Thank you," Katz said, seemingly relieved by Cohen's answer. "Like Roland Berger's devices in Der Bruder's house, Goldie was a way to get information. Among other things, about you."

"Why did Sophie kill her?"

"I think you know," the old man said. His crooked smile was meant to blame Cohen, not console him.

Despite the air conditioning, Cohen was sweating. He pulled futilely at the tuxedo tie, as he tried to order his thoughts. But the questions kept coming to him. "Roland Berger?" he stabbed at one. "Why did you let him use skinheads?"

The old man smiled wanly. "It wasn't the only mistake he made," he said.

"You shouldn't have let Berger use the rope," Cohen said.

"I went to beg forgiveness. Not to kill him," the old man said. "To beg that he forgive me and save us both. But Roland . . ."

"You and Der Bruder, or Katz and Manheim?" Cohen asked bitterly.

The old man smiled again, and again, instead of answering Cohen's question, he asked another. "Max Broder insisted on making his movie. Now be honest, Avram. You are famous for it in Jerusalem, no? Being honest? So tell me. Do you want that movie seen?"

Cohen repelled distress once more, shutting away his personal feelings to get to the truth. "It is being seen," he said. "Downstairs. Right now. The whole world will know about it," Cohen said. "It doesn't matter what I want." But he knew he had protested too much.

The man in the chair laughed, a coughing rasp that was as painful to watch as to hear. "You're so innocent, Avram Cohen. That movie won't be shown. Not in big movie theaters, not on broadcast television. Maybe a cult film. Maybe. But the whole world? You believe what is written about this place? Hollywood? America? The whole world is a big place. Who believes what they see from Hollywood? Fantasy. That's what Hollywood is about. Dreams."

"What happened at Broder's?" Cohen asked again.

"We had a long talk. Like we are talking now. I had to give him a last chance to take out his message about me. To put an end to the madness. But he wouldn't listen. You were coming. That gave him hope."

It was the confession he had been waiting for, but the questions continued bursting in Cohen's mind like the gunshots in the movie playing on the monitors. "How did he find out?" he asked. But before the old man could answer, Cohen figured it out. "Someone in East Germany," he said, finally beginning to understand. "They were blackmailing you. That's why they sent Sophie."

The old man nodded with a sad smile.

"Who was it?" Cohen asked.

"It doesn't matter. It's too late. He's dead."

"Who was it?" Cohen insisted.

"You don't want to know," the old man warned him.

"Who?" Cohen demanded.

"I should have told Broder," the old man said almost wistfully, with the same tone he had used when he said he should have told Broder about the circumcision, as if it were another lost opportunity. "It was true then and it is true now. You see the irony?" the old man answered himself, determined to take his own time. "The blackmailer set it all in motion but did not live to see it go the course. I'll give you a hint. You always underestimated his commitment to his cause. Max Broder didn't."

Cohen swallowed, his mouth dry with dread. Bernard Levine had survived. He had not died in jail. He had been one of the servants of his workers' state, and he had served it well. He had used Max Broder—not to reveal the butcher but to blackmail Katz.

Cohen could only wonder what obscure bureaucratic need deep inside the East German secret service originally required Levine to be declared dead and whether, already then, Bernard expected that one day he would so abuse Broder's loyalty in the name of a dying state, for the purpose of a private escape.

"The girl?" he finally asked.

"Is she really his daughter?" the old man asked for Cohen. "We'll never know, will we?"

"Her body has not come up," said Cohen. "She might be alive."

"Oh, she came out of the water alive," the old man said. "But Berger was better at his job than you give him credit for."

The matter-of-fact tone only added to Cohen's shock. "Why?" he asked. "Why was it all necesary? The killing?"

The old man smiled wryly. "The girl had only one instruction," he said. "If Levine didn't get out, she was supposed to let Broder know about Katz and Manheim. She didn't know that Levine died." The old man laughed. "Of natural causes. A heart attack on the night they started dancing on the wall. So he didn't get out. She set it all in motion."

"But you could have stopped it," Cohen charged.

The old man simply shook his head. "You don't understand. *I* couldn't do anything. It was up to Laszlo. He had buried Karl Manheim. Buried him deep inside this body. But Broder was already at work on the movie. Once she told him about Katz and Manheim, the Nazi had to protect himself. When this," he said, pointing at his one good eye, "saw the movie, it was Manheim who understood the message that Broder sent you. He came back from the grave Katz had dug for him. And now they're both gone. I had to step in. To bury them both."

"Who are you?" Cohen asked, aghast. It was true. The old man in front of him was neither Katz nor Manheim, but a third person who could speak about the other two with both familiarity and objectivity.

"Whoever you want me to be, Avram Cohen. You created me.

Brought me to life, so to speak. You forced me to take action, so all the good works that Laszlo began could survive."

Cohen shook his head, trying to clear his mind. But the old man interpreted it to mean rejection.

"What are you going to do? Kill me? Take your revenge?" the old man asked. "Revenge will pay for scholarships for the Holocaust Institute? Revenge will bring someone back to life?"

He had asked Cohen too many questions. "It's not revenge," Cohen said softly. "You conspired with Berger to murder. Katz or Manheim, or whoever you are, it doesn't matter. You killed. Max, Jacques. And all the others. Now. This week. And for what?" Cohen charged. "Who could have made the connection between Katz and Manheim, except me? You saw the movie. What did it say I did? I stopped. I stopped my killing."

"So did I," the old man said eagerly, protesting his innocence. "Don't you see? It was Manheim. Not Katz. You and Broder, you two made him come back, with all your questions."

"You tried to pay for your sins," Cohen shot back. "Even prayed for the souls you killed. Maybe you stopped killing. But you, Manheim or Katz or whoever you are, you started killing again. You thought I would look for you because of Max's movie. But I was looking for his killer. I wasn't searching for the missing Manheim. I searched for the killer of Max Broder, the killer of Jacques Rosen and Goldie Stein. I searched for the killer who sent those hoodlums. That is why I sought you out." He rose to his feet. "Not for the past. For now."

"What are you going to do?" For the first time, his voice was trembling. Cohen gazed down at him, seeing hazily behind his own welling tears.

"It's not what I am going to do," Cohen finally said. He looked at the gun lying limply in the old man's hand, resting on the blanket, and then back to the red-rimmed eye enlarged behind the spectacles.

The old man regarded the gun.

"It's what you're going to do," Cohen added, turning his back on the old man, uncertain if it was Katz or Manheim or that strange one-eyed magisterial observer of his own tragedy whose stare he felt on his back. All he had left were his instincts, and he obeyed them. He was marching past Madden's uncomprehending stare when the gunshot's blast echoed throughout the second floor.

"Ambulance!" Madden screamed.

But Cohen didn't go to the telephone. The gunshot had put an end to the old man's misery, leaving only the unanswerable question of who executed whom: Katz or Manheim or that third mysterious magistrate hiding in the crippled body.

He continued his slow march through the library, into the corridor to the wide stairs. A crowd was gathering in the foyer below, pouring from the ballroom where the movie was just ending, filling the air with the shouts and hushes of a brewing panicky mob.

Servants and security men raced past him as he descended the stairs. The crowd at the bottom parted. Faces peered in at him.

Blakely's, Barbara's, Hirsh's. For a moment, he thought of Madden, alone with the chaos upstairs. But then he smiled slightly to himself as in his trousers pocket he flicked off the switch to the Walkman wrapped under the cummerbund of the suit. He had his witness.

He stepped outside, onto the landing at the top of the stairs. The ponytailed chauffeur, waiting with other uniformed drivers below, tossed away a cigarette and came forward with his obsequious salute.

Cohen looked away to the ocean's horizon, where a skinny hand of electricity grabbed at the darkness. A moment later, the thunder rolled over him, bringing a wind that smelled of rain. He turned back to the house. Two servants were closing the tall white doors against the rising wind, shutting all the celebrated witnesses inside.

Witnesses are always participants, he thought, even if they only contribute their memories to the action. They had seen the movie. Now they were part of it. As for him, he thought, his vacation in Hollywood was over. He could go home.

Epilogue

AHUVA HAD FLOWN to Los Angeles, worried by the press reports that had followed Cohen during the week. Indeed, she had been inside the ballroom at the benefit, brought by the consul general. But they had arrived late, missing Cohen before the movie, and then, trapped in the panicked crowd, they missed him again when he left.

But Hirsh located Cohen at Broder's house, where he was doing his laundry after booking a seat on a flight back to Israel the next day. By the time Hirsh's limo dropped her off, Cohen had prepared a dinner for them both.

They spent all night talking. Cohen told the story from the start, leaving out nothing. She listened carefully, reserving her judgments until the end.

Just as dawn was coming up on the rainy Sunday morning, he finished the tale. By then they were in bed, almost asleep. But before she closed her eyes, she passed her sentence. Cohen woke Madden at home. The American made the rest of the arrangements.

And that afternoon, after lovemaking and a long, lazy sleep, they walked in the driving rain up the meandering path to the grave where the hearse was waiting with Jacques Rosen's body beside Broder's grave.

Cohen held the umbrella and Ahuva carried the *siddur,* the prayer book she had found in Broder's library. Madden was waiting at the top of the ridge.

"I thought you Jews needed rabbis to pray," Madden said from under his umbrella. "Or at least ten men."

Cohen shook his head and then nodded to the pallbearers from the funeral home. As they carried the coffin from the car to the hydraulic bier, Ahuva handed the opened prayer book to Cohen.

But he didn't need to look down at the page of Aramaic to remember the words he had heard at hundreds of funerals over the years.

"*Yitgadal veyitkadash, shmeh rabah,*" he began.

The rain swept across the field, almost drowning out the words of the Kaddish. But its damp breath on his face sweetened the tears he had waited nearly fifty years to cry.

Acknowledgments

SPECIAL THANKS to Barry Rubin, Michael Eilan, Dado Kessler, and Naomi Landau. All in their own way contributed to the telling of this second tale about Avram Cohen.

Without the generosity, hospitality, and loyalty of Shirley "Dolly" Rosenberg, Arthur and Nimi Rosenberg, and Sarah Stern from Café Tamar, it would have been impossible for this story to be told.

And of course, thanks to George Hodgman and Lisa DiMona, for keeping the faith with Cohen.

About the Author

ROBERT ROSENBERG, who introduced Detective Avram Cohen in his first novel, *Crimes of the City,* has reported for many leading newspapers and magazines. He lives in Tel Aviv.